HER PROTECTOR

Copyright © 2020 2025 by Rianna Campbell

All rights reserved.

Published by Gremlin Press.

This is a work of fiction. The story, all names, characters, organizations, places, and incidents portrayed in this production are either products of the author's imagination or are used fictitiously. Any resemblance to actual persons (living or deceased), events, places, buildings, and products is entirely coincidental.

No part of this publication may be reproduced, distributed, stored in a retrieval system, or transmitted in any form or by any means, including photocopying, recording, or other electronic or mechanical methods, without the prior written permission of the publisher, except in the case of brief quotations used in critical articles or reviews or as otherwise permitted by U.S. copyright law.

For information contact: riannacampbellwrites@gmail.com

https://riannacampbellwrit.wixsite.com/my-site

2nd Edition: May 2025

Hey, Reader,

Just a heads-up: this story touches on trauma, stalking, PTSD, and the aftermath of sexual violence. Nothing's shown in graphic detail, but if you're not in the headspace for that right now, take care of yourself first.

Her PROTECTOR

MacLachlan Security Group Book One

Rianna Campbell

For the ones who've been there.

For the ones who needed someone like Connor and never had him.

For the ones who needed to be seen, to be fought for, to be loved—
even when it got messy and painful and hard.

For *me.*

Chapter One

He'd only been waiting for ten minutes—tops—but that was more than enough time for Connor to identify what security measures they had in place. Four security guards at the entrance, two metal detectors, and a desk where employees flashed their badge and visitors signed in *if* they were on the list.

The elevators were keycard access only and every inch of the place had video surveillance. He didn't know who handled their security, but he was annoyed he couldn't seem to find a single hole. Whoever it was, he'd like to have them on his team.

It was a tight system, so why would a senior partner at Langston, Buchanan & Hughes want to meet with him? There was only one reason he could think of.

"Mr. Hughes will see you now." The secretary—blonde, petite, mid to late twenties—delivered the news like a memo: polite, professional, no response required. She was pretty, but forgettable. And there were two more just like her on the lower floors.

Apparently, Barbie comes in "Corporate," now…

"Thank you." He stood, buttoned his jacket, and pushed through the large, wooden doors. The office was exactly what he expected: spacious, well-lit and outfitted with what appeared to be expensive, dark wood pieces, hand-picked for maximum intimidation. It was slightly more eclectic than he anticipated, but the layout was precisely what he'd imagined, down to the large desk facing the door and the entire wall of floor to ceiling windows behind it.

It must be good to be the King.

Richard Hughes, probably in his sixties, could easily pass for someone twenty years younger. His hair was still more dark brown than silver, his hazel eyes sharp and intelligent, and he had a tall, athletic build. In his dark Armani suit, red silk tie and matching pocket square, he looked every inch the senior partner.

"Good morning, Mr. Hughes." Connor stopped in front of the desk and shook his hand.

"Thank you for coming," he replied. "And call me Richard. Please, have a seat." He gestured to a black leather club chair before settling into his own behind the desk.

"Call me Connor." He unbuttoned his suit jacket and sat. It wasn't Armani, but it was quality and perfectly tailored to his frame.

"Can I get you anything? Coffee? Scotch?" Hughes offered.

"No, thank you."

"You're sure about that?"

"Quite." The corner of Connor's mouth twitched up.

"Well, just remember I made the offer," Hughes said, a trace of humor in his voice.

Connor raised an eyebrow but chose not to comment.

"What can I do for you, sir?" he asked instead.

"I've heard a lot about your company from a friend of mine. He was very satisfied with your services last year and when I encountered a… *similar problem*, he recommended you."

"It's always good to hear our clients are happy with our work." Connor flashed his most professional smile. "May I ask who referred you?"

"Michael Pritchard. Good friend of mine. Mostly because I always beat him at golf or cards."

Connor offered the polite laugh Hughes was waiting for. These jokes were common from the corporate types who often retained his services, but he'd never enjoyed the glad-handing. It was part of running his own business—something he'd come to understand over the last three years-but he didn't think he'd ever be totally comfortable with this part of the job.

He recognized the name immediately and knew his earlier inference was correct. He'd hired them for private protection rather than a security consult.

"So, you need a bodyguard."

"Not me. I have excellent home security, and you've seen the office," Hughes began. "But there's an employee—a junior partner—who's become the focus of some… unwanted attention. We felt it would be best to bring in additional security as a precaution, until the situation is resolved."

"Does this happen often?" Connor asked.

"Not often, though once is too often in my opinion." He sighed, looking tired. "We have handled a lot of big cases, some more publicized than others. We have quite a few high-profile clients. Occasionally one of ours ends up the target of harassment or worse."

"Is this harassment, or worse?"

"I'm not entirely certain how to classify what's happened." Hughes frowned, deep creases appearing between his brows. He seemed genuinely concerned, and for a moment he looked every bit his age.

Hughes pulled a small manilla envelope from his desk drawer, sliding it across the desk like it might burn him.

When it was within Connor's reach, he took it and opened it. A small stack of photos—at least two dozen—all of the same woman. She was in her early thirties. Tall. Attractive. Dark hair that barely brushed her collarbone.

The first photo showed her exiting a black sedan from the driver's seat, briefcase in hand, cell phone to her ear. The next photo, apparently taken just moments later, showed her entering the office building, still on the phone, but the camera had caught her as she glanced over her right shoulder, frowning, like she'd felt someone watching her.

Some of the photos showed her looking all business—pencil skirt, pin-straight hair, looking focused. Others showed her in yoga pants or jeans, hair pulled back or in loose waves around her face. Caught mid-step. Unguarded.

Whoever was behind the camera had been watching her for weeks, if not months. They'd captured every outfit, every errand, every part of her daily routine like she was a celebrity… or a mark.

He shuffled through all the photos a second time, slower, taking in everything from her expression to what and who was in the background. The devil was always in the details.

"Who got these?" Connor asked.

"I did." Hughes scowled. Connor raised an eyebrow.

"When?"

"Two days ago."

"Any note?"

"None. Just the photos. No return address. No postmark." Connor resisted the urge to raise his eyebrow *again*. Apparently, that was his thing today.

"No postmark? Do you have a drop box of some kind?"

"No, too dangerous," Hughes replied.

Smart move. Drop boxes allow anyone to leave anything at any time, including everything from glitter bombs to pipe bombs.

"So how did it get in the building?" Connor asked. Hughes merely shrugged.

"It was handed to me with my regular mail Wednesday morning. No one seems to know how it got there. Mail gets dropped off and x-rayed before it's sorted and delivered. The security staff would have noted anything delivered by hand, and none of the mailroom staff recall seeing anyone or anything in the mailroom that shouldn't have been there."

Connor's brow furrowed. No demands. No blackmail. No sender. Someone wanted him to know that this woman was being watched but not why. And why not send them to the employee directly?

"The police have seen these?" Connor asked.

"They have. These are copies. The police, of course, insisted on keeping the originals, along with the original envelope. They couldn't get any usable prints, but said they would do what they could." Hughes looked skeptical, as he should.

Connor respected the thin blue line. He knew plenty of cops who worked damn hard, but they didn't have the resources to cover half the shit that came their way.

Something like this, with nothing to go on, had "low priority" written all over it. You might as well ask them to look into it "when they're not busy." If Hughes relied on the police to figure this out, he'd be up a creek, no paddle in sight.

"We've put our team of investigators on it, as well," Hughes added.

Connor nodded. That was a good call. And it was one less point Connor would have to make.

"Did she give you any idea who might do something like this, or why?" Connor asked, putting the photos back in the envelope. Hughes hesitated for a moment, his face tense, lips pursed.

"She know yet?" Connor asked instead.

"Not yet," Hughes admitted, squeezing his eyes shut and rubbing the bridge of his nose.

Connor held his tongue, waiting for an explanation.

"Alexandra can be… particularly *stubborn*. I don't think she's going to be very cooperative." Connor didn't roll his eyes. *Wanted to*, but didn't. Lord, save him from headstrong women.

"Well, sir, I think telling her would be a good place to start," Connor said flatly.

Hughes gave him a wry smile.

"You're certainly right. And that's something we're about to remedy—that is, if you'll agree to take the contract."

Connor thought about it for a moment.

"We'll have to go over the details, but I'm confident we can handle it."

"Excellent." Hughes smiled, looking relieved. He picked up his handset and pressed a button. "Send her in."

She was already irritated with this latest imperial summons. If he'd interrupted her trial prep to invite her to Sunday brunch again, she'd throttle him.

"You can go in now," Julie said, all Colgate smile and eerie calm. Alexandra was convinced she moonlighted as a toothpaste model—or the poster girl for a dental office. In five years, not a single frown. Even when Alexandra tried to catch her off guard. It was Stepford Wife levels of creepy.

"Thanks."

She pushed open the heavy door, once again missing Mrs. Miller, her father's former secretary. She'd always had a candy dish on her desk and would sneak her some little treat every time she visited. Ms. Whitestrips over there was probably the type to hand out floss on Halloween.

Her phone buzzed just as she stepped into the monstrosity that was her father's office. She glanced at the message from Charles and rolled her eyes.

"This better be important, old man, because—" She froze. They weren't alone.

Her father fought a smile, pursing his lips. He used to do the same thing when she was little—whenever she did or said something that he *knew* he should be scold her for, but it was just too funny.

"I'm sorry, sir," she said trying to recover. "I didn't realize you were in a meeting. Julie sent me in."

Her skin betrayed her—heat crept up her neck. She was twenty-nine. Junior partner in a multi-million-dollar firm. She'd tried cases in front of the toughest judges in the state. And she still blushed like a damn schoolgirl. Humiliating.

She wanted to turn around and run, but being contrary by nature, she did the opposite. Stepped forward, looked him in the eye—*Holy shit, he was hot*—and offered her hand.

She introduced herself, valiantly ignoring his surprised and slightly amused expression.

"Alexandra Hughes."

He took her hand in his—large, firm, warm—and her heart stuttered like she'd touched a live wire. His calloused fingers scraped lightly against her palm as he pulled away. She couldn't remember the last time she'd met a man with hands so clearly used to hard work. Had she ever?

"Connor MacLachlan," he replied. She was surprised to hear he spoke with a bit of a Scottish brogue.

He didn't sit once the introduction was done, merely put his hands in his pockets, and waited. She gave him a *very* thorough once-over before taking her seat.

He was tall. Over six feet. Broad shouldered. His suit was tasteful, moderately expensive, and clearly tailored. There was no way he'd find something off the rack that fit his proportions.

His hair was dark, almost black, and cut short. It was just long enough on top to curl slightly over his forehead. Devoid of hair products, she wondered if it was as soft as it looked.

But his eyes...

They were intensely blue and framed by thick, dark lashes. He was a gorgeous man regardless, but his eyes held warmth and intelligence. It would seem he was more than just a pretty face.

Good to know.

She crossed her legs, adjusted her jacket, and folded her hands in her lap. The man finally sat. Leaning back, relaxed, he turned slightly toward her with one elbow on the arm of the chair and his chin supported between his thumb and index finger.

She couldn't help but think that if he'd been a painting, it would be titled *Predator at Rest.*

She shook herself out of her musings and brought her focus to the man behind the desk.

Shoulders back, chin up, stay professional. Never let them see you rattled.

"Can I get you anything, DD?" her father asked, his tone solicitous.

So much for professional…

He knew better than to bring their relationship into the office.

He'd called her his "Darling Daughter" since she was six. It had made her feel special—until she hit puberty. Then it was cringey.

He'd shortened it to "DD" to keep from embarrassing her in front of her friends, and the moniker had stuck. It was still cringey, but now she was old enough to appreciate the term of endearment. At least *outside* the office when they were father and daughter instead of senior partner and junior partner.

Anywhere else, she'd have smiled and rolled her eyes. But here? She'd told him countless times that she wanted to be treated like every other employee. There were enough people in the building who thought the only reason she'd gotten her job was because of her father and she didn't want to add any more grist to the mill.

She and the partners might know how she really got the job, but no one else would believe it. It didn't matter. She worked twice as hard as everyone else to prove she deserved it.

"No, thank you, sir." Her tone was stiff. She risked a glance at the man seated beside her. He was still, but he watched with unnerving focus.

"I don't mean to be rude." Her half smile was meant to look calm. Controlled. "But I have hours to bill. What can I do for you gentlemen?"

Her father returned her smile with an almost identical one. It startled her at times how eerily similar they could be.

"I'm afraid something rather important has come up that requires immediate attention." Her father's face grew serious and she braced herself. He looked… worried.

"What is it?" She kept her voice even, trying not to show any sign of her anxiety.

"Well, it might be easier to show you." He turned and gestured to the other man. "Connor, if you would?" The man—*Connor*—picked up an envelope from the desk and handed it to her, watching her intently.

She opened the envelope and removed a small stack of photos. *So many photos.* It took her a moment to register that they were photos of *her.* Her pulse pounded in her ears. She forced her face to stay neutral—only a slight furrow of her brow.

She studied every photo—slowly, methodically. She mentally catalogued possible dates, times, and locations where each photo might have been taken.

Facts were what mattered. Emotions solved nothing.

When she'd examined every photo, she placed them back in the envelope. When Connor reached for it, she didn't give it to him. She tucked it beside her—guarding it like a secret.

"Where did these come from?" she asked, focusing on her father—letting him ground her.

"They arrived in the mail Wednesday morning," he replied. His eyes were searching, gauging her state of mind. He was looking out for any sign she was about to break down. She kept the mask firmly in place. She didn't let her shoulders sag. Chin still up.

"They were sent here?" She kept her voice calm and level.

"Yes."

"Any indication where they came from?"

"Not yet."

"But you've contacted the police?"

"Yes."

"Do they have any leads?"

He paused before finally answering as if he was afraid of how she'd react.

"No."

That hesitation. The one-word answers. She wanted to scream. He was trying to protect her again in the worst way possible—by keeping her in the dark.

She exhaled slowly and focused on what mattered. The wheels started to turn, and she tried to put the pieces together. She ran through clients—past and present—cases, files, interviews, anything that might give someone a reason to do something like this.

It had to be work related since she didn't have a social life to speak of. She hadn't done anything but work, eat and sleep for five years. One face flickered briefly in her mind but she quickly shoved it away. She refused to even consider it. Not yet.

"Assuming these photos are a threat—"

"That's a big assumption," her father cut in.

Always the lawyer.

"Not much of an assumption at all, as I see it. What other purpose could this conceivably serve? I doubt it's supposed to be fan mail."

Her father glanced at the man beside her—hoping for backup. Connor held his gaze, gave a subtle shake of his head. Nothing to say.

"As I was saying, if this was a threat, was it meant for me, or for you?"

Her father frowned. If there was one thing Richard Hughes hated, it was not knowing the answer to a question.

Connor cleared his throat, a quiet warning that he was about to jump into the fray.

"It's a fair question, sir," he pointed out.

His voice was deep. Rich. Distracting. It wasn't just the accent. It was the cadence. The inflection. His voice was... oddly musical.

"The photos are of you, Ms. Hughes, but they weren't *sent* to you." He turned to her father before he continued. "The threat is obviously *to her*, but it may be meant *for you*. It would certainly be a more effective tactic than threatening you directly. After all, a father would do almost anything to protect his daughter."

Alexandra glared at her father—hard enough to burn a hole through him. She was going to have it out with him the minute this meeting was over. Her father, on the other hand, was staring at Connor. He might look bored to anyone else, but she knew better. He was genuinely surprised. Damn near *amazed*, actually.

"You didn't have to tell me she's your daughter," Connor continued, his smile a little smug. "You're not just concerned about her safety. You're trying to guard her *feelings* as well. Seems a bit far to go for an employee. And I very much doubt there are many people you'd let call you 'old man' without battin' an eye. Not only were you not surprised, but you smiled which tells me it was affectionate—something you're used to."

Her father smiled and looked down at the desk.

"And she has the look of you when she smiles." Connor shot her a sidelong glance and winked. He hadn't turned his head—hadn't made a show of it. Just a flicker of mischief. Easily missed. Her father hadn't seen it. But she had.

It felt like a stolen secret, tucked away between them, and she hated the way it made her skin prickle with heat.

Alexandra swallowed, ignoring the funny little flutter in her stomach and nodded curtly, confirming his assumption. His smile broadened and—just for a moment—it stole the air right out of her lungs. He was gorgeous anyway with his chiseled jaw and high cheekbones, but that smile made him *scorchingly* hot. *Panty-dropping hot.*

The guys who modeled overpriced underwear and starred in every ad for expensive cologne with a ridiculous name had nothing on him. She turned away quickly—the moment she felt the blush creeping up her neck.

She resisted the urge to fan herself. Picking at a nonexistent piece of lint on her slacks instead. It bought her a second to think. And breathe.

"So, what do you propose we do?" she asked, steering the conversation back to safer ground. Her father took a deep breath and she could tell she was not going to like what came next.

"Personal protection. The threat is to your safety even if it's meant to get something from me. You'll have a bodyguard any time you're not at the office or in your apartment until further notice."

"No." She shook her head.

"Alexandra—"

"*No.* I'm not living with a squad of chaperones shadowing my every move," she said. "I rarely go anywhere aside from work, home, and the gym. All three buildings have security systems. I'll be fine."

"Coming and going from those three places is how they got those photos in the first place. He, or *she*, knows where and how you spend your time," Connor pointed out. "In fact, the more predictable your routine, the easier it is to plan a kidnapping. Or an *attack*." He was dead serious now and she couldn't help the shiver than ran down her spine at the thought.

"Fine, I'll drive to the gym. Problem solved." Her smile was too bright to be anything but sarcastic.

"Unless your gym has a valet, it still presents an opportunity," Connor replied.

"Alexandra, this is not up for debate."

She knew that tone. Low, firm and absolutely final. He *never* raised his voice. He didn't have to. But this was as close to it as he got.

"The police—"

"Have nothing to go on." Her father shook his head. "We've put

Archie on it, but miracle worker that he is, it will take time. And as you know, his place is here."

Archie was in fact a miracle worker. Which was lucky for everyone, because with her father's Rex Stout obsession, he would have hired him based on his name alone.

Back then, she'd teased him—asking if he thought he was Nero Wolfe now that he had his own Archie Goodwin. He'd laughed, patted his still trim waistline, and replied that he liked to think of himself more as Nathaniel Parker. Not New York's best detective, but the lawyer New York's best detective has on retainer.

She pursed her lips and considered the situation for a moment, eventually coming to the conclusion that her father was probably right. The police would need time, *Archie* would need time, and until one of them figured it out—her money was on Archie—she would be vulnerable. She *hated* being vulnerable. Almost as much as she hated being told what to do. It was a bit of a problem.

"Not to sound petulant—but with all due respect—you can't *make* me."

Connor had the audacity to snort with laughter before trying to cover it with a choking cough. She glared at him but he quickly and firmly averted his gaze.

"I can, and I will," her father replied. He reached for a folder that was sitting off to one side of his desk and handed it to her. She opened it and looked it over, recognizing the contract she'd signed five years ago when she joined the firm.

"And this proves… what, exactly?" she asked.

"Paragraph six, subsection D." She found the correct page and read it. Twice.

Damn him.

Connor studied her with a raised eyebrow, and she sighed, launching into the explanation.

"My contract outlines *quite clearly* how seriously the firm takes the safety of their employees and how, due to the nature of the work we do, if an employee should encounter a situation that puts their safety in jeopardy, the firm's senior management may enact such security measures as they deem fit to protect the firm and their employees."

She shook her head and tossed the contract back on his

desk—probably a little more aggressively than was strictly necessary.

"Two questions, counselor. Before I submit to this… surveillance," she said coolly. Her father nodded.

"Go ahead."

"Would you be this concerned if I were a man? And would you go this far if I weren't your daughter?" she asked, keeping the anger from her voice by sheer force of will.

Her father pursed his lips and looked down at his desk, frowning. She shot to her feet, fury boiling through her. But before she could speak, he looked up—his eyes sad, his face weary.

"Yes, I would… and I have," he said. His gaze was steady.

She narrowed her eyes. He'd never lied to her—*not that she knew of.* But she *did* know how far he'd go to protect her. And she hated that she'd ever had reason to find out.

"Do you remember Pete Sanders?" he asked quietly.

"Of course," she replied, slowly lowering herself back down. She perched on the edge of her chair. "He used to be in Criminal Defense until he went on sabbatical two years ago. When he came back, he switched to Matro and Family Court."

"Do you know why he went on sabbatical?"

She frowned, trying to remember the particulars. "No, I don't. We all just assumed it was for medical reasons. We thought maybe the stress was getting to him."

"It wasn't for medical reasons—not the sabbatical or the transfer." Her father said. His voice was quiet, serious. "He was in a similar situation. He'd received threats to his family that were eventually traced back to a case he was working on. We sent him and his family to stay with relatives out of state and made sure he was protected until it was sorted out."

Her father glanced at Connor briefly. There were things he couldn't say at the moment—*confidential* things.

"It still seems excessive. Especially for just two weeks."

Connor frowned. "What happens in two weeks?"

"I'm leaving the country."

Connor had just started looking forward to the assignment—then she dropped that little bombshell. He'd expected Alexandra Hughes to be like every other woman in the office—boring pantsuit, sensible shoes, zero personality. But when she'd started in on her father the *second* she was through the door, he knew she was going to be a handful.

Entertaining. Challenging. Absolutely his type.

Oh, she was professional, all right. She seemed to be keeping an iron grip on her emotions. She asked her questions, made her statements, and absorbed all the information thrown at her with poise and calm.

But he'd seen the battle light in her eyes, and he'd caught a hint of a flush creep over her face more than once. Cool, calm, and collected on the outside. But inside? Rioting.

You learn everything about people when you're in their shadow. He couldn't wait to see what he would find out about Alexandra Hughes.

He knew she had a personality under that cool exterior, and she certainly wouldn't be hard on the eyes. She had curves in all the right places. Ideal proportions, wrapped in Armani and sarcasm.

Her hair just looked brown in the photos, but in the sunlight? Chocolate, honey, caramel…

And those eyes were stunning. A golden hazel with a ring of jade green on the outside. Smart. Not just sharp, but *deadly.*

She was tall—statuesque. She had to be close to six feet in those three-inch heels. Those were anything *but* sensible. Like her dark suit and blunt hairstyle, they were a power play. They'd make her taller than almost anyone she would go up against, including most men. It was calculated dominance. And it was sexy as hell on her.

To him, they were "fuck me" pumps, pure and simple. They didn't intimidate him but the way she moved in them was… mesmerizing. For just a moment, he pictured her in those heels and a tight skirt instead of slacks.

He shut that thought down. *Hard.* He turned his attention back to Mr. Hughes, who was speaking again.

"Mr. MacLachlan, or one of his associates, or possibly *more* than one, will be accompanying you to London," he said. Alexandra's eyes widened—just a fraction. She shifted, crossing her legs again. The movement caught his attention.

"I don't think that's necessary. I doubt anyone's going to follow me across the pond." She smirked, but Connor noticed the stiffness in her shoulders.

Anxiety.

"Respectfully, ma'am, we have no way of knowing what they will or won't do. Until we know who they are and what their goal is, it's best to cover every contingency," Connor replied, evenly.

He thought he might have a bit more luck convincing her. At the very least, she might be less inclined to argue with the professional than with her presumably overprotective father. But Hughes wasn't overreacting.

If there was one thing he'd learned after twelve years in the Army and three running his own company, it's that people were unpredictable. You had no way of knowing how far someone was willing to go until you saw it with your own eyes. By then it was usually too late.

And if he knew himself at all—and he liked to think he did—he already knew who'd be going with her to London. *Him.* And he could tell himself it was because he was one of the few with a valid passport, or because he was familiar with London, but that wouldn't be entirely true. Still, those were damn convincing reasons.

Alexandra studied him for a moment, then stood. Connor rose too, slowly—deliberately—stretching to his full height and slipping his hands into his pockets.

"I suppose there's no point in arguing. If there's nothing else, I'd like to get back to work." Alexandra paused for a moment, waiting impatiently to be dismissed.

Mr. Hughes frowned, clearly unhappy, but resigned to the minimal satisfaction of knowing that the biggest battle was over—even if the war waged on.

And he pitied what the man would face when he next met his daughter outside the office. He nearly smiled at the bullocking he imagined Richard Hughes would be getting from his *darling daughter.*

"Of course. I know you're busy and I have things to discuss with Mr. MacLachlan."

She just nodded in response, resolute, and made her way out of the office at a businesslike pace. Connor tried not to watch her as she walked away—he really did. And failed miserably.

"That… could have gone better." Hughes shook his head and leaned back in his chair. He looked positively exhausted. "Of course, it also could have gone *much* worse. I warned you she was stubborn."

"You certainly did," Connor agreed, offering a wry smile.

"Care to reconsider my offer?" Mr. Hughes asked, reaching into his bottom desk drawer and pulling out a bottle of amber liquid and two scotch glasses.

Connor laughed, shaking his head. "Actually, I think I will."

"Good man."

Mr. Hughes poured two fingers into each glass and handed one to Connor. He took a sip, appreciating the smooth burn of expensive whiskey as it slid down his throat.

"Would you like to know how Alexandra ended up working here?" Mr. Hughes asked, setting his glass down on the desk and leaning back.

"I'll admit it. I'm curious."

Mr. Hughes told him the story as they nursed their drinks. Connor thought he knew how the story would go, but he couldn't have been more wrong. The more he heard, the more convinced he became. Alexandra was going to be a total pain in his arse.

And he couldn't wait.

Chapter Two

"So what did *Dear Old Dad* want?" Janie handed her a Starbucks cup like an offering—no eye contact, just flawless timing.

Alexandra took a sip and groaned. Her Assistant was the patron saint of scheduling, file organization, and keeping her caffeinated enough that *everyone else* survived.

"Business, for once." She shrugged, already debating how much she should share. Janie was her right hand but she was also a friend—one of the few Alexandra had. She needed all of them. Keeping her in the dark wasn't ideal but dragging her into this mess didn't feel right either.

The phone buzzed with an interoffice call. Alexandra cringed reflexively. Janie answered it with a practiced smile and a hint of venom "Yes, Patricia?"

Alexandra snorted and swept past Janie's desk into her office. It was smaller than her father's, which suited her just fine. The layout was nearly identical—including the wall of windows—but her office was warmer. Cozier.

Bookshelves lined both walls, with a large desk facing the door and two club chairs for clients. She and her father had similar tastes, but Alexandra prioritized comfort.

She'd only allowed herself a few personal touches. A family photo tucked away on her desk where only she could see it, and a tastefully framed portrait of Ruth Bader Ginsburg with the quote:

"Women belong in all places where decisions are being made."

Understated. Comfortable. Professional. But also, unmistakably *her*.

She stripped off her jacket and slumped into her chair. Her heels hit the floor with a thud as she kicked them off. The file she'd abandoned still lay strewn across her desk, exactly where she'd left it. She picked up her notes, trying to shift her focus back to the upcoming deposition.

But her thoughts kept drifting back to the meeting. And to Connor MacLachlan. She ran through her cases again, wondering if there was anything she'd missed—anything that would push someone this far.

If they wanted something—money, a better outcome in their case—why no note?

Would there be another package? A letter?

None of this made any sense.

Nothing she was working on seemed serious enough to resort to blackmail.

No high-profile clients. No criminal charges. Just the usual cases, completely unremarkable. She handled litigation cases—breach of contract, med mal, personal injury.

The worst outcome she usually saw was someone—or more often their insurance company—writing a check.

Only one case was headed to trial before she left for London—but even that was only worth *maybe* a million dollars. And she was almost certain they'd settle out of court after the deposition. The one she was currently *supposed* to be preparing for.

Enough. Stop obsessing. Get your head back in the game.

It didn't matter how much money was at stake—*every* client deserved her best. She wanted to help—to be part of the system where everyone was equal and treated with respect.

A system that was fair. Just. Impartial.

Except it hadn't been—not for me.

She shook her head like an Etch-A-Sketch, hoping to clear it. The system had failed her. That was all the more reason to stay focused. Committed. To make sure it didn't happen again.

She couldn't fix it from the outside. So instead, she'd find ways to beat it.

She took a few deep breaths, centered herself, and returned to her notes. It worked—*mostly*. She managed a few solid hours before her four o'clock deposition.

By five-thirty, Alexandra was walking out of the third-floor conference room, trying not to be *too* smug as the defendant and opposing counsel filed past. Their lawyer mumbled, "We'll be in touch next week," without meeting her eye.

Not that he could've met her eyes if he'd tried.

"Looking forward to it." She kept her tone gracious—with just enough edge to sting.

As soon as they were on the elevators with the doors closing behind them, she had to resist the urge to pump her fist and strut down the hallway like Queen Beyonce.

"Nice work." She felt a quick squeeze on her shoulder and looked behind her. Charles Bennett smiled at her.

"Thanks. You weren't so bad yourself."

Charles laughed. "Please. I was *clearly* only there for moral support. And aesthetics." He winked at her. "But, you crushed it, kid."

Alexandra rolled her eyes. Anyone else would have gotten the evil eye, and possibly a swift kick in the… *shin*. But Charles? He was her oldest friend. They'd known each other since their first year of law school, and it was sort of an inside joke. Since she'd graduated high school and college early, she was two years younger, and he'd been calling her "kid" ever since he found out.

"Thanks. Say it louder for the suits upstairs."

Charles laughed again, flashing that perfectly straight, perfectly white, movie star smile. Even Julie would be jealous of that smile. And because life was wildly unfair, that wasn't even his best feature.

Charles Bennett was objectively perfect. He looked just like the boy next door, or "the boy next door" as portrayed by a Hollywood actor. Golden blond hair, a jawline that could cut glass, stormcloud-blue eyes, dimples—the works. And he looked *damn good* in a suit.

"What?" he asked, giving her a skeptical look. "Do I have spinach in my teeth?"

Alexandra snorted and rolled her eyes. "Like you'd ever be caught *dead* with spinach in your teeth. No, I was just thinking what a handsome bastard you are."

"That I am," he replied without missing a beat. A smile that smug shouldn't be charming, but somehow it was.

"God, I love your face," Alexandra said with a laugh.

"I thought we just established that," Charles said, cocking his head to the side in feigned confusion. Then he smiled wide and shot her a wink. "I love your face, too."

Alexandra squeezed his arm, and they headed back to their offices, still basking in their pre-trial smackdown. "You joining us for drinks?"

"If you're buying."

"First round *only*," she warned. "Between you and Janie, I'd be broke by closing time."

"Closing time—"

"No. Singing," Alexandra said quickly.

"You know… you used to be fun," he sighed. "It's a shame that all work and no play has made you a dull boy."

"If I were a dull *boy,* I think our plans for the evening would look very different."

Charles laughed. "True," he agreed with nod. "I'll grab my stuff and meet you out front. Should I get a cab?"

"No cab. It's close. We'll walk."

Alexandra left Charles at his door and made a beeline for Janie's desk.

"How'd it go?" Janie asked without looking up. Janie cared about their cases, but she had more faith in Alexandra than she deserved. Alexandra was tempted to mess with her a little but decided to be nice.

"We killed it," Alexandra said with a shrug. Janie finally looked up at her and smirked.

"Of course you did. Between you and Charles they were probably too stunned to even *speak*. And when they did, I'm sure you gave them the verbal smackdown they deserved."

"Excuse me? I was the epitome of professionalism," Alexandra replied.

"Oh, I'm sure it was a *very* professional evisceration. The most professional in history, probably. Anyway, congratulations, killer."

Alexandra snorted. "Don't congratulate me yet. They might offer to settle, but if they low-ball us, we're definitely still taking it to court."

"I'm sure they'll cave. You've got them by the balls," Janie said with a wicked smile.

"Watch your language, Janis. This is a place of business."

Janie scowled. She hated her full name.

"Yeah? Language, yourself," Janie grumbled.

Alexandra laughed but decided to extend an olive branch.

"Sorry. Peace offering? Why don't we go to that new place you wanted to try?"

Janie practically jumped out of her seat, clapping her hands together. "Fabulous. I've only been *begging* to go for ages."

"Charles is coming too," Alexandra added.

Janie's arms dropped like someone cut her puppet strings. She rolled her eyes dramatically.

"Ugh, fine."

"Don't be a bitch. You *like* Charles."

"Oh, don't get it twisted, I *love* Charles," Janie said. "If he were straight, I'd climb that man like a tree and never come down. But he's too gorgeous. He scares away all the other men in the room just by *existing*."

Alexandra laughed, but she couldn't argue. That was part of why she invited him—he was a human buffer. Especially when it came to men.

She wasn't looking to meet anyone, and while she wouldn't mind a little harmless flirting, most guys saw that as an opening. Honestly, she just didn't have time, interest, or energy for that kind of hassle.

"Don't worry. I'll keep him occupied. And you can sample the entire buffet of toxic masculinity. Tastes like mediocrity and regret."

"Deal," Janie said with a grin.

"I'll be right there. Charles is probably out front already."

Alexandra ducked into her office, dropped the deposition file onto the growing stack on her desk, and grabbed her coat and bag. She was halfway to the door when her intercom buzzed.

"Seriously, Janie? You couldn't wait thirty seconds?" she huffed.

"Um, there's someone to see you, Ms. Hughes." Janie sounded nervous. Janie didn't *get* nervous. Alexandra's stomach dropped as the events from earlier came rushing back to her.

Shit.

She'd almost forgotten. She'd been so focused on work that she'd actually managed to completely block out the meeting with her father. That was probably him now—ready to rehash everything and make sure she'd play nice with the bodyguards like a good little girl.

"Send him in," Alexandra sighed. She tossed her bag and coat in one of the chairs and leaned back against her desk, folding her arms across her chest.

But it wasn't her father who walked through the door. It was Connor MacLachlan.

It took Alexandra a second to register Janie, still standing just outside the door. When she did, Janie met her eyes over Connor's shoulder and mouthed "HO. LY. SHIT." Alexandra subtly shook her head as she stepped around him quickly pushing the door shut.

She exhaled slowly, relieved that Janie was safely on the other side of the door. She paused, took a second to compose herself, and turned back to her desk.

When she finally looked at him—*really* looked at him—her jaw nearly dropped. Okay, gun to her head—he'd *briefly* caught her eye in her father's office. But now? There were no words for how good he looked.

Like the eighth deadly sin in grey cotton and denim…

He'd changed—*literally*. The suit was gone, replaced by faded jeans torn at the thigh, a black t-shirt stretched across a broad chest and flat stomach, an unzipped grey hoodie beneath a black peacoat, and worn work boots. The five o'clock shadow was just the cherry on top. The effect was…

Mouthwatering.

Clearly, she hadn't been expecting him. Connor had assumed Mr. Hughes would've briefed her.

Apparently not. She looked thoroughly baffled.

Which meant he'd have the pleasure of explaining it to her *personally*. She gave him a frank once-over. Maybe she was appalled by the casual clothes—or maybe she just liked what she saw.

When a blush crept over the collar of her crisp, white blouse, he had his answer.

Interesting.

She finally blinked—rapidly—and turned away, suddenly fascinated by the papers on her desk.

He didn't comment, giving her a moment to recover. He let her have that small semblance of control.

"What can I do for you?" she asked. Her voice cracked on the last word. He smiled, thinking she wouldn't notice.

But when their eyes met in the reflection of the darkened window, she froze. Her expression shuttered and she turned around, jaw tight, face stiff.

"Was there something you needed, *Mr. MacLachlan*?" She spat his name like it tasted foul. He didn't care for that. At all.

"No, ma'am," he replied. "I'm here to begin your protection detail."

Alexandra's frown deepened. "The old man left you to do the dirty work, didn't he?"

"I'm not sure what you mean," Connor said blandly, hoping she'd take it up with her father and leave him out of it.

She snorted and he bit the inside of his cheek to keep from grinning.

"Right," she said, drawing out the word. "Okay, I'm going to tell you what I think happened. Stop me if I'm wrong." She waited for a beat, but no more. She didn't require an answer. She just expected him to obey.

Adorable.

"I'm assuming that you and my father hammered out the details of this… *arrangement* after I left his office?"

"Yes, ma'am."

"And you either assumed—or he led you to believe—that he would relay the pertinent information to me before you began your duties."

She paused again, waiting.

"Am I under oath?" he asked, brow arched.

"Just answer the question—if you don't mind." Her tone made it clear: she didn't give a shit whether he did or not.

"That would be a fair assessment." He tried—not very hard—to keep a straight face. He failed.

Another mistake.

Her eyes narrowed. Every line of her body went tense.

"And what were the terms?" she asked.

"You'll have a protective detail any time you aren't at home or the office. Any off-site visits will be accompanied by one or more of my people, depending on the circumstances. Door-to-door escort."

"How many of your people?" she asked calmly. *Too* calmly.

"Five or six total, rotating shifts. One or two at a time."

"Beginning now, I assume?"

"Yes, ma'am." He nodded once, sharply.

"So, hours ago, you and my father discussed all of this. And you left with the impression that he would fill me in after you left."

"I—"

"And then, *knowing* that I was already… *displeased* with his decision, he failed to do so—instead leaving it to you to break the news when you arrived." She was locked on to him with laser focus. It was a little unnerving.

"Tell me… is that a fair *assessment*, Mr. MacLachlan?"

"It would seem so," Connor said, crossing his arms.

"In other words, he left you to do the dirty work."

Alexandra smirked and Connor thought she might actually say "I rest my case."

Instead, she just shook her head and muttered something that sounded suspiciously like "unbelievable."

"Honestly, the mistake was mine," Connor said. "I assumed your father would fill you in. That was an oversight on my part. Next time, I'll make sure we're all on the same page."

Her gaze sharpened—assessing.

"Tactful," she finally said—like she was surprised. "Make sure you're *very* clear with Mr. Hughes in the future. He's an expert when it comes to lies of omission. It's the only kind a lawyer can get away with."

"Thanks for the advice," he replied, his smile polite. "I'll keep that in mind."

"Please do." Her stare was unflinching. "Because contrary to what my father believes, I *am* petty enough to shoot the messenger."

She glared. And he believed her.

Yeah. He'd been right.

She was going to be a serious pain in the arse. Uncooperative clients made the job ten times harder. Constantly arguing about the rules, trying to ditch their detail.

He was there to protect her, not babysit. If she wanted to be a problem, he'd shut that down—*right feckin' now.*

Connor unfolded his arms and took two steps forward—slow, deliberate. Her eyes went wide as he leaned in and braced both hands on the desk, caging her in.

He kept his voice calm. Quiet.

He looked her straight in the eye, his face inches from hers.

Up close, he could see the flecks of green and gold in her hazel eyes. Her perfume was warm and sweet. Her skin radiated heat.

"I hear you," he said, voice low and rough. "And you can scream your fool head off all day if that's what you want. But I *will* do my job—whether you like it or not." He paused, letting his words settle into the silence between them.

"You don't have to like me." His hands flexed for a moment on the desk and the muscle in his jaw twitched. "But I'll keep you safe. Even if I have to throw you over my shoulder and carry you out of the office like a sack of barley every night."

She swallowed hard, her face flushing a tempting shade of pink.

"You wouldn't dare," she whispered.

"Feel free to test me anytime." His smile was a little—or maybe *a lot*—predatory.

If looks could kill, he'd already be six feet under and she'd be dancing at his wake. But she didn't say a word.

"So," he said causally, straightening away from the desk. "Any plans tonight?"

Her brow furrowed in confusion, blush deepening.

It took effort not to say something that would *really* make her overheat. No need look like more of an arsehole than he already did. *Probably.*

"Not really," she said. She glanced at the chair, then back to him. He stepped back—just enough for her to grab her coat and purse.

"A few of us are going for drinks."

"Brilliant. I could use a beer."

Her eyes snapped to his, startled. "You're really starting right now?"

"Yes, ma'am. Right now. Your father requested we start immediately… and I agreed. Seemed advisable."

"Okay, I get it," she said, exasperated. "And stop calling me *ma'am*. I have a name—two of them, in fact."

"Fair enough." He leaned in until their eyes were level. "*Ms. Hughes.*"

She turned to put on her coat, but he heard the shaky breath she took as she adjusted the collar.

She hesitated as she turned back—just for a moment—before squaring her shoulders, like she'd made a decision.

"Listen, I haven't…" She paused, chewing her lip. "I don't want the others involved."

Connor didn't say anything—just watched her carefully.

"Is there any way to do… *this*—" she gestured vaguely between them, "without making it obvious?"

Normally, he'd have told her he didn't give a rat's arse about office drama. Not his job and not his problem. But…

It was all over her face—fear, anxiety, uncertainty. All the things she'd bottled up. She'd let the mask slip.

And he wasn't prepared for that. Or how much it got to him.

Damn it all.

He took a deep breath and held it for a second, then let it out slowly.

"Look, I don't need to be on top of you all night."

She blushed.

Connor had to look away.

Christ.

"I need eyes on you at all times, and I've gotta be close enough to get to you—*fast.* But I'll be watching everyone else, not you. It's not like I'll be there to socialize."

"How close is *close enough?*" she asked, biting her lip again. It was damn cute. And *too* distracting.

"In a crowded place? Five feet."

"Ten."

He scowled.

This is what I get for trying to be accommodating.

"Five." He folded his arms. "This isn't a negotiation. This is your *safety. Five. Feet.*" He stepped closer, bending slightly—invading her space.

"If you try to ditch me, or duck out?" His voice dropped. "I'll be on your ass so fast your pretty little head will spin. And I'll *stay* there 'til the job's done. Get me?"

Alexandra glared silently up at him, cheeks burning.

Now what the hell am I supposed to do with that?

She wasn't sure if her mind had followed Janie's into the gutter… or if he'd pulled it down there on purpose.

On top of you all night…

On your ass so fast your pretty little head will spin…

Who the hell actually talks like that?

His tone infuriated her—cocky, condescending, menacing in a way that had no business being as hot as it was. A voice in the back of her head screamed that he needed to be taken down a peg or two.

So why the hell was all of that being drowned out by the surge of adrenaline suddenly roaring through her?

All she could hear was her own heart pounding.

She couldn't tell if she wanted to kiss him or gouge his eyes out.

And that was more than a little concerning. The idea that it was probably a little of both crossed her mind.

Even worse.

At this rate, she'd need stage makeup to hide all the blushing—or she'd just have to claim she had the flu and start wearing a surgical mask.

She just prayed that this whole mess would blow over before London—before she had to pay the checked luggage fee for all the extra baggage.

The last thing she needed while juggling Maid of Honor duties and trying to enjoy a much-needed break from work was to be stuck with a shadow.

A cocky, confusing, annoying, gorgeous, muscular—

Stop it.

Stop that right now.

She didn't say a word as she followed him out of the building. Janie had gone ahead, texting Alexandra that she and Charles would be waiting at the bar. It was October—*way* too cold to stand around waiting in the dark. Especially when there were drinks and men just down the street.

Unfortunately, that left Alexandra stuck walking three blocks in uncomfortable silence… with her surly, burly bodyguard.

Kill me now.

She nearly choked, imagining his reaction if she ever called him that out loud. Then he looked at her and quirked a damn eyebrow. She glowered, all of her humor evaporating.

Fine. Just walk fast and get this over with.

They pushed through the glass doors and she turned left—until a large hand caught her arm.

"Car's this way," Connor said, jerking his chin in the opposite direction.

"It's three blocks. I was gonna walk," she said, trying to tug her arm free.

"Then what?" he asked, tilting his head.

She could practically *hear* the implied "stupid" at the end of that sentence. And she didn't appreciate it.

"Then come back the whole *three* blocks for my car," she explained slowly, like he was three years old.

She knew *exactly* how condescending it sounded, but he deserved it.

He gave her a look that said he knew *exactly* what she was doing—and he wasn't taking the bait. "I think it's better if I drive you," he said. "I'll take you home afterward. You can leave your car here."

"I beg your *finest* pardon?" she laughed, her disbelief palpable.

"Escort. Door-to-door. Apartment and office," he said, enunciating each word slowly. Carefully. *Infuriatingly.*

"That was the agreement. I'll *escort* you home. Depending on your schedule, I can bring you back to pick up your car tomorrow."

"Wait… You're not planning to *sleep over,* are you?"

Nuh-uh. No way. Absolutely not.

Her apartment was sacred, and her personal space? Untouchable.

She didn't have friends over. Dinners were rare. And sleepovers? Never—except her sister.

Connor ran a hand through his hair, clearly as over this conversation as she was.

Good.

And he had the nerve to look even better afterwards.

Asshole.

What she wouldn't give to have *that* superpower.

"No, ma'am," he gritted out, grabbing her attention. "Unless you plan to sneak out in the middle of the night." He quirked an eyebrow.

She was really beginning to hate him. *And* his stupid, smug eyebrows.

"I hadn't planned on it, no," she said, her voice dripping acid.

"Good," he replied, unbothered.

Jerk.

"Then I'll take you back to yours, make sure you're safe and sound, then go home, sleep *in my own bed*, and come back in the morning."

"That's a relief," she muttered.

He finally let go and gestured for her to go ahead. She thought about it, decided it wasn't worth the argument, and followed him. He stopped in front of a massive black SUV that looked like it could—and probably *had*—carried a small battalion.

He opened the passenger side door for her and held out a hand, offering to help her climb up into the behemoth. One look at the step up told her she didn't have a choice.

Again, she noticed the callouses.

And the warmth.

And his grip—sure, but gentle.

Great. He even has perfect hands.

The drive was quiet, and that was fine with her. She couldn't figure him out. He went from playful and *almost* charming, to argumentative and stubborn in under thirty seconds. With detours through serious and politely professional.

She'd known him for maybe an hour total, and she'd already seen more sides of him than most men showed in decades. With the possible exception of Charles.

She was usually a decent judge of character—a few notable and *deeply regrettable* exceptions notwithstanding. It never took her very long. By the end of her first meeting, she already knew exactly what kind of client she was dealing with.

She'd known she was hiring Janie within the first five minutes of her interview. She'd known everything—*almost*—about Charles before he even opened his mouth. They'd been friends ever since.

More or less.

But Connor MacLachlan? He was a different story.

He'd been honest with her—answering her questions. He'd even agreed to give her space when she'd explained why she needed it.

Maybe she was being too hard on him. It was just possible that he was only doing his job. Since she had no frame of reference, she should probably trust his judgment—to a point.

The whole situation sucked. But that wasn't his fault. Honestly, she couldn't even really blame her father. He was trying to do the right thing, as her father *and* as her boss.

The truth was, she didn't have any *logical* reason to be upset with either of them. It was an inconvenience, but a necessary one. She just found herself… off-balance.

And *that,* she absolutely could not stand.

Connor pulled up to the curb, smoothly parallel parked—impressive given the monster he was driving—and hopped out. As he circled the front to open her door, she decided she *might* owe him an apology.

They'd just gotten off on the wrong foot.

And he would have gotten that apology if he hadn't opened his damn mouth.

"Well, I feel a wee bit overdressed, but at least I dinnae have any trouble finding it," Connor smirked.

Alexandra frowned at him like he'd just committed a felony. He grinned wider, pointing to the pink neon sign hanging above the bar's entrance.

G-SPOT.

Alexandra read the sign and flushed all the way to her hairline.

Damn, but she's easy to rile.

She muttered something under her breath, frowned again, and spun around to glare at him.

"Right," she snapped. "Five feet. No hiding. No sneaking away."

He nodded, confirming the rules.

"But," she continued, "in there? You don't know me."

Her glare was so cold, he'd swear he felt the temperature drop.

"Just because I have to tolerate your… *hovering*, doesn't mean I want you interfering with my life."

Connor frowned, opened his mouth to respond, but she raised a hand, silencing him.

"In other words," she said coolly. "I expect to *see* you… but not *hear* you."

Oh, I see. Kitten's got claws, huh?

He'd best not forget it. But the spitfire? So much more fun than Miss Emotionally Repressed.

And the fact that these little tantrums of hers came with those adorable blushes? Win-win. He'd take blushing and cranky over bland and boring any day.

He opened his mouth—locked and loaded with a comeback—but his phone rang. He glanced at the screen and grimaced as he accepted the call.

"What's wrong, Angel?" he said quietly, holding up a finger—asking Alexandra to wait a moment. She was positioned between him and the Humvee, well-covered. Still, he scanned the sidewalk. Watched the people moving. Eyes sharp, body ready. Alert.

"Can you come over?" Angel asked. Her voice was small, anxious. "I need your help. My car won't start. Melissa is covering my shift tonight, but I have to go in tomorrow. I'd take a sick day, but Maureen is still on maternity leave and Melissa has worked the last eight days straight…"

"I'm working right now," he replied with a sigh.

"Please, Connor? I know it's a lot to ask, but I can't lose my job." He took a deep breath and let it out in a short huff. Of course, he'd agree—he always did—but the timing definitely sucked.

"Alright. I'll come by as soon as I can but it might not be until late. Are you going to wait up for me, or should I just use the spare key?" He checked on Alexandra to make sure she was still there, just behind him. Satisfied she was still within reach as she should be, he went back to watching the crowd.

"I'll wait for you. Thank you for this. You're the best brother in the world."

"The best, huh?" He chuckled.

"Absolutely. Hands down," she replied. He could hear the smile in her voice and he couldn't help but grin. She didn't smile nearly enough. Just hearing it in her voice did his heart more good than he could say.

"Alright, I have to go. I'll see you later."

"Love you."

"Love you, too." Hanging up the call he turned back just in time to see Alexandra hustling toward the front door.

The hell…

He locked the car with the key fob as he jogged after her, his long legs eating up the ground between them. Catching up to her just as she slipped through the door, he grabbed her hand. She spun on him, all fury, eyes throwing sparks.

"You couldn't have waited two minutes?" he growled, tugging her out of the doorway.

"It's your job to stay with *me*," she snapped. "Not the other way around. Maybe you shouldn't be taking personal calls at work and you wouldn't get distracted and lose track of your… *person.*"

She yanked her hand from his, spun on her heel, and made a beeline for the back of the bar. He forced himself to wait a beat before following her, staying a few steps behind. He didn't know what her problem was this time, but they were definitely going to have a *wee* chat in the car later. And not a quiet one.

She threw her shoulders back, raised her chin and waved as she approached the bar. He recognized her assistant, but he didn't recognize the good-looking blonde guy in the expensive suit she was sitting next to.

Looks like Malibu Ken.

Connor snorted under his breath and took a seat halfway down the bar. He ordered a pint. It would no doubt taste like piss, but he needed to have something—to cool his head and to blend into the crowd.

He swiveled the stool to face outward and put one arm on the bar while he sipped his generic beer. From there he could keep an eye on the crowd, and Alexandra.

His first problem came in the form a blonde in a skintight dress and too much makeup. She caught his eye and smiled. Connor looked away pretending not to notice. He hoped if he ignored her, she'd get the message. She was party-girl pretty but not his type. Even if she was, he wasn't interested. Not tonight. Not while he was working.

She stopped just inches in front of him and leaned over. Her breasts were in his face, and he nearly gagged on her perfume. Some overly synthetic floral stench that made his throat burn and his eyes water.

Up close—*way* too close—he could see she was young. Possibly too young to be there. Her blonde hair was pulled up into a high ponytail and—

Is that glitter?

Sure enough, her hair, her face, her cleavage—all dusted with glitter.

You've got to be fuckin' kidding me.

"Buy me a drink?" she purred, breath warm in his ear. She'd clearly had two or three already. The last thing she needed was one more—but it was none of his business. She was an adult. Her choice. He should just gently refuse and let her go about her business so he could do his job.

He glanced over his shoulder. Alexandra and Janie were talking enthusiastically about something. There was a lot of gesturing and laughing.

The girl twirled a lock of hair around one glittery finger, and suddenly she looked twelve. And worse, it reminded him of someone who used to do the same damn thing.

Ah, hell…

"Sure," he said. He swiveled and signaled the bartender. He leaned in, ordered and pulled in a lungful of fresh air. Or what passed for fresh air in this place. She perched on the stool next to him—directly between him and Alexandra, blocking his line of sight.

"You come here often?" she asked.

"First time," Connor admitted.

"It's my first time, too," she said, leaning in to be heard over the music and placing a hand on his thigh to steady herself. Considering she barely looked legal, Connor immediately felt like needed a scalding shower, some steel wool and maybe—*definitely*—a priest.

He was relieved when the bartender brought her drink and she had to remove her hand from his leg to pick up the glass. She did a little shimmy as she took the first sip. She paused, took another—much bigger—sip and set the glass down with a frown.

"This is just soda," she said, craning her neck to see the bartender at the other end of the bar, trying to get his attention.

"That's what I ordered," Connor said, sipping his beer. He should have ordered the same for himself. His beer tasted like micro-brewed regret.

"What?" she asked, clearly confused. He sighed.

"How old are you?" He set his beer down and turned to face her.

"Twenty-two. Why?" she replied, instantly defensive.

Jesus Christ, she's a fetus…

Why the hell couldn't he just let things go? Always stepping into shit that was none of his business. He didn't know this girl. It wasn't his problem.

But every single time something like this happened, he just couldn't help himself. Sam—best friend and bane of his fucking existence—always told him he had a savior complex.

Apparently, he was right.

He spotted Alexandra again, exactly where she'd been the last half hour. It didn't look like she was leaving any time soon. On the contrary, she'd ordered a second round so it was almost guaranteed he had another twenty minutes or so. He'd have to work with what he had.

"You in school?" he asked, resting one arm on the bar and interlacing his fingers as he watched her face.

"Yeah." Her tone was suspicious.

Good. She should be…

"What's your major?" he asked. She hesitated for a second, and he could see the wheels spinning.

"Graphic design," she finally said. Connor nodded.

"That's a good choice," he said, nodding. "Do you like it?"

"I mean, yeah." She shrugged. "It's fun. I'm pretty good at it."

"Good. That's grand. Seems like you're on the right track."

"I guess," she said. "I mean, I hope so." Her laugh was a little self-conscious—her smile shy. Nothing like when she'd strutted up to him a few minutes ago.

"Look, you seem like a nice girl…" he began, struggling to find the right words. "Do you have a brother?" He braced himself for the weird look.

"What?" She blinked at him, bewildered.

"This will be easier to explain if you've a brother. Or maybe an older sister?"

"I have two older brothers. Why?"

"The thing is, I've got a younger sister. She's a bit like you—pretty, smart, talented." he paused. She blushed and looked away.

Shite… Not where I wanted this to go.

"But I worry about her a lot, you know?" He waited until she looked up at him. "The world's a scary place and I can't always be there to watch out for her," he added seriously. "I bet your brothers feel the same way."

She rolled her eyes but she smiled a little. "They are *so* overprotective. When I was in high school I had to tell them where I was going and who I was hanging out with. *All the time.* So annoying."

"Bet you're glad to have a bit of freedom now, yeah?"

"Absolutely," she agreed.

"But I'll bet your brothers still worry. Wondering where you are—if you're safe. That's how I was when my sister was far away. Drove me crazy."

She looked down at her hands, fidgeting with her rings. He let the silence stretch for a moment. Gave her space to think.

"And when I couldn't be there," he said finally. "I always hoped that someone might step in—make sure she was okay, see if she had a way to get home. Ask if she had a friend or two with her so she wasn't alone at night. You know what I'm saying?" he asked, giving her what he hoped passed for a meaningful look.

She glanced up at him quickly before lowering her head again.

Pease don't be crying, please don't be crying, please don't be crying…

He'd really feel like shit if he'd made her cry.

"My friends are over there," she said quietly. Looking across the room, he saw two girls who looked to be her age sitting at a table. With them were two men who *did not* look the same age. "We're sharing an uber back to the dorm. Just the *three* of us," she promised quietly.

"Ah, that's smart. Your brothers would be proud."

She smiled sheepishly—suddenly looking exactly like the little girl her brothers probably still saw. They'd have to get used to the fact she was grown sooner or later. But he understood the urge to put it off as long as possible.

"I better go," she said, slipping off the barstool.

"Hold on," Connor said, standing up and pulling a business card out of his wallet. "Take this. If you're ever out and find yourself in trouble, you can call me." She went to take the card, but he held on to it until she looked at him.

"Make sure you look me up when you get home. Don't just take my word for it, right?" He winked at her and smiled, letting go of the card so she could tuck it into her tiny purse.

"Thanks." She gave him a little wave before she turned and walked away.

"And call your brothers," he called after her.

She rolled her eyes, but she was smiling now—and trying to hide it. "I will."

Then she walked away, melting into the sea of people on the dance floor. When she emerged on the other side, he saw her whisper something to one friend and then motion for both girls to follow her. The other girls looked a little confused, but they did it anyway.

He watched in relief as all three walked out the front door—hopefully straight into a cab. And he sent up a silent prayer that she and her friends would stay safe and make good choices.

He glanced over at Alexandra again only to find her scowling at him. She was furious. The Ken doll in the suit said something to her and started to turn Connor's way. She shook herself, smiled and put a hand on his arm, drawing his attention back to her.

Connor frowned. Janie was nowhere in sight. And Alexandra was alone—with someone he didn't know and hadn't vetted. Even if *she* knew him, that didn't mean he wasn't a suspect.

He sipped his beer and then set it right back down. It was warm which did *not* improve the taste. The next time he caught Alexandra's eye her expression was unreadable. Her eyes were still flashing warning signs, but there was a smile tugging at the corner of her mouth—like she was *trying* to piss him off.

She turned her attention back to the blonde prick—laughing at something he said. She put her hand on his arm. Again. This time she left it there. Connor watched, growing more uncomfortable by the moment. It seemed like this was going to be his night for handing out life lessons.

Alexandra laughed again and ran her hands through her hair. It looked better a little messy—it suited her better than the pin-straight style she'd walked in with.

She ordered a third drink. Nothing frilly—a gin and tonic. From what he'd seen so far, the bartender was being generous. The drinks were stronger than usual.

Connor sincerely hoped he wouldn't have to carry her home tonight. If she booted in his Hummer—so help him God…

Alexandra slipped out of her suit jacket, undoing the top two buttons of her blouse. And that tiny sliver of skin? It grabbed his attention harder than anything else had all night.

She picked up a cocktail menu and started fanning herself with it. Head tilted to one side, hair swept off of her neck…

His mind was seething. And other parts of him were *definitely* taking notice. She was beautiful. That had been obvious from the moment he saw her—even if she did try to hide it behind the clothes and the tough-as-nails attitude.

She'd walked into that office in three-inch heels, lithe and graceful. He'd been mesmerized. The black suit might scream *power play*, but it was perfectly tailored to her every curve. Sharp. Professional. And flattering as hell. It had only made him more curious about what was underneath.

Now, it was like everything she did was designed to drive him mad. The tilt of her head and the curve of her neck as she listened. The way she crossed her legs, hooking one heel on the rung of the bar stool. The tension in his body was ratcheting up by the second.

And he was dangerously close to his breaking point.

The image of her full mouth wrapped around that straw was going to fuel his fantasies for *weeks*. When she lost the straw and her tongue darted out to catch it, he sucked in a breath through his teeth. The dull ache in his groin sharpened—sudden, intense, *immediate.*

Connor pushed his beer away. He'd clearly had enough.

Tastes like pish anyway…

Alexandra leaned in and whispered something in the man's ear. He laughed and put a hand on her waist. Connor's vision went red. He didn't know what the hell she was doing, but if she thought he was letting her go home with anyone else, she was out of her goddamn mind.

And if she thought for one second that she was taking this assclown home tonight, she was full-on fucking delusional.

Not a fucking chance in hell…

Connor scowled. She'd almost finished her drink already. She was gonna be steamin' at this rate. A slow smile spread across her face as she looked down at the bar. She looked up at the man next to her through a fringe of dark lashes. Then she bit her lip and Connor froze.

Oh, I think the fuck not…

This stops. *Now.*

He stood up and the movement caught her eye. When she looked at him this time, Connor could see a flicker of doubt—just a whisper of uncertainty. He grinned.

You brought this on yourself, lass…

Chapter Three

Okay. Maybe she'd gone too far. Alexandra *had* promised Janie she'd keep Charles occupied—keep her from getting cock-blocked. And that's what she was doing. At first.

But then he just had to open that smug, gorgeous mouth. She was angry—at Connor, at herself—so she'd decided to mess with him. Just a little. Just enough to make her feel better.

It wasn't like he hadn't been needling her from the moment they met. It *had* to be intentional.

And flirting with that blonde bimbo? Unacceptable.

And it had *nothing* to do with how he'd been intentionally provoking her all evening—charming her, teasing her. She wasn't interested. *At all.* She'd given up dating a long time ago and hadn't missed it. *Much.*

But that phone call early was so obviously from a girlfriend. Cheating on the clock? Unprofessional. Dishonest. *Despicable.*

She wanted nothing to do with him.

Maybe if he thought she was interested in Charles—or even better, that Charles was her boyfriend—he'd back off. Because here he was, flirting with her like it came naturally when he had a girlfriend. He hadn't even bothered to ask if she had a boyfriend. If she had to sit here feeling like an idiot, the least he could do was have the decency to feel like an asshole.

She sighed—body sagging.

She was lying to herself.

And she knew it.

She wasn't morally superior. She was *jealous.*

Jealous and uncomfortable about it.

And now her brilliant plan was looking more like a huge mistake.

He didn't look sorry. He didn't look like he felt like an asshole.

Just mad.

And smug.

A crowd had formed at the bar and by the time it cleared, he was gone. She'd lost sight of him, but she knew he hadn't lost sight of her. The hair on the back of her neck stood up and she tossed back the rest of her drink.

That made three—two more than she'd normally have. And it was starting to catch up with her. It had been a while since she'd really let her hair down. Her victory this afternoon seemed like a good reason to celebrate. And *Connor* had turned out to be an excellent reason to drink. *Heavily.*

She needed to step back and regroup. His self-satisfied smile told her something was about to happen. Something she wouldn't like. She needed an exit strategy.

She'd have to face him eventually—but not now.

Take a minute, pull yourself together and focus on getting home.

She could figure out the rest later. And maybe she wouldn't see him again. He'd said there were five other people on his team. Maybe he'd just hand her off after tonight. Would that be better... or worse?

The longer she sat there, the worse her nerves got.

"I'm going to use the ladies' room."

The bathroom was safe. No boys allowed.

She stood up—too fast. Instant regret. The room lurched and she teetered a bit on her heels. A pair of hands steadied her. Large, warm hands circling her waist.

Charles still sat on his stool around the corner of the bar. He hadn't moved. Or turned into Mr. Fantastic.

She blinked a few times and looked over her shoulder. She swallowed hard, knowing who she would find. Connor was there, grinning down at her. And it almost took her breath away.

Until she realized he was probably just so proud of himself for swooping in to rescue her in her moment of weakness.

"Whoa, easy there" he said, voice deceptively gentle. "You're mad wi' it, aren't ye?"

"What?" she said. His accent was thicker now—she had no idea what he'd just said. Or why his hands were still on her waist. And why was the room still spinning?

"You're drunk," he chuckled. "Sorry I'm late. I had to take a call."

Then he kissed her—quick and hard—leaving her stunned, confused… and a little tingly.

"Connor MacLachlan," he said, offering his hand. "Alexandra's boyfriend."

Boyfriend? BOYFRIEND?!

"You-" she stammered. "You…"

Her mind went blank. She stood there stunned.

"Charles Bennett," he said coolly. "Nice to meet you."

The familiar edge in his voice snapped her out of her stupor.

Oh, shit. This is bad.

"Boyfriend, huh? I didn't know Alexandra was seeing anyone." He smiled politely as he shook Connor's hand. It didn't reach his eyes and when he looked at her, she could practically feel the daggers he was throwing her way.

"It hasnae been long," Connor replied, smiling fondly down at her. One of his hands was still on her waist and he tightened his grip for a moment.

"Oh, uh, no—no it hasn't." She offered Charles a weak smile, but he simply nodded.

"That makes sense. We've been so busy at work, I guess she just… hasn't had the chance to mention it."

Yup. He was pissed.

"Well, like he said, it hasn't been long, and I hadn't really planned on telling anyone yet." She shot Connor a look that screamed: *Shut. The hell. Up.*

She had no idea how she was going to explain. And he'd demand answers. She told Charles everything. He knew her too well—her schedule, her habits, just how profoundly unsocial she was. Where the hell would she have met someone like Connor?

She didn't want to worry him. Or Janie. It was bad enough that her father had to deal with this. But if she wanted this to work, she was going to have to commit, and fast. Unfortunately, her brain was too pickled to figure that out at the moment.

One thing at a time. Damage Control.

"This is the friend I told you about," she said looking up at Connor with what she hoped was a convincing smile. "The one I went to law school with?"

Connor didn't miss a beat.

"Of course I do," he said smoothly. To Charles he added: "She can hardly shut up about ye. Grand to finally meet ye, Charlie."

Charles's eyes narrowed—just barely. It was so imperceptible Alexandra didn't *see it*. She *felt* it. Like a drop in barometric pressure.

"Ready to head home, love?" Connor winked at her. She resisted the urge to punch him. Barely.

"Absolutely. Just need to use the bathroom first." She grabbed his arm, holding onto his coat sleeve for dear life.

"I'd better help you get there. Doesn't seem like you're too steady on your feet at the moment." He grinned again and she wanted to kick him. Or kiss him. Maybe both? Probably both. *Definitely* both.

"See you around, Charlie," Connor called over his shoulder as he ushered her toward the bathrooms.

As soon as they were out of sight, she spun on him—wobbled—and caught herself with a hand on the wall.

"What. The. *Fuck*?" she gritted out. "I told you not to—to… invade my life! What the hell was that?"

"That was me doing by job and watching your arse. Like I'm supposed to. I had no idea who he was, and you've *clearly* had too much to drink."

"He's a *friend*," Alexandra shot back. Connor just shrugged, crossing his arms over his chest.

"Still a suspect as far as I'm concerned."

"He is not a *suspect*. I know him *very* well."

A muscle in Connor's jaw ticked and he took a menacing step forward.

"*Everyone* is a suspect until *I* decide otherwise."

"But—"

"And before you tell me *again* how well you know him, let me tell you something. Most stalkers? They're not strangers. They're someone you know."

"Charles is *not* a stalker."

Connor shook his head. "I don't know that."

"I can *guarantee* it's not him." she said through clenched teeth. She wasn't going to stand there and give him their entire history. And she didn't owe anyone an explanation.

"Looked like a lot more than a *friend* to me," he growled. He looked positively murderous. "You were sending him so many signals I expected planes to start circling overhead."

He almost sounded jealous. She ignored the way her breath caught—and the spike of adrenaline that hit her nerve endings like a fire alarm.

"Even if I had gone home with Charles—or picked up someone off the street—that's none of your damn business."

He scoffed, shaking his head. "It's my *job* to protect you, so *literally* my business. Picking up strange men in bars is dangerous."

"Oh? Is that what you were explaining to Bimbo Barbie earlier?" she shot back. She immediately regretted it.

"Yeah," he said simply.

She blinked. And stared. "What?"

"I bought her a *Coke* because I'm not even sure she was old enough to be here. Then I gave her a little free advice," he explained. "And hopefully the next time she goes out she'll be more careful."

He paused and then added under this breath: "We're not all so nice."

She frowned. "I saw you. You gave her your number."

"I gave her a *business card*. Told her to call if she was ever in trouble."

"You're lying," she said flatly.

"I'm not." He sighed, pinching the bridge of his nose.

For a second, she actually felt a little bad. Until she remembered the phone call from earlier. There was no way he could talk his way out of that one.

"So, you were just helping a damsel in distress, is that it?" she asked. "Wow. A knight in shining armor. I bet your girlfriend just loves when you *rescue* other women. In bars."

Connor's brow furrowed and he cocked his head. "What girlfriend?"

"Don't play dumb," she hissed. "I heard your phone call. '*What's wrong, angel? I can't come over until late, are you going to wait up for me? The best, huh?*" She imitated him, even—to her absolute horror—attempting an accent. A *terrible* accent.

He just stared for a moment... then burst into laughter. Not just a chuckle either—a full-body, head thrown back, clutching your sides kind of laugh.

Son of a bitch.

"I need to pee," she huffed and turned away.

He stepped around her, blocking her path and caging her in—hands braced on either side of her head.

"First of all, that accent was *feckin' awful.* Just *rubbish*," he said with a grin—stifling a laugh. "Second? That was my baby sister."

Alexandra felt her face go nuclear. New levels of humiliation achieved. She ignored his first comment since—well, she couldn't argue with him there.

"Right. You call your baby sister 'angel'?" she asked. She was skeptical.

"Aye. Because that's her *name*. Don't ask what my mum was thinking, but that's her name. I assume it had something to do with all the drugs."

She shot him an incredulous look—until his smile dissolved into a glare that sent a shiver up her spine.

He leaned forward and she pressed back against the wall. The exposed brick was cold and rough against her back. She could feel the heat radiating off him soaking into her skin.

The contrast raised the hair on the back of her neck. Goosebumps erupted all over her skin. She could smell his cologne—woodsy and clean with a hint of something spicy.

He smells so fucking good.

"I know you don't like me watching your every move. Few people would." He paused, until she looked him in the eye. "But this is my *job*. If I think you're in danger—even if odds are you'd be fine—I *will* step in. I won't gamble with your safety."

His eyes darkened—his voice gained an edge that sent a shiver down her spine. And it *wasn't* from fear.

"Not sure why you're so interested in my personal life, but that's *twice* now you've called me a liar. There won't be a third time. Ask me anything. I'll give you a straight answer. And when I tell you something? *That* you can bet on."

She stared up at him. Trying to ignore the way her body reacted to him was nothing but a pipe dream. But she wouldn't be intimidated. Her concerns were perfectly reasonable. She couldn't trust him to protect her—with his *life*—if he lied to her.

Before she could put any of that into words, he pushed off the wall and took a step back. He motioned her toward the ladies' room.

"Go ahead. I'll wait here." He leaned one shoulder against the wall, looking out over the dance floor.

Thankfully, there was no line for the ladies' room. She was even more grateful to find Janie inside, fixing her makeup in the mirror.

"There you are." Alexandra was so relieved she could've cried. All the adrenaline was draining away, taking the alcohol with it. Now she was just... *tired*.

"Here I am," Janie said with a grin gesturing broadly at the room.

Alexandra smiled. Only Janie could've made her laugh at that moment.

"Looks like you've been busy. I haven't seen you for more than five minutes all night."

Janie caught her eye in the mirror—a wicked grin spreading across her face.

"I'm on the prowl." She waggled her eyebrows in case Alexandra had any doubt about what she meant. She didn't.

As much as she resented Connor for marching in to "rescue" her from Charles, he wasn't *totally* wrong. If it *had* been some random guy, it would have been pretty stupid of her to drink so much. And anyone *other than* Charles, would have assumed she was flirting. Aggressively.

It wasn't fair that women had to be so careful about literally everything—their clothes, their words, how much they drank. But it was necessary.

Alexandra had been off the market so long, she'd perfected the art of saying no. Not too mean, but not nice enough to "lead them on."

Firm but polite. And always crystal clear: *you're wasting your time.* She was always careful and well prepared, just in case, but the easiest thing to do was make sure she wasn't a target in the first place.

And it made her furious—Every. Single. Fucking. Time. She was so tired of it, she just stopped going out. She didn't know how Janie did it.

"Any luck?" Alexandra asked.

"Some. Two numbers so far. Going to try for the hat trick before I head home." Janie shot her a wink in the mirror.

"Only two?"

"What do you want from me? I'm selective." Janie shrugged. "I only take numbers I plan to *use*."

"Good call," Alexandra said. She enjoyed the stories—*Janie's Adventures in Dating*. But she also worried about her.

"Any immediate plans for the evening?" she asked.

Janie's brows drew together. "No, why?"

"Just curious."

"Uh-huh. Sure," Janie leaned against the sink and crossed her arms. And waited. She had that "well, are you going to tell me or not?" look on her face. She didn't have to *call* bullshit. She could say it with a look.

"Promise me you'll be safe, that's all."

Janie smirked. "You sound like my sex ed. teacher."

"That's not what I meant," Alexandra said wearily. "There are a lot of assholes out there."

"Oh, trust me—I know. But don't worry about me, babe. I've *always* got an exit plan. And I carry a taser, just in case." Janie said with a grin.

"Good," Alexandra snorted. "Listen, I'm beat. I'm gonna head out. Can you do me a favor and make sure Charles makes it home okay?"

"You want *me* to make sure Charles gets home okay?" Janie looked at her like she had two heads. And one of them was suddenly singing opera.

"You know how delicate he is."

"Of course," Janie snickered. "I guess I can handle it. See you tomorrow."

"See you tomorrow. And happy hunting." Alexandra waved and rolled her eyes as Janie adjusted her cleavage on her way out the door.

She'd been quiet on the drive. *Too* quiet.

Connor felt a little guilty. He'd charged in without thinking about it. That wasn't like him. He'd put her in a tough spot with *Charles* by making up that story about being her boyfriend. He still didn't like him. But Alexandra clearly cared about him. Which somehow made him feel better *and* worse about it.

Not only that—they'd had a deal. He'd agreed to give her space and then went back on his word.

And then, just to top it all off, he'd given her a lecture. He hadn't said anything that wasn't true, but he'd been too harsh.

He couldn't help himself—couldn't stay calm, couldn't stop antagonizing her. She was beautiful, and those blushes were so fucking sweet. But that sass? That fire in her eyes when she was laying into him? Sexy as hell.

He was out of his depth.

The real hell of it was how quickly her mood shifted. One second she'd be fine—*almost* nice—and the next, she was biting his head off. He couldn't change tactics fast enough to keep up with her.

He'd planned to talk to her about the ground rules—for her own safety and his sanity—but when she'd come out of the bathroom she seemed… subdued. Even giving him a tight smile, trying to smooth things over.

They'd barely spoken two words to each other since. She gave him directions, but that was it. He already knew where they were going—he let her guide him anyway.

He pulled into a space in front of her brownstone and told her—*politely*—to wait a moment. Looking up and down the street, he got out of the Hummer. He scoped out the buildings, high and low, on both sides of the street. Nothing unusual.

Satisfied, he skirted the hood around to the passenger side and opened her door. He kept an eye on their surroundings, as he ushered her up the stairs—his body blocking her from behind.

At the top, she turned, keys in hand. She probably thought this was where he'd leave her. She thought wrong.

He motioned toward the door and her brow furrowed.

"Go ahead," he said.

She stared at him for a moment, rolled her eyes, and unlocked the door. He wanted to smile, but he resisted. Now wasn't the time to be playful. He was crossing a threshold, and not just physically.

It was one thing to flirt in her office or a bar—and he *had* been flirting. He'd admit *that much*, at least. But this was her home. It was a sacred space. She was most vulnerable here and that wasn't something to be taken lightly.

He wasn't here because she *wanted* him here. It was out of necessity—part of his job. He needed her to know that he understood the difference.

His job wasn't *just* keeping her safe, it was making her *feel* safe. Including from him.

She opened the door and, he gently took her elbow and escorted her through the door. He took a deliberate step back once they were inside—giving her space.

"Do you have an alarm system you need to disarm?"

"No." She hid it well, but she was uncomfortable—he could tell. She was fiddling with her keys as if she might need to use them as a weapon.

Good girl. Smart girl.

"I'm going to secure the house," he said, keeping his voice low and calm. She nodded stiffly

"Just stay right here. I'll be back in under three minutes. If I'm not, get in the Hummer, lock the doors, and call the police." He put his keys in her shaking hand.

"This is routine. Nothing to worry about."

A lamp on the hallway table was already on—probably on a timer. The rest of the house was dark, save for a nightlight here and there. The glow from the streetlights filtered in through the curtains, but it didn't help much.

He made his way silently from room to room on the first floor, turning on lights as he went. He went through the foyer and up the stairs—holding up a hand to Alexandra when she started to speak.

Two and a half minutes later, he'd checked both bedrooms and bathrooms and was descending the stairs.

"All clear."

Alexandra nodded and some of the tension drained out of her shoulders. She gave him a strained smile and something squeezed in his chest.

"I even checked under the beds," he added with a wink.

Her body relaxed a little more—her smile less stiff. The tightness in his chest eased.

He stood there a moment, just watching her. Making sure she was steady. He couldn't linger too long—just long enough to convince himself she was alright.

"Can I see your phone?" he asked, holding out his hand.

She frowned. "Why?"

"So I can put in my contact information."

She unlocked her phone and handed it to him—still frowning.

He typed in his numbers—all three—labeling them for her. He handed the phone back and put his hand on the doorknob.

"Make sure you lock up behind me. Call me first thing in the morning and let me know what's on the agenda."

She stared at her phone, not saying a word. He tilted his head, trying to get a look at her face.

"Alexandra?"

"Yes," she said, her head coming up. "Lock up, call you tomorrow. Got it."

"Good." He opened the door and stepped out—or tried to. A small tug on his sleeve stopped him.

"Wait."

He turned to look at her. Even *she* looked surprised.

"Do you have a minute? I mean, would you like a drink, water or something?" She seemed nervous. Maybe a little scared. Clearly she *wasn't* okay.

He could spare half an hour to try and make her feel better. Angel's piece of shit car wasn't going anywhere. Not without a tow truck.

"I could use a drink, since you're offerin'."

What am I doing?

She couldn't wait to get rid of him earlier. She'd have bolted the second he pulled up to the curb if he hadn't stopped her. Why did she ask him to stay?

Because you're scared.

This was the one place in the world where she could just *be*. The one place where she didn't have to worry about how she looked, what she said, or how she carried herself.

This was her safe place.

At least until now.

She was used to the anxiety she felt as soon as she stepped outside. She could deal with that. But she never thought for one second that she'd be anxious *here* of all places.

The idea shook her. *Badly.*

"I hope this is okay. It's all I have," she apologized, handing him a bottle of water.

"That's grand. Thanks." He took a sip and set the bottle down on the coffee table. The overstuffed chair he sat in was arranged next to the couch at an angle that made it convenient for conversation. He sat back, one elbow on the arm of the chair resting his chin on his closed fist. Casual, relaxed—everything she wasn't.

She sipped at her water, head still spinning slightly from alcohol. She tucked her legs beneath her on the couch, hugging a throw pillow to her chest.

From the outside, the brownstone might scream *money*, but on the inside? It said something totally different, and she liked it that way.

It murmured *comfort*.

It spoke *joy*.

It whispered *peace*.

The chair Connor sat in was a bright turquoise—matching the throw pillows on the grey linen couch. The walls were the same color and every inch of wall space was occupied. Prints of Van Gogh, Monet, Klimt—all the paintings she loved. A few miniature reproductions of sculptures by Bernini and Rodin dotted the bookshelves.

The family photos studded the walls and bookshelves in her bedroom, but the living room was a tribute to her favorite things—colors, textures, art, and books that made her smile. She looked around the room, but the contentment she usually felt was muted. Incomplete.

The thought of losing that—losing her soft place to land? She hated it. It made her feel sick.

She didn't realize how much time had passed until Connor broke the silence.

"You're thinking awfully hard over there," he said softly. He smiled, but his eyes were wary—concerned. He was leaning forward—elbows on this knees, hands clasped tightly in front of him.

"Sorry," she said, shaking her head.

"No worries." He studied her for a moment and she shifted uncomfortably, taking a sip of her water. "Are you alright?"

"Yeah. Fine," she replied. "This is all just a bit…"

"Unsettling?"

"I think so," she admitted, biting her lip. He surprised her by taking her hand. He stroked his thumb gently across her knuckles as he spoke.

"I know it's scary. Most people go their whole lives without worrying about something like this."

"I've lived in New York my whole life. You'd think I'd be used to taking safety precautions." She kept her tone light—lighter than she felt.

"You are. Out there," he said nodding his head toward the street outside her windows. "But once you're through that door and it's locked behind you—that's different."

A nod was all she could manage. She didn't trust her voice, and the last thing she wanted to do was fall apart—especially in front of *him.*

"I'll do whatever I have to do to keep you safe." His voice was low, but there was steel in it—a hard edge that surprised her. Even more unexpected was the relief she felt.

She cleared her throat.

"Thank you. I appreciate that," she said, eyes lowered.

"Hey." He nudged her chin up until she met his eyes. "I mean it. You're safe with me. I won't let anything happen to you."

She wanted to believe that. But that wasn't a promise anyone could keep.

"I'm sure you'll try." A hint of bitterness bled into her voice. She mentally kicked herself for letting it slip through.

"What did I tell you?" he asked with a hint of that same edge. "I won't lie to you."

She nodded, suddenly very tired. All she wanted was to change her clothes, fall into bed and pass out. She knew she wouldn't, but she could hope.

"I'm sorry to have kept you. I know you probably want to clock out for the night."

"Thanks for the drink."

"You're welcome."

He paused in the doorway, like he wasn't sure what to say.

"Lock up behind me and call me in the morning," he finally said.

"I will."

"Sleep well," he added quietly as he closed the door behind him.

"Shit." Connor swore as he slammed his car door, jamming his keys in the ignition.

Connor felt like he'd lost his damn mind. Alexandra had looked so lost and sad—curling in on herself, hugging a pillow against her chest like a shield. He'd seen every emotion she felt flicker across her face. Every one had made him want to wrap her in a blanket and hold her until she felt like nothing could ever touch her.

White Knight complex aside, he knew how strong most women were. Tough, independent, resilient. They *had to be*. They had it twice as hard as anyone. And nine times out of ten it was their own husbands, fathers, and brothers making it harder.

He knew a lot of women could protect themselves, but—goddamn it, they shouldn't have to. Just accepting a date, or *not* accepting one, shouldn't put anyone in harm's way. And when he thought about his sister having to live like that, the walls nearly closed in around him.

But, he'd never had that strong a reaction with anyone else. He had no trouble staying objective, knowing that doing his job right was the best way to keep them safe. With Alexandra, it went beyond keeping her safe. The look on her face told him everything. She was familiar with fear in a way that no one should be.

She'd been hurt. *Badly.*

Maybe so badly she hadn't fully recovered. It made his chest ache. And it made him furious.

When he'd asked her father if he knew of anyone who might have a grudge against either of them, he'd been given one name and one name only: Lucas Whitmore. Mr. Hughes didn't give him any details but Connor would bet he was the reason for the haunted look in Alexandra's eyes.

He squeezed his eyes shut and took a deep breath.

Get your shit together.

Connor opened his eyes. And froze.

Case and point: he'd been so distracted he'd nearly missed it. Opening his door slowly, one hand on his weapon, he looked around him. Seeing nothing unusual, he snagged the piece of paper tucked under his windshield wiper blade.

Once he was back in the car—door closed, he set it down on the dash. He fished a pair of latex gloves out of his center console, pulling them on. He opened the paper carefully, not touching it any more than necessary. Once it was unfolded, he could see it clearly:

"This is your only warning: back off if you don't want her to get hurt."

Connor studied the note, taking in every detail. No unique

characteristics—likely on purpose. Non-descript block print. Simple and straight to the point—no wording or syntax clues.

It *did* tell him a couple of things. For one, they'd been somewhere nearby when he and Alexandra had arrived. He wouldn't know where to leave the note unless they saw Alexandra get out of his car.

They'd been here. They'd watched them arrive and go inside. And Connor hadn't clocked them. Connor clenched his teeth, the muscle in his jaw twitching. As frustrating as that was, it told him something else. They had a regular spot—close by and *very* well hidden.

An apartment with windows overlooking the street, maybe. Or a spot they would be hidden from sight and out of the way, where they *knew* they wouldn't be interrupted. Stalking was a marathon. They must have been waiting here for hours considering when they'd left her office.

It was possible they'd been followed, but not likely. Connor hadn't noticed anyone following them. And leaving a note like this without even knowing who Connor was? It was impulsive. If they'd been followed to the bar, it's likely he would have left it then and there.

The impulsiveness itself was odd. Stalkers are thorough. They plan. They tend to gather information first and escalate slowly. Taking all those photos without being noticed took time and planning. Leaving a hastily hand-written note didn't fit the profile.

They might have acted out of frustration, anger, or jealousy, without thinking things through. Letting your emotions dictate your actions led to mistakes. It was a weakness. One they could exploit.

Connor put it all together. They had a base, or at least a regular spot very close by. Patient, calculating but emotional and impulsive when provoked. And they were here less than an hour ago.

He pulled out his phone and hit three on his speed dial. Sam answered on the second ring—surly and half asleep.

"This better be important."

"I don't care how you do it, but I need you to get any CCTV footage you can find from within a two block radius of Alexandra Hughes's townhouse between the hours of…" Connor looked at his watch. "Twenty-one hundred hours and Twenty-three hundred hours."

While he'd been at the office that afternoon he'd filled Sam in on the situation. They'd discussed options and Sam was working on putting things together as soon as possible. Unfortunately, that did *fuck-all* for him just now.

"Just say between nine o'clock and now, dude," Sam grumbled. Connor heard sheets rusting and then footsteps as Sam got out of bed. He was probably heading to his home office where he had the kind of computer set up that Connor was afraid to even *touch*. It was more expensive than his car. And more complicated to operate than a Blackhawk.

"Just do it, alright?" Connor snapped. "And I need you to find out whatever you can about the tenants of the buildings on this block— both sides of the street. I want to know if any units are vacant, especially ones that would be accessible from the ground floor, so basement and first floor apartments."

"Yes, sir." Sam made a sound of disgust. "Should I polish your boots for you, too, Sarge?"

Sam hated taking orders from Connor. They'd been the same rank when they'd mustered out and they were partners in the business. But since Sam wanted nothing to do with actually *running* the company—things like approving payroll or meeting with clients or even ordering *fucking* office supplies, Connor would give him any goddamn order he felt like, and he was just going to have to suck it up.

"Listen, I'm happy to do it myself if you want to finish putting together everything the accountant needs for the quarterly taxes," Connor replied.

"Uh, I—"

"Or maybe you'd like to take over the client presentation scheduled for Monday morning?"

"Well—"

"*Or* maybe you'd like to start looking through resumes and setting up interviews so we can hire more people?"

"*Fine!*" Sam snarled. "I get it, okay? You're the boss. I'll do it."

"You were *always* gonna do it," Connor snorted. "I just needed you to skip all the bullshit complaining and just fucking *do it.*"

"You're a real dick, sometimes, you know that?" Sam spat. He hung up before Connor could reply.

"Same to you," Connor muttered. He shot off a quick "thank you" text, anyway, knowing Sam wouldn't be mad for long. He had a short fuse, and even shorter cooldown.

Sam sent him back a middle finger emoji and Connor grinned

before he tossed his phone into the passenger seat. He read the note again before refolding it carefully and sliding it into a plastic bag. He sealed it shut and tossed it into the seat next to his phone. He'd call Mr. Hughes in the morning and then take it to the police department. But, he doubted it would do any good.

With one last look at Alexandra's townhouse, he put the car in gear and pulled out, heading for the Queensboro Bridge.

He was in a foul-mood the whole way to Angel's house. And working on her piece of shite car didn't help. His mechanical knowledge was limited and after two hours of banging and cursing, he'd given up. It was nearly midnight and he was too damn tired to waste any more time. He booked a rental car through their website and arranged for it to be dropped off at his sister's house in the morning.

When he went to give Angel the news, he found her curled up on the couch fast asleep. He covered her with a blanket, left a note on the coffee table, and let himself out, setting the alarm and locking the door as he went. He'd call a tow truck on Monday and decide what to do with her ancient Honda.

No matter how many times he offered to buy her a car, she always refused. She was stubborn—insisting she could take care of herself. He'd pointed out that calling him every other week because her car broke down—*again*—wasn't exactly being self-sufficient. But she hadn't budged. Apparently, big brothers were meant to come and fix things or move furniture or do yard work. They were *not* supposed to buy their sisters cars, pay bills, or give them money.

She needed to know that she could stand on her own two feet—and he got it. Really. And that was the *only* reason he hadn't pushed before now. But right now, Connor just wanted to buy her a damn car and be done with it.

He could afford it. And it was his job to make sure she was safe and had everything she needed. He *wanted* to do it. He *offered*, so It wasn't like she'd asked for it.

He argued with himself until he got home. And he was still arguing well after he'd climbed into bed. In the early hours of the morning he made two decisions and *finally* drifted off to sleep.

Chapter Four

Alexandra most definitely had a hangover. When her phone rang at nine a.m. on a Saturday, she knew exactly who it was. Only one person had such a knack for calling at the worst possible time.

"Hello?" Alexandra rasped.

"What the hell, dude?" Amanda shouted. Alexandra winced and pulled the phone away from her ear.

"Lower your voice, bitch, or I'm hanging up," Alexandra hissed.

"Oops! Sorry," Amanda whispered.

"She was, in fact, *not* sorry," Alexandra thought to herself, her inner narrator sounding suspiciously like Morgan Freeman

"A little hungover?"

"A little," Alexandra sighed. She blinked at the bright sunlight filtering in through the window and rolled over. "What do you want?"

"I called Dad this morning."

"Ugh," Alexandra groaned. Why couldn't anyone in her family keep their mouth shut? "*And?*"

"And... tell me what's going on! A security escort? Should you really be staying alone in that house if you have a stalker?"

"Sounds like Dad already told you *all* about it. What do you want from me?"

"Don't be a bitch," Amanda sighed. "I just wanted to check on you. You know, make sure you're not freaking out or anything."

"I'm *fine*." She loved her sister, and knew she was just concerned. But Alexandra was the big sister. It was her job to watch out for Amanda, not the other way around.

"You want to come stay with me for a while?" Amanda asked.

"Um, no, thank you. I couldn't deal with all of your roommates.

You have, what, five now?"

"Four. The fifth was just here temporarily until he went home to Germany. And they're all *super* nice guys."

"Sure. Whatever you say." They'd had this fight before, and Alexandra wasn't in the mood for it at the moment.

Besides, Amanda had been living there for over a year, and everything seemed to be going fine. She hadn't slept with any of them, none of them had done anything creepy, and they all seemed decent enough the few times she'd met them. Amanda was twenty-seven. She was old enough to make her own decisions. Alexandra just had to *remind herself* of that every once in while.

"Well, if you need anything, let me know." Amanda sounded anxious. Alexandra paused a moment.

"I wouldn't say no to a movie night."

"God, I wish I could. I'm working all weekend. And switching with anyone is impossible. Sergio is already on my ass this week."

"About what?"

"Hell if I know. He's *always* on my ass about something. It's simply his state of being. Some people are morning people, some people are dog people, and then there's Sergio—an *everyone-but-Amanda* person."

Alexandra laughed, flinched when it made her head hurt, and told Amanda she'd call her next week. She would have given anything to be able to go back to sleep, but she was wide awake, and her head was pounding. She needed painkillers. And a toothbrush. And coffee—preferably by the gallon.

She threw on gym clothes—sports bra, t-shirt, leggings. She put her hair half up—it was too short for a proper ponytail, but at least this would keep it out of her face.

Luckily, her stomach was fine, but her head felt like someone had taken a gavel to it. And she remembered *everything*. Unfortunately. She drank a large cup of coffee and ate two pieces of toast over the sink before downing two Tylenol with a full glass of water. She wasted a few minutes cleaning up, but she couldn't put it off forever.

She picked up her phone and tapped on Connor's name. For a moment she contemplated just skipping the gym entirely. It meant missing her session with Trey. Janie would send a barrage of angry texts over the next hour. And Trey would send one massive wall of text. One that would inevitably end with some version of "*I'm not mad, I'm just disappointed.*" She shuddered just thinking about it. He could be *truly brutal* at times.

But she was beyond embarrassed about—oh, *so many* things. She wasn't sure she was up to facing Connor, especially when she felt like death warmed over. But she'd have to do it eventually.

"I might as well get it over with," she muttered, hitting *send*.

She waited for him to pick up, thinking—hoping maybe, she'd get lucky and it would go to voicemail. All hope was lost when he answered on the third ring.

"This is Connor."

"This is Alexandra Hughes. You told me to call you in the morning."

"Good. You're up."

The doorbell rang and she jumped. Her heart lurched and then kicked into high gear.

Don't be stupid. Criminals don't ring doorbells. It's probably just a delivery.

"Sorry, I didn't sleep well so I slept in a bit," she muttered as she made her way to the front door.

"I didn't sleep well either," Connor replied. "Been up since six."

"Um, can you hang on a minute? There's someone at the door."

"Sure."

Alexandra wasn't sure why, but she thought he sounded… amused. As her security… *person*—bodyguard—shouldn't he be more concerned? Or at least tell her what she needed to do?

She peeked through the side window and saw a large man in baggy athletic shorts, sneakers and a hooded sweatshirt standing on her front steps. His hood was up and he was facing out toward the street so she couldn't see his face.

She took deep breath and told herself she was overreacting. She unlocked the deadbolt but kept the catch on, opening the door the two inches or so it allowed.

"Can I help you?" she asked. He turned around, cell phone held to his ear and smiled at her. She scowled. "You couldn't have just told me you were at the door?" she snapped as she ended the call.

"Just making sure you're taking proper safety measures." He shrugged. The smirk on his face told her that winding her up was, at the very least, the icing on the cake.

"Well, did I pass the test?" she asked.

"Oh, absolutely not," he said. "Failed miserably in fact."

"What?"

"But you did about as well as I expected."

"So, you expect abject failure?" Alexandra asked, crossing her arms over her chest and glaring at him through the gap in the door.

"I did, actually. But it's not really your fault. Almost everyone fails."

"Okay. What did I do wrong?"

"These catches?" he replied pointing at the chain keeping the door from opening all the way. "They're crap. One good shove or a hard kick and those links will give. Or the screws attaching the chain will come right out of the door. Don't worry, though. We can go over that later."

Alexandra rolled her eyes.

"Can I come in?" he asked.

"May I see some identification, please?" she replied coolly.

"Ha ha," he deadpanned. "Very funny."

"I'm sorry, but if we're testing my security measures, I would like to be thorough. Anyone I'm not familiar with needs to provide identification before I'd consider letting them into my house."

"And, under normal circumstances, I would applaud your due diligence, but I've been out here for three hours and I'm freezin' my arse off."

"Oh," she said, startled. She undid the catch and opened the door for him.

"Thank you," he said, gratefully, stepping in from the October chill.

"Have you really been here that long?" she asked. He shrugged, looking a little uncomfortable.

"I was up at six. I made some calls but I didn't have anything else to do and I knew I'd be coming here at some point today, so I figured I might as well familiarize myself with the neighborhood."

"Well, if you'd told me you were outside, I would have let you in half an hour ago."

"I'll live." He seemed a little tense, or maybe tired. That wasn't surprising if he'd been up for hours.

"Want some coffee? There's some in the kitchen. I'm supposed to meet Janie—Shit! I forgot to call her this morning."

"No need. She's expecting both of us in half an hour."

"What? How?"

"I introduced myself while I was waiting last night. I gave her my number—*for professional reasons,*" he said. "I asked her to text me when she got home. She told me about your plans and invited me along."

Alexandra felt a lot of things, all within the span of three seconds. Rage. Relief. Gratitude. Exasperation.

How dare he introduce himself to her friends as her boyfriend without even consulting her? After some thought, she'd decided it probably *was* the best way to handle things, but still—what right did he have to make that decision?

And, yeah, now she didn't have to be the one to make the introductions, meaning she didn't have to actually *lie* to them. She could just not correct him. It was a technicality, but it was better than nothing.

She also had to admit that it was sweet of him to check on Janie and make sure she got home alright. Unless of course he meant to use her number *after* the job was done. Or unless he just wanted to use Janie to keep tabs on her.

Which would honestly be smart. Alexandra didn't even know *her own* schedule as well as Janie did. But he wouldn't need Janie unless—did he really think she was going to *sneak away?* That was just insulting.

Well, technically, she *had* sort of slipped away the night before, but it wasn't like she'd run off. She just went in ahead of him.

While all of this played out in her head, Alexandra opened her mouth three or four times, only to close it again. She couldn't come up with an appropriate reaction—couldn't settle on an overriding emotion.

"You're doin' an excellent impression of a goldfish there, darlin'," Connor said with a smile. It wasn't a malicious smile, just genuinely amused.

And there it was. The overriding emotion.

Before Alexandra spun on her heel, heading for the kitchen, all she said was: "Fuck you."

Okay, so she was pissed.

Very pissed.

But with that fire in her eyes, and the way she walked away—spine straight, chin up, hips swaying—all he could think was how fucking gorgeous she was. By the time he'd followed her into the kitchen, that woman was nowhere in sight. All the fire was gone, replaced with ice.

She poured herself a cup of coffee dumped in a metric ton of sugar, added an equally obscene amount of cream, and then took a step back to lean against the adjacent counter.

Finally she looked up and met his eyes. He'd swear the temperature dropped ten degrees.

"Help yourself, Mr. MacLachlan," she said. He poured himself a mug and sipped it. He drank it black and wasn't picky. It was lighter than he was used to, but pretty much everything was. The Army didn't serve coffee; it served coffee flavored motor oil. But as long as it was hot and caffeinated, he didn't care.

"It's good."

"Have a seat." She gestured to the kitchen island.

There were three bar stools on the far side. He took the middle, just to see what she would do. But instead of sitting, she stood on the opposite side of the island. That told him everything he needed to know about how she saw things. As far as she was concerned, they were on opposite sides.

Connor kicked himself for being so quick to wind her up. He enjoyed seeing her all sassy. He enjoyed the back and forth. Their battle of wills at the bar had been the highlight of his week. Possibly his whole *month*. It was fun—and so, *so* easy. But he didn't want her to see him as the enemy. Not only did it make his job harder, he just didn't like it.

"Since you've pushed us irrevocably down the path of *deception*, we need to get a few things straight," Alexandra said calmly.

She didn't sound angry or upset. She sounded like this was a staff meeting. Her mask had slipped firmly into place. Connor cursed himself again.

"I don't appreciate you making decisions without my consent—" She raised a hand to silence him before he could even form a response. "When it comes to anything *other than* security. That's within your scope, and I'll respect that. But that is your *only* purview." She paused, taking a sip of her coffee. She set the mug down and crossed her arms.

"After some consideration, I've come to the conclusion that, although not my *first* choice, the boyfriend idea is probably the most convenient course to take."

He opened his mouth, intending to ask what the hell the issue was. Again, she held up a hand to silence him.

"Which I would have *told you,* had you bothered to simply *ask.* But since you seem to be *committed* to using your mouth first and your brain second, we're going to establish some ground rules moving forward."

She stopped and looked at him expectantly.

"Oh, so now I can speak?" He snorted.

"If you have anything relevant to add to the conversation, then please, feel free."

Damn it all, but he didn't really.

"That's the fanciest way I've ever been called an *eejit,*" he said instead. Which pretty much proved her point.

She raised an eyebrow and one corner of her mouth tipped up into a smirk.

"I'll take that as a compliment," she said. "Now, first of all, you will not tell them *anything* that we haven't discussed and agreed upon in advance. Even if the question is as simple as 'what did you have for lunch?' you will obfuscate."

She paused again, probably waiting for him to ask what it meant. Too bad for her, he didn't need to ask. He gave her a curt nod in response. And if she looked a little disappointed, it was probably just his imagination.

"Everyone will already know by Monday, if they don't already," she said with a roll of her eyes. "News travels fast in our office. You can thank Janie for that. People will be curious—they *will* ask questions, not all of them appropriate. Again—I'm primarily talking about Janie."

He said nothing. She took a deep breath and let it out in a long sigh.

"To be blunt, Janie will ask for *details.* And she won't be coy about it."

Connor grinned. He liked Janie already.

"You will not, *under any circumstances,* give her any."

"Not even a few innocent ones? Would make it look more convincing." He shrugged.

"Nothing—not even *Amish grandmother* approved 'details.' No implying, no suggesting, no innuendos."

"So, you want me to tell her we haven't had sex?" he asked, tilting his head. It was just to clarify—nothing to do with the way she blushed and glanced away.

"She'll assume we have no matter what you tell her. And that's fine. Let her make assumptions if she wants, but you will neither confirm nor deny."

"Name. Rank. Serial Number. Got it. But… why does it bother you so much?" He was suddenly curious. She didn't care if they thought she was doing the dirty, but she'd rather let their imaginations run wild than offer up even a fake first kiss story?

"Because it's nobody's fucking business," she snapped. She composed herself almost instantly and continued as if nothing had happened. "It's just something I'm not comfortable with. Janie knows that which means it would be probably be weirder for you to talk about it."

"But she'd still ask?" He looked for some kind of sign—trying to figure out what was going on in her head. But aside from that little outburst, she gave him nothing to work with. He hated it—not knowing what she was thinking, not even being able to guess.

"It's Janie," she replied dryly. "I'm pretty sure her personal philosophy is 'it doesn't hurt to try'."

"Fair enough."

There was a long pause and, even with her mask on, he could see she was a little uncomfortable.

"I want you to know that I do appreciate you checking on Janie. It was thoughtful of you. And, although I have *significant* issues with the way you handled things last night, I am nothing if not reasonable. Your intentions were good, and I recognize that."

He was surprised and a little pleased that she was giving him *some* credit. Even if the delivery was a little disappointing. It was less of a *thank you* and more of a logical acknowledgement that she *should* appreciate his concern for Janie's safety. She thought it, but she didn't really *feel* it. That made it feel a little hollow.

It also made him want to see her a little less reasonable—less composed, less in control. He wondered what *that* Alexandra would look like, sound like, *feel* like—

Nope. No. Nuh-uh.

He cleared his throat. "Anything else?"

"Yes." She paused and cleared her throat. "I'd appreciate it if you kept any other relationships you might have during the course of this ordeal *discreet.* A breakup is one thing, but I'd rather not be pitied because my fake boyfriend cheated on me."

"I see," he said tightly. "You done?"

She swallowed hard. "Yes."

"Good. Now, it's my turn." Alexandra visibly braced herself, her shoulders coming up and her whole body tightening. And he fucking *hated* it. "For one thing, we've already established I don't have any *relationships* ye need fash yerself wi'. I don't fuck around, and I'm no' the type of dobber who'd start this whole thing and then go around doggin' anything on two legs right under yer nose."

She blinked at him. "I have no idea what you just said."

He paused, taking a breath.

"I'm not a prick," he enunciated, regaining control of his language center. "I'm currently single, as previously established. And I don't fuck around. Does that clear things up?"

"Oh," she said quietly. "Yes. It does."

"Same goes for you," Connor added. "No *relationships* with other guys. It might be a fake relationship, but I'd rather not—"

—see you with another man.

"I'd rather not deal with the additional security risk."

"I don't date," she said flatly—no hesitation. She turned, placed her mug in the sink. "If that's all, we should go. We're already late. Janie won't have much time to grill you at the gym. We can sit down and come up with the backstory later." She walked away without another word, and Connor could only follow.

The ride to the gym was silent- uncomfortable. But at least it was short.

Janie was waiting for them and Alexandra quickly ushered her toward the treadmills, giving her no opportunity to ask questions. Connor stayed close enough to keeping an eye on the girls and the door at the same time, but didn't hover. He thought Alexandra could probably use some space.

He grabbed a couple of free weights, keeping the load lighter than usual—just enough to look convincing.

They warmed up, chatting away and occasionally glancing in his direction. He laughed to himself.

Looks like the inquisition has begun.

He almost felt bad. *Almost.*

Eventually the conversation stopped, both of them popping in earbuds. Janie kept up a brisk walk while Alexandra turned hers up to a jog.

He kept an eye on the surroundings—*mostly*. But he found himself watching Alexandra more and more. And his elevated heart rate *wasn't* because of the exercise.

She was stunning. Tall, toned, curvy in all the right places. Long, powerful legs, encased in those painted-on leggings, easily kept pace with the fluid motion of someone who knew their body and *exactly* what it was capable of. Her movements were sure. Graceful.

But those eyes…

Even though her face was a mask of concentration—carefully blank despite the sweat beading on her forehead—the spark had returned to those beautiful hazel eyes. He wondered where it came from. What made her light up from the inside?

He'd seen it flare white hot when she argued with him—at least until he hit that nerve that made her shut down. With her friends at the bar it had been a warm, golden glow, like a fireplace in the middle of the winter. Now it was quiet—private. A candle flickering in a dark room. Small, but there. And he saw it.

Connor cringed and shook his head.

You sound absolutely daft…

He looked around the room, clocking the other patrons, the exits. He checked the perimeter again. He looked everywhere but at her. Or at least, he tried. But soon enough, his eyes were drawn back to her. She was listening to music, mouthing the words to herself. He was riveted by her mouth—the way it moved. He could only make out about half the words.

Lost in her own world, she closed her eyes, turning her face up as she silently sang along. He was transfixed. Was that the same rapturous expression she wore when she…

Then all he could do was picture it—picture her. Writhing. Moaning. Under *his* hands. He was immediately, and *painfully* hard.

Fuck.

The last thing he needed was to get thrown out of the gym for walking around with an erection. He'd get arrested as some kind of pervert. There goes his license. And his company. And probably his dick because

Sam would castrate him.

He tore his eyes from Alexandra's mouth and sat on the weight bench. He focused intently on bicep curls until he could get his body under control. He watched the door and everyone else, limiting himself to quick glances in her direction—just enough to make sure she was still there.

And if he sang the national anthem in his head while trying to remember every goal from last year's World Cup? Nobody needed to know.

Alexandra wouldn't let herself look at him. Not until she'd had a chance to work off her frustration. A good run on the treadmill with her favorite playlist did the trick. Starting her cooldown, she finally looked around to see where he was. He wouldn't be far away given his hard and fast five-foot rule.

She spotted him directly in front of her. He was seated on a bench doing curls with what looked like a very heavy dumbbell. His shirt was damp with sweat, stretching across his broad back and sculpted shoulders. Her mouth went dry as she watched every muscle move under the fabric. She guzzled water and hid her burning face by wiping away the sweat with her gym towel.

When she looked again—because she couldn't help herself—all that work to reign in her hormones had gone to hell. He'd switched sides, working the other arm. His body was angled more and she could see the muscles in his bicep bunch and flex. Sweat dripped off his face and slid down the back of his neck. Lips slightly parted, his breathing quick. She could practically feel his panting breaths against her neck as he hovered over her.

What? Stop! Stop, stop, stop.

Her face felt like it was on fire. She quickly jabbed buttons on the machine until it stopped. Cooldown aborted. Before she could escape to the bathroom to regroup, Janie grabbed her and urged her to the next set of machines. Alexandra groaned.

"Really? I hate these."

"I know you do," Janie said, smacking her on the ass. "But they're fantastic for your glutes."

Alexandra rolled her eyes and climbed onto the machine. Climbing an endless staircase to nowhere was her version of hell. To Janie, it was "a good burn." The only *burn* Alexandra wanted right now was maybe a little beard rash from Connor's stubble on her inner thigh.

Jesus, Alexandra! Get a fucking grip.

At least the machine faced the opposite direction from the sweaty slice of beefcake. Being tortured by the machine was one thing. Suffering through that while watching Connor flex and sweat right in front of her? Unacceptable. She was pretty sure it was banned by the Geneva Convention.

Needing the distraction from both her burning muscles and her rioting hormones, she left the earbuds out so she and Janie could talk. Janie talked about her love life because she was Janie. And then it was Alexandra's turn. Only she didn't *have* a love life to discuss—not really. And she wouldn't discuss it even if she did. So she dodged questions about Connor—how they met, how long they'd been dating, why she didn't say anything—until they were both too out of breath to talk.

She paused for a moment, putting her earbuds back in and choosing a song, only to see that Connor was directly in front of her. On the opposite side of the gym from where he was before.

He stood in front of the machine, reaching up to grab the handles overhead. He pulled them down until his hands were side by side in front of his hips he stepped forward, pulling the cables tight. He stopped with one foot in front of the other, muscles flexing, jaw clenched and eyes focused. What Alexandra saw was a warrior. He was Achilles, Leonidas, Arthur. A Michelangelo—*no,* a Bernini sculpture in flesh and bone.

He spread his arms—up and out—and then pulled them downward again. It was smooth, controlled and it made every muscle in his chest and shoulders flex. The veins in his arms stood out and all she could picture were those same arms braced on either side of her, just like they were the night before.

The memory flooded her—his warmth, his scent, the weight of his stare. She forgot how to breathe.

She forced her eyes closed and focused on going through the motions of the machine. That worked for a while, until her mind started to wander, inspired by the music in her ears. Suddenly she was on the beach in Mexico laying on the warm sand, the sunshine kissing her skin.

And a shirtless Connor was walking out of the ocean in slow motion—water dripping from his hair and running in rivulets down his chest, over rippling abs and right down to where that delicious V disappeared beneath low slung shorts. Then before her imaginary self could blink, they were both down in the sand, her hand tangled in his dark, wet hair as he trailed kisses down her neck.

She may or may *not* have let out a little sigh. A sigh that sounded suspiciously like a soft moan.

She jumped, nearly falling off the machine when she felt a warm hand on her shoulder. She pulled out an earbud and was assailed by a throaty, masculine laugh.

"I didn't mean to startle you." Connor grinned.

He hadn't said he was sorry, because clearly *he wasn't*. The devil was in his eyes. Worse, she could feel her face burning. She wanted to slink away and take a cold shower. A long one. Instead, she tried to remember that there was no way he'd know what she was thinking. For all he knew, she was flushed from the workout.

He handed her a cold bottle of water and she mumbled a *thank you* before twisting off the cap and downing half the bottle.

"You alright, babe? You're looking really flushed?" His brow was furrowed but he didn't look concerned. He looked *amused*.

Oh, damn you.

"I'm fine," she said breezily. "These machines are just a lot of work."

"*I bet*." He smirked and winked at her.

"What's next, Janie?" She turned to her friend for rescue, but Janie gave her a positively evil grin.

"You know what comes next. Warm-up, Booty work—"

"Ugh," Alexandra grunted. "Abs. I *hate* abs."

"You hate *everything*," Janie pointed out. "But you'll do it anyway because you like the *results*. Now, go on."

"Yes, ma'am," Alexandra muttered heading toward the mats. She didn't dare look back.

Janie had put together a routine that was a combination of Pilates, yoga, and basic calisthenics. All abs and all pain. It hurt more than going for a Brazilian, and getting that one Russian lady who was clearly on steroids and had zero sympathy for your pain. Alexandra was convinced the only English she knew was "is not so bad" and "hold still."

But much like the Brazilian, the results were worth it.

Chapter Five

Connor felt like his head was going to explode from the sexual frustration. He'd handled the treadmill incident only for Alexandra to turn around, literally, and show off that perfect ass of hers by climbing on the fucking Stairmaster. Then, he'd repositioned again to avoid an embarrassing hard-on only to catch her ogling him while he did cable flies.

He'd figured the blushing meant she found him attractive. But that hungry look? That had surprised him. All the blood had rushed south and he'd started thinking with his dick—which was the same as not thinking at all.

Then her eyes had closed and—*God*, would he love to know what she'd been thinking about. He'd had to take a break to cool off. He bought a couple bottles of water, the coldest ones he could find, and for a second he debated whether he should drink it, or pour it down his gym shorts.

The plan was to pull her off that damn machine and call it a day. But that goddamn blush when he'd startled her made him think twice.

Maybe being alone in a car with her wasn't a great idea just then. Instead, he'd enjoyed watching her squirm a little and went back to his workout.

He hit the treadmill, jogging a couple of miles while Janie tortured Alexandra with her drill sergeant routine. Honestly, it was pretty accurate. He kept his head up, watching the surroundings, and by the time they were done, he was calmer, steadier.

Janie gathered up her things and waved at him as she headed for the door. Breathing a sigh of relief that it was finally over, Connor cracked open the third bottle of water.

"Ready?" he asked, taking a long drink.

"Not yet," she panted. "I have about five minutes before my training session." She was watching Janie leave, murder in her eyes.

"Training?"

"Yeah. I have a personal training session today—self-defense. It'll take about forty-five minutes. We'll be in one of the class rooms, but I'll be fine. You can keep going and I'll meet you here when I'm done."

Connor didn't like the sound of that. For a few reasons.

"No can do," he said, shaking his head. "I go where you go."

"So, you're just going to watch?" she asked. Her face was blank, but she shifted her weight nervously from foot to foot.

"I could train you myself," he offered with a shrug. "Throw in some Tae Kwon Do, Jiu Jitsu—a little Muay Thai if you want. Spice it up." She raised an eyebrow, clearly skeptical.

"We could grapple. Might be fun." He grinned.

She frowned. *And* blushed.

"I don't think that's a good idea."

"Why not?"

"You're bigger than I am and you're presumably highly trained. You'd have an unfair advantage."

"First of all, I don't think that *presumably* was called-for. A little rude, actually. Second of all, that's the whole point. You learn the most when you spar with someone better. Besides, an attacker isn't paying attention to *weight class.* And neither should you."

"True," she conceded. "Still, I think I'll stick with Trey this time." She turned around and made her way to the drink cooler. She chucked her empty bottle in the bin and grabbed a fresh one.

"Janie doesn't train with you?" Connor asked.

"No. Her motto is work smarter, not harder. She carries pepper spray and a taser and thinks that's good enough," Alexandra sighed.

"That's a little naive."

"We all start out that way," Alexandra said with a shrug.

"You, naive? *Never.*" Connor expected her to bite back—make some kind of crack about being born cynical. That wasn't what he got.

"I'm no exception," she replied, shaking her head. "I decided to go to law school because I actually had faith in the justice system. I knew it wasn't perfect but I figured, *overall* it was fair and impartial. Everyone's equal in the eyes of the law, right?"

"You don't think that anymore?" Connor asked cautiously. He

didn't know why she felt like sharing, but he didn't want to spook her. He found himself genuinely wanting to know.

She looked at him, her face screaming: "Are you kidding me?"

She snagged a chair at one of the little tables and sat. Connor took the other chair, positioning it on the other side of the table, between her and the door.

"I was… *disabused* of that notion pretty quickly. The system is all kinds of broken." She picked at the label of her bottle. He wanted to ask what exactly had changed her mind. But if he did, he knew she'd stop talking.

"Think it's fixable?" he asked instead.

"My father thinks so. It's sort of been his life's mission. Especially now that he's a senior partner. He doesn't have to answer to anyone anymore, really. He's actually working on an Amicus brief for a Supreme Court case next month."

"Impressive." And Connor meant it. He had brains, but something like that was way beyond him. And that fact that he was doing it with no other intention than trying to making things better? It wasn't just impressive, it was admirable.

"That's my father," she said. There was something like resignation in her voice. Like maybe there was something about it that bothered her, but she'd just learned to live with it.

"Is he why you became a lawyer? Because he wanted you to?"

"Oh, God, no," Alexandra laughed. "Everyone always thinks that. Truth is, he didn't give a damn what we did. When I was applying for colleges and trying to decide on a major, I thought he'd be disappointed if I didn't follow in his footsteps. He just told me that all this money he'd earned was no good to him if it meant we—my sister Amanda and I—couldn't do whatever we wanted. That as long as I did something I was passionate about, I didn't need to worry about making a living. At least not right away."

"Wow." Few parents were so unconditionally supportive of their children, especially parents with power and money. He always thought it was strange that the parents who could actually afford to let their children grow up to do and be whatever they wanted, often pressured their children the most to succeed.

Even his own father had wanted him to go to law school like he had. He hadn't pressured him about it, but he knows he would have been pleased if that was the path Connor had taken. The familiar guilt jabbed him in the ribs. He ignored it.

"Yeah. I really couldn't have asked for better parents." She smiled wistfully to herself. Connor filed the image away to pull back out later. "Of course, that doesn't mean he wasn't *thrilled* when I told him I was going to law school. Especially since it was my choice."

"I bet," Connor chuckled. He could tell just from meeting Richard Hughes that he was incredibly proud of Alexandra. "So what *was* your other reason?"

"It was a challenge." She shrugged and looked away, focusing on one of the televisions mounted on the wall. "It was competitive and fast-paced. No two cases are the same even if it might look like they are. And every once in a while, you actually get to make a difference."

Connor suspected there was more to it than that, but before he could figure out what and how to ask, he was springing out of his chair.

"You!" A large man snarled from over Alexandra's shoulder. "Get your scrawny ass up out of that chair and into my dungeon."

Connor was halfway around the table before Alexandra held out a hand to stop him.

"Connor, this is Trey," she said. "My trainer." A clear signal for him to back off. "Trey, this is Connor. M-my boyfriend."

The stutter in her voice registered somewhere in the back of his mind, but he was on high alert. His focus was elsewhere. Connor took a minute to study the man as he stepped forward and offered his hand.

He was a little taller than Connor, maybe six foot four. His shoulders were broader, and he was bulkier in general than Connor was. It was all muscle, but the showy kind—the kind you got at the gym, rather than through an occupation or activity.

Once Connor decided he didn't pose a real threat, his hackles lowered. But only a little.

"Nice to meet you," Trey said, smiling. His perfect smile was set off by his caramel colored skin. He was clean shaven, even his head, and he had dark, expressive eyes.

"Same here." Connor nodded as they shook. Then Trey turned to Alexandra and scowled, going from affable to intimidating in a heartbeat. Connor tensed again, but didn't move.

"What the hell you waiting for, *Ms.* Hughes? You don't need an invitation. *Move.*" Alexandra hopped up, chucked her empty bottle in the bin and grabbed her bag before hustling to the far end of the gym.

"Mind if I tag along?" Connor asked, already following. Trey pursed his lips.

"You gonna backseat coach, cheerlead, or otherwise disrupt my session?"

"No, sir," Connor said with a grin. Okay, maybe he could see what Alexandra liked him.

"Good. You might even learn a few things," Trey said with a wink.

Connor didn't roll his eyes. But it was a close call.

They spent the next forty five minutes in a windowless room only marginally larger than a boxing ring. It had a heavy bag and speed bag at one end and the entire floor was covered in mats.

Trey knew his stuff. It was mostly a mix of basic self-defense and some kickboxing for good measure. He was a hard taskmaster. Alexandra was sweating in minutes and he didn't let up on her until they were done with the session.

She practiced drill after drill, kicks, punches, combos, blocks—anything and everything—at least two dozen times.

Then they sparred for the last fifteen minutes.

Connor ground his teeth as he watched. Trey was pulling his punches, but he still didn't like it. They both wore gloves and headgear, but that wouldn't stop Trey from rattling her teeth if he put his full weight behind a punch.

She removed her head gear and Trey helped her take off the gloves and the tape. Connor looked her over, making sure she was uninjured. No blood. Some redness that might turn into bruises on her arms and legs, but nothing more serious.

Some of the tension eased and he rolled his neck a little to try and relax. He hadn't realized how wound up he was.

When he saw Trey approaching her with that perfect smile, his shoulders tensed again.

"Look at you, baby girl," he beamed. "You're gonna be kicking my ass pretty soon."

"Thanks," Alexandra said, breathless. Connor noted she didn't blush when Trey praised her. That somehow made him feel better.

"Don't thank me, you did all the work. I'm proud of you," he said putting one of his big mitts on her shoulders. Alexandra smiled up at him—*really smiled.*

Connor froze. He hadn't seen her smile like that before. Not a smirk. Not a polite, professional smile. A genuine smile.

If Angel's too-rare smiles warmed his heart, Alexandra's lit him up from the inside.

The only problem was, it wasn't for him.

Connor's arm was around her shoulders before she could even blink.

"Great job," he said with a smile. He leaned over and placed a soft, swift kiss on her temple.

"Thanks," she muttered. She turned to Trey. "I'll see you next week?"

"Same bat time, same bat channel," Trey replied with a wink. She couldn't help but grin and shake her head.

"Dork."

Trey just laughed as he packed up his things.

Trey had been training her for a little over a year. And they'd been friends from the first session.

She'd signed up as a way to learn self-defense. She couldn't stand the thought of taking a class with a dozen strangers, and she could afford private lessons, so she figured, "why not?"

Trey had come highly recommended by the owner of the gym. He had an impressive education, was a former boxer and had been a personal trainer for five years already.

But at their first session, she had been so nervous she'd hardly spoken a word. He'd pushed her hard and halfway through the class she'd just lost it. Angry with him but mostly with *herself,* she'd launched into a tirade, calling him every name in the book and comparing his class to torture and his studio room to a dungeon.

When she was done—gasping for air and shaking, she'd braced herself. She assumed he'd yell at her. At the very least she thought he'd tell her to leave and never come back.

To her surprise, he just *laughed.* And he had a great laugh—a deep loud, rumble, right from the gut. It had immediately put her at ease.

And when he stopped laughing, he'd told her that—just for that—he was never letting her quit. And he was extending every class by fifteen minutes, free of charge. He'd been a huge support for her ever since. She came in every week, worked out all her stress physically, and sometimes verbally.

He was a good listener, and he had a sister so he had at least the bare minimum of emotional intelligence.

"Tell Cassie I said 'hi' and to call me for lunch soon," she said as she picked up her bag and started for the door.

"Will do," he called after her.

"Who's Cassie? His wife?" Connor asked.

"No, his sister, Cassandra. She trains here sometimes. I like her," Alexandra said with a shrug. She was a professional boxer and built like a tank. Intimidating as hell.

But she was also loud and funny, much like her brother, but with much better style. Every once in a while, they went shopping.

Connor didn't reply until she looked at him.

"Are you showering here or at home?" he asked.

She hadn't really thought about it. Normally she'd just walk home and shower there. She didn't like the idea of climbing into Connor's car all sweaty.

"I think I'll grab a quick one here," she said.

She didn't keep toiletries in her bag, but at least she could rinse off and change her clothes. She kept a changes of clothes in her bag, just in case.

"Alright. I'll wait for you outside the locker rooms."

Fifteen minutes later, Alexandra had showered and dressed in the only change of clothes she found in her bag. They'd obviously been in there for a while because all she found was a pair of cut-offs and a white t-shirt.

But, with her fleece jacket, she'd be alright for the short drive home. Her legs would be a little cold, but at least she'd shaved them recently. And she was *clean.*

When he'd said he'd wait outside the locker room, she didn't think he meant *directly* outside. She probably should have known better, but it still surprised her.

He was leaning against the wall across from the ladies' locker room, head turned toward the main area of the gym. As soon as she stepped out the door his head turned, eyes snapping to hers.

He stared at her for a beat before his eyes traveled down her body, tilting his head as he took in her bare legs. He just looked for a second, clearly appreciating the view. She felt herself blush.

"I'm all set," she said, forcing her feet to move and breezing past him.

"Just a sec," he murmured, catching her arm. He stepped up to the desk and had a quick conversation with the girl behind it. He handed her his credit card and a moment later he turned and held out a pair of sweatpants with the name of the gym screen printed across the butt.

"Put these on."

"You didn't have to do that. I'll be fine."

"I didn't have to, but I *did*," he said. "Put 'em on."

When she didn't say anything or move to take them, he smirked and tossed them at her face. She caught them on reflex.

"Fine."

Alexandra dropped her gym bag and pulled on the sweatpants over her jean shorts. They were loose enough that it wasn't an issue, but not so loose they would fall off. He'd picked a good size.

"Thanks. I'll wash them and get them back to you tomorrow."

"Keep 'em." He waved her off as he picked up her gym bag.

"No, really."

"Keep. Them," he insisted. "They won't fit me. It's no big deal. Everyone can use an extra pair of sweats, right?"

"If you insist." Alexandra rolled her eyes and Connor grinned at her. She had to fight—just a tiny bit—to keep from smiling back.

"Let's go."

Connor grabbed her hand and tugged her out the door. She wasn't sure why, but she didn't pull away. His hand was big and warm and having it wrapped around hers made her feel safer, more secure. It felt *nice*.

Before she could stifle it, a sigh escaped. She tried to cover it with a cough, but from the half smile Connor gave her, she knew he wasn't fooled.

Connor unlocked the car and helped her in. He tossed her bag in the back seat and closed her door, circling around to climb into the driver's seat. This time the silence was a different kind of awkward.

When they parked out front, Connor grabbed her bag before

helping her out of the car. He kept a wary eye on the street as he herded her up the steps to her door. She unlocked it and he'd pushed her through and shut the door before she even knew what was happening.

He set her bag down on the floor and gave her a reassuring smile.

"I'll be right back." She waited, less shaky this time, and a few minutes later he gave her the all clear. Alexandra stood awkwardly for a moment, not knowing what to do with herself. "You want something to drink?"

"Sure. Thanks."

"I'm just going to run this to the laundry. I'll be right back." Connor nodded and she brushed past him. She walked through the living room and dining room, into the kitchen. She continued on to the laundry room—just off the kitchen at the back of the house. While she was there, she surreptitiously removed the sweats and the shorts, before putting the sweats back on.

"Is water okay?" she called from the kitchen. She grabbed two bottles of water from the fridge—almost dropping them when she turned and found Connor standing in the doorway.

"Water's fine. Thanks."

Alexandra handed him a bottle and then pointed toward the living room.

They sat down—him in the chair and her on the couch, just like they'd been the night before. She opened her mouth to speak, but he held up a hand to stop her.

"First things first. I know we have some things to talk about, but I'm starving. What do you want to eat?"

"Oh, I'm fine, thank you," Alexandra replied on reflex.

"Lass, ye haven't eaten for hours. You must be half starved after all that exercise. I'm not going to eat in front of you, either, so what will it be?"

She stared at him, eyes wide. Then she laughed. And laughed. *And laughed.* By the time she got herself under control, she was wiping tears from her eyes. She hadn't laughed so hard in years.

Connor said nothing. He just waited for her to stop, a ghost of a smile tugging at the corner of his mouth. But his eyes weren't amused. They were hot. Intense. The laughter died in her throat, replaced with something else—something that made her swallow hard.

"Anything you want to share with the class, Ms. Hughes?" It was barely more than a whisper giving his deep baritone a bit of a rasp. And she'd swear she felt it in her bones. It was intimidating. And sexy as hell.

"It's just that I've never actually heard anyone say 'lass' before. Not seriously, anyway. It was just a bit surreal."

And adorable.

She kept that part to herself. She shouldn't have even *thought* it.

He gave a slow shake of his head. His eyes never left hers. And what she saw in them made her shiver. She cleared her throat and stood, walking to the desk.

She opened the drawer and took a second to pull herself together. She pulled out a pile of papers and shut the drawer again.

"These are my usual places," she said, handing him the stack of menus she kept on hand. She liked to cook—and she was good at it—but didn't have the time. Over the years she'd found a lot of good places, mostly through trial and error.

Unfortunately, it meant she'd also eaten a lot of *bad* takeout in the process. Sort of like dating.

"Any preference?" he asked, fanning them out on the coffee table.

"Not really." She shrugged one shoulder and sat back down on the couch.

Connor took a few minutes to browse through the options before holding up a menu for her favorite Indian place.

"What's good here?" he asked.

"Everything I've ordered has been good. I'm not a big fan of spicy food so I can't vouch for the vindaloo, but the tikka masala is good. The tandoori chicken is my favorite. The saag paneer looks gross, but it's amazing. Oh! And the samosas? Phenomenal."

Connor smiled and picked up his phone, dialing the number on the menu. He ordered everything she mentioned and asked for extra garlic naan before she could even suggest it.

While they waited, she grabbed plates, napkins and silverware and set them on the coffee table.

"You want to eat here?" he asked.

"I usually do, but if you'd rather use the table, that's fine."

"Here's good. Just figured you'd be worried about curry stains on the furniture." He smirked and once again she had to fight—only a little—to keep from smiling.

"Please." She rolled her eyes. "You see that?" Alexandra pointed to a purplish stain on the rug under the coffee table. "Red wine from three weeks ago. And that," she added, pointing to a small brown smudge on the arm of the couch. "Chocolate, from last Halloween."

Connor laughed.

"Furniture is meant to be used—comfortable. At least mine is. It's not just decorative."

"Good to know," he said with a smile. After a moment, he cleared his throat and continued. "Speaking of things I should know, if we're going to pull off this boyfriend thing, you said we should agree on a story. You're right. But there are also some basic facts we should know about each other first, don't you think?"

"Okay. Makes sense," she said, nodding. "Would you like to start, or shall I?" She sat up straighter and took out her phone, opening the notes app.

Connor put his hand over hers, gently taking her phone and setting it back on the coffee table.

"Why don't we just wing it. If there's anything you want to know, just ask. And I'll do the same."

Alexandra frowned, confused. She didn't see why that meant she couldn't take notes, but it probably would be a little rude. Not to mention it would be difficult once the food arrived.

"Okay," she said, tucking her feet under her and leaning back into the corner of the couch.

"Good." Connor smiled at her. "For a start, I want to know about your family. I've met your da, so tell me about the rest of the Hughes clan." He cocked his head to the side and waited.

"Not much to tell, really." Alexandra shrugged. "I have a sister, Amanda. Parents are divorced, but civil. Neither remarried. Both of them are still in the city, and I see my mother every couple weeks. Give or take."

Connor nodded, sitting forward in his chair. He leaned forward, elbows resting on his knees, fingers interlaced.

"How long have your parents been divorced?"

"About… eight years now."

"So you would have been…"

"Twenty-One."

"Hmm."

"Hmm, what?" she asked, raising her eyebrow.

"Well, it seems like people either get divorced when the kids are little—they start fighting about how to parent them, or about money, or they just…drift apart because everything is about the kids—or when the kids are all grown up and leave the nest and they realize they've forgotten how to be a couple."

Alexandra thought about it for a moment and nodded slowly.

"That makes sense. Big life changes can be hard to deal with. I know my mom got a little restless when my sister went away to school. We were both in college and she didn't feel like we needed her as much. And my father wasn't slowing down at work the way she—the way we *all* thought he would. I think she was a little… *lost.*"

She thought about it a little more and found herself frowning.

"You know, I always wondered what happened. They both seemed happy. They were always affectionate when I was growing up. Sometimes, *too* affectionate."

Connor made a face and shuddered and she stifled a laugh.

"We all laughed a lot," she finally said.

And we all cried a lot.

"They never had any serious problems. There was no cheating. They certainly didn't argue over money. They just kind of drifted away from each other at some point, I think. Neither one of them really talks about it much."

"I'm sorry. It's never easy, even when you're an adult."

"What about you? Are your parents still together?" she asked, trying to steer the conversation away from herself. He shook his head.

"No. But at least I know why." He smiled bitterly. She waited for him to explain, but he didn't.

Instead he asked, "Where did you go to school?"

"I went to private school, then NYU for undergrad. Columbia for law school."

"Must have been a good student."

"Yup. I read a lot, and still do. I was a shy kid. Didn't get into trouble, never threw any wild parties. I was on a few teams, a lot of clubs, but mostly I just studied."

"So… you were a *nerd,*" Connor teased, grinning. She gave him a brief, sarcastic smile before taking a deep breath.

"I was," she admitted. "I didn't have much fun until I got to college. That's where I found myself a little bit, I think."

Before I lost myself…

"Takes longer for some than others," he said, nodding wisely.

"What about you? Were you a good student?"

"Terrible," he said with a devilish grin. "I was wildly popular. Threw loads of parties."

Alexandra scoffed, rolling her eyes and Connor laughed.

"No, I was born here, Brooklyn specifically. But I spent a fair bit of time in Scotland, especially as a teenager."

"Never would have guessed." Alexandra deadpanned.

"I ken. Hard to believe, isnae?" he replied.

"Very," Alexandra choked out. She absolutely *did not* laugh.

He paused, just staring at her for a beat before moving on.

"Got into a few scrapes here and there, but I made it through high school in four years and in one piece. Then I joined the Army, learned a lot more, and saved enough money to start my own business when I got out."

"What did you do in the Army?"

"I could tell you, but then I'd have to kill you," he replied with a wink. She rolled her eyes.

The doorbell rang, and he motioned for her to stay where she was. He went to the door, checked carefully, and then opened it. He paid the delivery guy, closed the door and locked it. Alexandra helped him unpack everything and once they'd filled their plates, they ate in silence for a while.

"So how did you end up spending so much time in Scotland," Alexandra finally asked between mouthfuls of naan. "Do you have relatives there?"

"My da is there," he said, not looking up from his plate.

"Oh. Did your sister enjoy Scotland?" she asked. He stopped chewing for a second before he eventually finished his mouthful and swallowed.

"She's never been."

Alexandra raised an eyebrow and waited. He didn't speak and neither did she. She stared and him until he finally looked up and met her eyes. He sighed, setting his plate down.

"Angel is technically my half sister. My father is from Scotland, and her father was—*is*—from Brazil. As far as we know, he still lives there."

"Wow." Alexandra couldn't think of anything else to say. She didn't want to pry, but it was killing her not to ask. The silence stretched on for ages. She picked at her food, sneaking glances at him every so often, hoping he'd say more.

"You're wondering how that happened," he finally said with a chuckle.

"Oh, my God, yes!" she blurted out. "I'm sorry, I don't want to pry, but *yes. Of course,* I'm wondering how that happened!"

He laughed again, shaking his head.

"My mother was a flight attendant. International flights were her favorite, apparently."

"Was?" she asked quietly. His face sobered and he nodded.

"She died while I was on my last deployment. About four years ago."

"I'm sorry," she said.

It was her turn to offer comfort, and she put a hand on his forearm and squeezed. She started to pull away when he surprised her by catching her hand and bringing it to his mouth. He kissed her knuckles, twice. His mouth was warm and soft. She couldn't help imagining those lips on other parts of her body.

"Thank you," he murmured. His warm breath and the brush of his lips against her skin as he spoke gave her goosebumps all the way up her arm.

As soon as he released her hand, she stood, suddenly nervous

"Would you like more water? Or something else?" She started gathering the dishes and closing up the takeout containers. He stopped her and when she looked at him, his expression was unreadable.

"Let me," he said. He took the piled up plates and carried them to the kitchen.

She followed behind him and put the leftovers in the fridge before grabbing a bottle of beer and holding it out to him. He looked at the clock on the stove and then looked back at her and raised an eyebrow.

"It's five o'clock somewhere?" she said with a shrug.

He shook his head but he took the bottle from her and twisted off the cap. She opened a fresh bottle of water and tapped it against his beer.

"Cheers."

She is so damn adorable I can't stand it.

Her laugh had made his heart stop. It was beautiful. She sounded free. *Happy.*

After how scared and lost she'd looked the night before, it was a relief to see her relaxed and enjoying herself—at least a little bit. He realized then that he'd do a whole hell of a lot to make her laugh.

He didn't know why but her mood affected his far more than it should. Her fear made him furious, and her laugh made him feel invincible.

What the hell is wrong with me?

Connor sipped his beer and watched as Alexandra nervously backtracked to the living room. She positioned herself more toward the center of the couch, farther away from the chair he'd been sitting in.

When he sat himself down on the couch—right beside her—her face was priceless. Her eyes went wide and her cheeks turned pink. Her lips parted on a surprised gasp before she clamped them shut again. She shifted nervously and looked away to set her water down on the table.

"So, what should I call you?" he asked.

He fought the urge to tuck a stray lock of hair behind her ear. Or brush it back from her face. Or wrap it around his finger. And he fought the urge to lift her chin so that she'd look at him. He caught the scent of something warm and sweet—almonds and honey.

"Whatever you want," she said. It came out as a whisper, and he bit back a groan. He reminded himself she was just answering his question.

"I don't think you mean that." He gave her a wolfish grin and she blushed, like he knew she would.

"I mean, most people call me Alexandra," she clarified. "But I don't have a preference."

"It's a beautiful name," he replied. "Alexandra."

She shivered a little and bit her lip and his brain nearly short-circuited.

Jesus, she's going to kill me.

"How about Alex?"

"One of my exes called me that," she said with a frown.

"Okay. No' a fan of that. You really don't have a preference?" he coaxed. She pursed her lips and cocked her head.

"You know, I'm not sure anyone has ever actually asked me before."

"Wankers," Connor mumbled. She laughed again and he had to cross his legs to hide the tent in his gym shorts.

"Janie and my sister—Amanda—they call me Lex. I don't mind that."

"Would you like me to call you that? Lex?" he said softly. She blushed, but looked him in the eye.

"I think I could tolerate it," she said with a wry smile. And she didn't look away. It felt like maybe he was seeing the real her—if only a little bit of it—for the first time.

"Lex it is." He didn't blink, afraid she'd slip back behind the mask if he did. Sooner than he would have liked, she did look away and he felt the loss of her eyes like an ache in his ribs.

"So what's our story?" she asked.

Connor took a deep breath and allowed himself a small moment to regroup.

"Well, I had an idea about that…"

They discussed every fictional detail of their pretend relationship until they agreed to stick as close to the truth as possible. And he flirted shamelessly with her the entire time.

He couldn't help it. Those sweet blushes, the rare mischievous grin, the accidental—and not so accidental—brush of their hands. They were like a drug. And he would've done almost anything for *just one more*.

By quarter after five, they had everything squared away and he'd run out of excuses to stay.

Unless…

"Any plans for tonight?" he asked.

Please say yes, even if it's just a grocery run…

"Not really," she said hesitantly, biting her lip.

I should ask her to go for a drink.

No, you fucking shouldn't. Your job is to protect *her, not* date *her. She's safer at home.*

It'll be fine, as long as I'm with her.

No. Do. Your. Job. Go home. *And let Jackson take over tomorrow morning.*

Fuck Jackson.

Get a fucking grip!

"Well, I'll let you enjoy your evening then." Connor smiled and stood up. She looked a little uncertain, but didn't say anything. He walked to the door and she followed. He turned around and she smiled up at him. It hit him like a punch in the gut, knocking the wind out of him.

"I'll be sure to lock the door behind you," she said, rolling her eyes. But she was still smiling. At *him.*

"Good girl," he murmured, running his knuckle down her cheek. Her skin was soft and the way her breath hitched slightly made him want to kiss her. *Hard.*

Instead, he forced himself to turn around and walk out the door.

Chapter Six

I should have asked him to stay.

But why would he? They'd straightened out what they needed to, and she was in for the night. He had no reason to stay. She'd taken up his entire Saturday as it was, he probably wanted to go home and relax. He might even have plans.

But…

If she called Janie, she'd probably invite her to come out with her tonight. Then she could call Connor and tell him that Janie was dragging her out and he'd have to come back. And they'd have to act all cuddly.

He'd have his arm around her, or his hands on her, and she could just enjoy it. She could pretend—just for a while.

Don't be stupid. This isn't a game. You're safer at home.

I've been safe for years. Safe and alone…

It wasn't the first time she'd thought it. She'd intentionally isolated herself. She didn't trust easily and it had never been worth the risk.

The more people you let in the more people had the power to disappoint you. To *hurt* you. And not just her. Her disappointment—her hurt—affected everyone who loved her. They'd been through enough.

Her decision made, she put her phone face down on the coffee table and walked to the bookshelf. She pulled out her old copy of *Pride and Prejudice* and got comfy on the couch.

She used to read through all of Jane Austen's novels at least once a year, but it had been a while since she'd had the time. She opened it to the first chapter and smiled at the familiar words.

For some reason, she couldn't concentrate. Words she knew by heart slipped away. She read the same page three times before she gave up.

She got up, went to the kitchen and pulled out her recipe book—the one that her mother had given her with all her favorites. She gathered ingredients, measured, mixed, and scooped and an hour later she had four dozen chocolate chip cookies cooling on the counter.

She tasted one and savored the warm melty chocolate. This was a good batch, but it still wasn't quite right. Her mother always insisted that the special ingredient was extra love. Maybe that was why she never got them right.

She was contemplating what she could do differently—*maybe a pinch more salt and a bit less flour?*—when her cell phone buzzed from the living room.

She jogged over from the kitchen, flipped it over and flinched.

"Charles, I can explain."

"I really fucking *hope so*. And you can start with explaining why *you* didn't call *me*."

"I'm sorry," she said, cringing. Because he was right. She should have called him first thing this morning.

"You know, I didn't expect you to call me last night considering the state you were in—and *who you left with*," Charles said, ignoring her apology. "But I thought you'd call me *at some point* today."

"I know, I'm *so*, so sorry, Charles. You're my best friend and I should have called you. And I should have told you about Connor sooner."

"*Am I* your best friend, though?" he asked, his voice pitching up.

Shit, he's really *pissed.*

"You *are*! And that's why I didn't tell you," she said quickly. Charles was quiet for a second.

"What do you mean?"

"I love you, Charles. You're *family* to me. And…" she found herself tearing up, the truth in her lie hitting a little too close. "When I get hurt, *you* get hurt. I just… I didn't want to do that to you over something I wasn't sure was… *anything*."

"Alexandra," Charles sighed. "You're so fucking dense sometimes."

"I know," Alexandra said. She was too relieved he wasn't mad anymore to even argue about it. Besides, it was true.

"You realize it hurts when you don't tell me things, too, right?"

"Yes," she said quietly.

"And are you going to do it again?" he asked.

"Not unless there's a really good reason," she said.

"Jesus… what am I going to do with you?"

"Forgive me?" she said hopefully.

"Of course, I'll forgive you. But you *owe* me. Big."

"Absolutely. Any favor, any time. No questions asked."

"Damn right," he muttered. "Now, tell me everything."

Alexandra took a deep breath and prepared herself to tell a very creative and highly edited version of the truth.

Half an hour later, Charles was appeased. And he'd only made six or seven more comments questioning their friendship. All things considered, it could have been much worse. And probably would be when and if he ever found out the actual truth.

She set her phone down and picked up another cookie. They were cool now, but still delicious.

Her phone rang again, and she rolled her eyes. Charles could be such a diva sometimes. What was he going to make her promise now?

She picked up her phone and saw Janie's name on the caller ID. She dropped her half-eaten cookie back onto the plate and answered the call.

"Hey, Janie."

"Lex! Thank God you answered. I *know* you screen my calls on the weekend."

"I don't… do that *all* the time."

"Uh-huh. Anyway, what are you doing tonight?" Janie asked. She sounded even more enthusiastic than usual. That couldn't be a good sign.

"Nothing, why?" Alexandra asked. Even though she'd thought about calling Janie earlier, she was getting the feeling Janie had something in mind besides a casual girls' night out.

"One of the guys I met last night is a drummer in a band and he put me on the list for his gig tonight. He said I could bring friends. You *have to* come."

"Uh…"

"Please? I wouldn't mind going alone, but this bar is outside my usual radius and I'm not sure what to expect."

"If you're worried about it, why are *you* going? Can't you just wait and meet him for coffee tomorrow or something?"

"A date… for coffee… on a Sunday?" she scoffed. "What am I, eighty? Besides, didn't you hear me? He's a *drummer*, Lex. So hot."

"This isn't some dive in Hell's Kitchen again, is it?"

"No. It's just in Soho. It can't be *that* bad."

"Where in Soho?"

Janie mumbled something that Alexandra couldn't understand.

"Where. In. Soho. Janie?"

"It's on Baxter Street," Janie said.

"Janie, that's *not* Soho!" Alexandra protested. "That's Chinatown!"

"So, it's a little south of Soho. Please? I promise we won't stay too long."

"Fine," Alexandra huffed. "But I'm bringing Connor so I'm not stranded when you ditch me."

"You know I wouldn't do that," Janie said. Alexandra could *hear* the eyeroll. "But I'm cool if he wants to come too."

"What time?" Alexandra sighed, though she couldn't help the flutter of excitement she felt.

"Show starts at ten. I'll meet you out front. Thank you, thank you, thank you. I really appreciate it."

"What do I even wear? What kind of bar is this?"

"Just wear whatever you'd normally wear to a bar. Gotta go. See you later!"

Janie hung up before Alexandra could explain she didn't normally *go* to bars. She hadn't been out in anything other than her work clothes in so long that she had no idea what that meant, let alone what that meant *to Janie.* Janie was unique and her idea of style, though it was perfect for her, was not the same as Alexandra's.

First things first. She called Connor. The phone rang and her stomach flipped. Would he be mad? He just left two hours ago. What if he *did* have plans? This was a bad idea. She nearly hung up the phone, but the ringing stopped.

"Lex? Something wrong?" he answered. The sound of his voice gave her butterflies. She froze.

"Are you there?" he said. His concern came through loud and clear.

"Yeah," she choked out. She cleared her throat and added, "Everything's fine. I, um… I hope I'm not bothering you. Are you busy?"

"No. Not at all." He didn't seem annoyed. He seemed *relieved.*

"Good," she breathed. "Janie called and begged me to come out with her to see some band. She's into the drummer, apparently. I hate to do this—I mean I know you were just here, and if you've got something more important to do I can just call her back and tell her that something came up and I can't make it."

She was babbling so she snapped her mouth shut before she could go any further. There was a beat of silence on the line that made her nervous. He was pissed for sure.

"You know what, just forget it. I-"

"Lex," he cut in. His tone was firm but soft. "Stop. What time do you need me to pick you up?"

"The show's in Chinatown and it starts at ten, so… nine? Is that okay?"

"That's fine."

"Are you sure? I mean I don't need to go."

"Do you *want* to go?" He asked.

"Not really," she said with a nervous laugh. "But I feel like I should. She doesn't know this guy at all and she's never been to this place before. I'd feel like a shitty friend if I let her go alone."

"Then we're going," he said simply. She could almost hear his easy grin. "You don't have to ask my permission, Lex. I go where you go, that's all there is to it. You're not bothering me, and nothing is more important right now. Got it?"

She couldn't keep the smile off her face. And since he couldn't see it, she didn't bother to try.

"Got it."

"Good. I'll see you at nine."

Connor showered, shaved, and ran his fingers through his damp hair. A club in Chinatown wasn't very specific, but he figured a suit and tie would be overkill. He went casual, putting on an outfit pretty similar to what he'd worn the night before—jeans, a band t-shirt, a hoodie over his shoulder holster, and a pair of work boots. He grabbed his coat on the way out.

By quarter to nine, he'd parked his Hummer on the street outside Alexandra's brownstone. He checked both sides of the street, as usual, before he got out and climbed the steps to her door. He knocked and a few minutes later he saw her peek through the window to see who it was. He stepped back so she could see him clearly and she opened the door.

"You're early," she said, pulling him inside and shutting the door behind him. She locked it automatically without him having to remind her. "I'm almost ready."

She didn't look almost ready. For one thing, her feet were bare. He found himself staring at her toes, which were painted a vibrant blue. They were… *cute.* The color was fun and different. Unexpected, but fucking adorable.

"My eyes are up here, you know," she said. He smirked, taking his time letting his eyes wander to her face. She wore tight jeans that hugged her hips and legs. Her t-shirt was black—and surprisingly familiar. He laughed, and when she gave him a curious look, he held his hoodie open so she could see his shirt.

He wore an identical shirt—a white four-leaf clover on a black background. Two snakes intertwined in the center and surrounded by a ring of green. White letters spelled out the band name.

"No way," she gasped. "Flogging Molly?"

"Yup. I've had this shirt since high school."

"Oh, my God. Me too," she laughed. "What are the odds?"

She turned and jogged up the stairs. His feet followed her without even having to think about it. She didn't object.

"I just need to finish getting dressed."

"Take your time," he replied. He looked around her bedroom and stopped in his tracks.

He'd seen the room twice before, including just that afternoon. It was a large room with an attached bathroom and a walk-in closet. She had a Queen sized bed with a cream colored comforter and an array of pillows in various shades of purple. There was a padded headboard in dark purple with a vine pattern stitched into the fabric and a large dresser dominated the far wall.

At that moment, every surface—the bed, the dresser, the floor—were all covered in clothes. It looked like her closet had vomited all over the room.

"What happened here?" he asked in mock horror.

"I couldn't decide what to wear," she said defensively. "Janie said to wear *whatever I normally wear to a bar.* I have no idea what that means. I don't go out much, except with Janie. And that's usually after work, which means I go in whatever I've got on." She sighed rummaging through a pile of clothes.

"You could wear a sack and still look beautiful," he said. He hadn't meant to say that out loud. It just sort of slipped out and he squeezed his eyes shut, silently cursing himself. She turned toward him, blushing wildly, muttered a thank you and went back to looking for… whatever it was she was looking for. And he couldn't stop watching her.

Her hair hung in waves around her face. It looked soft. Natural. Her makeup was subtle, only enhancing her naturally high, cheekbones, dark lashes, and warm, amber and jade eyes.

She was beautiful, just as she was. It didn't matter what she wore, she would look amazing in anything. Case and point, she bent to tug on a pair of socks and he noticed that even in jeans her body was a work of art. A living, breathing, warm, soft sculpture of womanhood.

Christ on a bicycle, what the fuck are you on about now?

She laced up a pair of black ankle boots with a chunky heel and wrapped a grey houndstooth scarf around her neck.

"I just need to grab a coat," she mumbled, heading for the closet again. Connor just stood there watching and keeping his mouth firmly shut. She came out of the closet with a black leather motocross jacket and did a little spin.

"What do you think?" she asked. He took a moment to look her up and down. As if drawn by a magnet, he prowled toward her. Her eyes grew wider with every step in her direction. And so did his grin. He didn't stop until they were toe to toe and she had to tilt her head back to see his face.

Fuck it. In for a penny…

He leaned forward to whisper in her ear.

"You look delicious," he said. She looked away but he could see the flush creeping up the back of her neck.

So damn cute.

The bloody club was in a strange no man's land between soho, Tribeca and Chinatown. The address was officially Chinatown, but it didn't *feel* like Chinatown. Instead of an Asian grocery store or restaurant, it was next to a bail bondsman. Convenient.

The place itself seemed nice enough. Clean, decently lit and it didn't have the stink of stale beer and cigarette smoke you sometimes found in seedier places. The bar was well stocked and the bartender wasn't a grizzled prospector type with a 12 gauge loaded for bear under the bar, within easy reach. Instead it was a clean cut guy, probably in this mid twenties, in a white dress shirt.

Connor relaxed a fraction and escorted Alexandra to a table in the far corner, off to the side of the dance floor. Alexandra was busy looking for Janie and her hand popped up when she spotted her at the other side of the room.

Janie made her way through the crowd, which was getting denser by the minute, and gave Alexandra a hug.

"Thanks for coming." She beamed. "You look *amazing*, by the way. Love this look." Janie gestured in her general direction as she gave her outfit a once over. A strange sense of pride filled Connor's chest. He had to remind himself that she was his *pretend* girlfriend. *Pretend*—as in *not real.*

Then Janie surprised him by giving him a quick squeeze as well. "You, too, big guy."

"Which? Thanks for coming or I look amazing?"

"Both," she shot back with a wink and smile.

"Any time and, of course I do."

Janie's eyes widened a little and she laughed.

"I like him," she said to Alexandra, hooking a thumb in his direction.

Alexandra caught him off guard when she muttered a "me too." She turned away from him, refusing to meet his eyes as she took off her jacket and draped it over the back of the chair.

"The band won't be on for a while, yet. Sound check and all that. Want a drink?" Janie asked, motioning to the bar. "I'm buying."

Connor pulled out a chair for her, and motioned for her to sit instead.

"I'll get 'em. What can I get for the two most beautiful girls in the room?"

Alexandra gave him a suspicious look and Janie simply gaped at him. "I know you want a G&T, don't ye?" He smiled at Alexandra and pecked her on the cheek.

Janie found her voice and held up her glass. "Another old fashioned for me, please."

"Coming right up."

Connor headed to the bar, glancing back over his shoulder every once in a while to check on them. Before he made it three feet, he heard Janie mutter, "If you ever decide you're done with him, I'm next in line." He didn't hear Alexandra's reply, but he heard Janie yelp a moment later. Connor chuckled all the way to the bar.

"Seriously. He's fucking gorgeous, Lex." Janie was practically swooning. She kept sneaking glances over her shoulder as he stood at the bar waiting for their drinks. "And that ass. Mmm, I could just bite it."

"Janie!" Alexandra gasped, blushing *for* her. "Keep your voice down."

"And that voice," Janie continued as if Alexandra had never spoken. "Hot, sexy and with a Scottish accent. It's like heaven. Hey, does he have a brother?"

"Sister," Alexandra gave her a saccharine smile.

"Hmm..." Janie thought for a moment. "If she's as hot as he is, I might be persuaded to switch teams."

"You're terrible," Alexandra laughed. "And no, you wouldn't. You like men too much."

"True," Janie replied with a sigh. "It would probably be so much easier if I didn't, but there's just no substitute for a hot, hard d–"

"Here you go, ladies." Connor said, placing their drinks on the table.

Janie bit her lip to hide a giggle at what he'd probably overheard. Alexandra closed her eyes and shook her head, hoping to sink into the floor.

"Thank you," she muttered as she took a healthy sip. It was cool and citrusy and had a delicious burn.

"You're welcome," he said, whispering in her ear. His breath on the shell of her ear made her shiver. He draped an arm over the back of her chair and his fingers began trailing lazily over her shoulder and down her arm. He leaned into her until his lips barely brushed her ear.

"She's right, you know. There's no substitute for the real thing," he said. His voice was pitched so low that she knew no one else would have heard him.

It sent a tingle down her spine and she had to repress a sigh of pleasure. He chuckled darkly at her reaction and she nearly melted out of her chair.

She forced herself to take a sip of her drink before she spoke. "I'm well aware," she said quietly. And she was. It had been an insanely long time since she'd had the real thing.

He pressed a soft, swift kiss to her neck, just below her ear and then turned his attention back to Janie.

"So, tell me about yourself," Connor said. "Lex has told me about you, but I always like to hear it from the horse's mouth, so to speak."

"I'm more interested in hearing about *you* since Alexandra hasn't told me *anything*. I was *shook* when I met you at the bar last night. First time I've seen her with anyone."

Alexandra glared at Janie, wishing she had the power to turn her friend into a pile of goo on the floor with just her mind.

"You haven't met any of her previous boyfriends?"

"What boyfriends?" Janie muttered before she caught Alexandra's glare. "No, I haven't," she quickly added.

"Good. Hopefully, it's one of many ways I'm different," he said to Janie, while looking directly at Alexandra. His look was scorching. He looked like he wanted to prove to her just how different he was. Possibly right then and there.

"Tell me about this drummer," Alexandra deflected, focusing on Janie.

Janie would gladly take over the conversation if she had the chance. She was a verbal steamroller sometimes. Once she got started you either got out of the way or you got flattened.

"His name is Luke and he's a drummer, which means his digital dexterity must be exceptional," she said with a waggle of her eyebrows that made Alexandra laugh. "He's twenty-eight, 6′1″ and he's originally from Texas. Can you believe that? An honest to God cowboy. It's like, on every woman's fantasy bucket list. And he looks it, too. He's lean and strong like he just spent the summer bailin' hay."

A bit of her own much suppressed southern accent came out. That was usually a sign of one of three things: she was either a little drunk, *really* pissed, or she'd been talking to someone with a similar accent. Alexandra would guess it was a little from column A and a little from column C.

"I mean, if I can talk him into wearing cowboy boots and a plaid shirt, you might just have to scrape me off the floor. As it is I could just sit and stare at him all day." Janie paused and eyed Connor up and down. "Though you're not hard on the eyes either, killer." She winked again.

Alexandra felt a flare of irritation.

Alexandra's eyes flicked to Connor for the briefest moment and it was a mistake. He was smiling like the cat that ate the canary. The phrase "tickled pink" had never entered into her vocabulary before, but he was the picture of it.

She didn't like that Janie's effusive praise irritated her so much, or the fact that Connor seemed to be eating it up with a spoon. She sipped her drink and tried to tune both of them out for a few moments. Then something caught her attention.

"... haven't even slept with him yet and it's all I can think about."

"*Jesus*, Janie," Alexandra said, lowering her head and covering her eyes. "You're going to give Connor the impression that you're just a walking vagina!" Connor chuckled and Janie laughed. She glared at both of them.

"I am way more than a walking vagina," Janie said haughtily. "I have *many* erogenous zones, and they *all* better get the attention they deserve."

"Oh. My. God," Alexandra groaned. Janie snickered and Connor laughed that genuine, *funniest thing you've heard in your life* sort of laugh. It was so sexy that Alexandra just stared at him.

His dark hair had fallen across his forehead. Wrinkles had formed at the corners of his eyes, and she realized he had a small dimple in his right cheek. His large shoulders shook and she could see the defined muscles of his stomach flexing as he laughed.

He was like some sort of romance novel character. Too handsome, too perfect, too... *vivid* to be real. She briefly wished she were heroine material. Strong, seductive, confident.

She could play the part pretty well, but inside she was awkward and afraid. She took a large swallow of her drink and then stood.

"I have to use the ladies' room," she said softly. She'd only take two steps when Connor's large hand caught hers.

"I'll walk with you," he said quietly as he matched her pace. In the hallway outside the restrooms he stopped her. He crowded her against the wall and she felt a sense of deja vu.

"We have to stop having conversations outside of bathrooms," Alexandra said dryly. "People will think we're talking shit." The corner of his mouth lifted, but his eyes were wary—concerned.

"Funny girl," he said. He stroked a knuckle down the side of her face before cupping her cheek in his hand, his thumb stroking softly across her cheekbone. "What's wrong, funny girl?"

She just shrugged. "Nothing."

"You're a bad liar."

"I'm a lawyer," she snorted. "It's what we do."

"Not you," he said quietly.

"You don't know that," she breathed.

"Aye, I do. The way you say what's on your mind, even if it's uncomfortable. The way you talk about your job and the reasons you do it. You're *honest*."

She looked away—thrilled and embarrassed at the same time. He'd been paying attention. He'd seen more than she expected him to—more than most people would.

"So, tell me what's wrong," he prompted.

"Nothing really," she sighed. "I just get in my own head sometimes."

"And what's going on in that pretty head of yours right now? What's causing you so much trouble?" he asked. His eyes bore into her as if he could see her thoughts.

"You." She shrugged again. "Me. *Life.*" He snorted and gave her that crooked half smile that she was coming to know so well.

"Nice and vague," he scolded. "But we'll talk more later." He stepped back and she ducked through the bathroom door.

The band was surprisingly good, and Alexandra had to admit that Janie's drummer was in fact, very cute. He had that "aw, shucks" vibe that made him seem sweet and innocent. Alexandra snorted to herself.

That won't last long.

Janie hadn't said a word the entire time. She'd just been making eyes with her good ol' boy while he played.

Alexandra hadn't met any of Janie's other conquests so she couldn't tell if this behavior was typical for her. It certainly wasn't what she'd expected from Janie. She's sort of expected her to be more... aloof? Disinterested?

At any rate, she and Connor were left to occupy themselves, which they did. Mostly by watching the band in silence. He seemed content just sipping his beer, one arm resting on the back of her chair, his thumb brushing over her shoulder in a maddeningly steady rhythm.

She wasn't content. Between the casual intimacy of his touch, the heat radiating off of his skin and the scent of his cologne, she was practically squirming in her chair. Her face felt flushed. Not a blush—a constant warmth that wasn't from the drink she'd been nursing.

She needed room to breathe.

"I could use another drink," she said, standing. "Anyone else?"

"I'll get it," Connor said, standing as well. "Stay put. Janie?"

Janie nodded absently and handed him her empty glass, not taking her eyes from the stage.

As soon as he was gone, Alexandra switch sides, sliding into the chair between Janie and the wall. Janie gave her a curious glance but quickly returned her focus to the band.

When Connor returned and saw the revised seating arrangements, he frowned, narrowed his eyes, and then handed Janie her drink. He set Alexandra's glass on the table in front of where she'd been sitting.

"Come sit with me," Connor said, smiling sweetly.

"I can see better from over here. I was getting a cramp from having to turn my head." Alexandra replied.

"Well, in that case…" He stood and moved around Janie to stand behind her chair. "You're right, the view is better on this side." He swept his hands across her shoulders and then began working the muscles with his strong fingers.

Alexandra couldn't help herself. She groaned and closed her eyes. He chuckled and inched his hands in towards her neck. He ran his thumbs firmly up either side of her neck and then back down. It was heaven.

She leaned farther back into his touch and let her head droop forward to give him better access. After a few minutes she was both relaxed and very, *very*, aware of her body. Every stroke, every brush of fingers, sent goosebumps down her arms.

"Up," he whispered in her ear. She shivered and hesitated, but eventually obeyed. He stepped around the chair and sat, pulling her into his lap.

"Thank you. For the massage," she quickly added. She felt his breath on her neck as his arms tightened around waist, pulling her closer to him.

"Happy to help," he said as he settled her more fully onto his lap.

Happy indeed. Either that or he was carrying a nightstick in his pocket. Her face burned and she looked away. She wasn't sure what to do with this information. She didn't know what she *wanted* to do with it.

Yes, you do, coward.

Alexandra shook her head trying to clear it, she sat up straighter, trying to gain some distance.

Connor sucked in a sharp breath when she shifted.

"Damnit, don't move," he growled. He punctuated the command with a nip to her earlobe. She squeaked and jumped, eliciting a hiss from Connor.

"Christ, woman, are ye tryin' to kill me?" His voice was thick, and his accent was thicker. "If you don't stop squirming, I'm going to have a real embarrassing situation to deal with when we have to get up and leave."

Alexandra glanced furtively around them, but everyone seemed to be focused entirely on the stage. She bit her lip and, heart racing, she leaned back against his chest and, reaching back, placed a hand on the side of his neck.

He went very still and his breathing became shallow. A thrill went through her at his reaction, and she felt… *brave.* Or maybe just reckless. She arched her back, rolling her hips in the process and pushing back against him.

Connor cursed, low and harsh, and his hands tightened almost painfully on her waist as he pulled her closer, his hips bucking upwards a fraction. After several long moments, Connor's grip loosened and his breathing evened out.

"Behave," he commanded. His voice was all gravel and whiskey—rough and deep. It washed over her leaving fire in its wake. And she closed her eyes, relishing the burn.

But even as she reveled in the feeling, a warning voice in the back of her head reminded her what happened when she played with fire. She pushed the thought away, but let her hand drop from his neck and sat very still.

"Or what?" she asked. Part of her was genuinely curious. She wanted to continue this little game, dangerous as it was. Another part of her dreaded the answer.

"Are you sure you want to know?"

Alexandra swallowed hard and licked her lips. She wasn't sure at all, but it was too late to back down now.

"Yes."

"Hmm," he purred. After a moment of thought he leaned in close to her ear. She felt the barest scrape of teeth against her neck and she shivered.

One of his arms snaked around her waist and his free hand wrapped itself around one of her wrists. Her heart began to pound.

"Handcuffs would be most convenient, but personally I think you'd look gorgeous with a pair of silk rope bracelets." His thumb swept back and forth over her pulse point.

Alexandra froze. Her breaths came in shallow pants and her vision tunneled.

No, no, no, no… not now. Not here. Not Now. Breathe. Breathe.

Connor must have sensed something was wrong because he immediately released her wrist and removed his arm from around her waist, resting his hands gently on her hips instead.

"What's wrong?" His voice was all soft concern now. Every trace of heat had vanished.

Her stomach flipped and nausea assaulted her—sudden, overwhelming. She jumped up and scrambled around Janie without explanation. She made a mad dash for the bathroom and made it just in time to puke her guts up in private.

She couldn't stop shaking and a cold sweat broke out on her forehead.

She was so dizzy. She sat on the cool tile floor and closed her eyes, trying to keep the room from spinning. She took deep, steadying breaths to try and calm her roiling stomach. She counted. She did all the things her therapist had told her to do—still the tears came and her hands trembled.

She didn't know how long she sat there trying to pull herself together, but she didn't recognize her name until someone said it for a third time.

"Lex?"

"Yeah," she croaked. Her throat was raw and her mouth tasted foul.

"God, are you okay?" Janie said.

"Sick," was all she could manage.

"Can you unlock the door?"

She didn't answer. Instead she knelt up long enough to unbolt the stall door before sinking back to the floor.

"Jesus! You look awful." Janie crouched down in front of her and, ignoring the smell of vomit, wrapped her arms gently around her, rubbing her back in soothing circles.

That was all it took for Alexandra to break down again.

Chapter Seven

Shit. What the hell is going on in there?

Something was very, *very* wrong. He'd known it the moment he'd felt her pulse skyrocket under his fingertips. Her breathing had gotten faster and shallower and she'd started to tremble.

He hadn't even been able to get an answer from her before she'd bolted from the table. He hadn't been able to catch her before she made it to the ladies' room.

He'd given her five minutes before he'd dragged Janie away from the table and sent her in after Alexandra. That was fifteen minutes ago and he was standing out here losing his shit.

He knocked twice on the bathroom door before he opened it crack.

"Janie? Lex? What's going on?" He waited a beat but got nothing but silence.

Fuck this.

He pushed the door open and walked down the row of stalls until he saw two pairs of feet. He rapped gently on the door.

"You alright, love?" he said softly.

"Connor?" Alexandra rasped. She sounded wretched. His heart broke.

"Aye. I'm right here. What's going on? Are you sick?" He had tested her drink and knew there was nothing wrong with it, and she was still working on her second. It couldn't have been the Indian food they had that afternoon because he felt fine.

"She's been throwing up," Janie said, opening the door and moving aside. Alexandra was pale and trembling. She was slumped against the wall of the stall, shoulders up and body tense. She'd wrapped her arms protectively around herself as she sat with her eyes closed, breathing steadily in through her nose and out through her mouth.

I know what this is…

He swore under his breath and bent down to scoop her up. Her whole body was shaking and the hair around her face was damp with sweat. She protested weakly but he just tucked her head onto his shoulder and carried her out the door.

"I'm taking her home," Connor said. Janie nodded and handed him Alexandra's purse. Then she draped both of their coats over Alexandra, tucking them carefully around her.

"Will you be okay?" he asked. He didn't like the idea of leaving her there alone, but he needed to take care of Alexandra. *Now.* She was his priority.

"Yeah, I'm fine. Go." He raised an eyebrow and she gave him a tight smile. "I promise I'll call you when I get home. Better?"

"Yeah. Thanks." He nodded, and headed out the door.

Alexandra was still shivering even though he'd helped her put on his sweatshirt before covering her again with both of their coats. Her eyes were still closed, and she hadn't said anything since he'd pulled away from the club.

Her breathing seemed to be steadier now, but she was still taking slow, deep breaths. Every once in a while he thought her mouth moved. She was probably counting.

"How long have you been having panic attacks like this?" he asked quietly. She opened her eyes and stared at him in shock, and then he saw it. The embarrassment, the shame. She didn't lie—didn't tell him he was wrong. Just said nothing.

She turned away and stared out at the city as it passed them by. He fought with himself for a few long minutes before he finally spoke.

"I still remember the first time," he said softy. He kept his attention on the road. This wasn't something he shared often. He didn't think he'd be able to get it out if he looked at her. She turned toward him out, but he couldn't see her expression. That was for the best.

"I was in the Army for twelve years. For eight of those, I was a Ranger. I was deployed to the middle east three times." He took a deep breath before continuing. "I came home three years ago. In June. Mom had been gone about six months. Angel was here all alone, so I moved in with her. Started trying to figure out what the hell I was going to do with the *next* twelve years."

His grip on the steering wheel tightened. Breathing got a little harder as his chest grew tight.

"People talk about vets transitioning back into civilian life—how hard it can be. But it's not really just finding a job and a place and starting over. Everything is different. *Everything*." He swallowed hard.

"Your brain is conditioned to work a certain way. You train constantly. Do drill after drill. You're broken down and built back up with all these new instincts—*reflexes* that are meant to keep you alive."

He paused, giving himself a moment to collect his thoughts.

"When you're in combat, all that training kicks. It's automatic. You just react without even thinking about it. When you get back? It's like being on another planet. The rules change and your reactions are expected to change—your *focus* is expected to change. All overnight. One day you're a soldier and the next you're not."

He cleared his throat and pushed on.

"Sorry, I'm getting off track," he said. "The transition was hard for me like it is for a lot of guys. I tried to hide it—that's just how we're wired. But Angel… she's a sweet kid and she knew I was strugglin.' So, she wanted to do something special for me."

He cringed at the memory. Just thinking about this gave him a pit in his stomach and had his hands shaking on the wheel.

"Her friend's family invited us to Long Island for the weekend. She didn't tell me where we were going. It was a surprise. We got there and it was this big party on the beach—food, music, drinks. Everything was fine. I had a beer, met her friends… I was actually enjoying myself." He couldn't keep the bitterness from creeping into his voice.

"But I hadn't paid attention to the date. It was the fourth of July." He felt a little embarrassed admitting that. After all he was an American citizen, and one who had served his country. The Fourth of July should have been one of his holiest days. He felt stupid for forgetting.

"I wasn't prepared when the bombs went off." He dragged in a breath. His hands clenched on the wheel. "It was just the fireworks, but suddenly I was back in Iraq. Explosions, gunfire, shouting—all that shit you see in movies when someone's having a flashback. Except what they can't show you is how it *feels*. Your adrenaline kicks in and it's not just a bunch of memories. It feels *real*. You can smell the smoke, feel the weight of the gear on your back. Taste the blood."

"PTSD," she whispered.

"Yeah," he sighed, focusing on the road in front of him.

"What happened next?" she asked cautiously.

"I freaked out," he said tightly. After all this time, the shame still lingered. Less of it, maybe, but it was still there. "After the flashbacks faded a little, I tried to remind myself I was home. I wasn't there anymore. But it felt like I was breathing through a straw. My hands shook. I wanted to puke."

He saw her nod out of the corner of his eye.

"Like I said, Angel's a sweet kid, but she had no idea what was happening. She saw me lying in the sand—shaking, gasping for air. Trying to get myself under control. So, she did what anyone would do. She put her hand on my arm. Except I couldn't tell what was real and what wasn't, and I—"

He gritted his teeth until his jaw ached with the pressure.

When he finally spoke it was just a whisper. "I shoved her. *Hard.* She went down and I… *lost* it. All I could think about was 'what if we'd been closer to the fire?'" He had to stop and swallow down the bile rising up his throat.

"I thought… 'what if I'd had a weapon?' I could have killed her before I even knew what was happening." To his surprise she reached out and took his shaking hand in hers and squeezed. He'd been trying to comfort her by showing her she wasn't alone, but now *she* was comforting *him*.

"I cried. Sobbing, hysterical…" He grimaced. It wasn't something he liked to admit. He was still learning how to deal with all of this, but being honest about it was a start. "The guilt…" His throat tightened and he couldn't finish.

So many people in her life had never understood and never would. And she was *glad* they wouldn't. The only way anyone could understand was if they'd suffered through it like she had. And she wouldn't wish that on anyone.

Connor had been so honest with her. And she knew just how difficult it was to share something like that. She'd had trouble even discussing it with her therapist. She took a shaky breath.

"That's the worst part," she whispered. "The shame. You keep thinking 'what's wrong with me? why can't I get it together?' You wonder if you'll ever be able to fix what's broken, and you feel like you should've been strong enough not to break in the first place."

He raised her hand to his mouth and brushed kisses over her knuckles. One, two, three. She felt a tear slip free and slide down her cheek.

"I'll tell you the same thing someone told me, once," he said quietly. "Everyone breaks. No matter how strong, no matter how tough, everyone breaks. What matters is how you mend."

And she understood exactly what he meant.

There was a time in her life—after everything came crashing down around her—when she'd had to make a choice. And a feeling in her gut had told her that the path she chose to walk through the aftermath would be the most important decision she'd ever make.

"Thank you," she said. "I appreciate you sharing that with me. I know how hard it is."

He nodded and kissed her hand again.

"I won't ask you," he assured her. "But I'd be honored to listen if you ever want to talk about it."

She nodded, grateful that he wouldn't push her. She was relieved that he understood how much trust it would take for her to share her story.

"I will," she promised. "One day." She didn't know why she made that promise when he might walk out of her life just as abruptly as he'd walked into it. Maybe she was trying to convince herself that wouldn't happen—that somehow, he'd still be there when the dust settled.

He gave her a warm smile, as if he was hoping for the same thing. She felt the knot in her chest ease a little.

He pulled up in front of her house and opened the door. He took his time moving around the front end, checking the street as he went, before opening her door for her. Rather than helping her out, he simply scooped her up and carried her to her door.

She dug the keys out of her purse, unlocked it so he could carry her inside. She didn't have the strength or the desire to protest.

He set her down, keeping an arm around her waist until he was sure she was steady on her feet. He disappeared without a word, but she knew the drill and waited until he came back.

He came downstairs after checking the second floor, but instead of telling her to lock up behind him, he did it himself. He slid the deadbolt home and then grabbed her hand, tugging her up the stairs. Her heart raced faster when it already felt like it was trying to hammer it's way out of her rib cage.

She swallowed hard and hesitated for a moment. He looked down at her and smiled, smoothing away the hair from her face.

"Don't worry, lass," he murmured. "I'm just gonna tuck you in."

She laughed, the noise sounding nervous, almost hysterical, to her own ears. She suspected he did that on purpose—made her laugh to put her at ease. It was sweet.

"Oh, alright." She rolled her eyes. "I suppose I can let the big, sexy Scot tuck me in." She was sure she turned bright pink the moment the words left her mouth.

She wasn't sure where she'd found the courage, but she enjoyed their playful banter. And their snarky banter. *Any* banter with him, really.

She couldn't look at him as she started climbing the stairs so she walked up the stairs in silence, holding his hand. She pushed open the bedroom door and groaned at the sea of clothes littering every surface. She'd forgotten about the mess she left, and now she was more embarrassed than ever.

Why in heaven would he want to stick around after he'd seen what a hot mess she was? She was obviously delusional.

Connor dropped her hand, and she ignored the disappointment she felt at the loss of his warmth. She assumed he was going to leave, but instead he grabbed her bedspread and yanked it down, tossing all the clothes on the floor. Then he meticulously straightened it, folding one side over neatly so that she could climb in.

"Problem solved." Connor smiled, spreading his arms wide.

"You are quite the problem solver, aren't you?" she replied, batting her eyelashes dramatically.

See? Delulu.

She ducked past him to the dresser and pulled out a pair of flannel pants and a t-shirt. She went to the bathroom to change and get ready for bed. She returned a while later—face washed, teeth brushed, hair brushed—in clean pajamas.

In that time, Connor had picked up the clothing off the floor, folded it, and piled it on her dresser.

Great. Not only had he seen her mid freakout, but he'd also had to clean up her mess.

"You didn't have to do that," she murmured, feeling self-conscious.

She'd felt like an idiot most of the night—panicking over what to wear, *actually* panicking at the bar, and now standing here in pajamas while he picked up after her.

Pathetic.

He shrugged and set the last carefully folded shirt on the pile.

"How else am I supposed to nick a pair of your knickers for my collection?"

She laughed and his answering smile was broad and radiant.

"Nah. It's habit at this point. My sister was a slob, leaving things all over the place. I was constantly goin' behind her and tidyin' up. It's the main reason I got my own place, frankly."

"Seems like you two are close," she said.

"Yeah, she's a good kid. Just a little high strung."

"It's good that you have each other," Alexandra sighed, opening the top drawer and pulling out a pair of thick fuzzy socks. If she was going to look ridiculous in front of this gorgeous man, she might as well be comfortable. She sat on the edge of the bed and pulled on the purple fuzzy socks.

"You're no' wearing those to bed, are ye?" he asked, horrified.

"That was my intention, yes," she answered, taking a play out of his book and raising an eyebrow. "Is there a problem with that?"

"You don't wear socks to bed. That's… *mental.*"

"Mental?" she repeated, raising both eyebrows.

"Mental," he confirmed with a grave nod. "Completely daft."

She burst into laughter. She laughed until her sides ached and tears streamed down her face. It felt good, but it was brief.

When she came to her senses, Connor was looming over her, his face hard, jaw clenched, eyes glittering. Her breath hitched when he gave her a predatory smile.

"What's so funny there, lass?" he asked, as if daring her to laugh again.

"You're adorable," she said with a shrug. Her face burned, but it was worth it.

The look he gave her was incredulous, and then positively horrified.

"*Adorable?*" he choked out.

"Yes," she replied. Her face heated even more, but she kept her eyes on his. "I find your… *Scottishisms* adorable."

"*Scottishisms?*" he said, offended and bewildered. "Surely, that's no' a real word."

"Idioms? Colloquialisms? Whatever you want to call them," she replied, suppressing a giggle. She'd never seen him so… flustered. She rather liked it.

He leaned over her, placing his hands on the bed on either side of her.

Instinctively, she leaned away from him until she was perilously close to lying down. She rested on her elbows and licked her lips nervously. She saw his gaze fasten on her mouth and her heart skipped a beat.

A cell phone rang, Connor's apparently. He let out a muttered curse and stepped back, digging the phone out of his pocket. He held up a finger, indicating he'd be back, and hustled out to the hall.

Was she relieved or disappointed at the interruption? She wasn't sure she wanted to know the answer to that.

Trying to recover her sanity and calm her frantic heartbeat, she climbed into bed and burrowed beneath the blankets. She closed her eyes and focused on her breathing.

She could hear Connor talking in the hallway, but only as a low rumble. She couldn't make out words, but she enjoyed the sound nonetheless.

Surprisingly, it was nice to not be alone for once. Even if it was only temporary. She let the deep timbre of his voice wash over her and she began to drift.

Connor spent twenty feckin' minutes on the phone. First, he'd had to reassure a hysterical client who'd received a phone call from the police because someone or *something* had tripped their security system. Then he had to hear the report from one of his guys so he'd know what *actually* happened.

They had an on-call rotation in case of emergencies like these. Their answering service was supposed to forward the call to the person on-call depending on the schedule. But it never failed that Connor got dragged into it, no matter whose night it was. Every. *Fucking.* Time.

He took a deep breath and reminded himself that it was just one of the many perks of being self-employed. Everything ends with you.

If something went wrong, he had to step in and fix it. If something came up that they weren't prepared for, he had to figure out what to do. If someone got hurt, either a client or one of his men, it was on him.

There were days he thrived on the challenge, and then there were days when the pressure made him want to chuck it all and retire to Inverness. But this was what he loved, this was what he excelled at.

And this was what kept Angel safe and provided for. She made her own money, but he made sure she knew that he had her back. No matter what happened, he was her safety net.

So, he took it one day—one crisis—at a time. And right now, there was a challenging woman waiting for him in the other room while he'd been standing out here with his thumb up is arse, playing phone tag.

He tucked his phone away after setting it to vibrate and returned to Alexandra's bedroom. Where he was greeted with the sight of her tucked in, eyes closed and snoring softly. He walked around to her side of the bed and stood there for a moment, watching her sleep.

It would be stupid and dangerous to get too involved with her. It went against his better judgment. But there was something about her. He craved those moments when he got to see the fire in her eyes, or when she was so achingly sweet and shy. He wanted to know what made her tick—how here mind worked, what she liked, what made her happy.

And he wanted to know what had happened to make her put on that mask she wore. Probably the same thing that was behind her panic attacks.

She was a bundle of contradictions. Vulnerable and strong, sassy and shy. Sultry one moment and self-conscious as hell the next. He didn't know what to make of her just yet, but he was having a hell of a lot of fun figuring it out.

He sighed, and shook his head. What the hell was he gonna do about this? Whatever it was, instead of standing there watching her like some creep, he should go home and get some sleep.

Though it seemed a shame to head home just to turn around and head back here in the morning. But she'd been adamant about having her own space, so he'd just have to deal.

He was nearly at the bottom of the stairs when he heard a scream. His adrenaline spiked and he drew his service weapon, keeping it down at his side. He sprinted up the stairs, taking them two at a time, sidling up to the door and gingerly pushing it open.

Alexandra was still in bed, alone, but she was thrashing—sheets and blankets twisted around her legs, pillows pushed to the floor. Connor quickly holstered his gun, rushing to the bed. He cradled her face in his hands, disturbed by the look of sheer terror on her face.

"Lex? Wake up, love. Wake up. You're okay. You're safe." He kept his voice calm and low, trying not to frighten her any more. She thrashed and whimpered and his chest squeezed. He could see the fear and pain etched into her soul.

"No! No, no, no, no," she muttered.

"Come on, sweetheart, wake up," he said more firmly. "Show me those beautiful eyes, love."

Her eyes flew open and her body went rigid. Her eyes were glazed and hazy and she immediately squirmed away, backing up to the headboard, pulling her knees to her chest, tears flowing freely down her face.

"It's alright, Lex," he soothed. "You're safe. You're at home."

Her eyes cleared a little and confusion slowly replaced the terror. And the shame followed swiftly on its heels. She lowered her head in her hands and sobbed. Her shoulders shook and Connor couldn't stand it any longer. He sat on the bed and pulled her to him, hoisting her up onto his lap.

She turned away, trying to hide her face, but he wrapped his arms around her and held her to his chest until some of the tension left her body and her sobs became less frequent. She wouldn't look at him as she sniffled and frantically wiped at her face.

"You want to tell me about it?" he murmured.

She shook her head quickly. "Can't. I c–can't," she whispered. He opened his mouth to tell her it was okay, but snapped it shut when her hand flew to her mouth.

"Sick," she gasped.

Connor scooped her up and marched to the bathroom. He set her down and she lurched for the toilet, retching violently. He knelt behind her, sweeping her hair away from her face.

He pulled a washcloth down from the towel bar behind him and turned on the cold water. He wet the washcloth and pressed it to the back of her neck. He ran his hand up and down her back—slow and gentle. Comforting her.

She heaved a few more times, her shoulders shaking, tears streaming down her face, before she slumped back on her heels. Connor continued to run his hand up and down her back as he wiped her face and mouth with the washcloth.

He was calm on the outside, but inside he was seething. Someone hurt her. And she was still suffering—the panic attacks, the nightmares. If he had to put money on it, he'd bet it something to do with Lucas Whitmore. The look of disgust and rage on her father's face when he'd given him the name had said it all.

If that was the case, Connor *hoped* he was their stalker. Because he'd hunt him down and make him pay. *Dearly.* Even if he *wasn't* the stalker, he still might.

Death would be too swift—too merciful for the monster who'd hurt her like this. He hadn't been told, and he wouldn't ask. But Connor had an idea of what he'd done. His jaw clenched and he fought the urge to slam his fist into the wall.

Then only reason Connor kept his composure was because Alexandra needed him. He promised himself that when he had the chance, Whitmore would pay. That fucker had no idea what was coming for him. Connor was a monster, too—cold, efficient, lethal. The kind he would never see coming.

"You alright?" Connor asked after several minutes of silence. She nodded weakly and tried to stand. She was shaking so badly that he didn't know if she'd be able to take two steps on her own.

He growled and swept her into his arms. She gasped in surprise but offered no other protest.

"Don't worry, lass, I've got ye." She seemed to be amused when he let his "Scottishisms" slip. And even though he'd normally rather bite off his own tongue than be called *adorable,* he would do anything to put a smile—even a weak one—on her face and chase the shadows from her eyes.

Rather than smile, or laugh, she frowned, confused. He set her gently on the bed and straightened out the blankets, tucking her back in.

He replaced the pillows behind her and then sat on the edge of the bed.

"Anything I can get you, love?" he asked, tucking a strand of hair behind her ear.

"Water?" she asked, still looking confused. He let it go. For now. He went to the bathroom where he'd seen a glass on the counter. He filled it with cool water from the tap and brought it to her, along with the bottle of mouthwash he spotted beside the sink.

She murmured a thank you and drank. Just a sip at first, and then another. Then a long gulp. She set the glass aside on the side table and he handed her the mouthwash.

"I imagine you'll be wantin' this," he said. She nodded, blushing, and took a small swig. She swished and spit it into the glass, which he promptly took to the bathroom, rinsed thoroughly, and refilled. He set it on the table and then sat back down on the bed.

"Why?" she croaked. Her voice was raspy, either from spewing her guts up or the emotions he could see churning in her eyes. Or more likely, both.

"Why what?" he asked, cocking his head.

She looked positively stricken, realizing what he'd seen.

"You didn't have to—" He held up a hand to stop her.

"I've been there. It's always better when you're not alone." He took her hand and squeezed it gently. "Besides, it isn't the first time I've had to hold a woman's hair back. I took Angel out for her twenty-first birthday and she was spectacularly pissed by the end of it. At least you didn't boot on my shoes."

She gave him a wane smile.

"Or in my car. Or on the carpet. Or in the bushes outside the pub," he finished with a grin.

Her smile grew slightly and she ducked her head.

"You're a good brother. A good man," she muttered. "Thank you."

Connor sucked in a sharp breath, and she knew she'd said the wrong thing. She just couldn't seem to stop humiliating herself. She wished the ground would just swallow her up, or that she'd wake up and find out the last twelve hours had been a horrible nightmare.

Dear God, she'd thrown up. Several times. While he held her hair.

Sweet baby Jesus, just take me now.

Rather than look at him and see what a fool she'd been written all over his face, she tried to bury her face in the covers.

"Alexandra." Her name came out as purr. She peeked at him briefly through her lashes, but quickly looked away.

"Look at me, love," he said. His voice was soft, but his tone was commanding. He reinforced his demand with a knuckle under her chin. She looked up, not sure what to expect.

"No one has ever given me a better compliment," he said. She could tell he was being sincere. "Thank you." She tried to turn away to hide her blush of pleasure, but he held her chin firm. "You've nothing to be ashamed of. You're a brave woman. You survived, and you're still functioning. That's no small thing. You should be proud of that."

She hadn't ever thought about that. She'd focused on all the things that had gone wrong, on all the ways she was still broken. She hadn't spent much time thinking about how she'd clawed her way back from the brink and kept going—kept living her life.

Am I living, though?

She was functioning, as he'd said. She had a few friends and her family. She had a career, she had hobbies. Was it enough to say she was really living? A few days ago, she would have said yes.

But now…

"Thank you," she said.

"You're welcome." He smiled at her. "Now if we're done thanking each other, we should get some sleep."

She frowned and before she could ask, Connor spoke up.

"I'm not leaving you in this state. I was on my way out before, but I can't leave you alone knowing you might need me again. It's for your own safety. Can't have you fainting in the bathroom and cracking your skull now, can we?"

Alexandra gave him a skeptical look and he offered her a sheepish smile.

"Besides, it's well past midnight and I'm knackered."

Alexandra closed her eyes, thinking she must be out of her mind, but at the same time, she was grateful to have him with her. She said nothing, simply scooted farther under the covers and rolled over.

She felt the bed dip and shift as he settled in beside her. Once he stilled, she risked a glance.

He was still fully clothed, except for his shoes—and socks, of course. He was on top of the covers and turned to face the door. It was sweet of him to give her as much distance as possible while sharing the same bed.

She might be an idiot for believing him, but it really felt like he only wanted to be there for her. No ulterior motive. No agenda. He just acknowledged that she was having an awful night and that she needed someone to be there with her—*for her.*

"Aren't you going to be cold?" she asked, concerned.

He rolled onto his back and his unbelievably blue eyes were amused. He shrugged. "Nah. I'm a furnace—or so I've been told. I'd just end up kicking the covers off in the middle of the night."

Alexandra scrunched her face in distaste. She couldn't imagine not having something—anything to cover up with. Even when it was unbearably hot, she still had a sheet draped over most of her at night. She just couldn't sleep without one.

"Don't worry about me. I'll be fine. Sleep now," he murmured. Alexandra reluctantly rolled over and closed her eyes. She was tired—hell she was *exhausted*—but sleep was a long time coming.

Chapter Eight

When she did sleep, it wasn't well. She woke up twice more in the early morning hours. Fortunately, there were no more nightmares, but her body just seemed too tense to let her to sleep for long.

Each time she woke, Connor was there murmuring soothing nonsense and rubbing her back until she fell asleep again. She must have finally relaxed, or maybe her body had just given up from exhaustion.

The next time she opened her eyes, the sun was streaming through the curtains. Her head ached a little, but her body felt warm and heavy.

Too warm.

Way too heavy.

She cracked an eye open never expecting to see Connor's sleeping face, three inches away from hers. She flinched.

But then she looked at him—r*eally* looked. In a way she hadn't let herself before.

God, he's beautiful.

People were rarely *better* looking up close. But Connor was gorgeous. His eyelashes were long and darker than soot.

Even messy—*especially messy*—her fingers itched to furrow into his dark hair. Or maybe toy with the strands that had fallen over his forehead.

She wanted to trace the bridge of his nose with her fingertip and outline his jaw with her tongue. Stubble and all.

Her eyes fell to his mouth, lips slightly parted as he slept. He had a beautiful mouth. She bit her own lip as she resisted the urge to kiss him.

Abort! Abort!

She needed to get out of this bed. *Fast.*

She lifted her head and realized that she was using his arm as a pillow. He was still on top of the covers, but his right arm was under her head and wrapped around her shoulder. His left arm—and leg—were draped over her.

She was wrapped in sexy Scotsman, and she had no idea how to extricate herself. Part of her didn't really want to, but the rest of her was panicking. He'd taken care of her all night, vomiting and all, and now here they were cuddling.

Cuddling, for fuck's sake. She couldn't possibly come off any clingier even if she tattooed "property of Connor" on her forehead.

Dammit, Alexandra! Get your shit together!

She took a calming breath and decided her best option was to slide out, very carefully. Hopefully without waking him. Then she could put some distance between them, so that she didn't come off like such a psycho.

Oh. My. God. What if he starts thinking this is all a set-up? And not just last night, but the whole thing?

She cringed at the thought. The whole 'let's pretend you're my boyfriend' thing certainly didn't help. Wait—that was *his* idea. He'd done that all on his own without even asking her. *And* she'd been pissed.

Okay, I'm clearly overreacting.

She took a few deep breaths. One thing at a time. She checked to make sure he was still asleep and then she very slowly, very carefully rolled onto her back. From there, she could slide out of the bed and make a run for the bathroom.

She shifted onto her back, being sure the keep her movements gentle enough not to jostle any of his… *appendages* enough to wake him. When she finally landed on her back she held her breath for a moment.

When he didn't move, she sighed heavily. Noticing an odd weight on her chest, she looked down. And found his hand on her right breast.

His arm had obviously shifted when she'd turned over. The real problem was she'd pushed the comforter down in the process.

Which meant there was only a thin piece of cotton between them. Thin enough that she could feel the heat from his hand. She squeezed her eyes shut and tried to stay calm.

Then his thumb twitched over her nipple, and she let out a gasp. She immediately clamped her mouth shut and held her breath. A quick glance told her he was still asleep, and she said a silent prayer of thanks.

She was trembling slightly as she slowly scooted sideways toward the edge of the bed. Which dragged his hand directly over her *other* breast in the process. Her heart was pounding—breathing quick and shallow.

After a small eternity, she slid one leg, and then the other, off the bed. Eventually, she slipped her torso free, dropping to the floor. She froze, waiting to see if the sound had woken him.

When she didn't hear any movement, she gradually stood up, breathing a sigh of relief. She walked backward to the bathroom, afraid to breathe too loud.

Once inside, she shut the door and sagged against it in relief. She locked the door and stripped out of her clothes.

She stepped into the shower and turned on the water, welcoming the shock of cold water that hit her before it finally warmed up. She stood here under the spray, letting the hot water sluice over her skin, while she tried to make sense of the last forty-eight hours.

She couldn't. Because ever since she met Connor MacLachlan, her entire world had been turned upside down.

I deserve fucking sainthood for this.

Connor immediately winced, knowing his Gran would be rolling in her grave at that. But what else was he supposed to say?

He'd been awake for at least an hour. At first, he'd just watched Alexandra sleep, taking in all the details of her face—the gentle curves of her jaw, the soft slope of her nose lightly dotted with freckles. Her fair skin. Her long, dark lashes.

He hadn't meant to wake up wrapped around her, but he'd be damned if he was going to waste the opportunity.

And then he'd been trying to decide what to do. She'd be embarrassed to wake up like this, even though there was no reason to be. But she'd had a hard enough night as it was. He didn't want her worrying about this.

He was just about to remove the limbs he'd thrown over her in his sleep before trying to slide his arm out from underneath her when she woke up. She stirred, her lashes fluttering slightly, and let out a soft sigh that almost made him groan.

He was already glad there was a thick blanket between them. It was even more lucky after hearing that.

As if waking up cuddled together wasn't awkward enough, he could just imagine what would happen if she woke up with his morning wood pressed against her leg.

"Good morning. And yes, that is *my tadger pokin' ye."*

Since his window to slip away had vanished, he decided the next best thing was to pretend to be asleep. And to *stay* that way, no matter what. He'd let her slip away—like he *knew* she would—preserving her dignity or whatever.

No doubt, she'd still be embarrassed, but at least she'd have the illusion that she was the only know who knew that they'd spent the night tangled up together.

He kept his body limp—the parts he could control—and focused on keeping his breathing deep and even. When his hand slid, *entirely by accident*, onto her breast, his hand had twitched before he could stop it.

He'd used every swear word he knew—in any language—to curse himself. And when it happened again, he'd used every ounce of willpower he had not to react.

But sweet baby Jesus, they were amazing. The perfect size to fit his hand. Firm. Soft. And natural. And judging by that little gasp that was going to haunt his dreams? *Sensitive.*

He held perfectly still, but as soon as he heard the bathroom door close softly, he cracked an eye open and groaned softly, adjusting himself. He rolled onto his back to take some of the pressure off but waited until he heard the shower running before getting out of bed.

He went downstairs into the kitchen and hunted for the supplies to make coffee, giving her privacy to shower and dress. She'd reasonably assume that the shower had woken him and he'd gone foraging for coffee. And maybe by the time she came down stairs, he'd have his lower half under control.

Alexandra kicked herself for bring in such a hurry to escape that she'd forgotten to bring clothes with her. She opened the door just a crack and peeked out.

Seeing that the bed was empty and Connor was nowhere to be seen, she wrapped a towel around herself and grabbed the first pile of laundry she could find before hurrying back to the bathroom.

She ended up with three t-shirts, a denim skirt, a pair of yoga pants, and a sweatshirt. No bra, no underwear.

She'd worn a cotton bralette under her shirt last night because

Connor was there. She could wear that again. But she wasn't about to put the same underwear back on.

She decided it didn't really matter. He'd be leaving soon and the pants would cover everything anyway. Clean, dressed and moderately more composed, she made her way downstairs.

Her stomach rumbled and she realized she was starving. She was going to have to go shopping today. She wasn't even sure what was left in her kitchen.

She bit back a smile when she realized, that meant she had a reason to spent at least part of the day with Connor. She had a brief moment of doubt. Maybe he'd gone home already.

She reached the bottom of the stairs and saw his coat hanging by the door. She let out a relieved breath and shook her head.

The scent of coffee floating out from the kitchen gave her a good idea where he might be. And sure enough, when she found him, Connor was leaning against the counter in the kitchen, sipping coffee from her favorite mug.

She looked from the mug to his face, narrowing her eyes. She walked to the cabinet and pulled out her *second* favorite mug—a tall black mug that said "We're going to be really cool old people" in gold script. It was a gift from Charles, and he had one to match. The only reason it was her *second* favorite, was because it was too easy to tip over.

Her *favorite* was a wide-mouthed white mug that said "People say I'm unapproachable, and yet, here you are." And that was the mug Connor was currently drinking from.

"That's my favorite one, you know," she said as she poured herself a steaming cup of coffee.

He took a sip and then grinned at her over the rim. "I ken."

"And you still decided to use it?"

"Sorry, lass." He shrugged. "You snooze, you lose."

"Excuse me, but *I* was up first," she shot back. She was struggling not to smile.

"Very true." He nodded. There was clear amusement in his eyes. "Tell you what. Next time, I'll bring my own mug."

Next time...

She stared, dumbfounded. Heat rose predictably on her cheeks, but she ignored it, looking him in the eye.

"See that you do," she replied

He raised an eyebrow in surprise and then a slow smile spread across that gorgeous mouth. She willed her hands not to shake as she took her time adding the right amount of cream and sugar. The right amount being a butt-load of each.

She hummed softly as the first perfect sip hit her taste buds and leaned against the kitchen island across from him. He was wearing the same wrinkled clothes he'd slept in and his feet were bare.

He looked relaxed drinking coffee barefoot in her kitchen with his hair a sexy mess. He looked like he belonged there. It filled her chest with something warm.

And her stomach with lead.

Connor's stomach grumbled and he gave her another one of those sheepish smiles that made him look so young and sweet.

"Hungry?" she laughed.

"Seems like," he said with a grin.

She yanked open the fridge's double doors and started scrounging. She pulled out what ingredients she could find hoping she could throw something together.

Eggs, shredded cheese, a package of ham, half a green pepper and half an onion. She also grabbed butter, and a couple potatoes from the pantry.

"Need help?" he asked, setting his coffee cup aside.

"Sure. Can you peel the potatoes?" she asked. He grinned as she handed him a paring knife and a glass bowl.

"It's pronounced *tatties*. And I think I can manage." He winked at her and she rolled her eyes.

She retrieved a cutting board—chopping the peppers and onions, dicing the ham. As she worked, she checked his progress with the potatoes.

He had some impressive skills with a knife. That should probably scare her more than it did. He was quick and efficient, like he'd had years of practice.

"You cook much?" she asked.

"Some." He shrugged, now dicing the potatoes into perfect cubes. "Da was a terrible cook. Burned everything, even water. It was either learn to do for myself or spend all my money at the chippy."

"What about your mom?" His hand stilled for an instant and his brows drew together a fraction.

"She was a decent cook. When she was home—which wasn't often. We always had plenty of easy meals in the fridge we could make ourselves, and she'd leave us a little money for take away."

"Sounds like you were pretty independent as a kid," she said quietly. She got the impression it wasn't fun for him. It seemed as though he hadn't had a choice.

He shrugged again dumping the bowl of peels in the garbage. He swiped the potatoes into the bowl and rinsed them a few times in the sink. Alexandra was just about to change the subject when he surprised her.

"It wasn't hard taking care of myself, but Angel… I felt bad in the summers when I was gone and she had to stay with our grandmother."

"I can understand that." She nodded. She'd put water on to boil and retrieved a cast iron skillet from the cabinet. She sipped her coffee as she waited for the water to boil.

"You seem pretty close to her. How old is she?"

"She's twenty-seven—she five years younger."

"What does she do?" Alexandra asked.

"She's a nurse—pediatrics," he said. It was obvious how proud he was.

"Wow." Alexandra was genuinely impressed. "That must be hard. I certainly couldn't deal with sick kids, especially every day."

"Ah, she's grand with the wee ones," Connor said with a wink. Alexandra laughed, shaking her head.

"She sounds remarkable. You must be very proud."

"I am. She's had a rough go of things since Mom died." His tone was more serious but he didn't seem upset.

"There's one thing I'm curious about," Alexandra said. "But if it's too personal, feel free to tell me to bugger off." Connor chuckled and she smiled. "You said your mom was a flight attendant and your father was Scottish."

"Mm-hmm."

"Were they every married?"

"For a while," he sighed. "They met at a pub in Glasgow. They talked and had a few drinks. One thing led to another and two days later he dropped her off at the airport with his phone number. About two months later, she found out she was pregnant, so she called him. He wanted to be involved so they kept in touch. They talked a lot and decided they wanted to give it a shot. I was born here, but we moved to Scotland when I was two months old. Da was done with law school and by the time I was born, he'd passed the bar." He turned to look at her. "He's a Solicitor."

"A Lawyer? Really?" Alexandra raised her eyebrows.

"Yup." Connor smiled. He set down the bowl and picked up his coffee. "Mom could really work from anywhere. And things were good for a while. But after about a year, Mom started working more and more. By the time I was three, she was working so much that Da had to hire a nanny. They fought about it. *Constantly.* She said she wasn't going to give up her career or her life and that was it. She left, and took we with her. We moved in with my grandmother so she could watch me while Mom was working—which was nearly all the time."

"How did your dad take it?"

"Badly. He'd loved her. And not only had he lost her, he'd lost me, too. She had no problem with him coming to visit, but she refused to fly me out there. He offered to pay but the cost of travel wasn't an issue for her. She just didn't want to. Then—when I was about eight—he decided that wasn't good enough. He threatened to sue for custody. He didn't want to, but he was out of options. Eventually, they came to an agreement: summers and two weeks in the winter with Da. As long as I was in New York for Thanksgiving and Christmas."

"Your poor father," Alexandra said, putting a hand on his arm. "That must have been so hard for him. What a shame they couldn't make it work even though they really loved each other."

Connor nodded. "A damn shame. But Mom just loved herself more."

Alexandra heard what he didn't say. That his mother had loved herself more than *everyone*, including him.

"I'm sorry, Connor," she murmured, squeezing his arm.

He gave her a strange look.

"What?" she asked.

"That's the first time you've said my name."

Alexandra shuffled a little nervously. "I guess it is."

"I like the way it sounds," Connor said softly. He touched her cheek with the backs of his fingers, dragging them along her jaw.

He tilted her chin up and brushed his thumb gently back and forth across her bottom lip. Her heart thumped wildly in her chest and her breath hitched.

His touch was electric. She shivered and goosebumps scattered across her skin. Her eyes flickered between those too-blue eyes to his mouth.

Kiss me, kiss me, kiss me…

His other hand found her hip and he tugged her closer. With their bodies pressed together, she could feel every muscle—his chest, his abs, even his thighs. They were rock solid. And warm.

Heat radiated off him as if he actually *were* a furnace. She could feel it through their clothes.

The brush of his thumb on her lip stopped and she almost whimpered at the loss. But he cupped her face instead and he leaned in closer, slowly—centimeter by centimeter—silently asking permission.

He was giving her a chance to stop him. To say no. He was offering her something—making himself vulnerable—while giving her the space to reject him. Not only was it painfully sweet, it was brave.

And that did it. That sweet patience washed away every ounce of self-restraint she had

Instead of just *letting* him kiss her, she decided she would be brave, too. She would make her 'yes' unmistakable. She tilted her head back and pushed up onto her toes, brushing his mouth with her own.

He let out a satisfied hum so low it sounded like a growl. One hand snaked around her waist, his hand splayed out on her back, tugging her closer. And the other slid into her hair, cradling the back of her head as he kissed her.

His lips were soft and warm, and they worked on hers in slow languid movements. He nipped gently at her lower lip and then soothed it with the slide of his tongue.

Alexandra had never been kissed like this. So slowly, so thoroughly. Her knees went weak, and all she could do was curl her fingers into his shirt and hold on.

So fucking sweet.

She tasted like coffee and sunshine. He moved his hand to the small of her back and pressed her more firmly against him.

She was soft and warm against him—her body melting into his

more perfectly than he ever could have imagined. He kissed her like they had all the time in the world.

He wanted to take his time and memorize every second of it. He wanted to *learn* her—what she liked, what made her squirm and sigh.

She sighed, her lips parting, and his tongue found hers. Her breath caught at the first tentative brush, but soon her tongue was sliding against his and she was pushing up on her toes—hands fisted in his shirt—begging for more.

He growled, the kiss turning hungry—urgent. His tongue tangled with hers. Her teeth nipped at his bottom lip.

Groaning, he tilted her head back, giving him a better angle. His hand moved to her hip and down her thigh, lifting her leg and guiding it over his hip.

She gasped as the bulge in his jeans nestled snugly between her thighs. He hitched her leg higher, rocking his hips into her until she was moaning.

He sealed his mouth over hers, devouring all those soft, sweet sounds until his lungs were screaming for air. By the time he pulled back, they were both breathing hard.

But they kept coming back together, again and again, unable to stand the distance. They kissed—hard and fast, soft and slow—they teased, the nipped.

His legs shook with how much he wanted her. He wanted to pick her up and haul her back to bed.

Or maybe strip her down, then and there, and lay her out on the kitchen table like his own personal feast. And he would taste everything—every inch of her.

His free hand slid down her side, slipping beneath the hem of her shirt skating over her skin as he traced her rib cage with his fingertips.

She trembled and her back arched further into him.

He kissed her again, hard and deep, claiming her mouth the way he wanted to claim *all of her*. His hand slid up over the soft cotton of her bra and he tested the weight in his palm.

And just as he had that morning, he swept the pad of his thumb over her nipple. He moved in slow, tight circles around it and she moaned into his mouth. He almost came then and there.

Definitely the table.

He pulled away just long enough to lift her up onto the counter. She squeaked a little—which was *fucking adorable*—but wrapped both legs around his waist, quickly tugging him back into the cradle of her hips.

Connor kissed her neck, just below her ear, and she looped her arms around his neck. He trailed soft, sweet kisses down her neck.

His tongue dipped into the hollow of her throat and he nipped gently. He planted open mouthed kisses up the other side of her neck, licking and nipping in between, until she was moaning and squirming against him.

His hands found the hem of her shirt gliding along her smooth, warm skin until he hit the band of her bra. He worked his fingers under the elastic until he was palming both of her perfect breasts—skin to skin.

"Oh, *God…*" Her back arched, legs tightening around him.

He rocked his hips into her faster, *harder*. Her heat taunted him even through layers of clothes, soaking into his skin. His heart was beating a frantic, staccato rhythm—w*ant, need, want, need, want, need…*

He trailed one hand down her stomach and traced just below the waistband of her pants.

Thank fuck for yoga pants.

It was easy to slip his hand underneath. It nearly killed him, but he waited. He looked at Alexandra—lips red and swollen, cheeks flushed and eyes blown wide with pleasure. He made sure he had her eyes before he slid his hand lower.

Jesus merciful fucking Christ… she's not wearing underwear.

He groaned, squeezing his eyes shut to keep from coming in his jeans. He opened them again and kissed her, hard and fast.

"Tell me," he gritted out.

She looked at him for a second, biting her lip. She opened her legs a little wider, but he wasn't going to rely on hints. He wanted the words.

"Say it, Lex," he growled. "Or I stop."

"Yes," she said, quickly. "Yes."

"Good Girl."

His hand slid lower, gliding between her legs. She was hot and so fucking wet.

For me.

A shrill noise rang out, piercing the haze.

He ignored it.

This is too good. She's too sweet…

It happened again and Connor realized it was his goddamn cell phone.

Connor pulled away and swore viciously. He pulled his phone from his pocket, his knuckles white as if he was trying to squeeze the thing until it shattered.

Alexandra hadn't even heard it ring. She'd been so lost in Connor's touch, his mouth on her skin, that a marching band could have swept through and she wouldn't have noticed. Or *cared*.

"What?" Connor snarled.

Alexandra flinched just a bit, but his hand was on her thigh, stroking lazily, reassuringly. He gave her an apologetic look and ran a hand through his hair in frustration.

"What? No," he snapped. "No, stay there." He hung up the phone without another word. He tipped his head, putting his forehead to hers and letting out a frustrated sigh.

"I have to go," His voice was thick—a mixture of frustration and regret. "I won't be long. Stay here and lock the door. I'll be back as soon as I can."

Alexandra nodded dumbly. Her head was still spinning and she didn't trust her voice. She slid off the counter, straightening her clothes, and he reluctantly stepped back, moving toward the door.

Half way there, he turned back, and kissed her greedily. He gentled the kiss and it ended sweet and soft. Without another word he walked away.

She heard him go upstairs, and return a few minutes later with his things. She met him by the door just as he was leaving.

He touched her face for a moment before he let his hand fall away. "I'll be back soon."

Alexandra locked the door behind him and returned to the kitchen in a daze.

What the hell just happened?

Chapter Nine

I almost had sex with Connor in my kitchen.

She couldn't even wrap her head around it. It *would* have happened. It had been as inevitable as death and taxes. And then what?

What would have happened *after*? Would they just go back to being client and bodyguard? Would they date? Trying to pretend nothing happened would be impossible. And awkward. But the thought of a relationship practically gave her a panic attack.

It wasn't that she didn't *want* to meet someone and fall in love, but she was… damaged. There was no way around it. She had panic attacks, trust issues, and was a serious control freak. She'd tried. It never ended well. At a certain point it became clear that they weren't interested in someone with so many issues.

And after the failures, there was every possibility she'd just be a basket case from the start. She'd just be waiting for the inevitable crash and burn.

She liked Connor—more than she wanted to admit. But she didn't want a hook-up and she wasn't sure she could handle a relationship, even a casual one.

And he was being *paid* to be there.

There was no guarantee that he'd stick around when the job was over, especially once he knew exactly how bad the damage was. The panic attacks were just the tip of the iceberg.

This wasn't getting her anywhere. She needed to put it out of her mind for now. When she was stumped or frustrated with a problem at work, she would take a step back, let her emotions settle and come back to it with a clear head. It had always worked for her before.

She decided she should finish making breakfast and eat before she did anything else. She boiled and fried potatoes, sauteed vegetables and whisked eggs. Pretty soon she had omelets and home fries for two.

She ate too much of both and then cleaned up the kitchen. She washed and put away dishes, wiped down counters, and cleaned the stove.

By the time she was done, an hour and half had passed. Connor still hadn't come back. He hadn't even called. She poured herself another cup of coffee and sat down to make a grocery list. Maybe she'd cook for Connor—*if* he came back.

She liked to cook but it was a little anticlimactic to cook for one. She'd occasional have Charles or Amanda over for dinner just to have an excuse to cook. And she'd rather hang out with them in her own space where she could relax than go out to dinner.

She grabbed a notebook and a pen and went to work. She planned out dinner and decided what she needed for the week. She went to the fridge to see if she'd missed anything and realized it needed cleaning out.

By the time she was done with that it was already early afternoon. She checked her phone for the tenth time—still nothing. She thought about calling him but decided against it.

You're being ridiculous.

Picking up *Pride and Prejudice* again she snuggled up on the couch with a throw blanket. She turned on the gas fireplace and settled in to read. But she couldn't stop replaying what happened that morning—over and over again.

She'd never wanted someone so badly and that was what really scared her. Hook-up versus relationship—all of that was still true, but the *real* problem was that she *wanted* him. And she wasn't sure she'd be able to stop herself, even knowing what might happen.

She set her book aside, and asked herself the scary question: What if?

What if all he wanted was a roll in the proverbial hay? She couldn't deny she wanted the same thing. If this morning was any indication, it would be mind-blowing. The memory alone would probably be enough to keep her warm all winter.

As long as I don't freak out and ruin it.

Okay, so what if she did? It would suck. But it wasn't anything she hadn't dealt with before. And eventually, their professional relationship would end and that would be that. She ignored the pang she felt and moved on.

So if it was just sex, it would either be spectacular—possibly several times—or, it would be embarrassing for a little while.

And what if he wants a relationship? That was a harder question. Higher risk, higher reward. The problem was, sex once was a one time risk for a one time reward. A relationship was a risk every day. And the stakes only went up the longer it went on.

She was still pondering the pros and cons, very rationally, an hour later. She sat brooding, staring into the fireplace until she gave up.

There was no point trying to analyze the situation. There was no predicting the outcome. But there was also no changing the past.

What had happened, happened. It might happen again but it might not. She'd cross that bridge when she came to it. Her therapist always told her to take things one day at a time. Although, she didn't think this is what Dr. Stein had in mind.

She picked up her phone, connecting it to the Bluetooth speaker in her living room, and started her favorite playlist. She dusted, vacuumed, cleaned the windows, and did anything else that needed to be done. And she did it all while dancing and singing.

By the time she was done, she felt much better. But It was dark and she was hungry. She debated ordering takeout. Was it safe?

Since she hadn't been told *not to*, she decided it would be fine as long as she was careful. Clearly, she wasn't going to get to the store tonight, and there was nothing for her to cook.

She ordered through an app and asked them to leave it on the steps. She watched them leave the food, get in their car, and drive away before she ducked out to retrieve the food. After she'd re-locked the door, she took it into the living room and watched *The Office* for the thousandth time.

She considered calling Connor again. She'd lost track of how many times she'd thought about it. But she was starting to worry a little. It had been hours and she hadn't heard anything. What if something had happened to him?

While trying to decide, Alexandra must have fallen asleep on the couch. The next thing she knew it was almost midnight. She wasn't sure what had woken her up until her phone chirped. She picked it up, opening the messages she'd received.

Connor MacLachlan: Sorry. Got held up.

Connor MacLachlan: This is Sam. He'll pick you up at 8:00am.

The third message was just photo of a man in his thirties. Clean cut, brown hair, blue eyes. And *hot*. The photo was only from the chest up, but his shoulders were massive.

He had a strong jaw, a straight nose, and a small scar on his left eyebrow. He looked fierce and just a little bit cocky. Just like Connor.

Were looks a requirement or something? Did they send in headshots with their applications?

She laughed at the thought. Maybe they figured if they only hired super-hot, intimidating men they could just scowl and bad guys would flee in terror. Or smile and they'd faint.

Her amusement quickly faded when she reread the terse messages and the time registered.

Thirteen. Hours.

He'd been gone for *thirteen* hours, and he was *just now* texting her? It was a good thing she didn't have anywhere to be today since she'd been left without a babysitter.

Even if he didn't owe her an explanation because they'd been playing tonsil hockey in her kitchen this morning, she at least deserved one as his client.

Instead, she'd waited around all day for him to call or text or show up. And apparently he hadn't even thought about her until now. She was angry.

And she was suddenly very glad she wouldn't have to see him first thing tomorrow morning. She couldn't go to court for her client if she was in jail for manslaughter. Although, if she packed the jury with women there was no way they'd convict her.

But if she was honest, underneath the anger, she was hurt. And that was even worse.

Connor was absolutely drained. Today had been a shit storm of epic proportions. He'd left Alexandra expecting to be back in a couple of hours, but everything had quickly gone tits up.

A client had insisted he come in person to deal with a *situation* at his house. The situation turned out to be his cat sneaking out of their house via an unlocked window and setting off a motion sensor.

In the middle of that, sis sister had called in a panic. She was at the dealership car shopping, but she couldn't find anything she could afford. Apparently she'd been counting on using her car as a trade in and the dealership wisely declined to give her anything for it.

While he was ignoring her protests and signing the paperwork for her new car at the dealership, he'd gotten a call from Jackson who was currently supposed to be working a short term detail. Some hot shot from Atlanta had hired them for his trip to New York.

His *one-day* trip to New York.

Jackson had picked him up from the airport and taken him to his meeting. Then he was supposed to take him directly back to JFK for his return flight.

He'd basically wanted a chauffeur with a gun. And he assumed if he was paying, he got to make the rules. It didn't matter that Jackson had been a marine for eight years and done three tours in Afghanistan and knew what the fuck he was doing. He insisted they make a "quick stop" on the way, despite Jackson's *strongly advising* against it.

The "quick stop" turned out to be for the purposes of acquiring very expensive, very illegal, recreational drugs. Whether he intended to take them back to Atlanta or partake of them in the car on the way to the airport was unclear.

Honestly, Jackson didn't give a fuck, and neither did Connor. Anything shady got reported to the police. Connor wasn't about to lose his license for *anyone*, especially this fucker.

And if that had been the worst of it, it would have been one thing. But no, the idiot had to go and get himself shot.

Never mind the fact that Jackson told him the neighborhood was dangerous. Never mind the fact that Jackson reminded him that our contract explicitly says any illegal activity will be reported to the police.

Dumb fucker only made it out alive because Jackson managed to disarm the drug dealer, apply pressure to the gunshot wound in his leg and call an ambulance. Now the moron was in the hospital, cuffed to a gurney, threatening to sue everyone at the top of his lungs.

He wasn't worried about it. Their contract was solid and if the asshole had bothered to read it, he'd know that. But Connor had to get a statement from Jackson before he spent the rest of the afternoon with his attorney—at his *weekend* rate—making sure he was covered.

After that disaster, there had been an emergency with one their biggest clients that turned out to be an actual, non cat-related security breach. Normally he would have let one of the guys handle it, but he'd given Jackson the rest of the day off, Sam was working Alexandra's detail first thing in the morning and everyone else was busy or off for the night. Someone had to be there to hold the client's hand through the process.

Nothing had been stolen, no major damage had been done and the system they'd installed had functioned perfectly. And yet, the client *still* wanted to spend an hour discussing possible upgrades.

Some would be thief had broken a damn window. They tripped the alarm, the police were contacted immediately and the metal bars on the windows kept them from getting inside.

And thanks to the security cameras, the cops would have a good chance of catching them. The perimeter hadn't actually been breached. Which was the whole point. So what he was talking about, was literally trying to avoid a broken window.

Or maybe he just wanted to know how to keep people from trying to rob his house.

If Connor knew that, he'd be out of a job. Which would be fine because he'd also be a millionaire. So, in the absence of a magic bug-zapper for burglars, they'd discussed ballistic glass.

But he wasn't very happy when Connor told him how much bullet-proof glass usually costs. In the end, they'd decided to stick with what they had.

To call it a cluster-fuck would be an understatement.

By the time he dragged himself back to his apartment, it was after eleven. He took a shower, changed his clothes, and texted Alexandra so she wouldn't be scared or surprised when someone else showed up tomorrow morning to take her to work. As much as he would have loved to do it himself, he had a meeting in the morning that had been on the books for a month.

He would have stopped by on his way home, but he didn't want to wake her if she was already asleep. And he was exhausted. All he wanted was to pass out and sleep for a week.

He'd call her tomorrow and explain. Maybe he'd even take over for Sam in the evening and pick her up after work. He'd look at his schedule tomorrow and see what he could do.

He hadn't worked protection personally in over a year. Once they'd really gotten the business up and running, he'd had to act like a CEO.

He'd only done it this time because Richard Hughes had wanted them to start right away. Under the circumstances, Connor had agreed that was the smartest move. With as busy as they'd gotten lately, all his guys were otherwise occupied, so he'd stepped up.

Thank God I did…

He didn't even want to think about "what if."

He really should start looking to add a couple more guys soon. They were turning away jobs and still booked out for months. They could afford to expand a bit.

As Connor climbed into bed and closed his eyes, thoughts of work disappeared and all that he could think about was Alexandra. Her face, her mouth, her body. The smell of her hair and all the sexy sounds she'd made when he'd had his hands on her.

He would have given his right arm to be able to finish what they'd started that morning. He decided then and there that whatever he had on his schedule tomorrow afternoon could be rescheduled. He'd pick her up from work, take her to dinner and then they could pick up where they left off.

I hope.

Monday crawled by.

Sam had been polite and professional when he arrived. And Alexandra tried to be nice. It wasn't *his* fault Connor had been an ass.

And speaking of… Connor called the office twice before lunch. She was still mad so she told Janie to tell him she was in a meeting and take a message.

She'd never replied to his text messages from last night and she'd ignored every one he'd sent that morning. She worked through lunch so she was famished by the time she texted Sam at five thirty to let him know she was almost ready to go.

Janie was long gone, so she locked up a few minutes before six and went to wait for Sam in the lobby. She heard the elevator doors ding before she reached the bank. That was odd, but she hoped it was just Sam.

Maybe he'd gotten there early and decided to come up for her. She hoped he hadn't been hanging around all day waiting for her. It hadn't occurred to her to ask what he'd do while she was at work.

She turned the corner toward the elevator and froze. Connor stepped off the elevator and was just standing there staring at her.

Instead of the jeans, t-shirt, and hoodie he'd worn all weekend, he wore dress clothes. A pair of perfectly tailored grey slacks that hung low on his hips. Fitted black dress shirt, open at the collar. And of course, his black wool peacoat with the color turned up against the October chill. It was as if he'd stepped right out of an add for Gucci.

God, he's delicious.

NO! You're mad at him. Don't get distracted!

He gave her a slow, sexy smile filled with filthy promises and Alexandra's heart practically stopped. But she locked that shit down and gave him a nonchalant glance as she brushed past him toward the elevator.

"Where's Sam?" she asked. He blinked, and pursed his lips, the smile disappearing.

"Home, probably. I told him to let me know when you called and I'd pick you up."

"Ah."

"Ah?" He raised an eyebrow.

"That's what I said," Alexandra replied flatly. The doors opened with a ding and she stepped in, pressing the button for the lobby.

"You're mad," Connor said, stepping in beside her.

"I'm not mad." She shrugged. "I'm mildly annoyed."

"Really?" he asked. "Because it seems like you're mad."

"Yes, *really*. I had things to do yesterday," she replied, picking a piece of imaginary lint off the sleeve of her coat. "And instead, I sat at home all day."

"So, it was just an inconvenience because you couldn't go out." He turned to stand in front of her. "You're not upset that I had to leave and didn't text you for twelve hours?"

Thirteen, asshole.

But she wasn't going to take the bait. "Yes, and no. Respectively."

He gave her an appraising look which she ignored. She focused instead on the floor numbers as they lit up, silently wishing the elevator would move faster.

He took a step forward and braced his hands on the wall of the elevator, caging her in. His voice was a low growl.

"So, you're not disappointed that we didn't get to fuck like bunnies—right there on your kitchen counter?"

She could smell his cologne, that cedar and pine scent that scrambled her brain. She felt herself blush as she imagined them lying naked together on a bed of pine needles.

She tried telling herself that it would probably be horribly uncomfortable. It didn't help.

"No." She shrugged, her eyes focused on the numbers behind him.

"Bullshit." He moved closer, leaning down until they were eye to eye. His face softened and he frowned. "I'm sorry, Lex. A million things happened, and I didn't even have time to *breath* until I got home."

"It's fine," she said flatly.

"It's *not* fine." His voice was quiet but laced with tension. "I should have called, and I didn't. I'm sorry."

"Really, it's not an issue," she said, keeping her expression and her voice neutral.

The doors opened and she ducked under his arm and marched out into the lobby. He caught up to her and escorted her toward the Hummer.

"I'd like to get my car," she said. "It's been here all weekend. I understand I may not need it for the foreseeable future, but I'd rather leave it parked at home or a parking garage for the duration instead of leaving it here."

"I'll have someone get it for you tomorrow," Connor replied.

Alexandra stopped walking and dug in her four inch heels.

"I'd rather do it now, if you don't mind."

Connor sighed and ran a hand through his hair.

"Fine."

He walked her to where her car had been parked since Friday morning. He motioned for her to wait, and to her surprise he got down on the pavement. Lying on his back, he examined the undercarriage using the flashlight on his phone.

When he was done, he asked for the keys. He popped the hood and looked it over before searching the interior and the trunk. When he was done he gave her a curt nod.

"Follow me and don't leave the vehicle until I give you the all clear."

He waited while she got in, locked the doors, and started it. She turned on the seat warmer and the heat and backed out. When Connor saw her pulling out of the garage, he pulled into traffic and stopped, giving her a space to pull out behind him.

Alexandra chewed her lip all the way home. She was afraid of what would happen if he came inside. She wasn't afraid of him, but she was scared that she wouldn't be able to resist and things would go the way of Sunday morning.

She didn't know how to handle this and she was sure it would end badly for her.

She liked him—was attracted to him. And she wanted to trust him, but that impulse had proven to be dangerous in the past. This was precisely why she'd given up on men a long time ago. Too much work for what was usually too little reward.

He pulled into the first of two open spaces in front of her townhouse and got out. He scanned the street and, once satisfied, walked backed to where she'd parked and opened her door. He kept his hand on her back as she mounted the steps and opened the door.

Once unlocked, he slid inside and began his sweep.

She waited, fidgeting. When he returned he was noticeably agitated and for a moment she was afraid he'd found something. He seemed to read her mind and he sighed.

"Everything's fine," he said. "At least in the house."

"Good. Thank you," she replied, removing her coat and hanging it on the hook by the door. She took off her shoes and tossed them by the stairs so she could grab them when she went upstairs.

She waited to see if he would stay or go and held her breath. He shut the door and locked it and took a step toward her.

"Can we talk about this?" he asked, a stubborn set to his jaw.

"What is there to talk about?" she said, turning into the living room.

She kept going straight through to the kitchen. She pulled a bottle of water from the fridge and opened it, taking a long sip.

"Do you want to just forget yesterday happened?" he asked, eyes smoldering. He was looking at her like he was a hungry lion and she was a porterhouse. This was dangerous.

"Maybe," she said with a shrug.

"Do you feel like it was a mistake?" he asked. His voice was deceptively calm. He was prowling toward her. There was no other way to describe it. He moved with an easy grace but the power in his body was unmistakable.

"I don't know what to think," she admitted. "I can't deny there's… chemistry between us, but I don't know what it means. I'm not good at this."

"What aren't you good at?" he asked. He was still moving closer.

"Casual sex? Dating? Relationships? Take your pick." She shrugged again. "I don't know if this means anything or if it's just because of proximity. I mean we were together Friday night, most of Saturday and yesterday morning. It's possible any two reasonably good-looking people of the opposite sex might develop an attraction if they spent enough time together, even if it's only temporary."

"Reasonably good-looking?" he smirked and arched an eyebrow.

Uh-oh. Oh, no. No, no.

"You're missing the point," she said, pointing her bottle of water at him.

"Do elaborate," he said. He had stopped roughly a foot in front of her and shoved his hands into his pockets, drawing her attention to those enticingly lean hips. She focused on drawing in steady breaths.

"The point is, this is an unusual and complicated situation. There's a professional relationship here that needs consideration and I think it's best we try not to muddy the waters with any interpersonal issues we might have."

He pursed his lips in thought and she hoped, and also feared, he was getting her point.

"Let's look at this rationally." He nodded.

The look in his eyes said that he was prepared to fight this out and for once, she wasn't sure she would win.

"One, we have a legally binding contract with your employer. We've made a commitment. I would never let *interpersonal issues* interfere with my ability to do my job. If, for some reason, I didn't think I could be objective, I have five employees that can more than handle your protection." His jaw ticked and she could tell he didn't really like the idea of leaving her in anyone else's hands.

"Two, I can assure you that I have been thrown into close quarters for extended periods of time with members of the opposite sex, some of them *reasonably good-looking*, and I haven't wanted to fuck a single one of them." He paused, leaning toward her. "Three, this is more than just *chemistry*, and I think you know that."

He shifted forward, backing her into the counter. It seemed to be an irritating habit of his. She licked her lips nervously and his attention focused on her mouth.

Mistake.

You didn't beard the lion, you didn't bait the bear, you didn't tug on Superman's cape.

"Four, you are not *reasonably good-looking*, Alexandra. You are fucking *impeccable*. Does that address your concerns?" he whispered. His lips were inches from hers and her brain was glitching. Her mouth hung open but nothing came out.

Connor closed the distance, kissing her like he was making a closing argument—like he was proving a point. Lightning coursed through her veins. Her whole body went on high alert as he bit her bottom lip, pulling it into his mouth. She arched into him like he had his own gravity.

His hands landed on her hips, pulling her flush against him. His tongue teased her lips and she opened for him without a thought. The kiss turned molten—slow, hot, liquid and quickly building pressure until her head felt like it would explode.

She was dizzy and the room spun as she gasped for air. But who needed air when he kissed her like that? At that moment she didn't need anything—air, food, water, sunlight—as long as he kept kissing her. And touching her. And-

Stop. This is insane.

Connor took a deliberate step back as if it caused him actual physical pain to stop touching her. He put a hand on her jaw, stroking with his thumb.

"You're confused, and a little freaked out," he said gently. Alexandra just nodded. "I'm not a complete asshole. I'm not going to push you. I want you to be sure." Alexandra nodded again. Too overwhelmed for thought or speech.

"But this isn't going to go away, and I don't want to ignore this." He seemed so sincere that she wanted to believe him. "I'll give you time and space if that's what you need. Just not *too* much." He winked and flashed that oh-so-sexy smile that made her heart race.

He took her hand and threaded his fingers through hers, tugging her away from the counter. He led her to the foyer.

"I can't be here tomorrow. I have meetings I can't reschedule. Jackson will be here instead. I'll text you a photo so you know who you're looking for." He searched her face like he was struggling with something, or like he was trying to commit it to memory. Alexandra flushed under his gaze but didn't look away.

"I *am* sorry," he said. "I was an arse. I should have taken a minute to let you know what was going on."

"Yes, you were," she said, smiling to take some of the sting out of her words.

Connor chuckled, looking relieved. Some of the tension drained from his body. He swept her to him, one hand on her waist, and one on her neck, and kissed her again—swift and brutal—leaving her lips tingling.

"Lock up behind me," he whispered, against her lips. "And get some sleep." One more soft press of his lips, and he turned away.

She did lock the door behind him, but it was hours before she could sleep.

Chapter Ten

Jackson, as it turned out, fit the job requirements perfectly. Tall. Ruggedly handsome, with the kind of face that made you question your feminism. A close-cropped beard and hair long enough to pull back into a knot at the base of his skull—if you put him in flannel and gave him an ax he could be a lumberjack.

Swap the flannel for a hat and boots, he could be a cowboy. He had the accent for it. Alexandra wondered what Janie would think of him. Her drummer boy had been cute, but this was a *man.*

Instead of flannel or a cowboy hat, he wore a dark suit. Expertly tailored, it made him look like an A-list celebrity on his way to a premiere. Chris Hemsworth maybe? No… more like Jason Momoa. Jackson's hair was a dark, rich brown, as were his eyes, and his skin was a glowing bronze. She'd given up on her pasty ass ever getting that kind of color.

He introduced himself, handing her his ID. Polite, professional, with a smile almost as easy as Connor's. She double-checked her bag, locked up, and he opened the door to a black Range Rover, helping her inside.

"What, no Hummer?" she joked as he pulled into traffic. Jackson laughed. A rich baritone rumble that rolled over her like honey. All of these men were lethally hot. She could easily have a heart attack in the next week.

"I prefer the Range Rover. Mr. MacLachlan doesn't much care what we drive, as long as it's reliable and properly outfitted."

"Outfitted?" she asked.

"Yup. Every work vehicle we use is armored and fitted with ballistic glass."

"Wow. No wonder he didn't want me driving around on my own. My Beamer definitely doesn't have bulletproof glass."

Jackson chuckled again and nodded.

"So is Jackson your first name or last name?"

He glanced at her, raised an eyebrow, and gave her a rueful smile. "First name. Nobody's ever asked that before."

"Do you prefer to be called Jackson? Or is there something else you're more comfortable with?" she asked. It was the same tactic she used with her clients—a subtle, personal way to say "I care bout *you*, not just your money."

"Jacks, Jackson, Hunter—anything's fine."

"Well, Jacks…" she said.

He grinned and she couldn't help but smile back.

"Are you stuck on babysitting duty all day?"

"Yes ma'am. I'm afraid you're stuck with me."

"Dear God, don't call me *ma'am*. Call me Alexandra, or Lex. Either is fine—just not *ma'am*. And I'm sure I'm lucky to have you on my team."

"Thank you very much, ma—Lex."

He beamed at her. You'd think she'd just given him a raise. Or a puppy.

"In that case, you and I are going shopping after work. Do you mind?"

He gave her an odd look again, like he didn't quite know what to make of her. "Not at all. Groceries, shoes, or clothes?"

"Groceries. Why?"

"Just thinking ahead. If you wanted to go shoe shopping, I'd have to call someone to bring an extra car."

"Ah. I see. You're a smartass," Alexandra said with a nod.

"Better than a dumbass." He grinned.

"You know what? I like you, Jackson. I think we're going to get along just fine."

He looked startled. A little uncomfortable.

"I hope so."

"Good. That should make this easier."

He frowned, suspicious, but said nothing.

Jackson pulled up in front of the building and parked in the nearest empty spot. He got out, walked around, and opened her door for her.

He escorted her to the security desk, and she gave him a friendly smile.

"Thank you. I'm not sure when I'll be done tonight, but I'll call you about half an hour before I plan to head out. Okay?"

Jackson gave her a dazzling smile and a wink. "Sounds like a plan."

He turned and walking away—just as Janie came in, balancing a cardboard carrier of coffees.

Jackson held the door open for her, treating her to an appreciative smile as she slid past him.

Janie openly gaped, walking backward through the lobby—eyes glued to him until he was out of sight.

"Careful, Janis," Alexandra warned.

Janie spun around, startled. The coffee carrier wobbled, but Janie juggled it like a pro.

"Did you *see* him? Jesus, Mary, and Joseph." She peeked over her shoulder even though he was long gone.

Alexandra laughed. "What happened to your cowboy drummer?"

"I'm not *dead*, Lex. I can still look, can't I?"

"Shall we?" Alexandra gestured to the elevator, ignoring the question. She snagged the largest cup from the carrier—hers, obviously—and took a long sip. Venti whole milk caramel macchiato. Extra caramel.

"You're an angel, Janie," she sighed, taking another sip.

Though her aforementioned pasty ass wouldn't thank her.

"I know," Janie said smugly.

"Seriously though. How'd it go Saturday night?" Alexandra pressed.

It wasn't like Janie to be tight-lipped—frankly, she wanted to talk about anything *other than* Jackson.

"Fine."

Double uh-oh.

"That bad, huh?" Alexandra grimaced.

Janie sighed. "I mean, he's gorgeous and all that, but he was so… *wholesome.*"

"Wholesome?"

"Yeah. Like he belonged on the fucking Waltons. Or in Mayberry."

"So, too… nice?"

"Nice isn't bad. But he was so bland. Even his drumming was bland. Not bad, just not… thrilling."

"Ah. No spark." Alexandra nodded.

"Exactly!" Janie exhaled, exasperated. "Am I being crazy?"

Alexandra frowned.

Janie wasn't the type to second guess herself. If she wasn't into it, she moved on—no drama, no shame.

She wanted what she wanted and made no apologies about it. Rearview mirror? Never heard of it.

"No, Janie. If there's no spark, it's not really worth it, is it? It's not like you didn't give him a shot."

"Yeah, I guess."

Janie sounded *dejected.*

Janie didn't *do* dejected.

The doors opened. Alexandra motioned her to follow, leading the way to her office.

"What's going on, Janie?" she said, dropping her bag and settling into one of the client chairs. "Why do you seem like someone kicked your puppy?"

"I don't know." Janie sank into the other chair and sighed again. "I guess… I've never really been the relationship type. But, I think—*maybe*—I might want something more… serious. *Possibly.*"

Janie looked so miserable just *thinking* about it, Alexandra had to fight the urge to laugh.

"And what changed?"

Janie shifted, looking uncomfortable.

"I think it started a while ago. It just doesn't seem as much fun as it used to. I used to be totally fine with casual dating, a good roll in the hay now and then. But lately… it's just not as satisfying."

She hesitated, then added, "And then I saw you and Connor the other night. The way you looked at each other. And the way he took care of you after…"

After I freaked out.

"It was… sweet. Nice." Janie looked away. "You guys left and I sat there thinking. And I found myself wanting to actually *get to know* him. Luke, I mean."

Janie looked absolutely *appalled* at the idea—like the words tasted wrong.

"So I did. Instead of going back to my place or his, we sat and talked. And he was sweet… but boring. If I'd just fucked him, I wouldn't have known. Because I wouldn't have bothered to talk to him *afterward.*"

Alexandra laughed. She couldn't hold it anymore.

"Oh, Janie. You're growing up." She faked a sob, wiping away imaginary tears.

"You are such a smart-ass." Janie rolled her eyes and stood up. "Why did I bother?"

"No, wait. I'm sorry. Don't go," Alexandra said quickly. "I couldn't help it. I don't think you're crazy—I just think maybe your priorities are changing. You're starting to want something more… well, just *more*. Dare I say… something a little more permanent?"

Alexandra shrugged softly. "I never judged you before, I'm not about to start now. You deserve to be happy—whether it's hooking up or shacking up."

"Thanks." Janie gave her a wan smile. "I never thought I'd see the day. But I guess it had to happen eventually."

Alexandra pulled her in for a hug, then gave her a gentle shove. "Now get to work. Be productive."

The rest of her day went by in a blur. Meetings ran back to back all morning, and the afternoon was swallowed up by trial prep. They hadn't received a settlement offer yet—even after Friday's slam dunk deposition—and until they did, she was preparing like it was going to court.

Maybe if they settled it, she could take a couple extra days off. She'd left most of next week open just in case.

Alexandra was in the middle of packing up for the day when there was a knock on her door. Before she could answer, it opened—and her father stepped inside, closing it behind him.

"Hi," she said, eyebrows raised.

Her father rarely deigned to visit the fourth floor. None of the senior partners did.

"What's up?"

"Just wanted to see how you were." He shrugged.

She narrowed her eyes, suspicious. He shook his head.

"None of that. It's after six—you're off the clock."

"Alright, then." She smiled.

"Does that mean I can get a hug, too?" he asked, his eyes—so much like her own—twinkling.

She walked into his open arms and hugged him without a word, not even when he squeezed her tight before letting go.

"So, how are you?" He shoved his hands in his pockets. Relaxed. Poised. And not looking a day over forty. She could only hope to age as gracefully as her parents had so far.

"I'm okay." She shrugged her shoulders. "It's certainly…strange—but not as uncomfortable as I thought it would be."

Especially when Connor's mouth and his hands were mapping every curve of her body…

The thought caught her off guard—rattled her. *Again.* She looked away and cleared her throat before her face could betray her.

"They're taking good care of you then?" he asked.

She turned, continuing to collect her things, mostly to hide the blush creeping up her neck.

"Very. I've only met three of them so far, but they've been very nice. Professional."

She left out "gorgeous" and "charming" and omitted how one of them in particular had crawled under her skin and, apparently, into her brain.

"Good. I don't want you to have to worry about this overmuch."

"I'll be fine, Dad. I'm a big girl. I've been taking those classes, and I'm sure I'm in very good hands with MacLachlan Security Group."

"No matter how big you get, I'm still going to worry about you, DD."

He gave her *the look*. The one that said "you're still my little girl, even when you're arguing case law and wearing three-inch heels."

"You and your sister are my heart and soul," he said, quieter now. "I don't know what I'd do without either of you."

She could hear what he didn't say. He'd lost a piece of himself when her mother filed for divorce. He'd poured every ounce of what was left into them ever since, and that devotion had been the thing that got him through it.

And he'd almost lost Alexandra once. One horrible night, nine years ago.

The memory of her father's face in that hospital room was always there in the background—just waiting to remind her what she'd put him through.

"I know, Dad." She gave him a soft smile. "Connor and his guys have it under control. Try not to worry too much."

"I'll try," he said. When his smile returned it came with a flicker of mischief. "*If* you let me take you to lunch this week."

She rolled her eyes.

"Talk to Janie tomorrow. She'll pencil you in."

"This is what I'm reduced to?" he said, dramatically. "Having to make an *appointment* with my own daughter?"

"When your daughter has a malpractice suit to win? Yes."

Her father walked her to the lobby, where Jackson was waiting. She made introductions, they said their goodbyes, and her father kissed her cheek before turning back toward the elevators.

She watched him go, worry aching behind her ribs. He was still working too much. Still… lonely.

She and Amanda were busy with their own lives. They rarely found time to spend together—the three of them. Herding cats might be easier than coordinating their schedules. The same was true with their mom.

Alexandra was too pragmatic to fantasize about her parents getting back together. She was an adult. She understood that some relationships simply *didn't work*.

She just wished they could both be *happy*. Not just… less sad.

Jackson took her briefcase and laptop bag without being asked, carrying them to the car like it was second nature.

"Your dad seems nice," he said.

"He is." She smiled. And even though she gave him a hard time for being overprotective, she knew she was lucky.

"You alright?" he asked once they were on the road.

"Long day," she said with a shrug.

He nodded, and they drove in comfortable silence for a while. After a few minutes, Alexandra shook off the lingering heaviness and turned toward him.

"Is the suit uniform or something?"

Jackson chuckled. "Sort of. Most clients expect it, but it's not required. When it makes more sense to blend in a little, we dress accordingly."

"Like Connor did this weekend," she said, nodding.

Jackson have her a look, one eyebrow raised. "Connor?"

"Yeah. He was on my detail. Did I say that right?" she asked. "*On my detail?"*

"Yeah, that's right," Jackson replied. But his tone had gone quiet—distracted.

"What?"

"Nothing." He shook his head. "It's just… odd, that's all. Conor doesn't usually do detail work personally."

"What do you mean?"

"He owns the company. These days, he's mostly behind the scenes—systems, logistics, client meetings. Don't get me wrong, he's more qualified than anyone. It's just… not usually what he does anymore. He's the big picture guy."

"He said everyone else was already assigned for the weekend," she said. That was a good enough reason—it had to be.

But…maybe there's another reason.

"Makes sense," Jackson said after a beat. He still didn't sound convinced.

"Alright, where to?"

Their shopping trip was quick and efficient. She hated it, so the less time it took, the less likely she was to catch an assault charge in the cereal aisle

There had to be a better system. You put everything in a cart, only to take it out again at the register—just to put it back in the cart, then out again at home. *Ridiculous.*

Jackson, to his credit, was a good sport. He ignored her grumbling and even insisted on carrying everything in for her.

"Jackson, you really didn't have to do that," she said as he brought in the last load.

But he didn't stop there. To her surprise, he started unpacking bags, helping her put the groceries away like he'd done it a hundred times.

"Were you a Boy Scout by any chance?" she laughed.

"Yes, ma'am," he replied with a sheepish grin.

"Boy scout, Marine, and handsome to boot. Your Mama must be proud."

"I hope so." His smile dimmed—turning a little sad.

"Does she live close?"

"No. Texas."

Called it. Another cowboy.

"That must be hard, being so far away."

"It is. But I've got two younger brothers who take good care of her. I talk to her once a week—at least. And I try to visit twice a year."

"That's sweet. How old are you brothers?" she asked, stacking yogurt containers in the fridge.

"Twenty-six and Twenty-three," he said with a fond smile. "Trent's an architect and a volunteer fire fighter. Justin just finished college—criminal justice degree. He's headed to law school next."

The pride in his voice was unmistakable.

"Sounds like your mom has a knack for raising heroes."

He stilled. His smile slipped, eyes dropping to the counter.

"I'm not a hero," he said quietly.

She blinked at him, caught off guard by the conviction in his voice.

"You were a Marine?" she asked, abandoning the groceries and taking a stool so she could give him her full attention.

"Yes, ma'am. Eight years, three tours."

"Lex, remember?" she said gently, placing her hand lightly over his. "That's a long time to serve."

"Yeah."

"Why did you join?"

He shrugged. "The boys. Pop died just before I enlisted. Mom had some savings, but I knew things would be tight. She wanted all of us to get an education. I wasn't a great student—no scholarships. But Trent and Justin were smart. I knew they'd make good if I gave them a shot."

"So, you enlisted so your brothers could go to college?"

"Yeah. Seemed like the best way. I sent my pay home and figured if I still wanted to go to school when I was done, I could."

"That's incredibly selfless of you." Alexandra blinked hard. "I know I don't know you… not really. I don't know what you've seen or done—and I don't need to. But doing that for your brothers? That already makes you a hero."

"Aw, hell. Please don't cry." He looked *positively horrified.*

"I'm not crying," she said, wiping her eyes. "*You're* crying."

He reached over and gave her a slightly awkward side hug—*and it was adorable.*

She offered him a reassuring smile. He smiled back—a little shy, a little haunted, but it was a something.

Her heart ached a little for him. Without overthinking it, she made a decision.

"Are you hungry?"

His smile widened. "Always."

An hour later they'd finished dinner—a simple grilled salmon with dill sauce, caprese salad and roasted potatoes. Jackson had gone back for seconds and thanked her profusely before insisting on helping with the dishes.

Dinner had been enlightening. Jackson had a great sense of humor. He was genuinely decent—even sweet. And he was a smart ass, which she appreciated, but easy going and fun, too.

That—and his Texas twang—gave her an idea. Once the seed was planted it quickly sprouted and grew until she couldn't contain it.

"Are you single?"

His eyes went wide. His mouth opened and then quickly closed again. The look of panic on his face had her laughing almost instantly.

"Oh, God—I'm sorry. That wasn't what I meant," she gasped, still laughing. He relaxed immediately, relieved, then reddened slightly.

"No offense, Lex. I don't want you thinking it's you. You're beautiful—and a killer cook. I'd snatch you up in a heartbeat… but I value my job." Jackson paused. "And my balls," he muttered.

She blinked at him. "What?"

Jackson winced. He clearly hadn't meant for her to hear that last part.

She raised an eyebrow and waited.

"Connor would castrate me if I so much as laid a finger on you. And that's… pretty much a direct quote."

What the hell?

So Connor had issued a warning. To Jackson… Or to all of them?

"Jacks," she said, voice calm but cold. "Was this a *private* conversation?"

Jackson shook his head slowly, guilt written all over his face. At least he had the good sense to look contrite.

Her face flamed. Humiliation clawed at her. She silently prayed for the ground to swallow her whole.

Christ, did he circulate a fucking memo?

"I'm going to kill him," she muttered, eyes squeezing shut. Her body was rigid with embarrassment. And *rage.*

Jackson chuckled. Her eyes flew open, and she fixed him with her deadliest glare.

"Keep it up and you're next."

That shut him up. Sort of. And that's when she had a thought—one that quickly snowballed into a plan. By the time she said goodnight to Jackson, it was unstoppable.

Oh, yeah. You're gonna pay for this, Connor.

She checked her phone as she plugged it in for the night—and there it was. A message from Connor. Even now, when she wanted to kill him, her stomach flipped when she saw his name.

Connor MacLachlan: How was your day?

Sent thirty minutes ago. She stared at it—thinking.
She finally typed:

Alexandra Hughes: Wonderful. Jackson just left.

He responded immediately.

Connor MacLachlan: Busy night?

Alexandra Hughes: Just a quiet dinner at home.

Connor MacLachlan: ??

Connor MacLachlan: With Jackson?

Alexandra Hughes: Yes. He's lovely. I like him.

Several seconds passed in silence. She grinned—imagining look on his face. And if a shiver went down her spine, she blamed it on the cold.

Connor MacLachlan: Lovely?! What does that mean?

Alexandra Hughes: Goodnight, Connor. :)

Connor MacLachlan: Lex…

Connor MacLachlan: Alexandra??

Connor MacLachlan: You there??

She snickered. And set her phone to *Do Not Disturb*.

Chapter Eleven

Alexandra awoke on Wednesday to three missed calls, a new voicemail, and several text messages, all from Connor.

Alexandra snorted. She didn't believe him for a *second*, but the jealousy was downright adorable. She almost felt bad, but he'd brought this on himself.

A photo of Parker followed, as usual.

Ugh, of course. Gorgeous.

Sandy blonde hair that hung to his collar and hazel eyes that were heavy on the green. Thick stubble and the tattoo peeking over the collar of his shirt gave him that yummy bad-boy vibe.

She put the phone on speaker and listened to her voicemail while she did her makeup.

"Alexandra," Connor growled her name. "Your last text was only five minutes ago. I know you're still awake. Call me back."

It shouldn't have made her shiver, but it did. Heat bloomed across her skin, and she shifted, thighs pressing together. But she wouldn't be swayed. He deserved a little comeuppance, and she was going to give it to him.

And if he wants to come find me, let him.

What surprised her most wasn't the thought itself—it was how much she liked it.

Parker wasn't as friendly as Jackson, but she made it a point to smile and ask him all about himself on the drive to work. She told him she would call when she was done for the day, then she went to work.

She pulled Janie into her office as soon as she had a spare minute and told her what she was planning, and what she needed. She left out the "why," of course. By six o'clock, everything was ready and there was no turning back.

She met Parker in the lobby, and he gave her a tight, professional smile. No doubt Connor had probably reminded everyone about his "hands-off" policy after their exchange the night before.

But she refused to feel bad. *She* wasn't getting them in trouble; Connor's stupid rule was. She was in no way responsible for his possessive macho bullshit.

"Good evening, Parker." She smiled, relieved. She had been half afraid that Connor would drop everything to pick her up himself, but apparently, he had better things to do. She definitely wasn't disappointed—even a little.

"Evening, ma'am."

"Please, call me Alexandra. Or Lex—anything other than ma'am." She gave him her most disarming smile, but he kept his face carefully neutral.

"Yes, ma'am," he said flatly.

"I don't bite. I promise."

"Yes, ma'am."

He led her to the car and ushered her in, without touching her. He pulled into traffic, and she let him focus for a few minutes before launching her assault.

"So, do you like working for Connor?" she asked.

"Yes," he said, keeping his eyes on the road.

"He must be very demanding."

He didn't even respond, he merely shrugged. It was clear this one was going to be a tough nut to crack. She'd have to try a different approach.

"You look familiar, have we met somewhere before?"

"No," he said confidently.

She narrowed her eyes. He was like a brick wall.

"Are you sure? Are you from New York?"

"No."

"Where are you from?"

"Montana. Then Texas for a while."

"Really?" Alexandra said, excitedly. "I don't think I've ever met anyone from Montana before. I hear it's beautiful there—I always wanted to visit. What part are you from?"

"Great Falls," he said, sparing her a sideways glance.

"Do you miss it?"

"Sometimes."

"What do you miss about it?"

He seemed to struggle with himself. He clearly wanted to answer but he was wary.

As you should be…

"The sky. And the quiet."

"Must be a big change from New York," Alexandra said with a laugh. "I've heard you can see the aurora borealis from there sometimes. Is that true? I bet it's spectacular."

"You can. And it is." His mouth twitched like he wanted to smile—but he shut it down almost instantly.

"Sounds amazing," she said. She suddenly straightened, eyes wide. "Oh shoot. I promised Connor I would call him. Is he in the office now?"

"No," he said flatly.

Good.

"You guys do have an actual office, right? With desks, conference tables…a coffee machine?"

"Yes," he said slowly—warily.

"Great. Can you take me there, please?"

"Ma'am?" Parker's brow furrowed. He looked confused. And concerned.

"Just for a second. I just need to drop something off. That's okay, right?"

"Yes," he said reluctantly.

"Then I'd like to go, there. Please and thank you."

Parker gave her a long look. He didn't know what to make of her or what she was up to—and he clearly didn't want to get involved. But he was smart. He didn't argue.

The ride was silent. Tense—at least for Parker.

They pulled up in front of a sleek modern office building. He opened the door for her, ushered her inside without a word, and led her to the elevator. He pressed the button for the sixth floor, and they ascended in silence.

The doors opened on a large, clean reception area—tasteful furniture, cool lighting. And completely empty. Parker Stopped.

"Is Jackson here? Or Sam? I just want to say hello."

He looked like he *desperately* wanted to ask her what the hell was going on—but also didn't want to know. He picked up the phone at the reception desk and punched in a number. He kept an eye on Alexandra as if she might bolt or… explode.

"Someone to see you." There was a pause, then he hissed, "just get out here."

A moment later Jackson turned a corner and froze. He stared at her for a beat, brow furrowed in confusion. His eyes shifted to Parker. Parker didn't move, but he must have made some kind of face because Jackson offered her a tense smile.

"What brings you here? Connor's not-"

"Oh, I know," she quickly cut in. "Which is why I'm here." She pulled out the box of almond cookies—just squeezed into her briefcase—and handed it to him.

"Thank you?" Jackson said, bemused.

"Just a little something to say thanks." She smiled sweetly, and produced a stack of envelopes from her bag. "And here. These are for you guys. You'll hand them out, won't you?"

Parker looked at her sideways—well looked at her *bag*. Like he was worried about what else might be lurking in there.

Jackson blinked down at the linen envelopes, hand-addressed in her best cursive. He thumbed through them, confused. Until it hit him.

Inside each envelope was a hand-written invitation to dinner on Friday.

"We'll be spending a lot of time together," she said innocently. "So I thought it would be good if we all got to know each other properly."

Then she smirked—a wicked, knowing little smile—and Jackson lost it.

He double over, laughing so hard it turned to wheezing. When he finally straightened—clutching his side and wiping tears from his eyes—he glanced at Parker and then looked at her.

"Oh, man," he gasped. "He is gonna *lose his shit.*"

"Good," Alexandra said smugly, tuning on her stiletto with military precision. She walked away like the unholy union of a runway model and a five-star General who'd just declared war.

Parker hurried to catch up, shell-shocked.

Back in the car, he finally gave in.

"Okay—what the hell just happened?"

Alexandra grinned and extending her hand. "Nice to finally meet you, Parker."

Cookies. Jackson was "lovely," and now she'd brought them *cookies?*

What the hell is she playing at?

Connor wanted nothing more than to march over to her brownstone and demand an answer. And once he had it, he'd remind her who'd been there first—*thoroughly.*

Unfortunately, his entire week had been a disaster and he was still catching up with the clients he'd cancelled meetings with on Monday.

Connor growled, raking a hand through his already disheveled hair. "What's the point of being your own feckin' boss if you're still chained to a desk?" he muttered.

Someone knocked on his door and he sighed. "Yeah."

The door popped open and Parker leaned in. Connor quirked an eyebrow and looked at the clock. Didn't seem like he'd hung around long. Parker was reliable that way. Loyal. Trustworthy.

Not like Jackson…

"She's in for the night," Parker reported. "I'm taking off, unless you need anything else from me."

"Depends. You got any idea what the hell is goin' on around here," Connor replied.

A corner of Parker's mouth ticked up for a second. To anyone else it would have seemed like a twitch. But if you knew Parker, it was practically a grin.

Before Connor could interrogate him, Jackson stopped in the hallway outside his door. He tapped Parker on the shoulder, handing him a cream-colored envelope.

"Don't forget this," Jackson said. He was speaking to Parker, but his eyes—and his *smirk*—were directed at Connor. Parked frowned and his eyes darted to Connor before taking the envelope.

"Something you'd like to share with the class?" Connor pinned Jackson with a hard stare, scowling. Jackson's answering grin was gleeful. He stepped around Parker and handed Connor an envelope.

It was addressed to Jackson. Of course. He opened the envelope and skimmed the contents, and felt the dull ache behind his eyes turn into pounding. Like a war drum.

He stuffed the hand-written card back into the envelope and shoved it back into Jackson's hand.

"How many?"

"One for each of us—except you, boss," Jackson replied, still grinning like the devil.

"Didn't I fire you yesterday?"

Jackson shrugged. "You tried."

"Get out, before I try harder."

They left, closing his door behind them, and Connor grabbed his phone.

What. The actual. Fuck.

Connor MacLachlan: I have rehired, and re-fired Jackson. In fact I sacked the lot of them.

He stared at the screen waiting.

A minute passed. Then two.

Alexandra Hughes: Good! That means they'll all be free Friday. How thoughtful. :)

He dragged a hand down his face, but he couldn't stop the grin tugging at the corners of his mouth. Damn, but she was a right handful.

But you do realize, this means war.

Connor MacLachlan: Yes, they will...

Connor MacLachlan: Of course that means I'm the only one left on your detail. See you Friday.

Check.

Connor MacLachlan: Oh, no. I know exactly how dangerous your dinner guests can be. I wouldn't feel safe leaving you alone with them.

Connor MacLachlan: See you Friday. ;)

And mate.

Thursday was busy—just like the rest of his week. He realized, not for the first time, that he *desperately* needed to expand his team. Including someone who could handle logistics and consultations. Before he lost his damn mind.

And *women.*

Not a single female applicant in the stack of resumes on his desk. He'd have to find a way to fix that.

I should've done it years ago. Then maybe I wouldn't be in this mess.

Friday wasn't any better. They hours crawled by, dragging his patience with them. His normally unshakable focus was beginning to slip. After his last client meeting, he ducked out early.

Two hours at the gym had helped in burn off some of his restlessness—just not nearly enough.

He went home. Showered. Changed.

Then headed to the offices of Langston, Buchanan & Hughes.

"So what's the occasion?"

"Nothing special. I felt like cooking," Alexandra lied.

She'd begun this plan, and she intended to go through with it, but she'd realized—almost immediately—that it might be a bit uncomfortable having dinner by herself with six strangers. Especially when those strangers were *men.*

So she was calling for backup. Janie was on board—*of course*—so she just had to convince her sister to show up.

"Ah, one of your culinary explosions. Let me guess—you've baked cookies in the last week, too, haven't you?"

"Guilty."

"Chocolate chip?"

"Please. Is there any other kind?"

"As a pastry chef, I'm offended. But I'll let it go. Now, what's on the menu for tonight?" Amanda wheedled.

"I'm making my paella." Alexandra grinned. Amanda *loved* her paella. If this didn't convince her, nothing would.

"Oh, you are ruthless."

"I know."

"Who else is coming?" Amanda was suspicious—with good reason. Alexandra didn't make Paella for anything less than a small army. It was too much work for just one or two people.

"I've invited some new… friends."

"What kind of 'friends?'"

"…Male ones?"

"Okay, you had me at paella. But *male 'friends'*? Bonus." Amanda paused and Alexandra braced herself. "No offense, but… where did you meet these '*friends*?'"

And there it was.

"They're kind of, my bodyguards?" There was a brief silence. And then Amanda laughed hysterically—for several minutes.

"That is *so* you, it hurts. And I'll bet this isn't the first time you've cooked for them, is it?"

"And what exactly do you mean by that?"

"I'll take that as a yes." Amanda snorted. "And *I mean* that it's very like you to take in a bunch of strays."

"Strays?" Alexandra couldn't say why, but she was a little offended on their behalf.

"Oh, calm down." Amanda sighed. "I don't mean that in a bad way. I mean, you have a way of… collecting people—from the most *random* places. And once you feed them, they never leave."

"I do not."

"Charles?"

"He's a friend from law school. Totally normal."

"That's not what I'm talking about—and you *know* it. Fine. Janie?"

"Janie is amazing at her job, thank you very much."

"Yeah, but what qualifications did she have when you hired her?"

Alexandra's pressed her lips into a thin line. She said nothing.

"See? You tend to collect people. Especially one's who need fixing"

"That's not fair," Alexandra snapped. "I'm not trying to *fix* anyone. Who the hell am I to fix anyone else?"

Her laugh was bitter, harsher than she meant it to be. But she felt called out—and she didn't like it.

"Maybe that's exactly why you do it," Amanda said softly. Then, more brightly, "Anyway, I'm in. What should I bring?"

"Yourself. And maybe a bottle of wine. You know I'm terrible with that."

"Got it. See you at seven." There was a pause, then Amanda added, "you know I love you, right?"

"I know. I love you too."

Alexandra glanced at the clock as she ended the call. Nearly five o'clock and the weekend couldn't come fast enough.

She wasn't sure if Connor was serious about crashing dinner. She dreaded—and hoped—he was.

She'd missed him. And hated herself for it.

They'd only known each other a week. A very eventful week—but still.

And she didn't actually know the rest of the team, either. She was comfortable with Jackson. And Parker had started to warm to her. She'd been extra nice to Sam yesterday—to make up for her Monday morning grumpiness.

But Ian and Cam? She'd only met them that morning. Not a lot of quality time. They were complete opposites in every conceivable away. The only thing they seemed to have in common was insanely good looks.

In retrospect, this whole plan was stupid. And Reckless. Not like her.

She didn't know what the hell she was thinking.

Yes, you do. You saw a glimmer of jealousy—and wanted more.

No, I'm just making a point. Nothing more.

It didn't matter. It was too late to turn back. She'd made her bed—and invited six dangerously attractive strangers to lie in it with her.

She shot off a text to Cam—the one who'd actually spoken to her that morning—and let him know she was ready to go.

Janie was just finishing up for the day.

"You promise you're coming, right?"

"Are you kidding? Free food, free booze, and a side of hot guys? Yes, *please*." Janie's grin was positively indecent.

Alexandra rolled her eyes. "Dinner's at seven. Don't be late!"

Janie gave her a saucy salute as she headed toward the elevator. Alexandra laughed, shaking her head.

Her own ride to the lobby felt like it took an eternity. And she couldn't blame the flutter in her stomach on the descent. She took a deep breath as the car slowed, trying to calm her nerves.

The doors slid open with a soft *ding*, and her heart stuttered to a stop.

Connor was there—leaning against the opposite wall like he owned half of Manhattan. Dark jeans, snug in all the right ways. A gray button-up with the sleeves rolled up over his muscular forearms. His dark hair was still damp and tousled from the shower. He looked like sin and sanctuary.

And more dangerous than ever.

Her mouth went dry.

Heat washed over every inch of her skin. She wanted to grab him by the front of his shirt and drag him into the elevator. Her office had a working lock.

And a desk.

Connor looked up—and caught her staring.

Those sapphire eyes made her breath hitch. Dark. Smoldering. Lit from within. She was starting to learn his expressions—amused, concerned, serious, playful. But this one? This one was new.

He pushed off the wall slowly, deliberately, straightening to his full height. And prowled toward her without looking away. The smile that curved his mouth was slow. Wicked. Dangerous.

He looked *feral*.

Predatory. Focused. Not just hungry—*starving*.

Fixated. Wasn't that the word?

He looked at her like she was the only person on earth. Like he was calculating the distance—and how fast he could close it.

She had the intense urge to run. She just couldn't decide if it should be *away* from him… or *toward* him. Possibly shedding her clothes on the way.

The scariest part? She *wanted* him to catch her.

She snapped her mouth shut and forced herself to move. Three steps forward—solid and steady—praying she didn't trip.

"Where's Cam?" she asked, licking her dry lips. His eyes tracked the motion, and the fire in his gaze flared hotter.

He stepped closer until only inches separated them.

"If you keep this up, you're gonna hurt my feelings, love," he said, voice low and teasing.

"You're a big boy. I'm sure you'll survive."

He smiled—crooked and full of heat, leaning in until his breath ghosted over her neck, making her shiver.

"I am a *verra* big boy."

Before she could respond, he took her hand, threading his fingers through hers.

"Car's this way."

The ride home was steeped in charged silence. Alexandra was off-balance. She didn't know where to go from here.

Bed. Couch. Foyer. Hell, just ask him to pull over.

She shifted, forcing herself to look away. She needed distance. But she couldn't help herself for long.

The sun was setting, and the fading amber sunlight outlined his profile. Bathed in a golden glow, his features turned into a work of art—too beautiful to be real. His eyes looked impossibly blue. His cheekbones were high, and his jaw was a sculpted line of strength and restraint.

How the hell is this man real? Let alone interested in me.

She knew she was attractive. But she wasn't a supermodel. Her hair was a natural chestnut brown—fairly common. But she liked it. It suited her. She didn't have time or energy to deal with roots ever four to six weeks like Amanda.

She worked out, mostly to relieve stress and stay sane, but she also liked to cook. And eat. She had curves. Her thighs touched. Her stomach wasn't flat. And her breasts had *never* been perky.

Her face was a little too soft—too round—and there was a permanent crease between her eyebrows which she called her "what the fuck" wrinkle. For obvious reasons.

And then there was the RBF—Resting Bitch Face. Amanda and Charles just loved to point it out. People constantly asked her what was wrong—and then kept asking until there *was* something wrong. Then they got the Active Bitch Face.

"What's wrong?" Connor asked.

She flinched. "Nothing," she snapped. She caught herself, realizing she'd overacted. "That's just how my face looks."

He didn't miss a beat. "No, I don't mean the RBF," he said casually. "You were staring at me while making your '*what the fuck*' face."

She blinked at him.

Are you a mind reader?

He looked at her expectantly.

She let out breath.

"What can I say, I'm trying to restore your wounded ego."

"Well, in that case, I've got a few suggestions…" he said with a lethal smirk.

"*Annnd* we're done." She turned to look out the window.

He chuckled. "Seriously, though. You alright? You looked…"

"Annoyed?" she offered.

"No, I'm *familiar* with annoyed." His voice shifted, going serious. Soft. "You looked… sad, maybe? Confused?"

She wasn't about to admit she'd been thinking about how *gorgeous* he was—or how he was probably out of her league. So she did what she always did: deflected with humor… and just a sprinkle of truth.

"If you must know," she huffed, rolling her eyes. "I was just thinking how unfair it is that you're so handsome. I always assumed those Calvin Klein models were airbrushed to hell—Photoshopped to within an inch of their lives. But here you are, in the flesh, proving me wrong."

He looked at her, bemused—lifting one brow slowly. Apparently he'd expected her to say something snarky. *Cutting.*

But there was no point in denying she found him attractive. That cow had already left the barn.

Still… he looked way too smug. And if there was one thing she hated, it was not living up to expectations. So, fine. She'd give him a little snark.

She gave him a long, deliberate once-over and rolled her eyes. "Disgusting."

He laughed, and she turned back toward the window to hide her smile.

"You always surprise me," he said, with a shake of his head and that maddeningly sexy, irresistibly crooked grin.

"I do my best."

The woman was going to kill him.

She was clearly attracted to him—and not even trying to hide it. But all week long, she'd done nothing but intentionally aggravate him. Flirting with Jackson, inviting everyone to dinner *except* him.

"Where's Cam?" For fuck's sake.

She drove him *mad.* That sexy pencil skirt. Those fuck me heels. The way she looked at him like he was her favorite dessert. And then? She'd slam the shutters closed and lock him out.

It made him want to kiss her. Or maybe strip her down and fuck her right there in the damn lobby just to see that mask crack. Just to see that spark when he got past the wall she kept putting up.

Because he'd *seen* her—really seen her—and now he needed more.

The flirt who teased him.

The shy girl who blushed when he touched her.

The razor-sharp attorney who gave as good as she got.

The woman with scars, and the strength to survive them.

She was complicated. Real. And hiding behind that mask like it was armor. He got it—everyone had their own way of dealing with pain. But he couldn't understand was why she hid the good parts, too.

When they were alone, she relaxed a little. She smiled more. Let herself *breathe.* And he liked it. Probably too much.

He didn't just want to protect her.

He wanted her to trust him—with her smiles. Her tears. Her fears.

He didn't get a chance to unpack that dangerous realization, because the doorbell rang.

He checked the window and saw a young woman standing on the stoop, balancing a duffle bag on one shoulder and carrying a large white cake box in her arms. Instinct kicked in and he assessed quickly. There were a lot of places she could be hiding a weapon. But he had a hunch she wasn't a threat.

He exhaled and opened the door.

She blinked, surprised, then smiled—and there it was, the confirmation he'd been looking for. The resemblance was obvious. Same bone structure, same smile, same confidence. But where Richard Hughes and Alexandra had hazel eyes and dark hair, the woman in front of him had vivid blue eyes and honey blonde waves.

"Amanda?" he asked. "I'm Connor."

"Hey," she said simply, stepping around him and into the entryway.

"Need a hand?"

"Yeah. Take this, would you?" She handed him the cake box. He saw an artful arrangement of pastries through the clear lid.

"No problem." He closed and locked the door behind her.

He eyed the gym bag slung over her shoulder. "Planning to stay over?"

She quirked an eyebrow and gave him a slow once-over. "Are *you?*"

He chuckled. "I haven't been asked."

Yet.

"Neither have I." She adjusted the bag. "I just left work. I didn't have time to change." She gestured at her white jacket, black pants and black sneakers—the kind that screamed "I'm on my feet all day."

"You're a chef?" He knew the answer already. Even knew *where* she worked. But it was easier to pretend he didn't. People got *uncomfortable* about that sort of thing.

"Pastry chef," she said with a nod. "Lex got all the talent with *real* food." She shrugged.

"Hey. Pastry *is* real food," Connor said solemnly.

Amanda snorted. "Tell that to my boss." She tilted her head. "Speaking of Alexandra…?"

"Upstairs." He motioned with his chin.

"Thanks," she tossed over her shoulder as she bounded up the stairs.

He put the box on the kitchen counter and his mouth watered at the scent of coming from the stove. Whatever Alexandra was making smelled *incredible.* The pot was enormous—enough to feed an army. Or four of his guys. And him.

Cam was on the job, so the guest list was limited to Jackson, Sam, Parker and Ian. Jackson had made a point of letting Connor know that he'd be there. Gleefully. And repeatedly. Jackson was a good guy, one hell of an asset to the team, and one of his best friends.

Which is the only reason Connor hadn't throat-punched him. *Yet.* The night was still young.

Janie arrived next. Like Amanda, she went straight upstairs to Alexandra's room. Connor wasn't sure what made him uneasy about that—three women locked in a room together, plotting—but warning bells were blaring in the back of his mind.

Oh, to be a fly on that wall.

The guys all arrived together. No surprise there. That left him to play host while the girls stayed out of sight—which worked in his favor. He needed a few minutes with his team.

"Anything?" he asked, voice low.

"Nothing yet," Sam said, shaking his head.

Connor swore under his breath.

Sam had been able to pull footage from five different cameras in the area, but none of them had a clear shot of the street directly in front of the brownstone. They'd caught a few people in the general vicinity around the right time, but nothing conclusive. The angles were wrong, the images were blurry—useless.

Now Sam was digging into the building owners and tenants on that block. Owners were easy—they were public record. Tenants took a little bit more work. Still, he'd ID'd more than half. So far, no red flags.

There were two vacant apartments on the block. One was on the ground floor, two buildings down from Alexandra's brownstone—same side of the street. The other was a basement unit, three doors in the opposite direction and across the street.

Both were easy to break into. Both had good sightlines. Either would be perfect for a stalker.

Connor had already reached out to the owner of the building down the street. The first floor unit was being cleaned out after the last tenant—a hoarder—had finally vacated. Cleanup would take weeks.

There was no guarantee, but he doubted that was the hidey hole they were looking for.

The basement unit across the street had already been rented. The tenants were supposed to move in the first of November. It would be empty for a couple more weeks, but they refused to show it.

If that was where the stalker had been camping out, it was about to disappear. That could work in their favor. Until then, they'd just have to watch. And wait.

Connor turned to Ian who—as usual—stood slightly apart, silently watching.

"Anything?" he asked.

Ian just shook his head.

"You're sure? Nothing suspicious? Nobody followed you this morning?"

Ian narrowed his eyes and shook his head again. Only slower this time.

Connor understood him, loud and clear: *"Isn't that what I just said?"*

"Fine" Connor muttered, pinching the bridge of his nose. "At least tell me Cam behaved himself."

Ian raised a single eyebrow. Read: *"What do you think?"*

"Dammit."

Connor hated this—all of it. He'd never been this unsettled before. His focus was shot. Every second Alexandra was out of his sight, his nerves frayed a little more. This week had been torture. More than once he'd been on the verge of snapping.

The guys had checked in regularly, but that wasn't good enough. He didn't completely trust it unless he could confirm she was safe with his own eyes.

He was seconds away from going up there to see what the hell was taking her so long when Janie and Amanda appeared in the doorway.

Janie looked good—curvy, confident. Her dark green dress hugged her body and set off her pale skin, red hair and striking eyes.

Amanda had swapped her work clothes for fashionably shredded jeans, a plain black tee, and a pair of black heels that Connor was pretty sure had *red bottoms.*

But the moment Alexandra walked in, everyone else faded into the background.

Her hair framed her face in soft waves. A worn pair of jeans hugged her hips and skimmed her long legs. Her sweater—a soft cream cable-knit—molded to her body as if it was custom made for her.

His breath caught and he refused to blink.

She looked relaxed. Comfortable. Cozy. Effortless.

It was so *her.*

And she was fucking radiant.

Chapter Twelve

When Alexandra went to check on dinner, he followed her back to the kitchen.

"Need any help? I'm pretty handy in the kitchen after all."

"Yes, I remember," she said dryly.

"Do you?" he asked as he stepped closer. Her cheeks flushed and he wanted to kiss her on those glossy pink lips. *Badly*.

"It's a bit… hazy, if I'm honest," she said.

"Would you like me to refresh your memory?"

He leaned in, keeping his hands in his pockets to make sure he behaved. The next kiss—and so help him God, there *would* be a next one—would be because *she* kissed *him*. He'd told her he would wait. And he meant it.

He wanted her to be sure.

She looked him in the eye, still blushing. "Maybe later."

Her smile was sarcastic, but it still took his breath away.

Two hours later, dinner was nearly over. Alexandra smiled at the people gathered around her table. It felt good to put it to use again after so long. Aside from needling Connor about his "hands-off" edict—and asserting her independence, of course—she'd wanted to throw Janie and Jackson together and see what happened. In a totally casual, no-pressure sort of way. If it worked, wonderful. If it didn't? No harm, no foul.

So far, there had been a few stolen glances, on both sides. Jackson was obviously interested. Janie was eyeing him like ribeye but had been oddly quiet about it. Maybe she was feeling shy.

Alexandra snorted at the thought. Connor tilted his head at her, curious.

He'd been far too at ease all evening, so she turned to Jackson, who was sitting on her left.

"So how's your mom, Jacks?" she asked innocently.

"She's good, thanks." He gave her a warm smile and her heart squeezed. It was so sweet how much he loved his family.

"Are you going to Texas for the Holidays?" she asked, sipping her wine.

"She's comin' here for Thanksgiving," he said, clearly excited. "Then I'm headin' to Texas for Christmas." He glanced at Connor, as if confirming. Connor rolled his eyes but nodded, smiling.

Connor might joke about firing them, but there was no doubt that he cared about his team. Damn. She didn't need any more reasons to like him. She pointedly ignored him and turned back to Jackson.

"You should bring her over for dinner while she's in town. I'd love to meet her. She sounds incredible." Alexandra smirked and reached across the table to shove playfully at his shoulder. "And I want a chance to tell her how awesome her son is."

Alexandra meant every word, but Jackson blushed, looking uncomfortable. Whether it was the praise or Connor glaring at him, she wasn't sure.

"So, where in Texas are you from?" Janie asked, from Jackson's other side.

"Outside Dallas." His eyes lit up, and he stared at Janie for a beat before realizing he should probably say something else. "What about you, where are you from?"

Alexandra smiled and tuned out their conversation, satisfied.

Her work there was done. Time to move on to the next victim. She spent the next half hour pretending Connor didn't exist and trying to pry open Parker and Ian. Sam was a little aloof, but he had a wicked sense of humor—if you appreciated snark. Luckily, she was fluent.

Parker was quiet. He'd hardly spoken at all, and when he did it was mostly to Jackson. He was observant, though. He spent a lot of time watching everyone else. Especially Amanda. Interesting. She'd have to keep that tidbit in her back pocket for now.

Unlike Parker, Ian wasn't quiet. He was silent. And still. The man was essentially a statue. He didn't say a single word to *anyone*. He'd eaten—*a lot*—but the rest of the time he just… sat there. Arms crossed, staring at the wall. It was like he'd been dragged there at gun point.

Ian, blink twice if you need help.

The thought alone had her almost spitting out her wine. Ian was the largest man she'd ever seen—by far—at well over six feet. The idea he'd been brought there against his will was ridiculous.

Alexandra stood to clear plates, and Connor immediately followed. He didn't offer—he just started helping. To her surprise, Amanda stood up as well.

"I've got it," Amanda said, with a wink at Connor.

An unpleasant sensation crept through her. Alexandra told herself it wasn't jealousy.

She was lying.

This was all pretend, she reminded herself. She didn't have any right to feel any kind of way about it. And Amanda was *Amanda*. She was fearless and social and more than a bit of a flirt. It was just how she was. Still…

"Thanks," Alexandra said with a smile as Amanda picked up a stack of plates.

As soon as they were in the kitchen, Amanda pulled her aside with a quick glance back to the dining room.

"What the hell?" Amanda whispered.

"What?" Alexandra said, surprised.

"Are you fucking the bodyguard?" Amanda asked.

"Which one?" Alexandra shot back archly—though the effect was probably ruined by the way her voice cracked. She was as red as a lobster, judging by how hot her face felt.

"I think you know who I'm talking about." She wasn't going to let this go. She was like a dog with a bone when she thought you were hiding something. "He's been staring at you all night, and *not* as a security professional."

"I have not had sex with Connor," Alexandra said firmly, setting her stack of plates in the sink.

"Yet," Amanda said with a grin, bumping her shoulder. Alexandra sighed, but she couldn't stop the corners of her mouth from turning up.

"Yet," Alexandra confirmed sheepishly.

"I knew it!" Amanda hissed, checking behind her again to make sure they hadn't been overheard.

"He's hot, okay?" Alexandra explained. "And he just… *says* things that make me…"

"Feral?" Amanda asked with a wicked laugh.

"*God*, yes. That's *exactly* what it feels like."

"I totally get it," Amanda said, glancing back into the dining room. "Excuse me?"

"Oh, don't worry. I'm not gonna poach your man," Amanda replied, never taking her eyes off of her target. As long as that target wasn't Connor…

"So, you really like him?" Amanda asked, finally looking at her.

"Yeah." Alexandra let out a shaky breath. "I really do. And I think he likes me, but there's a professional relationship and you know I'm…"

"What are you, Lex?" Amanda asked quietly.

"You know. I'm… *broken*."

"You're *not* broken," Amanda insisted. Alexandra knew better than to argue with her. They'd had this argument more times than she could count.

"I'm *something*. It's… complicated." The look Amanda gave her said she didn't buy that for a second.

"Well, I'm pretty sure he more than *likes* you. He's been looking at you like you're water in the desert. What did you do to the man? And can you teach *me* how to do it?" Amanda asked, steepling her fingers like a supervillain and rhythmically tapping them together.

Alexandra flushed and gave Amanda a whispered, highly abridged version of what happened last weekend.

By the time Alexandra finished, Amanda stood there wide-eyed with her mouth hanging open. Alexandra put a finger under Amanda's chin and gently pushed her mouth closed.

"Holy. Shit."

"I just don't know if it's a good idea. What if, when this is all over and the adrenaline has worn off, he's not interested anymore? Besides, I'm pretty sure last weekend was an anomaly. He's been so busy I haven't seen him all week."

Alexandra was absolutely *not* pouting. At least that's what she told herself.

"Are you sure that's what it's about?" Amanda looked at her with pity. Alexandra shut down instantly.

"Of course," Alexandra said. "I'm just not sure it's going anywhere, that's all. He's cute and fun, but I don't think we'd work out in the long run. Aside from sarcasm and Indian food, I don't even know if we have anything in common."

"Isn't that the point of dating? To see if you have anything in common?"

"I don't have time to date if I'm going to make partner by thirty-five." She knew she sounded cold. And she hated it. But she'd rather be cold than be pitied. Every time her sister or her parents gave her *that* look, she wanted to explode—or just shrink into nothing.

She was *fine*, dammit. She didn't need them feeling sorry for her for the rest of her life. Every time they looked at her, they saw her frozen in that awful moment. Nothing before or after mattered.

But she refused to let it define her.

"Will you take the pastries in while I make coffee?" Alexandra asked.

She turned away but Amanda caught her arm. "Lex-"

"Don't," she snapped. "I'm *fine*."

"Okay. I hear you," Amanda said, raising her hands in surrender. They were quiet for a minute while they each focused on their tasks. Finally, Amanda broke the silence.

"So… what can you tell me about Parker?" There was a wicked gleam in her eyes that said she was already planning. But Alexandra recognized this for what it was. An apology. And she accepted it.

"Poor man." Alexandra smiled and rolled her eyes. Amanda grinned and, just like that, everything was back to normal. At least, on the surface.

Alexandra was exhausted but satisfied by the end of the night. She was actually glad she'd pulled this silly stunt. She genuinely liked Connor's guys—the ones that actually spoke to her.

Janie had whispered a "we'll talk tomorrow" when she'd hugged her goodbye, which Alexandra took as a good sign. She wanted Janie to be happy and Jackson seemed like a great guy. Hell, she wanted Jackson to be happy.

As she said goodbye to everyone, she noticed Connor was nowhere to be found.

"Connor?" she called, wandering into the kitchen. To her surprise, he was loading the last of the dishes into the dishwasher. The counters were clean and all the food had been put away.

"Wow." She raised her eyebrows. "You didn't have to do that."

Connor simply shrugged. He picked up his wineglass and finished it before loading it, too, into the dishwasher.

"But thanks."

She took a step forward, wrapping her arms around her middle, unsure what to say or do next.

"So, did you have fun?" he asked. His tone was light, but he didn't appear to be amused.

"Yeah. I really like your… employees? Friends?"

She noticed Connor's jaw clench and unclench a few times and he stepped forward until they were almost toe to toe.

"Last week I would have said both, now I'm not so sure."

"Why is that?"

"Because now I have to try not to throw punches every time I see them," he said. The softness of his voice somehow made it sound *more sinister* than if he'd shouted. She swallowed, but forced herself not to move.

"Because *now* I find myself wondering how much you like them. How much I can *trust* them. What I might do if…"

His voice trailed off. He swallowed hard.

He shifted closer until she could feel the heat rolling off him. He ran a knuckle down her cheek, tracing her jawline, then dragged it down the column of her throat until it met the neckline of her sweater. She shivered and her eyelids fluttered closed for a second.

She blinked them open, looking up at him.

"I'm selfish, Alexandra. I want you to want *me*. *Only* me."

Her breath hitched and she took a step back—shocked by his admission and the naked desire in his eyes. She didn't know how to deal with him—with his honesty.

The teasing, the jokes—she could handle those. But this intensity? The kind that gave her goosebumps? She was completely lost.

He was tall, handsome, charming—although she'd never tell him to his face—and he was jealous.

Because of *her*.

Asshole.

How was she supposed to stay mad at him? How was she supposed to make her point when all she wanted to do was close the distance between them and climb him like a tree?

"I do. Want you," she stammered.

His slow smile was sinfully seductive. She had to muster every shred of righteous indignation in her body just to keep going.

"But I'm not a parking spot, or the last can of beer, or—God—a *donut*. You can't call dibs on a *person*." She raised an eyebrow, silently asking if he understood what she was saying.

"It's a guy thing," he said with a shrug, never looking away from her.

She scoffed. "A *guy thing*? Unacceptable answer. Try again." She crossed her arms. The anger surging through her was enough to make her forget how close he was and how delicious he smelled.

"Those guys are family," he said, stepping back and shoving a hand through his hair. "We work together, drink together, eat together—hell, Sam and I *served* together. We're *brothers*, Lex."

"Okay," she said. She didn't really see what his point was.

"Men lose friends one of two ways—money or a woman. So, there's a code—"

"If the words '*bro code*' come out of your mouth, I swear to God, Connor—"

"Just listen," he cut in. "Think of it as a *pact*. Is that better? When we find a woman we want, we let our friends know she's off limits."

She glared at him, still not seeing the point. And still pissed. He had no right whatsoever to tell *anyone*— friends or not—to stay away from her. She had serious issues with any man who thought he had the right to control a woman. Period. *Full stop.*

He crossed his arms over his chest and looked up at the ceiling, clearly frustrated. That made two of them.

"It's not about *controlling* you. It's about keeping my friends. Who I also happen to work with every damn day. They're good guys. If I were bringing you in and introducing you as my *girlfriend*, it wouldn't be an issue. But when we're not there yet— if we're just *interested*—we *tell* people. To avoid having to beat the shite out of each other later on. Sometimes *that* doesn't even work."

She continued to stare, wondering how deep a hole he'd dig himself if she just let him keep talking.

"Listen, lass," he huffed, clearly exasperated. "Men are

daft—absolute eejits, really. We're very simple and *very* dense."

Alexandra pressed her lips together to keep from laughing. But she nodded—emphatically.

"We have to communicate in the most basic way possible."

She was pretty sure he was doing this on purpose now. There was a flicker of mischief in his eyes.

"I'm lucky they shaved their unibrows and put on pants for the evening," Connor added with just the slightest lift at the corner of his mouth. Alexandra choked on a laugh, disguising it with a cough.

"You met Ian," he said, motioning toward the dining room where they'd all sat not even an hour ago. "That lot still communicate with *grunts* most of the time."

"I'm going to tell them you said that," Alexandra taunted.

"Please do. They'll tell you I'm no' lyin'."

Alexandra narrowed her eyes at him, very much doubting that.

He put one hand on his hip and used the other to pinch the bridge of his nose.

"Look, how would you feel if Amanda—or Janie—went after a guy you liked? Isn't that what half of high school drama's about? '*Suzy went out with Timmy even though she's best friends with Betty and Betty likes Timmy—like* likes *him.*'"

She bit her lip, trying not to laugh at his falsetto. She couldn't quite hide her smile, though. His mouth quirked up at the corner and his eyes lit up as if sensing he was close to a victory.

"How would you feel if Janie had slipped me her number before she left?" he asked quietly, taking a step toward her.

"That's different." She shook her head. "Janie *thinks we're dating.* That'd be a total betrayal."

"What about Amanda then? She knows the story. She wouldn't be breaking any rules if she'd asked for my number."

I'd punch her stupid face.

Alexandra shrugged. "I wouldn't be thrilled with the idea," she said coolly. "But I would expect anyone interested in *me* to ignore it. I'd like to know that someone *chose* to be with me *despite* having other options."

"So you wouldn't be jealous? You wouldn't want to take her aside and tell her to back off?"

"I didn't say that." She frowned. Damn, she was losing ground.

Connor chuckled, just to rub it in.

"Listen, Braveheart." She scowled, leaning into the snark because she hated that he might be right. "The point is, you don't get to decide who I, or any other *lass*, gets to be with. It's not up to you."

"I *know* that. I'm not sayin' it's a perfect system, but it's the best thing we've got. And it's not about forcing you to do anything or… taking away your choices. It's about keeping us from killing each other. If one of them came in and swept you off your feet because he was lookin' for a quick hookup, then I'd have to break his legs. This way, they know that they had damn well *better* be serious if they're gonna get in my way. And they'd better be prepared to lose a friend in the process."

Connor was serious now, desperately trying to make her understand. And she could tell it was something he was really concerned about. She wondered if he'd lost friends that way before. She had to admit that maybe—*maybe*—he had a point.

"Okay," she muttered. "I guess I see where you're coming from."

"I hope so. I really would hate to lose them," he said. And he didn't appear to be joking this time. He looked sad. Haunted. The last of her resolve dissipated. But she still needed him to understand where *she* was coming from.

"I just…"

How was she supposed to explain this in a way he'd actually understand?

"I have issues with people taking away my choices. I need to know that… certain things are mine to choose."

Great. Now you sound like a control freak. Men love those.

"I wouldn't dream of takin' *anything* away from you, Lex. But a man's gotta do what he can to skew the odds in his favor." He gave her a small crooked smile. "Think of it as self-preservation. If that means growling at the competition then I'll growl."

"Are you saying I can expect *more* of this behavior?" she asked, appalled.

"Maybe just a wee bit. Maybe just Charles."

Her brows shot up.

"*Especially* Charles," he muttered.

"What?" She blinked, genuinely confused.

"Your *friend,* Charles. The Ken doll from the bar."

Alexandra was struck momentarily dumb. Several things occurred to her at once.

First, that Connor hadn't just been looking out for her safety—or trying to piss her off—he'd been *jealous*. The thought sent a tingle all the way down to her toes.

Second… *Ken doll?*

Her laughter was uncontrollable for a few minutes. By the time she managed to pull herself together, Connor looked positively murderous.

"Oh, God. I have to tell Charles you called him that. He'll either be flattered as hell—or you'll be on his shit list for life." She swiped at the tears running down her cheeks. "I'm going to have to film his reaction."

"Alexandra…" Connor warned. He was clenching his teeth so hard that all the muscles in his jaw stood out. It was actually kind of sexy. But she was also a little afraid he might have an aneurysm at any moment.

"Charles and I are just friends," she said.

"So you've never dated?" he asked, stepping in closer. "You've never fucked him?"

Shit.

Sensing her hesitation, Connor's body went rigid.

"Once. In law school," she admitted.

"*What?*"

"Not that it's any of your business," she snapped. "We dated—very briefly—in law school. We only had sex once—actually not *even* once. It was more like we *tried*. But it didn't do it for either of us so we broke up."

She held her breath for one tense, silent moment.

"You're still friends with an ex?" he said, stunned. Like it was the most unnatural thing he'd ever heard—like putting milk in the bowl *before* your cereal.

His eyes narrowed and his chest began to rise and fall dramatically as he took several deep, angry breaths.

"I knew I should have knocked him on his arse."

"Listen," she spat.

And just like that, she was pissed again. All goodwill and understanding evaporated in a heartbeat. She'd worked so damn hard to make peace with her past, and she sure as hell wasn't going to let anyone judge her for it.

"You don't get to be pissy about who I've slept with, who I'm friends with, or how I spend my time. You don't get an opinion *at all.* "You're not my boyfriend. And even if you were?" Her voice sharpened. "I'd still tell you to go *fuck* yourself. I'm a grown woman and I make my own choices."

She was yelling, hands curled into fists at her side. She was debating the merits of slapping him versus punching him in the gut when he kissed her.

As furious as she was, her body reacted on instinct. All the pent-up frustration—sexual and otherwise—boiled over. She kissed him back like her life depended on it, grabbing fistfuls of his shirt even though he couldn't get any closer.

He kissed her with a hunger that heated her entire body. His tongue in her mouth was insistent and relentless. He wasn't just kissing her, he was conquering her mouth. She moaned and he probed further with a growl of satisfaction. In that instant she would have done anything he asked of her just so he'd make that sound again. And again, and again, and again.

He slanted his head to deepen the kiss, and she opened wider—giving both of them better access. Her tongue slid over and around his, seeking the fullness of his lips with just the tip. When she nipped his bottom lip—a bit harder than she meant—he made that low growl again, and Alexandra felt ten feet tall and bulletproof. That and his very obvious, very large erection.

Every muscle in his body was bunched tight and she reveled in the feel of all that coiled power surrounding her. His rock-hard chest pressed against her aching breasts, solid arms wrapped tight around her, and the proof of his attraction pressed hot and insistent against her thigh while he kissed her senseless.

God, she wanted this. *So badly.* She didn't care about the macho bullshit. His explanation had made sense, sort of, and she had to admit she was a little flattered. No—if she was really honest—certain parts of her found his possessiveness hot as fuck. He'd literally claimed her as *his* and the primitive part of her brain reveled in it.

And he'd made himself vulnerable in a way that most men wouldn't. He'd been honest—not just about his feelings, but his uncertainty too. Not only was that incredibly sexy, it was also incredibly endearing.

When they finally came up for air, she looked at him, bewildered. His expression pretty much matched her own.

"Charles is gay," she blurted out.

"So is Sam. Doesn't mean I want his feckin' hands on you," Connor muttered. He frowned but she could see he was a little relieved. "Go on."

"We were friends in law school and we were both single. We got along really well, so decided we might as well try dating. He was… *safe* and comfortable for me and he was in denial about his sexuality. Neither one of us was in it for the right reasons. When we had sex—or tried to, at any rate—we both realized what a *huge* mistake it was. There was no real attraction on either side. I wasn't a man and he wasn't…"

It had all come out in a rush, but she couldn't figure out how to finish the thought. She'd never really understood what Charles lacked that made his revelation that he wasn't attracted to her such a relief. But it *had* been a relief.

They'd been close friends and she hadn't wanted that to end. If he'd been invested in the relationship, she wasn't sure how she would have managed to get out of it. Maybe she wouldn't have. Maybe she'd be married to him by now with a mini Charles running around. Something had been missing but she hadn't been able to pinpoint it then.

She had a better idea now, but she was conflicted about what it meant.

"Wasn't what?" he asked. He seemed genuinely curious.

"Hard enough?" she said. Connor sputtered out a laugh and she blushed at her inadvertent innuendo. "That's not what I meant—though that *was* an issue, for obvious reasons," she muttered. "I just mean he was so… nice?" she said lamely.

Connor had loosened his hold on her, no longer fearing she'd slap him or run away, she supposed. Instead, he held her loosely with one hand at her lower back, the other stroking her upper spine and occasionally squeezing the back of her neck. The touch of his hand was hypnotic and she found herself talking freely while he watched her with fascination.

"He makes an excellent friend for the same reason he made a terrible boyfriend—at least for me. He's a great listener, but he doesn't offer advice or present a counter argument. He believes in boundaries and personal space, but he's too afraid of overstepping to give you the push you might need. He's flexible and accommodating about most things but that means he leaves too many decisions up to me. He's… compliant. He's a peacemaker everywhere but in the courtroom. Great in a friend, not in a lover."

"He's not really engaged in the relationship," Connor said, nodding.

She looked up at him stunned. "That's exactly it. I could never quite put my finger on it before… but you're right. I mean I can guess why he wasn't particularly invested in the relationship when he probably knew from the beginning that it wasn't what he really wanted. It was just what he thought he was supposed to want."

"You need someone you can fight with," Connor said with a smirk.

"Is that why you're so difficult?" she asked, tilting her head as she considered him. He laughed, a low rumble she could feel all over her body, and kissed the tip of her nose.

"Aye. And that's why you're such a handful. You need to be challenged. You want to fight for it—and you want to know your man will fight for it, too."

Your man… is that what he is?

"I mean I obviously don't want a bully—someone who just takes what he wants and doesn't respect the word 'no,' but sometimes you need a push. Sometimes you need someone to call you on your bullshit, and sometimes you need someone to take control so you can turn your brain off for a while."

She looked up at him and blushed. She couldn't believe she'd overshared so much. She felt exposed and vulnerable. She took a step back and Connor let her go, albeit a little reluctantly.

"Speaking of fighting…" she said dryly, crossing her arms over her chest. Connor put his hands back in his pockets and sighed.

"I understand where you're coming from," he said. "Just… do me a favor, okay?"

"What's that?"

"I know you need time, and I'll do my best to let you have it. But if for some reason you're not interested in the fine male specimen standing in front of you," he said with a cocky grin. "Just… please try not to fall for one of my guys. There's only so much my lizard brain can take."

He tried to sound joking, but his eyes were earnest, and a little anxious. He really wanted her to take the chance on him. It seemed like maybe Amanda was right. Maybe he did more than like her, for whatever reason. Now she just needed to decide if it was worth the risk to trust him.

"I will do my best." She rolled her eyes. But then, wanting to reassure him, added, "If it makes you feel better, I have to admit, you are the finest male specimen of the bunch."

His answering smile was joyful—and more than a little wicked. She couldn't help but return it. Still feeling a little uneasy at how much she'd told him, and how much she seemed to lose her head in his presence, she needed some space to think.

"Well, I'm absolutely exhausted. Thank you for helping me clean up. I'd have been up half the night otherwise—and right now, I just want to crawl into bed and sleep for days." As if she'd planned it, a yawn crept up on her just then, and Connor gave her a soft smile.

"I reckon that's my cue," he said with a chuckle. She followed him to the foyer where he retrieved his coat and put it on. To her surprise—and delight—he pulled her into his arms for a soft, lingering kiss before murmuring, "Good night," and slipping out the door. She found herself sighing as she locked up and headed up to her room.

Gah! Nut up, will you? Stop crushing on him like a high schooler and figure out what to do like the intelligent adult that you are.

So she thought about it like a rational adult. She liked him. They obviously had amazing chemistry and it had been… three *years* since she'd had sex.

Jesus. Has it really been that long?

Why shouldn't she enjoy whatever this was? There was only one thing standing in her way. The same thing that had been an issue with every other guy she'd dated in the last six years. It wasn't going away, and her only options were to deal with it or become a nun.

She'd tried to make relationships work in the past. And at first, they all understood. She'd explain everything without getting into too much detail, and they'd all respected her boundaries. But eventually, they got sick of the rules—sick of all the things she couldn't bring herself to do. She couldn't really blame them, she was sick of it too.

Connor seemed like he might actually understand. He'd witnessed her epic panic attack last weekend and still seemed to be interested. That was a good sign, right?

But how long before he decided her baggage was too much to deal with just like the rest of them had? How long before he wanted something from her that she wasn't willing to give—*couldn't* give?

There was only one way to find out—and the odds of getting hurt were pretty damn high. Maybe higher than they'd ever been. She'd liked all the guys she dated, but she hadn't *loved* any of them. Still, each rejection stung, chipping away at the fractured soul she'd been trying to rebuild.

She had a feeling that Connor's rejection would mean something... more. It would cut that much deeper and take much longer to heal. Would a few good memories be worth all the pain if things didn't work out?

Of course, she figured the memories would be damn good. And nothing was certain. Maybe things would actually work out? Miracles happened everyday, or so she'd heard. And if she was going to live in celibacy for the rest of her life, she might as well have some steamy memories to keep her company.

She made up her mind then and there that she wanted to try. God help her, but she wanted to know if she had any tiny scrap of hope of finding someone who would be able to accept her as she was. Someone who would take what she could offer and think that it was enough. That *she* was enough.

Chapter Thirteen

Connor woke at five the next morning, the last bits of his dream fading and leaving him restless. He groaned, knowing sleep was out of the question. He was too unsettled. Too eager.

He'd dreamt of Alexandra all night—her smart mouth and all the things it could do. It was wreaking havoc on his restraint. The taste of her on his tongue still haunted him and the scent of her had clung to his skin for hours last night. Almonds and honey—warm and sweet, just like her.

He threw on a pair of gym shorts and spent a good hour pounding the heavy bag in his spare room, trying to burn off some of the nervous energy coursing through his body. After a five-mile run on the treadmill, he was ready for a long, hot shower—and a mountain of carbs.

He was showered and dressed by eight o'clock, but rather than eating a bowl of cereal at his kitchen counter, there was something far more tempting waiting for him. He grabbed his coat and his keys and locked the door on the way out.

An hour later he pulled up outside of Alexandra's brownstone—anticipation jangling every last nerve. He'd stopped at a bakery on the way and picked up a selection of pastries. Amanda had brought a variety to dinner last night, and Alexandra had practically drooled over them when she set them on the table.

Walking into the bakery had been a test of his self-control. The entire place had smelled like almond cookies and all he'd been able to think about had been Alexandra. As if he hadn't been thinking of her all night and most of the morning as it was. Jesus—he'd thought of little else for the past eight days. She'd worked her way into his brain and now invaded his every thought.

He climbed the steps and knocked. Music played inside—he

thought he could just barely make out her singing along. He chuckled to himself. He could just picture her face the moment she opened the door.

She'd be slightly irritated because she wasn't expecting him. She'd probably blush a bit because she was secretly pleased to see him. And hopefully she'd be remembering how they'd ended the night before.

A moment later, the door opened. Alexandra blinked at him—clearly surprised—wearing faded yoga pants and a t-shirt that read: *"Dear Monday, Nobody Likes You."*

"Nice shirt," he chuckled, staring blatantly at her chest.

Dear God. Is she not wearing a bra?

She glared at him, crossing her arms over her chest. Unfortunately for her and fortunately for him, the action had the opposite effect she was going for. It plumped her breasts up rather than covering them. Connor just grinned wider, knowing full well it would only make her angrier.

"I don't recall summoning you this morning." Alexandra said, cocking her head and giving him a once-over. Which was fine by him. The more she looked at him the better.

"I come bearing gifts," he said, holding the box out like an offering. "But, if ye dinnae want it…"

Her eyes went wide at the box he carried, then narrowed at him.

"It's from Amy's," he added, opening the box and waving it beneath her nose.

"I *love* Amy's."

"I ken," he said with a smug smile.

Alexandra laughed in surprise. She probably didn't think he'd been paying attention. Some day she would learn not to underestimate him.

Alexandra stood back, opening the door wider. "Alright. Come in."

Connor set the box on the coffee table while she locked the door.

"Coffee?" she asked, heading for the kitchen.

"Please."

He wanted to follow her, but the kitchen seemed to be a danger zone for them. Every time they were alone in the kitchen together they either fought, or kissed. Or both. He'd promised he would be patient, and he would. Even if it killed him.

And it bloody well might…

She returned from the kitchen with a cup of coffee for each of them.

He took a sip while she got comfortable on the couch. When she flipped the lid open, her eyes went wide.

She pulled out a chocolate croissant, took a bite and tipped her head back, closing her eyes and moaning.

Yeah, this was *definitely* going to kill him. He'd been fighting off an erection since the moment he woke up. Even the workout and cold shower hadn't killed it.

"These are my favorite," she said, taking another bite.

"I know," he said. She gave him a curious look, but he just smiled and shot her a wink. "Though personally, I prefer almond."

He snagged one from the box and then licked a bit of chocolate off his thumb before taking a bite. She glanced at him—and blushed.

"So, what brings you by at nine fifteen on a Saturday morning?" she asked, sipping her coffee.

"You."

He didn't see any point in beating around the bush. He liked her. He *wanted* her. And she already knew it.

"Oh," she breathed. She fiddled nervously with her cup but her expression remained otherwise unchanged.

"I wanted to see you and I thought I might be able to bribe you into keeping me company."

He took another bite of pastry, chewing slowly while she processed what he'd said. He'd noticed that about her. Sometimes it took her a minute to think something through.

But he had all the time in the world and he couldn't think of anything he'd rather do than watch the gears turn in that remarkable brain of hers. Okay—so he could think of a few things…

"What did you have in mind?" she asked.

"Pity date?" he asked with lopsided smile. "Would you want to go out and do something? With me, I mean."

She blushed again, looking down at her coffee cup. She was quiet for so long that he was convinced she was going to turn him down. But then she surprised him.

"Where would you like to go?" she asked.

"Wherever you want. Beggars can't be choosers. We could go to the movies, maybe stop for lunch. We could go to a show. Or shopping. We could take a walk in the park, go to a museum—"

At that last suggestion, her whole body perked up.

Bingo.

"Even the Met?" she asked, giving him a sidelong glance. She was still studying her coffee mug. "It's been a while since I've been."

"I reckon that settles it, then. We'll have breakfast and go to the Met. And after that…" He shrugged. "Who knows?"

He grinned. And when she smiled back, his heart skipped a beat.

They finished off the contents of the box while Alexandra told him about all of her favorite exhibits. And when he admitted that he'd never been, he thought she would die of shock. But she recovered quickly and started planning out all the things he just *had* to see.

The fact that she was so excited to share the experience with him—to show him around someplace that was special to her—filled his chest with warmth. She was so damn sweet.

He told her to take her time—no rush. But apparently, she was too excited. She dressed in a hurry, insisting they wouldn't have enough time to see everything if they didn't get there early.

When she came downstairs, she wore jeans, canvas sneakers, and a navy sweater. She carried a jacket over one arm and a tote bag printed with a very famous painting. Probably. Connor had no idea what it was called, but he assumed he was about to find out.

Her hazel eyes were glowing, looking more gold than green in the autumn morning light. Her hair was half-up in a messy little knot, with a few strands escaping to frame her face.

At the Met, she held his hand and all but dragged him through the different exhibits. She pointed out details and gave him trivia about nearly every piece. To his relief, she wasn't an art snob. She just really liked art. She knew what she liked and agreed with him that some of them were clearly shite.

Either it spoke to her or it didn't. That was it.

He'd never been into art, but he enjoyed exploring the place with her. They liked a lot of the same things, and their conversation covered a lot more than art. They talked and laughed, and before they knew it, most of the day was gone.

There were no awkward silences, no struggle to keep the conversation going. Even through lunch—and then dinner—there wasn't a single a lull. She talked about her family, her job, books, art, music.

Everything that interested her.

And she asked him questions. She seemed genuinely interested in getting to know him.

He told her about places he'd traveled in the Army, funny stories from his time in Scotland—even about Angel and some of the guys.

"So what now, *Fergus*?" she teased after he'd paid the dinner bill.

"I knew I shouldn't have told ye," he grumbled. That only made her laugh harder. He'd made it his mission to make her laugh as much as possible. So far? He was crushing it.

"If it makes you feel better, my middle name is Matilda," she said. Connor laughed and she rolled her eyes. "It was my grandmother's name."

"Aye, I'd hope so," he said. "That's just about the only reason that makes sense." She smacked his arm and he caught her hand, tucking it into his elbow as they walked.

"How about a movie?"

"Nothing I really want to see," she said.

She turned away, pretending to window shop. But even the tip of her ear was bright red. He smiled to himself but pretended not to notice.

"How about we watch something at my place?" she said.

It took him by surprise and he whipped his head around to find her smiling at him, pink cheeks and all. "I have popcorn," she said. Then, in a whisper: "And cookies."

As if you have to bribe me.

He reached over, tucking a stray lock of hair behind her ear. She bit her lip and he winked at her.

"Sold."

Alexandra was excited and so nervous she thought she might puke.

Last night she'd decided to just see where things with Connor would go. But she hadn't expected to have to put that in to practice first thing this morning. She'd been cleaning and scheming when he'd knocked on her door bearing heavenly pastries.

The day had gone better than she ever could've hoped. As far as dates went—which she assumed this was—it was the best she'd ever had. Hands down.

She'd been taken out for fancy dinners, the opera, the theater—all of which were fine. But she'd never been out with someone who was so easy to talk to. Or someone who made her laugh *half as much* as Connor had.

He'd been a good sport, letting her drag him all over the Met and listening to her ramble about all sorts of things. And he hadn't just been humoring her. He'd paid attention. Asked her questions. He was interested, not just in the art, but in what she had to say about it.

The movie suggestion had been spontaneous—completely spur of the moment. She hadn't wanted the day to end just yet.

But now she was imagining all the ways it could go wrong. And all the ways it could go so, *so* right.

Back at the townhouse, she left him with her vast array of DVDs and Blu-Rays and the remote, telling him to pick something while she made popcorn. Whatever he wanted to watch was fine with her. She wouldn't be able to pay attention, anyway.

She arranged a plate of chocolate chip cookies, wondering what he'd want to drink. Soda, beer, wine? Milk?

Oh, hell.

"What do you want to drink?" she shouted from the kitchen. "I have water, milk, soda, beer, wine…"

"Beer, please," he said—right behind her.

She squeaked, jumping about a foot. She put a hand on her chest as if it would do anything to calm her frantic heartbeat.

"Asshole," she muttered, punching him on the arm. But she was smiling, and he chuckled. God, that throaty laugh of his was so low and sexy it made her knees quake.

"Here," she said, handing him the bowl of popcorn and the plate of cookies. "Take those out. I'll grab drinks."

He obeyed, and she took a moment to enjoy the view as he retreated through the dining room. He looked as if his jeans were made just for him. He'd stripped off his jacket and now wore a plain white t-shirt that she was sure would shred to pieces if he flexed too hard. God, he was gorgeous.

She sighed as she opened a beer and poured herself a glass of white wine.

"So, what's the verdict?" she asked, handing him his beer.

"Well, it was a tough call." He smirked, sipping his beer. "You have quite an interesting selection."

"I have eclectic tastes," she said haughtily, sinking into the couch's far end. He set his beer on the coffee table and crouched in front of the shelf that housed her collection. That white t-shirt stretched tight across his broad back, and Alexandra bit her lip—suddenly feeling just a little too warm.

"I mean, I don't even know what some of these are." He pulled out a box set and Alexandra panicked.

Oh, crap.

"What's this one?" He held up the boxset, bemused.

"Um, well… it's a TV series I used to watch," she said, gulping a mouthful of wine. He stood up, holding the box and turning it slowly to look at each side.

"Why is she blue? And why does this guy have tentacles on his face?" he asked, grinning—clearly enjoying her discomfort. She bolted out of her seat and grabbed the boxset out of his hand.

"They're not tentacles," she muttered, blushing.

Lord, take me now.

"They're aliens, okay? It's a series about an astronaut who gets sucked through a wormhole and joins up with a ragtag group of aliens while trying to find his way home." She put the box back in its place on the shelf.

Connor tried to suppress a laugh but failed.

"I know, I know. I'm a nerd. Just get it out now," she said, rolling her eyes. To her shock and irritation, he *did* laugh. And laugh, and laugh, and laugh some more. She was sure she looked as red as a beet.

"Well. This was fun," she said, clapping her hands together and reaching for the plate of cookies to take it back into the kitchen. He came up behind her, wrapping his arms around her, pinning her arms to her sides.

"I'm sorry, lass," he said, still laughing. "I think it's adorable. And… if it'll make you feel better…" He took a deep breath and let it out slowly as if psyching himself up to share some deep, dark secret. "I own every season of *Doctor Who* on DVD."

She went still and he loosened his grip until she could turn around and look at him.

"Woooow," she said, eyes wide. "And you had the nerve to laugh at *me*."

"I wasn't laughing *at* you…" he said. She pulled her head back and raised one eyebrow.

"Okay, I was. But the same way you laugh at… babies. Or puppies. You're just… so damn adorable."

She narrowed her eyes at him, looking for any hint he was mocking her.

"Okay, fine," she said, rolling her eyes.

"Am I forgiven?" he asked. When he was smiling like that it was *really* hard to stay mad at him.

"*This* time," she warned. "So what are we watching?"

He crouched down, picked a movie, and slid it into the Blu-Ray player without saying a word. She gave him a curious look and he rubbed the back of his neck. His cheeks turned a little pink.

And it made her want to launch herself at him.

She hit play and recognized it almost instantly—*The Philadelphia Story*, one of her all-time favorites. She'd spent a lot of time watching TCM while the other kids her age were watching cartoons. Her mother used to joke she'd been born in the wrong decade—and honestly, Alexandra kind of agreed. She'd always wanted to be Katherine Hepburn when she grew up.

"Interesting choice," she said with a smirk. She loved it, but she couldn't resist teasing him after the way he'd laughed at her earlier. "Does this mean there's a warm, gooey center underneath all those muscles?"

He gave her a slow smile that made her toes curl.

"Wouldn't you like to know."

They watched the movie, ate popcorn and cookies, and laughed. After the popcorn was gone, Connor draped an arm across the back of the couch and occasionally stroked the back of her neck with the pad of his thumb. It was enough to make her shiver.

Every. Damn. Time.

It was driving her so crazy she couldn't focus on anything else. Her whole world had narrowed to the feel of his thumb on her skin. Needing… more, she shifted closer, until their thighs touched and her arm rested against his side. He was warm and the smell of his cologne and the man underneath made her head spin.

His arm tightened around her and his thumb now stroked her shoulder in lazy circles. She tilted her head and rested it lightly against his chest. He tensed a little, but he squeezed her shoulder, tugging her closer.

Encouraged, she rested her hand—light, unsure—on his chest. The muscles shifted beneath her touch, and her fingers ached to slip under his shirt, to trace the lines of him. Then—God help her—she wanted to follow those trails with her tongue.

His heart thudded against her palm, quick and hard, and his breathing was just a little too fast. The rush of satisfaction sank straight to her bones. Feeling daring and needing to touch him—taste him—she tilted her head back and placed a soft kiss to his jaw. The stubble tickled her lips.

When she opened her eyes, Alexandra saw him looking down at her, eyes so dark they were nearly black.

"You're missing the movie," she whispered. She raised a slightly trembling hand to his chin and coaxed his gaze back to the screen. He obeyed, confused, and she nuzzled his neck, inhaling the woodsy masculine scent of him. She kissed her way up his jaw and—in a moment of daring, gently nipped his earlobe. He hissed and jerked slightly, but didn't move away.

She continued from his ear down his neck, keeping her kisses soft, teasing. The angle was awkward, and instinctively, she shifted—searching for something closer, something more. She knelt up and turned, straddling Connor's lap. He gave her a startled, hungry look and his arms wrapped around her as she resumed her kisses.

When she reached his shoulder and the collar of his shirt, she began moving sideways, kissing along the base of his throat and then up the other side. His breathing was heavy now, chest heaving beneath her hands.

She could feel the hard length of his erection pressed into her thigh and knew that he wanted her as much as she wanted him. She lifted her head and looked into his beautiful face—only to find him staring back, in wide-eyed awe, as if she were made of starlight.

She kept her eyes on his as she leaned slowly forward and pressed her lips to his. He'd been so sweet, and so understanding, letting her set the pace, telling her he would wait until she was sure. She wanted him to know that she wanted this. That she was choosing this—choosing *him*.

She closed her eyes and fell into the kiss, lingering on each of his lips—sucking, nipping, then soothing with the soft flick of her tongue. He let her lead, matching her slow, sensual rhythm. He opened for her and she tasted popcorn and chocolate and Connor. Salty and sweet and so, *so* sinfully good.

His grip shifted and tightened. Every muscle in his impressive arms and chest seemed to tense, his body was practically quivering with the strain of holding himself back.

She wanted this. She wanted *him*. She didn't want him to hold back. Alexandra pulled away, keeping her focus on his face and those eyes that seemed to devour her. She reached for the hem of her sweater—but his hand closed over hers, stopping her.

She blinked, confused. His mouth crashed down on hers and one of his hands cupped the back of her head. He tugged the tie from her hair, then fisted his hand in the fall of it, kissing her breathless. He tilted her head to deepen the kiss and she was surrounded by him. His hands, his mouth, his tongue, the smell of his skin— he blanketed her senses until there was nothing but the warmth and feel of him.

"Connor," she murmured when he pulled away to take a breath.

"Be sure, Lex," he said, voice rough, chest rising and falling like he was barely holding himself together. "Be sure. I don't do one offs. I don't do casual. This happens, and you're *mine*."

"Yours?" she breathed. It made her heart race, but she didn't know what that meant to him.

"Mine," he growled. "Your joy. Your pain. Your fear. I'll carry every damn piece of it. I told you I was selfish. I want to be your fuckin' world, Lex. I want your sun to rise and set with me. I want you to think I hung the moon just for you. Because you? You're my whole universe."

Alexandra's breath left her in a rush and she couldn't find the words to answer. That sounded serious, more serious than she'd planned on from the teasing, playful Connor she'd met just a week ago. Wasn't this too fast? What if he meant every word right now—but didn't, later? He didn't know what he was getting into, how could he say all of that and mean it?

"Connor…" she whispered. His eyes softened, already sensing her anxiety.

He brushed a strand of hair from her face and kissed her—soft, slow, reassuring. "I ken, sweetheart. It's a lot to take in. It's okay if you need more time."

"There are things… I can't do." Her voice broke on the last word, and to her shame, so did she.

He stroked her hair and pressed her to his chest, cradling her in his warm strong arms. That spark of hope in her chest glowed a little brighter.

She felt safe.

"I would never ask anything from you that you're not willing to give," he said quietly. "And whatever you choose to give me would be a gift. And I'll treasure it. *Always*."

God, she could so easily fall for him.

Alexandra pushed back from his chest to look him in the face.

"I'm sure," she said, surprised by the strength in her own voice.

The smile he gave her in reply was filled with such joy that her heart melted, then and there. He kissed her, a series of sweet gentle presses of his lips to her.

"We'll talk about all this later," he murmured between kisses. "Tonight, you tell me what you need."

He began trailing kisses down her throat, occasionally nipping and sucking, as his hands ran up and down her back. Alexandra let her head fall back, closing her eyes as he made her feel valued and cherished and safe.

"Tell me what you want, love," he whispered, his breath hot on her neck. "Let me spoil you."

"Just like this," she said, running her hands through his hair and urging him closer.

Connor had a name, now he wanted blood. The man who hurt her? He would suffer.

But that would have to wait. Right now, he needed to show her how precious she was—how good she deserved to have it. He'd meant it—whatever she gave him, it would be a gift.

Someone had taken that gift and crushed it under their boot. He wouldn't have blamed her if she'd closed herself off completely. The fact that she was here—offering him *anything at all*—humbled him.

Her body, her pleasure—even for one night—was sacred. But it wouldn't be just her body. And it sure as hell wouldn't be just one night.

Mine.

He pulled her closer and then let his hands drift to the hem of her sweater. He brushed his thumbs across the bare skin beneath her sweater and saw her tremble. He slid the sweater up and over her head and tossed it aside.

Connor spread his hand across her belly, reverent. Her skin was warm, impossibly soft beneath his rough palm. She was breathtaking. She wore a lacy bra in a soft blush color that offered a mere hint of her nipples straining beneath the fabric. He skimmed his hands up her sides and grazed the tips of her breasts with his thumbs until she was moaning.

"Beautiful," he breathed, trailing open-mouthed kisses across one breast, then the other. He undid the clasp and her bra slid down her arms, landing on the floor.

They were perfect. Just more than a handful, soft and pale, with rose-pink peaks that begged for his mouth.

He bent down and took one into his mouth, then the other, rolling his tongue slowly over each tight bud. Alexandra moaned, her fingers threading through his hair as she clung to him, urging him on. He grazed her with his teeth and she gasped. He soothed the sting with his tongue, then gave the other the same slow, teasing care.

She was writhing on his lap and his already aching cock twitched with each movement. He growled against her skin, delivered one last teasing bite, then stood—lifting her effortlessly with him.

He set her down slowly, savoring the slide of her body against his. Then he reached for her waistband, tracing the edge with a single finger. He paused, searching her face—making sure she was still with him.

She was breathless, flushed, and so unbelievably sexy that she took his breath away. She realized he was waiting, and reached up to pull him into a swift, hungry kiss. He had to restrain himself from tugging her back into his arms when she stepped back.

She scooted her jeans down and underwear down, and he held out a hand to steady her as she stepped out of them. He took a moment to simply look at her.

She was glorious.

And she was his.

He turned her around and she lowered herself to the couch. Keeping his gaze fixed on her, he dragged his shirt over his head and let it fall to the floor. He toed off his boots and unbuttoned his jeans to relieve some of the pressure.

She took him in, eyes lingering on the hard length straining against his jeans, and licked her lips. All sorts of images involving her mouth came to mind, but he shoved them away. This was about her—her wants, her needs.

He knelt on the floor in front of her and ran his hands up her calves, over her knees and thighs. She was fit, but soft in all the right places.

Generous hips, smooth waist, full breasts. *Heaven.*

He leaned in to nuzzle the underside of her breast, his hands roaming her legs, her arms, her stomach. He lost himself in the feel of her—in the smell of her honey and almond skin mixing with the scent of her arousal. The soft pleading moans she made as she ran her hands through his hair.

With his hands on her thighs, he coaxed them apart. She didn't hesitate, but her blush deepened and her breath hitched. The sight of her—bare save for a strip of close cut curls—made his mouth water. Soft. Flushed. Trembling—all for him.

Leaning forward, he kissed her thigh, inhaling the scent of her. He used his thumb to spread her slick heat up and around that tight bundle of nerves, making light circles until she was moaning.

Tugging her forward, he slid her legs up onto his shoulders and gripped her thighs, anchoring her to him. He groaned at the first teasing taste and every kiss, every stroke of his tongue only made him crave more. What started as slow, deliberate worship turned greedy—*hungry.*

"Connor…" It was a whispered plea. And the way she said his name tested every shred of his self-control.

He looked up at her, watching her face as he worked his middle finger inside her, starting shallow and going deeper with each slow thrust. She watched him, mouth open, eyes hooded.

She tangled her fingers in his hair, each desperate tug urging him on. He closed his mouth around her and focused his efforts—sucking gently, grazing her with his teeth. He noted every gasp, every moan, every time her fingers tightening his hair—learning what she liked.

After a few minutes she was moving her hips against his mouth. He added a second finger and curled them forward. She gasped. Her back arched, eyes fluttered closed.

"Please, Connor—" Her voice broke on a moan. He growled against her, his restraint snapping. He devoured her—teeth, lips and tongue—using everything he'd learned to send her over the edge.

Her whole body tensed. She inhaled sharply, breaking apart with nothing more than a whimper. He felt the rush of warmth as she pulsed around his fingers.

He slowed, but didn't stop until the aftershocks had stopped. .

She hummed, satisfied and boneless, as he kissed the inside of both of her thigh. Flushed and dazed, her lips were swollen, her hair wild.

He'd never seen a more beautiful sight. It made his chest ache.

He wiped his face with is discarded t-shirt before pulling her into his arms.

He kissed her, slow at first—a reverent benediction—then deeper, until they were both breathless again. She looked at him, eyes hazy, a dreamy smile spreading across her face.

And just like that, he was gone.

Alexandra had never come like that before. Not even on her own. But instead of feeling sated, she was restless, aching—like that had only been the prelude.

Connor kissed her again—messy, desperate, all teeth and tongue. No seduction, just hunger. When they finally broke apart, gasping, the need to have him—feel him—shoved everything else aside.

She dropped to her knees, hands unsteady with anticipation, and worked open his jeans. He hissed through his teeth when she slid her hand inside and stroked him through the soft cotton of his briefs.

She eased his jeans and briefs down his hips, revealing him inch by inch. Thick and hard—flushed tip already leaking. Her fingers twitched, aching to touch. Mouth watering to taste.

He was gorgeous. And hers.

She licked her lips, looking up at him from under her lashes. The look he gave her—hot, possessive, reverent—set her skin on fire and stole her breath.

The ache between her legs sharpened, but she took her time. Wrapping her hand around him—the weight, the heat—she stroked slowly from base to tip. He groaned, low and ragged, hips flexing toward her touch.

She felt powerful. Wanted. Worshipped.

She kissed the tip, soft as a whisper, and his whole body went tense.

She ran her tongue up his length, adding a gentle flick of her tongue beneath the head. He grunted. She did it again—and he groaned.

Taking the tip in her mouth she gently—almost teasingly—swirled her tongue around it. His hands clenched at his sides and she felt a surge of pride.

She'd never particular cared for this sort of thing—never understood why some women claimed to enjoy it. But with Connor? She craved every part of him. And she wanted him as desperate for her as she was for him.

Connor's hands slid into her hair, pushing it back from her face and holding it there—his grip firm but not painful. He didn't try to guide her—he just held on.

He swore under his breath as she took him deep. She could only take so much, but when she felt him at the back of her throat, she moaned around him. Connor shuddered in response.

She set a slow rhythm with her mouth and hands—and occasionally the barest hint of teeth—until the muscles in his thighs were tense with restraint.

"So fucking good," he growled. Then, to her surprise, he backed away. "Not yet," he explained, pulling her to her feet. He kissed her, not caring where her mouth had just been.

When they separated, he pressed his forehead to hers, hands flexing on her hips, and swore softly.

Her heart stopped. "What is it?"

He ran his hands up and down her arms—soothing her.

"I didn't expect this," he said, his tone apologetic. "I don't have a condom."

Alexandra felt her face heat as all the blood that had drained out of it a moment ago quickly returned.

"Um, there's some in my nightstand," she said quietly, quickly adding, "Janie gave them to me last night. She thought we might need them and that I wouldn't think to buy them."

She covered her face with her hands, thoroughly mortified.

Connor chuckled and kissed her temple. "God bless Janie. Be right back."

A few moments later, Connor strolled back into the living room a grin on his face. He pulled his hands out from behind his back and held up two boxes of condoms.

"She gave you options?"

"What? No! There was only one—" Alexandra squeezed her eyes shut and covered her face again.

Apparently Amanda had the same idea. That would explain what they'd been laughing about last night while she was getting ready.

"Let's see… we have *XL Bareskin or… XXL Raw*."

"I'm going to murder both off them."

"Wow. Hundred pack. Generous."

"Oh, God! Stop!"

She felt the warmth of his body before his arms wrapped around her waist from behind.

"There's nothing to be embarrassed about, love." He kissed the back of her neck and she shivered. "In fact, we should send them a thank you note. Maybe a muffin basket?"

Alexandra let out a surprised laugh. Conor's hands found her hips, running up her sides. He trailed kisses across her shoulders and she forgot why she'd been upset. He swept her hair to one side, kissing her neck.

She turned in his arms and he kissed her, slowly, coaxing her to open for him. When she did, he deepened the kiss until she melted against him.

"What do you need?" he asked. His mouth found the pulse point under her ear and his teeth scraped against her skin.

He palmed her breast, pinching her nipple gently—rolling it between his fingers. Just like that, her own name, his question, the entire English language—gone.

"Alexandra…" he growled, his voice a deep rumble she felt in her bones—in her *soul*.

He pinched harder and she gasped.

"Couch. You. Sit."

She felt him smile against her neck, no doubt pleased that he'd shorted out the speech center of her brain, reducing her to monosyllables.

"As you wish," he whispered, his breath hot on the shell of her ear. He kissed her shoulder softly before he turned and sat.

She took a moment to just admire him.

He was stunning. And it wasn't just the thick, dark hair, the piercing blue eyes and the smile that promised sin. Every part of him looked like it had been sculpted in muscle—chest, arms, stomach. Firm thighs. Strong hands. That delicious V of muscle at his hips that she wanted to memorize with her tongue.

He retrieved a small foil packet from one of the boxes—she didn't notice which one—and as she looked on, he opened it with his teeth while he stroked himself with his free hand. The motion was hypnotic and she found herself suddenly curious what it would be like to just… *watch him.*

He stopped, smirking like he could read her mind. Her face flushed but she didn't look away. He kept his eyes on her as he rolled the condom on and the way he looked at her banished any remaining scrap of embarrassment.

He held a hand out and she took it.

She knelt on the couch, straddling his lap. Her legs were already trembling and she steadied herself with her hands on his shoulders.

One of his hands rested on her hip, his thumb sweeping across her skin. The other slipped between them, and he slid two fingers inside her, pumping slowly.

"You ready for me?" His voice was like gravel—the sound raising goosebumps on her skin.

She nodded, biting her lip.

His free hand cradled the back her neck, tugging her down until his mouth ghosted over hers.

"I need to hear you. Are you ready for me, love?"

He pushed into her again and there was a stretch that hadn't been there before. She gasped, her fingers digging into his shoulders.

"I need the words, Lex," he said through teeth clenched.

"God, *yes*," she breathed.

As soon as the words left her mouth, Connor was there, taking her mouth in a savage kiss—a kiss so deep her jaw ached by the time they came up for air.

He positioned himself under her and she sank down, slow and steady, until her body gave way and he slid in the barest of inches.

He groaned, hands tightening on her hips.

She whimpered.

She sounded needy—*desperate*. She didn't care. She *was* desperate.

Once her body had adjusted, she sank lower, taking him in one inch at a time. She moaned at the fullness—the stretch—when she'd finally accepted all of him.

Connor groaned, his hips jerking upward, driving deeper. The muscles in his jaw ticked as he got himself under control.

"You alright, love," he asked, chest heaving with the effort of holding back. He put a hand on her face, brushing her cheek with his thumb.

Her heart squeezed.

How can he be so…

"Perfect," she whispered.

She kissed him slowly and sweetly. He cradled her face in his hands, his eyes on hers as he started to move—slow, shallow thrusts at first, making sure it wasn't too much.

Soon the stretch was a sweet ache—one that only Connor could soothe. She began to move on instinct—hips rising and falling in counterpoint. His strokes deepened but remained slow. Controlled.

He was holding back. For her.

But she didn't want him to hold back. She didn't want him to be careful. She wanted all of him.

She leaned forward, kissing his throat and scraping her teeth along his jaw. She bit his earlobe, pulling it into her mouth for a moment before she pressed her mouth to his ear, lips brushing against his skin as she spoke.

"I want it all, Connor. Give it to me. Please."

"Fuck," he groaned, his hands gripping her hard. His hips moved faster—the motion sharper.

"Yes," she gasped, increasing her pace to match his.

Soon they were panting and sweating—mouths clashing, bodies colliding.

"So perfect," he rasped, grinding his hips up into her as he pulled her down onto him. She gasped and circled her hips, pulling a groan from deep in his chest.

She rode him harder, everything inside her tightening like a spring.

Connor slipped a hand between them, finding that perfect spot as if he had a map of her body. The perfect pressure, exactly where she needed it—he made her body sing for him.

"Come on, Lex," he growled. "Come for me, love."

That was all it took.

Her climax washed over her—sudden and intense—and she screamed his name. His rhythm faltered, but never stopped as she shuddered and tightened around him, over and over again.

He thrust into her twice more before pulling her down hard on his cock and grinding up into her. His head fell back and he came with her name on his lips.

She tightened her muscles around him, and his whole body jerked upward.

"*Fuck!* Lex—" he groaned, shuddering one final time.

Alexandra collapsed onto his chest and he wrapped his arms around her, holding her tightly. They were still joined and she had no desire to move. She felt safe and warm and treasured, especially when Connor kissed the top of her head and ran his fingers through her hair.

"Mmm."

She felt weightless—like Connor's arms were the only thing tethering her to earth.

No panic. No fear. Just peace.

"You okay?" he asked, his hand drifting idly up and down her back.

"Mmm."

"You sure?"

"Uh-huh."

"Did I melt your brain?" he chuckled.

"Mm-hmm." She loved the sound of his voice, the way it rumbled through his chest and into her bones.

"Come on. To bed wi' ya," he drawled, lifting her off of him. She whimpered but he shushed her, lifting her as if she weighed nothing and tucking her head against his shoulder.

Alexandra sighed as he carried her upstairs, tucking her into bed.

Connor took care of the necessary clean up and then climbed into bed behind her, pulling the covers up around them.

"Sleep now," he whispered into her hair. He kissed her shoulder and wrapped an arm tightly around her middle, holding her close to his chest.

Her eyes drifted closed and she fell asleep, warm in Connor's arms, listening to the sound of his even breathing and marveling at how safe she felt.

Chapter Fourteen

"Mornin'."

"Good morning." Alexandra smiled.

Connor was unfairly handsome for so early in the morning. His kisses trailing along her shoulder and neck already had her tingling. His hands skimmed her body almost idly, as if he just couldn't stop touching her. A continuous caress—down her arm, over her hip, up her back.

His touch made her shiver—but it wasn't purely sexual. It was tender and almost reverent. She felt… worshipped. He continued placing small kisses along her shoulder and her neck. Back and forth in a hypnotic rhythm.

He chuckled against her neck and she opened eyes she didn't recall closing. She cleared her throat as a blush crept over her face.

"Did you sleep well?" she asked, cringing even as she said it.

Brilliant.

He laughed louder and she buried her face in the pillow to hide her awkwardness. It had been so long since she'd had to deal with the morning after and even then, there usually wasn't much to be embarrassed about.

They were guys she'd dated for a while—decent sex, lights off. They *weren't* gorgeous gods of sex whom she'd fucked on her couch with all the lights on after knowing them for a week.

She assumed this was why people who had casual sex didn't spend the night. No awkward mornings for them.

This isn't casual sex… is it?

What Connor had said the night before made it seem relatively serious, right? They were at least exclusive. She thought.

Fuck!

"Don't," Connor said, firm and low. She risked a glance up and his face was serious.

"What?" she asked, trying to seem casual.

"You're spiralin', love. Don't." He kissed her on the forehead and hugged her tighter. He rolled and pulled her with him until she was lying on his chest. She shifted, straddling his hips, and was surprised to find him hard. Her heart raced, breath catching. He gave her a devilish grin.

"Sorry."

"I'm not sure I believe you." She laughed even though she was still blushing.

"God, your blush does me in," he growled, pulling her down and nipping at the skin beneath her ear.

"Really?" she squeaked. He flexed his hips to prove his point.

"Really." He sighed, releasing her and settling back. "But there are a few things we need to settle after last night." Alexandra gulped.

This is where it all goes to shit.

"Relax," he said, running his hand up and down her back, soothing her. She forced herself to relax, bracing for the worst.

"First, do you remember what I said to you last night?"

"Yes," she said cautiously.

"Good." He smiled. "I meant every word. You need anything, you just tell me."

She blinked at him. She didn't know where to start. "So, this means we're..."

"Together." He frowned. "Dating. Exclusive. Whatever word works for you."

"What would you call it?" she asked.

He laughed and she couldn't help but smile.

"You're mine. I'm yours." He grinned. "That's what matters. Everything else is semantics," he added with a shrug. Relieved and more than a little thrilled, she smiled.

"So, was this is your plan? 'Fake it 'til you make it?'" He gave her a quizzical look. "You were pretending to be my boyfriend and now you actually are."

He thought about it for a second and then gave her a wry smile.

"I did at that." He leaned up and kissed her, a quick smooch thankfully since she was sure she had terrible morning breath. "Now, second thing," he continued. "I know you're not keen on me making decisions unilaterally—"

Alexandra raised an eyebrow. He rolled his eyes at her but smiled. "That means without consulting you."

"I know what the word means, douchebag." Alexandra smacked his arm.

"Right, Ms. Fancy Law Degree. Anyway—" he continued. "I wanted to let you know that I made a decision, strictly in a professional capacity, that I would have made in any situation like yours."

He was more serious now. She was worried at his change of tone, but she nodded.

"Your security system's getting installed tomorrow."

"What?"

"Your place isn't secure. Ground floor windows with no alarms, just a deadbolt on each door. Any client would be getting one. First thing."

She studied his face, searching for any sign this was more than just standard procedure.

"And for the record, I called our guys and made the appointment last Friday afternoon, before you got out of work. It's not personal."

"Okay," she sighed. "Thanks for telling me."

"Besides, the firm's paying for it. Why not?" He winked and gave her a wicked grin.

She laughed despite herself and, before she knew it, Connor was kissing her senseless. Morning breath completely forgotten, she wrapped her arms around his neck and returned his kiss with everything she had. He groaned and cupped her bottom, stroking and kneading as his erection grew beneath her.

"Shower," he groaned, sitting up. She giggled as he chased her into the bathroom.

What are you a fucking schoolgirl?

Connor took his time helping Alexandra dry off. He hadn't suggested the shower just to keep her naked a while longer, but that didn't mean he'd pass up a perfectly good opportunity to appreciate the view.

He should be more than satisfied after last night but he couldn't seem to get enough of her. She was beautiful.

Jesus, I'm mad for her.

He kept his focus on the task at hand, and when he'd dried every inch of her skin, he wrapped the large towel around her and shooed her out of the bathroom before she noticed that he was hard. Again. At this rate, she was going to think he had a medical condition.

He toweled off briskly, avoiding his… *situation* and wrapped the towel around his hips. He ran his hand through his hair a few times, trying to arrange it into some semblance of a style, but as usual, it was hopeless.

Alexandra was frowning into her dresser drawer when he exited the bathroom.

"So what's on the agenda today?" he asked.

"Apparently, laundry," she said with a sarcastic smile. She closed one drawer, and opened another, pulling out a pair of sweatpants—the pair he'd bought her at the gym last week. She dropped the towel and slipped on the sweatpants. No underwear. And he just stood there, gawking like a teenage boy with a stolen Playboy.

He stepped toward her, helpless against all that petal soft skin and the knowledge that only a thin piece of fabric separated him from heaven. She turned and her eyes widened as she registered the hungry look on his face. And saw what his towel was failing to hide.

"Connor." Her voice was low, unreadable. He couldn't tell if she was shocked, appalled or impressed that he seemed to be preparing to ravage her again so soon. Her eyes said impressed, and maybe even eager.

"No one to blame but yerself, love," he said, grinning like the devil.

He dropped the towel and her eyes went wide. Her tongue darted out and ran across her upper lip, still swollen from their kisses in the shower. He groaned and took his shaft in hand as he advanced toward her.

Her cheeks flushed, and she bit her lip—until the phone rang.

Who the fuck has a fucking landline?

It took her a second, but she tore her eyes away and checked the caller ID on the portable phone on her dresser. She frowned, but picked it up. "I have to take this. Sorry," she muttered as she answered the call.

"Not as sorry as I am," Connor mumbled under his breath as he picked up the towel and headed downstairs to retrieve his clothes.

He gathered his clothes from the living room floor and dressed—in everything but the boxer briefs. He ventured into the kitchen and started a pot of coffee.

When it was done, he grabbed two mugs, smiling as he filled her favorite mug and added an ungodly amount of cream and sugar, just the way she liked it.

Since Alexandra still seemed to be occupied, he carried the mugs upstairs and found her laying on the bed, now also wearing a t-shirt, talking on the phone. He couldn't help but grin when he noticed that she lay on her stomach, legs bent at the knee and crossed at the ankle, swaying back and forth in the air.

Alexandra was a competent, intelligent, professional woman—who had no idea what to wear to a club, got shy at the worst times, and still gabbed on the phone like a teenager.

He stepped around the bed and into her field of vision, setting the coffee on her dresser. He leaned against it and took a sip from his cup. She flashed him a sweet smile when she noticed him. It widened when she noticed the cup he inched forward with a finger.

"I still can't believe it," she said into the phone. "I know, but I still think of you as the topless table dancer of Sigma Pi." Alexandra laughed at something she heard and Connor cocked an eyebrow. "Oh, I'm going to tell that story, but maybe not at the wedding. Maybe at the Hen Night." Alexandra rolled her eyes. She listened a moment and laughed again.

Connor thought he could listen to her laugh forever. It was the sweetest sound he'd ever heard.

"Okay, Madonna," she sighed. "I have to go. I'm very busy and important you know. Love you. See you next week."

Alexandra ended the call and chuckled to herself. She sat up and smiled at him, clearly having enjoyed her conversation.

"Sorry. That was Megan. She's one of my best friends. We went to college together. She's getting married in a little over a week in London."

"Ah." Connor nodded. "That explains a lot."

"Her fiancé is a great guy. He's in finance. Very British and sophisticated… unless he's had a few pints."

Before he realized it, Connor had set down his coffee and knelt on the bed in front of her. He braced his hands on the bed, one arm on each side of her legs, and leaned forward, taking her mouth in a slow, possessive kiss. He took his time exploring and tasting until she kissed him back, melting under his mouth.

He pressed her back into the bed, never breaking the kiss. Resting on one forearm, he cradled the back of her head with his free hand, his fingers sifting through the strands of her hair. Suddenly she broke the kiss, panting. She pushed at his chest.

"Let me up, Connor."

"What if I don't want to?" He kissed the arch of her neck.

"Connor," she pleaded. But there was no need in her voice—only fear.

Fuck!

Connor scrambled back and sat up, moving off to the side. Alexandra sat up quickly, tugging her knees to her chest. Her face had gone pale, and Connor's lungs seized—his heart cracking wide open.

"God, Lex—I'm sorry." He didn't touch her; afraid he'd make it worse. "You're okay, love. You're safe."

"Y-yes. I'm okay," she whispered, squeezing her eyes shut too late to prevent a single tear from tracking down her cheek.

"Jesus, love." He touched her shoulder, tentative. When she didn't flinch, he eased beside her and gently gathered her into his lap. He made sure to keep his arms loose. He held his breath—waiting to see if she would push him away. After a few tense moments, she leaned her head against his shoulder and wrapped her arms around his neck. He exhaled slowly, winding his arms around her and holding her tight to his chest.

Alexandra buried her face in his neck and took several deep breaths. And he simply held her, rocking gently as she collected herself. After a few minutes, she straightened enough to wipe her face and look up at him.

"I'm sorry," she said.

"No reason to be sorry," he said gently. "I get it, remember?"

She nodded weakly and lowered her eyes. With one hand on the back of her head, fingers woven into her hair, he pressed a kiss to her temple. He tucked her head back against his chest, and for a while, neither of them moved.

"Thank you," she said, moving off of his lap. He let her go—reluctantly—but he didn't let her go far.

"Wait here." He climbed off the bed, picked up her coffee, in her favorite mug, and handed it to her. Then he disappeared into the bathroom, rummaging through drawers until he found what he was looking for. She gave him a curious look, but he just smiled and sat on the bed, leaning back against the headboard.

"Come here."

He reached for her cup, and she handed it to him so he could set it on the nightstand. She crawled toward him—slowly. Looking a little wary.

"Sit here and I'll brush your hair," he explained, holding up the brush he'd retrieved from her bathroom.

"You want to brush my hair?" she asked slightly amused and a little incredulous.

"Yup."

She shrugged and sat between his outstretched legs. Once she was settled, he gave her back the mug and she took an appreciative sip.

"Did I get it right?"

"Perfect." She turned, her smile so soft it knocked the air from his lungs. "Thank you."

He was pleased—and relieved—that she liked it.

Connor threaded his fingers through her damp hair, toying with the strands, admiring the way they dried in loose waves.

"When Mom was workin' and it was just us, I had to learn how to do Angel's hair. She could bathe herself, thank God, but that mass of tangles? Thick as rope, long as sin. Took me hours sometimes." He picked up the brush and began working gently through her hair. "And she was such a brat. If I didn't do it, she'd let it snarl into a rat's nest."

Connor chuckled at the memory and Alexandra laughed with him.

"I used to have to make up crazy stories to get her to sit still. Then, when she got older, for some reason, I kept doing it. I even learned to braid it, for Christ's sake." His cheeks warmed when she turned to gape at him. He gently turned her head forward and went back to work.

"Instead of telling her stories, she'd tell me all about her day—school, boys, drama. If anything was bothering her, I'd listen, brush her hair, and by the time I was done, she'd feel better."

Connor hoped she would see it for the invitation it was. He wanted her to open up—to trust him with her scars. He wanted to understand her. *All of her.*

But it needed to be on her terms—in her own time.

After several minutes of quiet, Connor's hand stilled for a moment when she finally spoke.

"When I was in college I had a boyfriend," she said quietly.

Immediately his heart began to race. He kept his strokes smooth and gentle. He didn't want to interrupt her now that she'd started talking.

"Lucas." She spat the name like vinegar. Connor's blood boiled.

He'd never hated being right more than at that moment.

He took a slow breath and pushed the rage down deep. Right now, she needed all of him—his focus, his calm. She needed him *there*, anchoring her so she didn't get lost in the dark.

He'd have plenty of time to hunt down that piece of shit and feed him his own dick once he'd taken care of his girl.

"We started dating our senior year. I'd graduated early from high school, took extra courses—finished college in three years. I was twenty. He was twenty-two." She paused, lost in thought for a moment.

Connor kept brushing—gentle, steady—grounding her with each stroke.

"I looked up to him. Thought he was so mature." She scoffed. "God, I was such an idiot. He was charming. At first," she mumbled, almost as if she was talking to herself. She shook her head as if she couldn't believe she'd fallen for his lies. Connor wanted to tell her she wasn't an idiot—then or now. He was just a lying sack of shit. And good at it.

"We dated for a couple of months before we—" Her throat caught on a sound somewhere between a sob and a gag. He rubbed her back, making large soothing circles—reminding her he was there and she was safe. He knew what it was like when your memories turned on you, dragging you back to a hell you once barely escaped.

He wouldn't let that happen. Not to her.

She took a deep breath, letting it out slowly through her nose.

"We dated for a couple months before we slept together," she finally said, her body going rigid under his hands. She held her breath for a second—waiting. But for what?

Did she think he was going to freak out?

Had other people freaked out?

Who the fuck would—

Connor shoved the thought aside, focused on staying calm—his breath, his touch. All of it steady. The most important thing was showing her that nothing she could say was going to change how he saw her.

She'd been so strong and she was so brave. He had to be rock solid. If he couldn't be that for her, he didn't deserve to be there.

She relaxed a fraction and her breathing returned to normal.

"I was a virgin. I thought it was sweet that he didn't pressure me."

Connor's blood ran cold. That absolute waste of fucking space had been her first—had tainted a moment meant to be unforgettable?

As more of the pieces fell into place the picture that was taking shape made him feel sick. It explained so much—the bar, why she didn't date, her reaction that morning.

And he'd played a part. Intentional or not, his words had triggered her. He'd fucked up. And even if she forgave him, he'd never forgive himself.

After he sealed that fucker in a barrel and dropped him in the Hudson River, he should just jump in after him.

But his feelings didn't matter. She was all that mattered right now.

She paused, sipping her coffee. Connor resumed brushing her hair—quiet, steady, waiting.

"Things were... okay at first," she said at last. "But after a few months, he wanted to... try things. Most of it was fine. It was nothing crazy—fuzzy handcuffs, scarves, blindfolds." She shifted nervously, pulling her legs up to her chest and wrapping her arms around them. She took a shaky breath before she continued.

"But it kept escalating—he'd push the line a little farther every time until it was clear..." She swallowed hard. "He just liked hurting people—hurting *me*."

Connor's knuckles went white around the brush, his hand barely steady. He swallowed down the bile that rose in his throat. Part of him didn't want to hear the rest, but the rest of him—the largest part—knew that he needed to hear it. She was trusting him with something private. Painful.

He would honor that. And keep it safe.

"And then one day he just... didn't stop. Even though I told him to." She paused. "We argued. He apologized, but kept insisting I was never really in danger. That he'd never hurt me." She snorted, the sound dripping with disgust.

"But I'd had enough. I told him I was done—that we wanted different things. I even thought I was being mature about it."

She looked up at the ceiling, shaking her head. Then she took a slow, steadying breath.

"At the end of the year, after finals, I went to a party to celebrate. Megan was my roommate then, so we went together. We went, had a few drinks, but we didn't stay long. She and her boyfriend walked me back to our room and then went back to his dorm together."

Her shoulders tensed, and she leaned away, curling slightly inward.

Connor's jaw already ached from clenching his teeth, but his heart ached more.

"Ten minutes later, there was a knock at my door. Lucas. He wanted to talk. And I stupidly let him in. We sat and talked—well, *he* talked. Gave me some sob story about how he hadn't been able to concentrate since we broke up. Couldn't eat, couldn't sleep. He'd tanked his exams. He was afraid he was going to fail his classes and not be able to graduate." She scoffed angrily. "He said I was his best friend. That he loved me. That he wanted me back."

Connor's hands stilled. They were shaking too badly to continue. He barely stopped himself from reaching for her. She'd slowly folded in on herself, and that told him all he needed to know—she needed space.

He couldn't change the past, or take away the pain. He couldn't even comfort her beyond just being there. His chest felt tight and it was hard to breathe.

He'd never felt so helpless. Not even when—

He shook his head and forced air into his lungs by will alone. He had to keep it together.

"I told him I was sorry he was upset, but my mind hadn't changed. Honestly, I'd been relieved. I should've ended it sooner, but I thought I needed a real reason. Not just... realizing I didn't like him as much as I thought. And then afterward I noticed a lot of red flags that I'd overlooked—or ignored altogether." She fell silent, lost in thought.

She shook her head sharply and continued. "I asked him to leave. He got angry. Told me it would be my fault if he didn't graduate. Said if his life was already ruined, he might as well ruin mine too. Then he hit me." Her voice thickened, and she wiped her eyes with the back of her hand.

Connor snapped. He couldn't sit still another second.

He wrapped his arms around her and pulled her back against his chest. He kissed her hair, her temple, her shoulder—anywhere he could reach. He squeezed his eyes shut, swallowing the roar of fury building in his chest.

Alexandra took a deep breath and plunged ahead, like she had to get the words out before they choked her. And he understood—God, did he understand. Once you started you had to see it to the end, if only to prove that you could.

"He raped me. Beat me. I had a broken jaw, two fractured ribs, and bruises everywhere." Her voice was tight—raw with everything she still held back. "I prayed I'd black out. It hurt so much, and I just… wanted to escape. Go somewhere else until it ended. But I knew if I did, he might kill me. So I held on. I survived. But I remember every second. And it was hell."

Her breaths came fast and shallow—she was barely holding the panic at bay.

"You're safe now, love," he rasped—throat tight. "It's over. You're safe."

Connor held her tight, murmuring softly into her hair—reassuring her—and hating himself for ever reminding her of that hell—even for a second.

No amount of suffering would be enough—there was no proportionate response for this. He deserved every agony imaginable.

I'll show him hell. I'll torture him for days—in ways he could never even imagine—before I slaughter him like the animal he is.

After several long minutes, Alexandra finally spoke.

"Megan—bless her flighty little heart—forgot her retainer. They came back and caught him. In the act. Ryan beat the living shit out of him while Megan called the police."

"Good." Connor grunted. "I'd like to buy him a beer someday."

"Maybe you'll get your chance," Alexandra said with a weak laugh. "Who do you think Megan's marrying next week?"

The ache in his chest eased a little now that she was starting to sound more like herself. He didn't want to drag this out, but there were things he needed to know.

"He was arrested?"

"And convicted," Alexandra replied, her tone tinged with anger—resentment. She took a deep breath, and he stayed silent, sensing there was more.

"Given the state I was in, and with two eyewitnesses, it should have been an open and shut case. I didn't really want to testify in court, or ask Megan and Ryan to do testify, but I knew we'd all have to."

There was more—he could feel it.

"But, it never went to trial."

"Why?" Connor asked trying to keep the outrage from his voice.

"My father," she said sadly.

Connor made a sound he didn't recognize—rage, frustration, and something primal.

"Not directly," she added quickly, startled by his reaction. She turned, placing her hand on his arm to calm him. He was ashamed of himself for making her comfort him at a time like this. He caught her hand, kissed her palm, and threaded his fingers through hers. She relaxed, leaning back against his chest.

"He was hell bent on making sure he was prosecuted. Told the District Attorney not to even think about offering a plea. But the defense produced… a video—several actually. Not from that night, obviously, but from while we were dating. I had no idea he'd been filming me—and I certainly hadn't consented to it. But his lawyer essentially threatened to file a motion asking they be admitted as evidence if it went to trial."

"Evidence of what?" Connor snarled.

"That we'd had a previous sexual relationship that included BDSM. Their defense was basically that what happened that night started consensual and just '*got out of hand.*'"

Connor swore under his breath, vibrating with rage.

"There was also the small detail that I'd been drinking underage. The DA didn't think any of that would hold up in court, but they asked me what I wanted to do. My father didn't care about the tapes. He still wanted to go to trial."

Connor's opinion of Richard Hughes improved a little more.

"He said he'd support me no matter what, but that he thought we should go to trial. But… I couldn't do it. Not because I was ashamed—I mean, I *was*, but I could have handled the embarrassment. It would have been a small price to pay to see that bastard sentenced to fifteen to twenty years in Sing Sing. But my father *lived* in that courthouse. He knew everyone—the judge, the DA, the ADA, the clerks, court security. He knew every single person in that building and if it had gone to trial, every single one of them would know about the videos and half of them would probably have seen them. The idea that he'd have to face them day in and day out? It made me sick to my stomach."

"Amanda had just started college. I didn't know what she'd face if it got out. I couldn't do that to her. So I told the DA to offer him a deal—to get it over with. He got five years for felony assault and was out in three for good behavior. He didn't even make it on the registry."

When it was obvious she had no more to say, Connor squeezed her and encouraged her to turn. She did so reluctantly. He pressed a tender kiss to her forehead and wiped away the rest of her tears with his thumb as he cupped her face. He looked her in the eye and gave her a small, proud smile.

"Thank you for telling me," he said softly. She tried to look away, but he wouldn't let her.

"Look at me." His tone was quiet but firm. She looked up, wide-eyed. "You're very brave, lass."

She gave him a watery smile, and he pulled her close—rocking her gently until her body softened completely, exhaling the last of her tension in one long sigh.

And all the while, he was planning out how he was going to find this prick and disembowel him, slowly, with something dull and rusty.

Chapter Fifteen

Alexandra collected the hamper from upstairs and carried it down to the laundry room, adding it to the overflowing basket beside the washer. She put on music and started sorting laundry, trying to regain her balance. She'd told that story to exactly three people—well, four now—and it drained her every time.

This time was a little easier, but she still felt like she'd gone a few rounds with Trey. She winced and made a mental note to call him and apologize for skipping yesterday's session. He'd make her pay for it next time.

She sorted laundry into piles, trying to quiet the anxiety that always followed reliving the worst night of her life. Connor had handled it well. He'd held her and comforted her, but didn't offer any of the empty platitudes she'd heard too many times before. He simply listened and acknowledged how hard it had been to share.

She'd told a few guys a simpler, watered-down version—just two or three sentences—and they'd all seemed fine with at first. It wasn't until weeks, or sometimes months, into a relationship that they realized just how much that night still haunted her. That's when they decided it was more than they'd signed up for.

Would Connor be different? Or was she just postponing the inevitable?

She'd gone back and forth a million times and finally accepted there was no way to know without trying. She'd already made her choice, and this time, she wasn't looking back.

To distract herself from the uneasiness creeping in, she cranked the volume and sang along as she sorted laundry. Connor had a few calls to make, so she'd left him in the spare room she used as a home office.

She started the first load and headed to the kitchen to scavenge for—well, brunch, given the hour. She refilled her mug, took a sip, and stared blankly into the fridge.

Fifteen minutes later, Alexandra was chopping vegetables and whisking eggs for a frittata when one of her favorite songs came on. She cranked the volume and sang, already smiling. This one always made her feel like herself again. She swayed her hips, dancing in place with a quiet smile. Mid-chorus, she jumped at a deep, smokey voice that definitely *wasn't* Mike Doughty's.

Alexandra whipped around, blushing with surprise. Connor stood there, smiling as he sang in perfect pitch. His voice washed over her like a caress. He strolled toward her, still singing along to *I Hear the Bells*.

Alexandra laughed, and Connor's grin widened as he pulled her into his arms, dancing her around the kitchen island. He was… *good. Too* good. And his voice in her ear made her shiver down to her toes.

The song faded into a slower one, but he didn't let go. He tightened his hold and kept swaying with her, as Ed Sheeran crooned in the background, voice low and sentimental. Connor sang along, and Alexandra rested her head against his shoulder, letting his voice wash over her.

She melted into him, feeling warm and… hopeful. Connor was so easy to be with, when he wasn't driving her up the wall. She loved how many sides he had—and how he always seemed to know exactly what she needed, even when she didn't.

Maybe that's why everything felt like the first time—but better. Like a second chance at a first love.

Love? Wha—

She didn't even get to finish the thought before Connor leaned in and kissed her neck, still crooning softly in her ear. Her stomach fluttered with butterflies, and she nearly melted as his hand slid to the small of her back. He took her other hand, laced their fingers together, and rested them against his chest.

There was no way this man was real.

She'd thought that before—but never in a way that didn't come with a sarcastic eye roll and a *"you've got to be fucking kidding me."* He was constantly surprising her.

Like now—giving her that sexy, slow-burning stare with those sapphire eyes and a grin that could melt steel. She'd felt more in the last week than she had in the last year. He was funny and sexy, warm and strong, gentle and passionate. Who didn't want all that?

"I like your music," Connor said with a grin, spinning her as she laughed.

"I like your voice," Alexandra said, biting her lip.

"Oh, really?" he laughed, the sound rumbling through her. She closed her eyes, a shiver sliding down her spine. She just hoped he hadn't noticed. She hadn't thought a man's singing voice could do it for her—but clearly, she was wrong. And kind of mortified about it.

Judging by the way he kissed her, he'd definitely noticed. His mouth took hers with heat and hunger, making her flush all over and her nipples tighten. Heat pooled between her thighs, and she pressed them together in a vain attempt to ease the ache.

Connor pulled back just enough to murmur against her lips

"Why is it that every time we're alone in this kitchen I want to bend you over the counter and have my wicked way with you?"

"I haven't the slightest," Alexandra breathed. "But it seems to apply to the living room too. And the bathroom. Want to test the rest of the house?"

"I love the way your mind works," he growled, then kissed her again—hot and deep. So good, she wanted to wrap her legs around him and—"

The doorbell rang. Connor groaned, loosening his grip and stepping back with obvious reluctance. Alexandra stood there, dazed, before shaking her head and turning for the door—only for Connor to stop her.

"Let me." He gave her quick kiss and strode toward the foyer. Alexandra sighed and went back to the frittata. She assembled everything in the cast iron skillet—the one she'd used for the peppers, onions, and mushrooms—and was sliding it into the oven just as Connor returned. And he wasn't alone.

"Archie?" Alexandra looked up, startled. Archie gave her a tight smile. She rounded the island to give him a quick hug. Connor frowned.

"I see you've met Connor," she said, gesturing both of them toward the table. She tugged at her t-shirt and ran a quick hand through her hair, praying she didn't look freshly groped in the kitchen. Archie was perceptive and the last thing she needed was rumors getting back to her father.

Connor took one side of the table, Archie the other. Alexandra sat at the end—putting a little distance between herself and Connor, just in case.

"We've met," Archie said flatly. Unlike his fictional namesake, he wasn't much of a conversationalist. He was, however, reliable—and damn good at his job.

Archie was in his early forties and she had to admit he was handsome. He had a square jaw perpetually covered in stubble, deep set brown eyes, and a full mouth. If he ever smiled—and got a haircut that didn't scream *boot camp flashback*—he'd probably be beating women off with a stick.

He was tall, muscular, and taciturn to a fault—intimidating, and he knew exactly how to use it. If he didn't work so closely with her department, Alexandra might've found him intimidating too—but she knew better. He was frighteningly competent. She could easily believe the rumors—less ex-military, more ex-military intelligence.

"You want some coffee?"

"I'm good," he replied. He didn't really smile—just sort of... stopped frowning for a second. That was about the best you could expect.

"So, what brings you out here on a Sunday? Must be something important," Alexandra said, trying to put on her professional face to mask her anxiety. Archie didn't say anything, but he definitely noticed—*that's* what made him so damn good at his job.

"Got a couple pictures I want you to look at." He slid two photos which looked like still images from security camera footage across the table. She looked, but there wasn't much to go on. A man—average height, average build. He wore a hat, sunglasses, and a tan jacket. He was placing a small package on top of a bin of mail while the postman's back was turned retrieving something from his truck.

"Look familiar?" Archie asked.

"No... I don't think so. With that hat and jacket, it's hard to tell what he really looks like enough for me to even hazard a guess."

Archie gave her a curt nod and slid the photo over to Connor. Connor studied the photo as Archie slid another toward her. This one was of a black sedan. Four doors, very nondescript. The license plate was partially visible, but nothing about it seemed familiar.

"Is that his car?" she asked. Archie nodded, sliding that photo over to Connor as well.

"Can you send me digital copies of these? Maybe the raw footage too? I'll see if my tech guy can get anything."

Archie gave him a skeptical once-over but just said, "Already done."

"Don't worry, we're on it, Ms. Hughes," he said, standing. "I'll call if anything new comes in."

He stood to go.

"Thanks." Alexandra smiled. Archie gave her a nod before he walked away.

"I'll walk him out," Connor said, giving her shoulder a quick squeeze.

While Connor was gone, Alexandra went back to making breakfast. When he returned several minutes later he was scowling at his phone.

"Sam's got 'em now. He might be able to get us a better look," he said, not looking up from his phone. His jaw was tight, his hair mussed—like he'd been dragging his hands through it.

"Okay."

She picked up her cup and took a sip, anxiety creeping in. It was strange—she hadn't forgotten about the photos, not really. But she'd been so wrapped up in Connor, she'd shoved it to the back of her mind. Archie's visit had snapped everything into focus, and the wave of worry hit hard.

Connor must have noticed—he tucked his phone away and wrapped his arms around her.

"Don't worry, love," he murmured, rubbing slow circles on her back. "I'll keep you safe."

And somehow, Alexandra believed him.

Connor could have kicked his own ass for making a promise he might not be able to keep. After all, he'd failed before. But he wouldn't let it happen again—not this time. Alexandra had been through enough. She'd survived all of it and managed to come out the other side a strong, vibrant woman. He wouldn't let anyone hurt her again.

He'd asked Sam to find Lucas Whitmore a week ago, but he'd been so focused on finding the stalker's hideout, he hadn't pushed him hard enough to follow up on Whitmore's location. That had been a mistake. Now more than ever, he needed to know where that fucker was—and what he was planning.

The note Archie found on his windshield was like the first—plain blocky letters on unremarkable white paper. Short. Not much to go on.

It read: "How was it? Enjoy it while you can."

"You slept over," Archie had said when Connor walked him out.

It wasn't a question, simply a statement of fact. Connor set his jaw but nodded, not seeing any reason to deny it. Archie looked at him—sizing him up. Trying to decide if Connor could be trusted or if the older man needed to do something about him. He was welcome to try. Connor wasn't going anywhere.

"You're Army, right?" Archie asked. Connor nodded again.

"Ranger," Connor said, tone clipped.

"I know," Archie said matter-of-factly. "You scored a seventy-two on your ASVAB. Pretty impressive. I'm surprised you only made it to Staff Sargent before your discharge."

Connor narrowed his eyes. Knowing he was a Ranger was easy enough—but how the hell did he get Connor's ASVAB score?

"Of course, if it hadn't been for that incident in Mosul, you probably could have made it to Master Sargent before you hit your twenty year mark."

Connor took a step forward, slow and menacing, anger simmering just under the surface. He closed the gap until they were toe to toe.

"I don't know how the fuck you know that—and I honestly don't give a goddamn. You and I have one job—*one*—keep Alexandra safe and find the bastard behind this. Can you do that?"

Archie's face stayed blank, unconcerned. Connor forced himself to rein in his irritation.

"Can *you*?" Archie replied.

"Or die trying," Connor shot back. He meant every word. Archie looked at him for a moment and nodded.

"Good." He turned on his heel and left.

Connor was quietly furious—mostly with himself. He'd been too busy thinking with his dick to actually do his damn job. He needed to find Whitmore, confirm he was behind this, and make him disappear. Then he could focus his attention where it belonged—on Alexandra.

And he would. He wanted her—and not just for now. It had happened fast—like being struck by lightning. The odds had been small—but never zero. And somehow, he'd gotten lucky. Right now she was his. And he was going to keep it that way.

He would've suited up and checked the neighborhood himself, but the note was damp from the early morning drizzle—meaning it had been there for hours. Maybe since the middle of the night. Whoever left it was long gone by now.

Instead, he'd texted Sam—double-check the photos, and find Lucas Whitmore. *Yesterday.*

When he came back to the kitchen, Alexandra was quiet—shaken. They'd both been distracted the last couple of days. This morning? A brutal reminder of what they were really dealing with. He'd wrapped his arms around her—comforting her, and grounding himself in the fact that she was safe. Here. With him. If it were up to him, they'd have stayed that way—*more or less*—the rest of the damn day.

Alexandra's phone rang, and he reluctantly let her go so that she could answer it. She winced at the caller ID, but answered it anyway.

"Hi, Mom."

Connor raised an eyebrow but she shook her head slightly.

"I know, I'm sorry. Work's been insane, and I've been trying to tie up loose ends before I leave for London—I've barely had time to breathe." There was a pause before she continued. "Um, yeah… maybe. I fly out Saturday afternoon, so I'll have to pack and stuff on Friday night."

Alexandra paced, unable to keep still. She twirled the ends of her hair before checking the oven—breakfast smelled amazing.

"Okay, okay—I get it, Mom. It *has* been a while since we had a girl's night."

Her gaze flicked toward Connor, and he clocked it immediately. She wasn't sure how to explain him to her mother. Given she was estranged from Mr. Hughes, she probably had no idea what was going on—especially with how determined Alexandra was to keep the situation quiet.

"Why don't we do dinner here? I'll cook, and you and Amanda can help me pack." A pause. "Okay. See you then. Love you."

Alexandra ended the call with a sigh and a roll of her eyes.

"You haven't told your ma, have you?" Connor asked.

"No," she said miserably. "I even made Amanda promise not to tell her. She doesn't need to know—she'd just worry. But I hate lying to her, you know?"

"Yeah, I do."

"I mean everyone lies to their parents, right? It's basically required when you're a teenager. But I've always hated it. I just knew if she ever found out… she'd be so disappointed. That was my biggest fear. Still might be."

"Ah, the classic '*I'm not mad, I'm just disappointed*' look," Connor said, nodding sagely. His father had been the same. His mother—when she'd been around—just screamed the house down. He never knew which hurt more: her rage or his father's disappointment. But the disappointment? That one stuck.

Maybe it was because his father had actually cared about him in a way his mother never had.

She'd loved him—he knew that.

She'd just loved herself more.

"Exactly. Although honestly, it was mostly self-imposed. They weren't cold. They always made it clear they'd love us no matter what—but they were just so… capable. I didn't want to let them down. They never pushed us to be high achievers like some parents do, but they believed we *could be*. I love them so much for that. But it makes failing at anything feel like… failing *them*."

Alexandra checked the oven again, pulled out the pan, and set it on the stove. Then she grabbed two plates from the cabinet and placed them on the counter.

"You felt like you had to live up to their confidence—instead of their expectations," Connor said.

She blinked, then gave him a small, disbelieving smile.

"Yes. How did you know?"

Connor grinned, shrugged, and took a sip of coffee. "I'm not just a pretty face, you know."

"Clearly," she said, dryly. "But, your face *is* very pretty."

She blushed, but her smile turned playful anyway.

"Pretty?" he scoffed.

"Your word, not mine," she shot back. And yeah—she had him there.

She sliced and served breakfast, and he marveled at how something so simple could taste so damn good. He wasn't bad in the kitchen, but he cooked for fuel—not flavor. His meals were basic at best.

Alexandra smiled and blushed under his praise—and he had half a mind to haul her back upstairs and spend the day making her blush over and over again. Something about her had him completely hooked. He hadn't struggled this much with self-control since he was sixteen and ruled by hormones.

Still, everything she'd told him that morning stuck with him. It didn't change how he felt—*not even close*—but ever since, something had been nagging him. He thought about telling her that Lucas might be involved.

She hadn't made that connection—at least out loud—and he didn't want to dredge up those memories. Or make her more afraid that she already was. But it was always easier to fight the enemy you knew.

She'd been so damn strong that morning. He knew how hard it was to relive trauma like that—and there was no point dragging her back through it until he had something concrete.

"So, after conquering the laundry," he teased as she pulled a load from the dryer, "what's next on the agenda?"

Alexandra gave him a coy smile as she set the basket on the table. Then she leaned in, placing a hand on each arm of his chair. His gaze dropped to her mouth as she bit her lower lip. She looked up at him through her lashes, and he swallowed hard—wanting nothing more than to claim that mouth. For starters.

"Something very exciting," she breathed, giving him that slow, wicked smile. "Something… indulgent."

"What's that?" he asked, voice rough even to his own ears.

She leaned in and whispered into his ear.

"A mani-pedi."

…What?

She leaned away, flashing him a mischievous grin as she laughed at his confusion.

"I promised Janie I'd take her for a nail day to make up for skipping our workout," Alexandra said.

"Naughty wench," Connor growled with a grin. He stood and planted a hard kiss on her mouth. "You'll pay for that later."

"Is that a threat?" she asked, breathless. Her narrowed eyes didn't match the blush creeping up her neck.

"A promise, lass."

Connor followed Alexandra's directions to the nail salon, where he waited—impatient and flipping through the only decent magazine in the place: a National Geographic from 1986. He kept an eye on the door while he texted Sam to see if he'd made any progress. Sam had been snippy, reminding him that it was a process, and these things took time.

Blah, blah, blah.

Connor watched Alexandra laughing at the far end of the salon, perched in some crazy chair with a built-in footbath. He was glad they were in the back, away from the windows—but damn, he wanted to know what they were whispering about. Especially with the way they kept glancing in his direction.

He was trying not to replay the night before—and this morning—but it wasn't working. It had been a while since he'd met someone he liked—and Alexandra? He liked her.

A lot.

He *should* be focusing on the job. But getting close to Alexandra made everything else fade away.

He'd spent too much time thinking about her when he should've been scanning his surroundings—and now he was emotionally invested. It killed the cool detachment he needed to do the job right. Emotions were messy. Messy meant mistakes. And mistakes got people killed.

He'd learned that the hard way.

"What do you think?" Alexandra sidled up to him, holding out her hand. Her nails were short, square, and painted mint green. The color was subtle, feminine—unexpected. And it sparkled.

Just like her.

"Brilliant," he said, smiling. "Suits you."

"Thanks. My toes match," she whispered. Janie joined them and Connor frowned.

"Didn't you get yours done?" he asked, frowning. She nodded and held her hand up by her face. The nails looked like natural nails except maybe smoother and shinier. "Looks like you got swindled, lass—they didn't do a thing."

"It's supposed to look natural, but better. I like to keep my beauty effortless—nails, makeup, the whole illusion." Janie tossed her red mane for effect, and Connor laughed.

Yeah, he liked Janie. Total spitfire.

"But, my toes? Fire engine red. In this weather, if a man sees my toes, the jig's already up." She winked and Connor barked out a laugh.

"Janie, heaven help the poor bastard who falls for you."

"Damn right," she said with a smug smile. "Speaking of which, I'm off." She waggled her eyebrows and sauntered out, waving over her shoulder.

"She on the prowl again?" Connor asked, raising a brow. Just last week, she'd been hot for some drummer.

"Perpetually," Alexandra sighed. "But… hopefully not for long."

"What does that mean?" he asked, eyeing her warily.

"Nothing you need to worry about," she said, looping her arm through his. "Now feed me. I'm *starving*."

Chapter Sixteen

They'd ordered in and eaten in front of the TV, watching the first two episodes of *Doctor Who*—which Connor insisted she'd eventually learn to love. The jury was still out on that, but she thoroughly enjoyed just hanging out with Connor.

When his sister called and he had to leave, she was a little disappointed. Her only consolation was that Connor seemed just as reluctant to leave as she was to let him go. He'd left her with one last spine-tingling kiss and a promise to call in the morning.

The security system was scheduled for installation Monday while she was at work, and they'd agreed that Sam would be there to supervise. Sam picked her up Monday morning looking a little worse for wear. When they stepped outside, she was surprised to find Ian standing by the car—a massive Hummer, just like Connor's.

She smiled and greeted him, but he just nodded and opened the door for her. Given her escorts for the day, Alexandra wisely kept the conversation to a minimum during the drive to work. At least it gave her time to organize her thoughts about... oh, *so many things*.

She had so much to do before her trip—giving Janie instructions on the high-priority files, confirming the wedding plans (for the third time), picking up her dry cleaning, and packing her bags.

Oh, shit. I still need to give Janie my itinerary in case of emergency.

She had just whipped out a pen to jot it down when Sam pulled up to the curb.

"Just one sec," she said, scribbling a note in her planner before tossing it back into her bag and collecting her things. Ian stepped out of the passenger seat and circled back to open her door. Sam came around and offered her a hand. She took it—she'd rather preserve her ankle than her pride.

She headed to the front door, flanked by two very large men in black suits. Somehow, having *two* of them made it worse. She stuck out like a sore thumb. Nothing screamed *bodyguards* more than two of them walking silently at her sides—unless they added sunglasses, earpieces, and started talking into their watches.

Thankfully, they walked her to security, then turned and left without a word.

Honestly? She was a little insulted—but mostly she was relieved to be out of the spotlight.

She swiped her keycard and headed for the fourth floor to start her day.

Nine hours later—after a successful but hectic day—Alexandra rode the elevator down to the lobby, eager to get home, change her clothes, and have either a cup of tea or a glass of wine. She hadn't decided yet.

"Good work today," Charles said, holding up a hand for a high five. She gave him one, but without much enthusiasm.

"You too," she muttered. "God, I'm exhausted."

"Same," Charles said, eyes on the numbers as they counted down. The dark circles under his eyes weren't subtle—he clearly hadn't slept in days.

"You okay?" she asked, her concern obvious.

"Fine," he said, flashing a weak smile. She recognized that one.

"Your dad?" she asked softly.

"Gee, how could you tell?" he quipped.

"Lucky guess," she said, bumping his shoulder with hers.

"And here I thought I was acting completely normal. There goes my dream of becoming an actor."

"One: we both know you have no such aspirations. You'd hate it."

Charles tilted his head sideways and shrugged. "Got me there."

"And two: your performance had one fatal flaw—you're not normal," Alexandra said with a half-smile.

"Truer words…" he said with a grimace.

"Hey, none of us are normal."

"Well, yeah. You're a total freak—so next to you, I'm Joe Average."

"Dick," Alexandra muttered, grinning.

"Yes, please." Charles winked, and she laughed harder, shaking her head.

"That's more like it," she said. "You sure you're okay?"

"Yeah. Just the usual," he said with a shrug. The usual being his father grilling him about his job, his life, his future—and being disappointed with every answer. Then his mother probably stepped in, trying to smooth things over while very deliberately ignoring the fact that he was gay. The military might have ditched "don't ask, don't tell," but the Bennetts had *not*.

"Sorry. That sucks."

"Yeah, but it's a predictable kind of sucky," Charles said with a smirk. "I can deal."

"You shouldn't have to, though."

"Agreed. Sadly, you don't get to choose your family. If I could, I'd probably be Richard Hughes, Jr."

"Oh, God, Dad would've *loved* that. You're already the son he never had. You should have seen how disappointed he was when he realized there was no hope of you becoming his son-in-law. Heartbroken." She made an exaggerated sad face, and Charles chuckled.

"I can't say I share his disappointment—"

"Rude," Alexandra muttered.

"But, if there were any option that didn't involve a lavender marriage or him adopting a grown-ass man, he'd have a son before you could say 'who's your daddy?'"

"Oh, God, please don't say that when talking about my father."

"He's not my type, but he *is* a bit of a silver fox."

"Ew! Just—stop," she groaned.

He raised his free hand in surrender.

She sighed and leaned her head on his shoulder. He wrapped an arm around her, and rested his chin on top of her head. When the doors dinged open, they walked out into the lobby like that—leaning on each other for support. Mental. Physical. Emotional.

After everything that had happened in the last ten days, this bit of normalcy felt like a haven. She was finally regaining her equilibrium—maybe even a little peace.

She'd needed this.

"We should do a movie night soon," Alexandra said, lifting her head from his shoulder. "I'll even let you pick this time."

"Sure. You cook, and I'll bring dessert and booze."

"Deal."

"We'll pick a day after you're back from London," Charles said, checking his watch.

"Remind me why you're not coming with me?" she asked.

"I told you—*one of us* needs to stay."

"No, we don't. Especially now that the Peterson case settled. You've got the whole trial week free—use it to get your shit together and take a few days off. At least come for the wedding, if not all the pre-wedding chaos."

"Weddings just aren't my thing, Lex," he sighed. "You know that."

"Ah yes—commitment gives you hives, as I recall," she said with a snort.

"Not really. It's just… you heteros are so gross. What you do behind closed doors is none of my business, but do you have to shove it in my face?" he deadpanned. "It's everywhere these days."

Alexandra narrowed her eyes. "Uh-huh. Sure."

"Seriously," he said. "It'd be too awkward. I wouldn't know anyone besides you—and you'll be busy with maid of honor stuff."

"You know the bride and groom, Charles. That's *usually* the important part."

"And they'll be busy getting married. Besides, we're basically friends by proxy—it's not like I ever really talk to them."

"But still, you—"

"Alexandra," he cut her off—quiet, but firm.

That was her cue. He only used her full name when he was done talking. She backed off, grudgingly—pushing him now would just earn her a couple days of the cold shoulder.

He could be so closed off about the weirdest shit. But there was nothing she could do—he'd tell her when he was ready… or never. That was just Charles. She knew what it was like to have things you didn't want to talk about. Hell, they'd been friends for nearly a decade, and there was still plenty she'd never told him.

They reached the doors, and Alexandra hesitated.

She was technically supposed to wait for Sam or Ian to walk her out—but how the hell was she supposed to explain that to Charles?

She spotted Sam approaching and decided to be proactive. She pushed the door open, caught his eye, glanced subtly toward Charles.

Sam froze.

He looked bewildered—rattled. Almost panicked.

Kind of an overreaction in her opinion. But whatever.

"Well, I'm over here," Alexandra said, giving Charles a quick hug. "See you tomorrow."

He squeezed her tighter than usual, his voice a little too soft. "See you tomorrow."

"You sure you're okay?" she whispered.

"Yeah. Just need to sleep for a week."

She wasn't convinced, but she let it go. He pulled back and walked off, waving over his shoulder. Something still felt off—more than usual. She called after him on impulse.

"Hey!"

He turned to look at her, an eyebrow raised. "Yeah?"

"I love your face," she said, smiling.

Charles smiled back—finally looking a little more like himself.

"Love your face," he echoed with a wink. He turned and walked away. This time she let him go.

She turned to head toward the black monstrosity parked down the street—and nearly ran straight into Ian.

"Jesus," she gasped.

How could someone that massive be so damn quiet?

She looked past him and spotted Sam, who'd returned to the Hummer.

Weird. But okay…

She looked up at Ian. He raised an eyebrow. And said nothing, of course. He moved alongside her, his hand hovering behind her lower back—like he was trying to guide her without touching her.

Or maybe he was afraid she'd make a break for it.

Honestly, they were all a little weird. But like she'd told Charles: nobody's normal.

Ian opened the door for her, and she collapsed into the back seat. Ian slid into the driver's seat this time. Sam rode shotgun. He'd looked tired this morning—now he looked wrecked.

She hoped Connor wasn't pushing him too hard.

"So, how'd it go?" she asked, leaning forward to peer around the passenger seat.

She got no response.

"Did everything go okay?"

"Oh." Sam glanced back at her. "Yeah. Fine. Everything's up and running."

"Good. Thanks."

"Yeah," he said absently. "Of course."

Before she knew it they were pulling up outside her townhouse. She must've dozed off in the quiet car.

Ian helped her out while Sam led the way up to her door, and Ian fell in behind. She felt a little claustrophobic between the two of them. She wasn't petite, but Sam was still a few inches taller—and Ian… was a damn giant. At least six-foot-four. Even standing two steps below her, they were nearly eye to eye.

They filed into the foyer, and Ian took up position directly in front of her while Sam swept through the house. Stuck between him and the front door, she felt like an Alexandra sandwich. Luckily, it only lasted for a few minutes

She was used to the routine by now, and she didn't even want to think about how quickly she'd accepted it as part of her normal life.

Sam came back down the stairs and gave them the all clear. Ian nodded at her, then stepped back outside—presumably to wait in the car. Sam walked her through the new security system, helped her program the code. He showed her how to arm it and disarm it and then he walked around the house with her to show her where the sensors were on each door and window.

Finally, he guided her to the dining room and sat her down at the table. There was already a laptop open and he tapped a couple keys to get it going.

"This is what you'll use to monitor the security cameras."

"Cameras? Where?"

She didn't like the idea of cameras in her house. The thought that she might be on camera—that she could be filmed even now, without knowing—made her stomach turn.

"Exterior only, here… here… here… and here," he said, pointing to each of the four feeds being shown simultaneously on the computer screen. "Front door," he said pointed out the top two screens.

She could clearly see Ian standing out on the sidewalk in front her building, looking up and down the street. They'd positioned two cameras so that they overlapped directly in front of her door but each camera also showed a good portion of the street on either side.

"And back yard," He continued, pointing to the bottom two sections of the screen. Again, they'd arranged them so that the entire back yard, small as it was, was covered completely. You could see the fence that enclosed the other three sides, and you could clearly see the door that led into the yard from the kitchen.

"And I'm assuming you'll be monitoring these from your office too?" she asked. She still wasn't thrilled—but this, she could live with.

"Yes. Not all the time, obviously," he said. "But the feed's available 24/7. The alarm…"

His voice trailed off and he stared out the window for a moment.

"Sorry. When the alarm goes off, it notifies the police and us."

"Are you okay? You seem tired."

"Yeah. Fine," he said.

"Okay. Well… thanks," she said, rising from her chair. She just wanted to be alone—get comfy, relax, maybe exhale for the first time all day.

And she *really* wanted to call Connor.

She hated to admit it, even to herself, but… she already missed him.

It was totally ridiculous—*absurd* really—considering they'd only spent a total of four days together out of the last ten, but it didn't seem to matter. She was so damn tired she could sleep standing up—*and* now more than a little freaked out. The security walkthrough had dragged everything she'd been avoiding right back into the spotlight.

"So," Sam said, clearing his throat. "If you have any questions, call me. Aside from remembering the code, you don't need to change anything about your routine."

"Got it," she said with a nod. She walked him to the front door so she could arm the system once he was gone.

"Make sure you get some sleep," she said, offering him a tired smile. "Personally, I'm about to pass out for the next three to four business days."

"Yeah. I'll do that." He flashed a tight smile, then turned and left.

She set the alarm and went straight upstairs. Stripping off her clothes she turned the shower on—*as hot as it would go*. She stepped in and sighed, letting the heat and water pressure work their magic.

Her body relaxed. Her mind? That took considerably more effort. By the time she felt human again, her skin was warm and pink.

She threw on sweats and a t-shirt before going foraging. She ate leftover pork lo mein—cold—while standing at the kitchen counter. Afterward, she poured a glass of wine and carried it upstairs.

She checked the time as she climbed into bed. Nearly eight.

Was Connor home yet?

She picked up her phone and—after half a second's hesitation—pressed *call* under his name.

It only rang once before he picked up.

"Hello, love," he said.

She could *hear* the smile in his voice. It was like painkillers for her soul.

"Hello, yourself. Is now a good time?"

"It's always a good time with me," he said with a chuckle.

And don't I know it…

"Hmm. Debatable," she said, grinning.

"Really?" he said.

Alexandra shuddered. How did he make just *one* word sound so… promising? How did he make her believe, with nothing but his tone, that he was going to make her rethink those words the next time he saw her?

"I'll have to make sure you're properly entertained next time."

"Entertained?" he snorted. "What, are you planning to put on a show?"

A low, wicked laugh rumbled through the line. She realized too late what she'd implied. She slapped a hand over her face and seriously considered hanging up.

"Would ye like that?" he purred.

Her brain short-circuited.

Delicious, dirty, absolutely *unspeakable* images flooded her mind.

"Oh, God," she groaned, clapping a hand over her mouth. She silently called herself every word for idiot that she could think of—which turned out to be a lot. Still didn't feel like enough.

He chuckled again—probably imagining how red her face was. And that sound did strange, traitorous things to her. She bit her lip to keep from blurting out something even more embarrassing.

She didn't understand what was happening to her. She'd never thought of herself as having a particularly high sex drive. Her last relationship had been… what, two years ago? Three?

Sure, she'd had the *occasional* date with her battery-operated-boyfriend, but even that was rare. Weeks—sometimes months—would pass without a second thought. And now? She was one low chuckle away from combusting.

She felt like she'd been bewitched. All sorts of naughty things she'd never even considered suddenly tempted her. And if Connor had been there, they'd probably be trying every single one.

If she had the nerve to ask for them, that is.

"You're awfully quiet, Alexandra," Connor said, his voice—warm and smooth as whiskey—sending tingles dancing across her skin.

"Sorry," she said, voice cracking. She cleared her throat, trying to sound normal. And nominally intelligent. "Just… lost in thought for a second."

"Hmm? Do tell."

"Now you're just doing it on purpose," she accused, knowing how feeble it sounded. "You enjoy making fun of me, don't you?"

"Maybe just a wee bit," he agreed. "But only because I like you feisty."

"*Feisty?*" she asked, dumbfounded.

"Aye. You get this look in your eye and you purse your lips just so… it makes me want to tame you."

"Now, that's just insulting," she muttered. And if she sounded a little breathless—well, she hoped he didn't notice. His laughter told her she hadn't been so lucky. "So you like me *angry?*"

Connor made a thoughtful noise.

"I suppose so. I like your smart mouth and your snark. And I like your wit and your sarcasm—your jokes and your laugh. I even like your silences."

"Wow," she breathed. "That's a lot."

"Yeah," he said softly. "There's a lot to like about you."

Alexandra bit her lip hard, trying to calm her heart, hold back the tears—because *of course she'd cry*—and stifle the dopey grin she could feel pulling at the corners of her mouth.

"I mean, you're a handful," he said. "But it's worth it."

He was clearly trying to lighten the mood, but instead, she took a shuddering breath, blinked hard, and exhaled slowly.

"That might be the sweetest thing anyone's ever said to me," she confessed.

He was quiet a little too long, and panic flared—too serious?

She quickly added, "But don't get a big head. The bar was literally on the ground."

He didn't laugh. Not even a chuckle. Her heart sank and she kicked herself. They'd been having a perfectly fun, flirty conversation—and she'd gone and ruined it with *feelings*.

"Well, thank God you found me," he said, voice teasing, but thick with something she couldn't quite name. "Clearly your taste in men up to now has been terrible."

"Can't argue with you there," she said dryly, voice dripping sarcasm. "It's a shame that my best boyfriend so far was the one who turned out to be gay."

Connor let out a breathy laugh, low and soft. "Then clearly, I'll have to raise the bar."

Alexandra smiled into the phone, biting the inside of her cheek. Her face heated, but she spoke anyway.

"You're off to a *very* strong start."

"You know what they say—'begin as you mean to go on.'"

Alexandra smiled to herself in her office for the eighty-seventh time in the last three days. Connor's words kept echoing in her head.—*all of them.*

She kept drifting off, only to come back to her senses staring at the wall with a stupid grin on her face and no clue how long she'd been out of it.

She was smitten. And disgusted with herself.

She forced herself to get back to work—flipping through her files, trying to see what she still needed to do. The answer? Not a whole hell of a lot.

She buzzed Janie. There must be something. There was no way she was caught up.

Janie settled into the chair in front of her desk, legs crossed, legal pad ready.

Alexandra had offered to buy her a tablet—several times—but Janie didn't trust technology. Or *herself.* She was convinced it would either crash or she'd hit the wrong button and erase her whole career. She backed up her computer three times a day and kept enough handwritten notes to choke a member of Greenpeace.

"You rang?"

"What am I working on right now?" Alexandra asked.

"Right now? Nothing. The Diaz deposition isn't until the week after you get back. We've already prepared and filed our Answer and Counterclaim to the Holland Complaint, *and* the Motion to Dismiss for Van Der Burg. We're waiting for Dave Lang to send us a draft of the Settlement Agreement on Peterson—but you know him. I doubt we'll have it before the second coming, let alone before you're back from London."

"What about the pro bono stuff?" Alexandra asked.

She tried to volunteer at a few local community centers when she could—mostly tenants' rights, insurance claims paperwork, or filling out small claims forms. It wasn't much, but it mattered to a lot of people. And she liked to help.

"Miracle of miracles," Janie said. "They didn't need you this week. Apparently they had all the volunteers they could handle right now. But they said, and I quote: 'Keep calling. *Please.*'"

Alexandra frowned.

"Wait—are you… *bored?*" Janie gasped dramatically, *horrified.*

"I… think so," Alexandra admitted, shifting in her seat. "It's weird. I don't like it."

Janie snorted. "Talk about first world problems."

Alexandra ignored that.

"Stay and talk to me for a minute. What's going on with you? Any luck on the *meat market?*"

"No." Janie huffed and slumped back in the chair. "I don't know what's wrong with me—I'm just not feeling it lately. With *anyone.*"

"Maybe it's time to cast a wider net. Someone outside of your usual type."

"Maybe," Janie said, chewing a freshly manicured fingernail.

"Hey—Stop. That cost you sixty dollars," Alexandra said.

"Shoot, you're right," Janie gasped, examining her nails. She put her pen in her mouth instead.

"What did you think of Connor's friends?" Alexandra fished. She'd been dying to know, but she didn't want to ask. She didn't want to make things weird, and Janie could be stubborn—like a mule-ox hybrid with commitment issues. If Janie thought Alexandra was trying to play matchmaker, she'd probably hate Jackson forever—on principle.

"Are you sure Connor isn't a Chippendale's dancer? I mean—*yowza*. All his friends are *crazy* hot."

"I'm sure," Alexandra laughed, rolling her eyes. "But you're not wrong."

"Where does he hang out to meet guys like that? And do you think he'd take me there?"

A pang of guilt hit her square in the chest. She hated lying to Janie, so she tried to stay as close to the truth as she could.

"Some of them are Army buddies, I think."

"Ooh, you don't think he's secretly gay, do you? Remember Greg?" Jane grimaced like she'd been handed a kale smoothie.

"Ugh, please. I'd rather not."

One of Janie's exes. It ended badly when Janie found him canoodling with his '*business partner*' during office hours.

"Trust me—Connor is definitely straight." The blush swept in fast, but she tried to play it cool. If she didn't react, maybe Janie wouldn't notice.

"Ohhh? What's this?" Janie grinned, leaning forward in her chair. "Spill the tea. Every detail—omit nothing. Did you use my gift? How many?"

"Nope. My lips are sealed." Alexandra smiled, but her skin felt too tight.

She didn't want to talk about it.

She loved Janie. Knew she wouldn't judge—not that there was anything to judge. Friends discussed this sort of thing all the time, right? It wasn't like she had some kind of weird kink. She wasn't…. turned on by *houseplants* or anything. Or licking doorknobs.

It was just sex. Really *good* sex. With a super hot, wickedly charming man who called her 'lass' like she was on her own private episode of Outlander.

Intense.

Spontaneous.

Mind-blowing.

But in no way deviant.

Just—*fucking unbelievable.*

Part of her wanted to gossip. Maybe even brag a little. But the fear of being exposed, of it being used against her…

It was irrational—and she knew it—she just… couldn't get past it.

"You are such a buzzkill," Janie pouted, her facial expression one mimes would call over-the-top.

"That's me," Alexandra said with a shrug.

She needed to change the subject.

"I think Parker is probably the hottest—aside from Connor."

"Oh, he's hot. That bad-boy biker vibe with the tattoos? *Yum.* But, Sam's got that clean cut, boy-next-door-thing going on," Janie said.

"Jackson has that sexy cowboy twang and that '*aw, shucks*' southern charm," Alexandra said, watching Janie's face.

"He's okay," Janie shrugged casually. She scrutinized her nails, glanced at Alexandra's bookshelf, and pretended to pluck nonexistent lint off her skirt.

This was decidedly un-*Janie*-like behavior. She was always direct—brutally honest. Especially about men. Jackson was objectively handsome. No woman in her right might would call him just *okay.*

And he was exactly her type. That could only mean one thing.

"You *like* him," Alexandra gasped.

"What?" Janie actually blushed. Janie *never* blushed.

She could teach a class on blowjobs to a group of elderly churchgoers—including her own grandmother—without batting an eye.

"You *do!*"

I knew it! I was right!

"Shut up, would you?" Janie hissed, but she couldn't stop her lips from turning up at the corners—just enough to show it was true.

"Janis Joplin Carpenter! Are you feeling *shy?*"

"Ew. No. I don't get shy, *Alexandra Matilda Hughes*," Janie shot back. You'd think she'd just been told her new book club didn't serve wine. "Now, unless you need something, some of us actually have things to do."

Janie got up, flicked her hair over her shoulder, and walked out.

This information was too good to waste—and she had nothing better to do.

She texted Jackson.

She suddenly felt like doing some shopping.

Connor paced his office, reading the same proposal for the third damn time. He'd pulled it together last week, then asked the team for notes. He liked getting their perspectives before locking it in.

Some of their notes were solid. He'd been tweaking his pitch to fit them in, but time was tight. He'd bumped up the meeting to clear his schedule for Alexandra's trip.

He knew it was probably a terrible idea.

His objectivity was shot to hell—nonexistent. He wasn't even supposed to do person protection anymore. The smart move would be to send Jackson and Parker.

No. Not Jackson. *Ian* and Parker.

He didn't do it anymore—but he still *could*. He was still fully qualified. And she'd feel safer with him than anyone else. Especially Jackson.

You're so full of shite…

He was going because he wanted to. He knew it. Everyone else knew it.

It was selfish. Probably stupid. But hell would freeze over before he let anyone else take her to that wedding.

No one was taking his place beside her.

And he wanted a full goddamn week with nothing to do but take care of her.

Saying it had been hard to leave her in someone else's hands was a feckin' understatement. He'd been on edge. Wanted to text her twenty times a day. Just to check in.

And he was calling her detail too often. *Way* too often. Parker hadn't said a word. Neither did Ian—*shocker*. But Jackson…

He thought it was funny—at first. But even he had limits. When Connor had called this afternoon—for the tenth time—Jackson had ripped him a new one.

Jackson never had trouble telling him to get his head out of his ass. It was one of the reasons Connor trusted him. Relied on him. Considered him a friend.

He'd told Connor flat out: If he didn't trust Jackson to do his job, he could either find a replacement—or do it himself. If he wasn't going to do either, then he needed to back the fuck off.

Then he'd had the balls to tell Connor not to screw it up with

Alexandra.

What the fuck was that supposed to mean? Like he'd ever let that happen.

He tried to refocus on the damn presentation when his phone chimed.

Alexandra Hughes: Playing hooky. Out shopping with Jacks and I need your opinion.

Alexandra Hughes: Red or black?

The photo hit him like a punch to the gut.

Jesus.

She wasn't even wearing them, and he could already picture her in them.

And then out of them.

He shifted—*adjusting*—before he could even think about reply.

Connor MacLachlan: Both. In every color.

Alexandra Hughes: Jackson agrees.

His vision went red.

He gripped his phone until it creaked in his hand.

Connor MacLachlan: Jackson can go fuck himself. And you can quote me.

Alexandra Hughes: Rude.

Connor MacLachlan: You haven't seen rude yet...

Connor tossed his phone on his desk and dragged a hand over his face.

He took a deep breath, trying to calm down.

It lasted thirty seconds.

Then he cursed under his breath and slammed his fist into the wall.

When Jackson parked that godawful Range Rover in front of Alexandra's townhouse, Connor was already waiting—arms crossed, eyes locked. Every inch the wolf at the door. She climbed out, laughing at something Jackson said, until she spotted Connor. Her eyes went wide.

He pushed off the railing, giving her a slow predatory smile.

She tossed her hair and grabbed her bags—playing it cool. By the time they met on the sidewalk, she looked calm. But he could see the flush creeping up her neck. She wasn't unaffected. Not even close.

Jackson passed him the bags, looking smug.

Connor set them down—

—and punched him in the stomach.

Jackson let out a grunt, doubled over slightly—then quickly straightened, like it was nothing.

Connor shook his head. "Hell mend ye."

"Connor!" Alexandra snapped, stepping between them.

He scowled.

"Don't fash yourself, love. Jackson's a big lad. He'll live."

Jackson nodded and shot her a crooked grin, rubbing his stomach.

"Just a love tap. No harm done," he said. "Besides, he's right. I knew better."

He raised both hands in surrender and stepped back. Then he winked at Alexandra as he turned and walked off.

"What the hell was that?" Alexandra hissed, unlocking the door as Connor hauled her bags up behind her.

"Guy stuff," he grunted.

"More macho, territorial crap?" Alexandra asked, punching in the code while he locked the door behind them.

"Aye. Keep tryin' to make me jealous, and it'll keep happenin'."

She blinked at him, blushed and looked away. She looked guilty—for about a heartbeat. Then she looked up at him from beneath her lashes, smiling slyly.

"But you're so hot when you're jealous."

"Is that so?" he murmured, dropping the bags at his feet.

She bit her lip and nodded—a challenge in her eyes.

He stalked toward her.

Slow. Deliberate.

He wanted her to see it coming. To feel it, and know there was no escape. She'd brought this on herself. Now he'd remind her who she belonged to.

The word hummed beneath his skin:

Mine.

He buried one hand in her hair, cradling the back of her head. The other hand slid up her throat, settling on her jaw—his thumb pressing gently on her chin.

He tipped her head back. Controlled. Measured.

She licked her lips. Her breath hitched.

He dipped his mouth to hers—just barely brushing her lips. A tease. A warning.

She pushed up, chasing the sensation.

He pulled back, stilling her with hands.

"Greedy girl," he murmured, his mouth ghosting over hers. His thumb swept across her jaw and he breathed her in—honey and almonds with a hint of crisp autumn air.

He fingers fisted in her hair. She whimpered as his grip tightened, tugging slightly. He searched her face

No fear. Only desire.

Frustration.

Need.

Her eyes blazed—molten gold, lit from within.

He kissed her with devastating care, every movement intentional. He memorized every press, every glide—savoring her like a luxury.

She melted against him, hands twisted in his shirt, pulling him closer. Her lips parted on a moan, hungry for more—but he wouldn't be rushed. They had all night and he planned to use every second.

He was patient.

Far more patient than Alexandra.

Her body was pressed tightly against him.

Each soft sound was a plea.

Needy.

Desperate.

Exactly how he wanted her.

With her heels on, she was the perfect height. When he backed her into the wall, his thigh slid between hers like it belonged there. That little pencil skirt—just like the one he'd imagined her in from day one—bunched up around her hips.

He traced her jaw, down her neck, all the way to her hip. The silk of her stockings teased his fingertips as he dragged his hand along the back of her thigh. He urged her leg up over his hip.

He shifted his hips, pressing into her until he could feel the heat of her body through his slacks. She gasped, tilting her hips.

Still, his mouth moved with predatory precision.

And Alexandra became more and more persistent—trying to deepen the kiss.

But he wouldn't give it to her. Not yet.

She surged forward again, demanding more—

He tugged on her hair and broke the kiss.

She whimpered.

He smirked. "Behave."

She bit her lip, and for a split second, he considered fucking her right there against the wall.

"Come," he said, voice low and rough.

He took her hand, silently leading her upstairs. At the foot of the bed, he paused. One hand on her lower back, the other at the nape of her neck, he kissed her.

Still slow. Still deliberate. But deep—consuming.

He pulled back, reveling in the dazed, wrecked look of her face. He pushed her jacket off her shoulders and folded it carefully, setting it on the dresser. He took his time shrugging off his own coat and laid it neatly over hers.

She watched him silently.

He held her gaze as he rolled up his sleeves—slow, precise.

"Strip for me," he said softly.

She blinked, shifting on her feet.

Connor slid his hands into his pockets and leaned against the dresser.

Waiting.

Come on, love. Just trust me.

Her blouse was white. Pristine. Buttoned all the way to the throat.

Her hands trembled slightly as she unfastened one cuff, then the other. She tugged the shirt free from her skirt and began unbuttoning—slowly, from the bottom. Each button revealed another inch of soft, pale skin.

Her confidence grew with every button. By the time she reached the ones beneath her breasts, a seductive smile curved her lips.

Connor shifted, not bothering to hide how much she affected him. Her smile widened as she slid the blouse from her shoulders—slow, unhurried.

She stood before him in cream-colored lace. Breathtaking.

She reached behind to undo the clasp—

He stopped her.

"Let me."

She turned around as he stepped forward. Instead of unclasping her bra, he slid down the zipper of her skirt. He pressed a kiss to her shoulder—soft, reverent—and stepped back.

She turned back to face him, then slowly pushed the skirt down over her hips. She leaned forward—just enough for her breasts to spill over the lace.

The skirt pooled at her feet, and he reached for her hand, steadying her as she stepped out of it. Seeing her in nothing but matching lace and thigh-high stockings had him clenching his fists—fighting the instinct to drag her to him.

Not yet…

But Christ and all the saints, she's bewitching.

Connor circled her slowly, taking her in from every angle—reveling in the way her skin flushed beneath his gaze. He placed a hand on her hip, his fingers trailing across the soft curve of her stomach as he moved.

She shivered in response.

He traced up her arm, over her shoulder, and down the center of her back—slow and steady—until he found the clasp. He unhooked it, letting it slide down her arms to the floor.

He sank onto the edge of the bed and took her hands, guiding her between his knees. He kissed each palm, lingering for a breath before letting her hands fall to her sides. His hands slid to her hips as he leaned in, pressing a kiss to her stomach.

He heard her breath catch and he looked up at her with a smug smile.

He pressed a kiss between her breasts, hands gliding up her sides—thumbs brushing the tender skin just beneath her ribs.

Her breathing quickened, shallow and shaky, her back arching toward his mouth.

"You're beautiful, Alexandra," he whispered, staring up at her.

She gave him soft, radiant smile. He leaned his forehead to her stomach, breathing deep—steadied by the scent and the nearness of her.

He guided her forward until she straddled his lap, then pressed a trail of kisses along her collarbone. His hand slid up, cupping her breast.

She moaned, eyes falling shut, head tipping back.

"Eyes on me," he said, voice hoarse.

Her eyes snapped open, cheeks flushing as she looked down at him.

He closed his mouth around her, teasing her with his tongue before sucking—slow, deliberate. She gasped when he dragged his teeth over her sensitive skin—and squirmed when he mirrored it on the other side.

He stood, setting her gently on the bed. She sat, knees pressed together—demure. Tempting.

"Spread your legs for me, love."

She shuddered, breath stuttering—but obeyed, parting her thighs until she was open to him.

"Good girl," he rumbled.

He dropped to his knees in front of her—ready to worship.

"Lean back for me, lass."

His hands slid slowly up her calves, then her thighs—tracing the shape of her like she was something precious. Treasured.

She lowered herself onto her forearms, eyes locked on his. He hooked his thumbs into her underwear, dragging them down to mid-thigh—leaving them there like a promise.

He leaned in, pressing open-mouthed kisses along her inner thighs, on her hips, then across her stomach. She shifted restlessly beneath him, fingers curling into the sheets.

Her scent was driving him mad—warm, sweet, *real*. A hand beneath each knee, he settled her legs on his shoulders with careful precision. She gasped at the sudden movement, but didn't pull away. Her knickers were now behind his neck, trapping her thighs around him—right where he wanted her.

He leaned in, tasting her with long, slow strokes of his tongue. Soft. Hot. Perfect. He could spend hours like this—devouring her. She moaned, hips rolling—so he stopped.

"Hold still… or I stop." His voice was low, laced with command. She froze—frustrated, surprised, and completely undone—and even more beautiful for it.

He lowered his head, breath skimming her skin—hot and cruel—before he moved lower still. This time he delved deep, tasting her fully, relishing the way her body clenched to keep him there. Her hips stayed still—barely—but her muscles pulsed with every stroke of his tongue.

He moved higher, lips closing around that tender bundle of nerves—teasing her with slow, swirling strokes until her hips jerked beneath him. He paused again. She whimpered, breathless and pleading.

He smiled—slow and wicked—dragging his tongue over that sensitive spot as she trembled, fighting to obey. He closed his mouth over her again—teasing with flicks of his tongue, gentle pulls of his lips, keeping her right on the edge. Her breathing turned ragged, her thighs trembling, muscles fluttering beneath his hands. She was close—so close.

He worked two fingers inside her—unhurried, but relentless—pulling a soft, drawn-out moan from her lungs. A long-overdue sigh as her body relaxed for him. Her hands tangled in his hair, holding him fast.

He loved the gentle pull on his scalp—loved that she reached for him.

He curled his fingers, seeking that secret place that drove her wild. Her hands tightened almost painfully and he knew he'd found it. He repeated the motion, again and again, with agonizing patience.

Every brush of his finger tips drew a short, soft cry from her lips—all breath and need. Her body tightened around him, instinctively pulling him deeper.

Connor made small, tight circles with his tongue, matching the rhythm of his hand. She writhed—uncontrollable, reflexive.

He didn't stop.

Not this time.

He kept worshipping her, driving her higher and higher, aching to see her break for him. Her body tensed, back arching off the bed. Her voice echoed in the quiet room as she cried out his name. He didn't stop, didn't slow down. Wave after wave rolled through her, drawing out everything she had to give. And he pushed her through each one until the bed was soaked and her body went limp.

"Good. Fucking. Girl."

His voice was rough. Raw.

He kissed the inside of her thigh, sucking the skin into his mouth until he'd marked her. A self-satisfied smirk pulled up the corner of his mouth as he wiped it on his sleeve.

She whimpered when he pulled away, lifting her head—barely—to look at him. Flushed and trembling, her body still moving lazily with the fading aftershocks. She was a fucking goddess. Sensual. Divine.

She looked farther down, squeezing her legs together and covering her face with her hands as realization dawned.

"Eyes on me," Connor said sharply.

She pulled her hands away, eyes wide.

"Don't," he said, with a quick shake of his head. "Look at you—you're perfect. And you did so good for me."

He popped the button on his slacks and dragged the zipper down shoving fabric out of the way, until he was free. He grunted, wrapping a hand around his erection and squeezing gently.

Then he groaned as he started stroking himself slowly with the same hand that had made Alexandra come undone. Her eyes were glued to him and it only stoked the fire.

Connor had never felt anything like this. He didn't have a name for it—but it was primitive. Visceral. Possessive.

It threatened his control—his sanity. Made him question everything he thought he knew about himself.

But that could wait.

Alexandra was right in front of him—glowing and more lovely then ever.

And he was nowhere near done with her.

Chapter Seventeen

"Up on your knees, love. Hands on the headboard."

She sat up, running her hands through her hair. He marveled at how beautiful she looked—stockings and heels still on, skin flushed, hazel eyes dark and hooded.

She turned to watch him unbutton his shirt, stripping it off and letting it fall to the floor. He kept his eyes locked on her face, watching her watch him.

Her gaze dropped, hungry, and she licked her lips when it landed on him—bare and hard, waiting. He growled, toeing off his shoes and stripping out of everything else in one smooth motion. If she kept looking at him like that, her eyes were going to be the death of him.

He dug a foil packet out of the drawer, and quickly rolled the condom on, hands shaking slightly.

He crawled onto the bed, kneeling behind her. He slid his hands from her hips up her ribs, savoring the smooth heat of her skin and the soft weight of her in his hands. He pulled her flush against him and kissed her neck and shoulders, slowly, softly.

She sighed, shuddered, and leaned her head to the side, offering him more of her. That one small gesture filled something in his chest he hadn't even known was hollow.

He worshipped her skin, breathing in her warm, sweet scent as he kissed and nipped his way from her ear to the curve of her shoulder.

"Connor," she whispered.

She was symphony—her sighs, her moans, every helpless whimper and gasp. They came naturally. No pretense. No design. No calculation. Just *her*.

"Shhh. I've got ye, lass."

He trailed his hand down the curve of her waist, sliding over her hip. She was still sensitive—she flinched at the first brush of his fingers. She arched, pressing herself against him as he slowly, gently stoked the fire inside her back to a blaze

She whimpered when he withdrew, then gasped as she felt him position himself against her.

He pressed into her just an inch, gritting his teeth. Trying to savor the warmth of her, the way her body stretched to take him—fighting the urge to rush.

"Ready for me, love?" he asked his voice low and rough with effort.

"Yes. *God*—yes," she moaned.

His grip on her hips tightened, jaw clenched—then he slammed home, filling her in a single, brutal thrust. He growled as she clenched around him. He held still, overwhelmed—already on the verge of unraveling.

Alexandra was panting and shaking, pressing back against him—wanting, needing more. He pulled out slow, dragging a long, low moan from her lips—stopping when only the tip remained. He inhaled once—then buried himself to the hilt again.

She pressed back against him, head falling to his shoulder, eyes shut, mouth open on a gasp.

"Yes, Connor… please." A breathless, whispered plea.

That soft surrender snapped something inside him.

"Arch your back," he rasped, nudging her knees wider with his own. She tilted her hips, changing the angle. They both groaned as he withdrew, then drove into her with one fluid motion. This time, he wouldn't stop.

He took her with long, deep strokes—lost in the feel of her, and the string of soft, broken cries that escaped with every snap of his hips.

"*Mine*," he gritted out.

His hand found her jaw—firm but gentle—tilting her head aside so he could drag his teeth down her neck.

"Yes," she moaned.

"Say it," he growled.

"*Yours*."

"Say my name."

He didn't know why, but he felt like he might die if she didn't fall apart with his name on her lips. He needed it like air.

He moved faster—hips and fingers in sync—until the only sounds were ragged breaths and the rhythm of skin on skin.

"I'm yours, Connor." It was a plea… and a vow.

Her body tightened like a coiled spring.

"Again," he snarled, jaw clenched.

"Connor…"

"That's it. That's my girl." He was panting, voice raw. His lips grazed the back of her neck. "Come for me, love."

She screamed, shattering in his arms, and he was ready to break. But he held her together until her body started to relax.

Then he let himself go.

Three more hard, claiming thrusts and he buried himself deep—fingers biting into her hips.

"Mine," was all he managed to choke out as his body went rigid.

He forgot how to breathe.

By the time he remembered, he was only sure of one thing.

She was his.

And nothing and no one would take her from him.

Alexandra sat soaking in her bathtub, replaying the way Connor had taken her just a little while ago. It puzzled her, and excited her. Sex with Connor had been incredible the first time, but this time had been something… *more.* He'd given her intense pleasure, and taken his own, but he had been commanding, determined…

Dominant.

Normally, the word would make her stomach turn.

Her perception of that kind of sex had been so badly skewed by past experience that she'd been sure she would never be willing to try it again. But Connor wasn't like Lucas. And she wasn't the young and naive girl she had been. With the benefit of knowledge and experience, surely she would be able to spot any red flags this time. So far, there weren't any.

Connor had been genuinely kind. Sweet, considerate, funny, and caring. He'd been careful not to push her too far. She'd noticed how closely he watched her reactions and she knew it was because he wanted to make sure he wasn't crossing any of her many, *many* lines.

No, Connor was nothing like that sadistic bastard. And she'd enjoyed his control—control that didn't come from physical restraint or force. She knew she could've said no—but she hadn't *wanted* to. That made all the difference.

It still confused her—but she hadn't been afraid with Connor. Not for a single second. Uncertain, maybe—but never afraid. She'd never thought she would tolerate, let alone enjoy letting a man take control in the bedroom. She never had before. Connor was different, but she couldn't quite figure out what it was that made her feel safer with him than with any other man she'd ever been with.

After nearly an hour of soaking and overthinking, the water had gone cold. She got out and dried herself quickly before wrapping the towel around herself and venturing out into the bedroom. She stopped short.

Connor was propped against her headboard in just his suit pants, bare feet crossed at the ankle, laptop perched on his thighs. His dark hair was mussed, stubble shadowing his jaw. His blue eyes were focused, intense, as he glanced between some papers on the bed beside him and the computer screen, his fingers flying over the keyboard.

She found the whole scene so ordinary, so domestic, and so, *so* sexy. She tried to push aside visions of them working side by side—quick smiles, teasing kisses, soft touches—but it was no use. It was joined by images of them cooking together in the kitchen, sitting on the couch together watching TV, and going to bed together, snuggled in each other's arms.

A *life* together.

She shook her head and crossed to the dresser in search of clothes. It was still fairly early, so she debated real clothes or pajamas. She decided on pajamas since she didn't want to have to change again later, but then hesitated between comfortable or sexy.

She chose comfort—she didn't know if Connor planned to stay. They hadn't actually spoken much so far. Either way, she didn't think he would complain. He seemed to like her in pretty much anything, though lord only knew why.

She smiled to herself, dropped the towel, and pulled on a plain white t-shirt and panties. She put on a pair of sweatpants and grabbed a pair of socks. She sat to pull them on, then scooted up beside Connor—careful not to disturb his papers.

He looked up and gave her a sheepish smile.

"I'm a *wee* bit behind since someone dragged me away from work early. Not naming names, of course."

"I did no such thing," she said.

"Alright, maybe not. But nonetheless, I've a bit of work to do. Do you mind?"

"Not at all." She smiled. "Beer?"

"You're a goddess," he said, stealing a quick kiss.

She went downstairs and browsed the takeout menus. She was starving and she figured Connor would be too. She ordered ordered Thai—one of every favorite—then returned upstairs with two cold beers.

She opened her book, tried to read—but her mind kept circling back to everything she was feeling. She brooded over them, trying to sort out, logically of course, what she thought she should be feeling and then how to reconcile that with what she *was* feeling. Except… she couldn't quite figure out what she felt.

The doorbell rang, and Connor jumped up to get it. She stayed put and in a moment he returned with a bag of food. They unpacked it together and ate right there on the bed, sharing bites straight from the container. It felt effortless. Intimate. Like they'd been doing this for much longer than just a week.

Had it really been just a week? That was another thing she couldn't wrap her mind around. She'd gotten much closer to him, physically and emotionally, in just a week than she'd ever thought possible.

"You're quiet," Connor observed.

"Eating," Alexandra replied between bites of pork dumpling. Connor gave her that crooked smile, but there was something in his eyes as he watched her. Anxiety perhaps?

"I was starving." She shrugged.

"Me too. Thanks for thinking of this."

"Sure." She smiled, wiping a bit of sauce from the corner of his mouth with her thumb. He grinned—broad and boyish, dimples in full force—then sucked her thumb into his mouth, licking it clean.

"Cheeky," she admonished him with a smile. He raised an eyebrow and went back to his Pad Thai. The silence lingered for a few minutes before he spoke again.

"Sure you're alright?" he asked. That uncertain look again. Alexandra couldn't brush it off. She wanted to reassure him.

"Absolutely." She smiled, and this time, she meant it. "You're very sweet, Connor MacLachlan. And very sexy."

"Yeah?" He grinned, hopeful.

"Like that's news to you." She snorted.

"It's news that you think I'm sexy. Headline news." He leaned in and kissed her, soft and sweet. "But you've got that look. Like you're thinking too hard about something."

"I'm just not used to this." She shrugged.

"What?"

"This. Being close to someone. And before was…"

"Was?" He grimaced, apparently expecting the worst.

"Amazing," she said quickly. "And confusing," she added.

"Why?" he asked, setting his container aside and taking her hand.

He was so goddamn sweet it made her want to cry. She wasn't sure how to explain. She didn't want to compare Connor to Lucas in any way, but she didn't have another way to communicate what she was puzzling over.

"I told you about… what happened," she began.

He just nodded, waiting patiently for her to continue, his thumb making soothing circles on the back of her hand.

"I hated the idea of ever letting anyone take control again. I never wanted to be that… vulnerable, that helpless, ever again. But earlier was… amazing. It shouldn't have been, though. I let you… direct things, and that should have made me uncomfortable. But it didn't. It was just the opposite, in fact. I'm just trying to wrap my head around it. How I could feel that way when I shouldn't have."

Connor nodded, silent, but his fingers tightened around hers in gentle reassurance.

"First of all, there are no rules for how you feel. You can't help it, and you can't force it. If you're being honest with yourself, then it just… is. If you enjoyed it, you enjoyed it. I understand why you think you shouldn't have, but there's no point in feeling guilty about feeling something that you don't think you should, or *not* feeling something you think you should." He shook his head. "Am I making any bloody sense?"

"Yes." She nodded, frowning. It did make sense.

"Second—I'm not him. I know you know that. I just hope you *feel* it."

"I do," she said, looking him in the eye so he could see she really meant it. "I'm sure of that much."

"Good." He nodded and dropped a quick kiss on her forehead to seal it. "Now here's my theory, and if I'm wrong, feel free to tell me to fuck off." He took a deep breath and let it out on a sigh before he continued.

"I think that piece of shit scared you, but I think he also made you ashamed of enjoying something a little less traditional. You said it yourself—you didn't want anyone to know about the videos because you didn't want you father to be embarrassed. Same with your sister. Thing is, lovely girl"—he tilted her chin, gently but firmly—"there's nothing in that to be ashamed of. Like I said, there's no 'should' or 'shouldn't' when it comes to feelings."

She thought about it and felt the truth of it. Sex… *after* had always been carefully controlled—and decidedly mundane. She realized now—it wasn't what they'd done she was ashamed of, it was *trusting him*.

The fear was still there—just under the surface. There were still a lot of things she didn't think she'd want or be able to do, but Connor was right. She'd jumbled everything together when her wants and needs had nothing to do with what happened—what Lucas had done.

"Lex?"

Alexandra looked up at him and realized she'd been in her own world for a few moments.

"I think you're right—actually, I *know* you are."

"But these things take time," he said. "If you want, I'll help you reclaim that bit of yourself," he continued softly.

She began to panic. Isn't this what happened every other time? After a while they always wanted to change her. They wanted her to "get over it" and be normal. Was he saying the same thing?

As if sensing her rising panic, Connor took both her hands in his.

"I'm not going to push, Alexandra. I'm not a Dominant, and I'm not looking for a submissive." He smiled, trying to lighten the mood. "And I meant what I said when I told you that whatever you gave me was a gift. I'm more than happy with that. But whatever you need, I'm here."

She was relieved—happy. And something else she couldn't name yet. She leaned in and kissed him. Sweetly. Thoroughly. Hoping he would understand what she couldn't say.

She pulled back and grinned at him.

"Even if I decide to tie you to the bed and have my way with you?"

she teased.

"If that's what you needed, I would tolerate that—*for you,* of course," Connor said, voice was warm with humor and eyes full of mischief, despite his serious expression.

"Thank you," she said.

And she meant it. In her experience, men were not as understanding and patient as he had been under similar circumstances.

"Anything for you." He smiled, kissing her cheek.

The rest of the evening passed in quiet companionship. Connor worked on his proposal while Alexandra sat with a book in her lap, lost in thought.

Connor slipped from the bed where Alexandra slept. It was nearly two in the morning, and Connor was as prepared as he could be for his meeting. He'd tried to sleep, but couldn't.

He was anxious about the trip—about more than just being away from work. For one week, Alexandra's safety would rest solely on him. But he'd promised her from the beginning that he would keep her safe

He said he wanted to be her world, and for a whole week he'd be just that. Everything would fall on his shoulders in a way it hadn't in years—with someone who was more important to him than he should probably admit.

He was afraid.

Not of the danger. Not of the risk. Of failing her. Of not being able to do the one thing he wanted and needed to do most. Protect her.

He grabbed his phone and crept downstairs.

"Connor!" his father answered. "Jesus, what time is it there? Ye must be burnin' the midnight oil, eh lad?"

"A wee bit." Connor smiled. "I didnae wake you, did I?"

"Nah, ye ken I'm up wi' the sun most days. I haven't heard from ye lately. Everything okay?"

"Aye, Da. Busy with work—but things are good. How's Mary Fran?"

"Ah, brilliant—just brilliant. Dinnae ken how I survived without her for so long."

Mary Fran, now his father's wife, had been his secretary for years before he finally pulled his head out of his arse and married her. Connor had never seen him happier—like a pig in shit, as the saying went. And he deserved it.

"That's easy—you had me cookin' and cleanin' for ye. And when I wasn't there, the maid and the chippy stepped in," Connor reminded him.

"Ah, ye're right, of course. You weren't half bad, either."

"Thank ye very much."

"No' as good as the chippy, but…"

Connor laughed. "No, but I was cheaper."

"That's debatable. I only had to pay for maself if I got takeaway—and ye used to eat like a damn horse."

"That's fair," Connor said with a laugh.

"Anyway, she's a godsend and I'm a lucky bastard," his father said. Connor could hear the smile in his voice. "An' how's yer sister?"

His father had always been a sweet man, and Connor loved him even more for taking an interest in Angel—just because Connor did.

Connor filled him in on work and Angel, as he always did. He usually confided in his dad—there weren't many people he could. Angel worked hard to stand on her own, and he wasn't about burden her with his problems. It was his job to support her, not add more stress.

His father told him funny stories from work, filled him in on the latest town gossip, and updated him on what the cousins were up to—which never changed: drink, brawl, bail.

And like he did every year, he invited Connor to spend the holidays with them—and to bring Angel. She'd never been keen to go, and though she insisted she'd be fine, he would never leave her alone for Christmas.

Maybe this year, he'd ask them to come visit him. Now that he was home for good and had a place of his own, he could finally have his family together for the holidays.

And maybe this year… there'd be someone else to share it with.

"Can I ask ye something?" Connor said.

"Course ye can."

"How did ye ken it was right—wi' Mary Fran?"

"Ah. I see. Met a lass ye fancy, have ye?"

"Aye," Connor said with a laugh. "Ye could say that."

"Well…" He paused, thinking. "It's hard to say, really. I never thought about it much."

"Very helpful, Da," Connor said, rolling his eyes.

"Maybe if I *had,* it wouldn't have taken me twenty years to marry her. But I didnae. It jus'… *happened.* I looked at her one day and realized—I'd rather do the rest of ma life wi' her than without her."

Connor swallowed hard, his voice a little rough when he finally spoke. "I think I understand."

"Seems ye already figured it out," his father chuckled.

"I reckon maybe I did," Connor agreed.

His chest felt full and warm but he wasn't quite ready to give it a name.

"If she's got *you* this turned around, she must be somethin'."

Connor laughed. "Oh, she's somethin'."

"I'm happy for ye, boy," his father said, his voice warm. "Now—jus' make sure ye dinnae cock it up."

"Grand advice. Thanks for that, Da," Connor said dryly.

"Anytime," his father said with a laugh. "Well, I'd best get on wi' it if I'm gonna make it to the office by nine."

"You're no' retired yet?" Connor teased.

His father had never shown the slightest intention of slowing down.

"Course no'. What would I do wi' myself all day long?"

"Play golf? Travel?"

"Aye, an' drive Mary Fran to drink, no doubt."

"Right. Best keep workin', then."

"Right. Love ye, ye wee rascal."

"Love ye, Da."

Connor made his way back upstairs and slipped into bed beside Alexandra. He felt lighter—but the moment he looked at her, sleeping peacefully, his chest felt tight. The thought of losing her filled him with dread. He didn't know when it had happened, but she'd burrowed deep into his heart and soul. It was too much, too soon. But there was no going back.

He tugged Alexandra tight against his chest and buried his face in the crook of her neck, breathing her in. She fit perfectly in his arms—her warmth soothing every bruised and battered part of him. Just like her fire chased away the shadows in his soul.

Eventually he relaxed into sleep dreaming about the future for once… instead of reliving the past.

Friday morning came too early, and Connor left a sexy, sleepy Alexandra with nothing more than a kiss. His meeting went well and the new clients approved of the contributions his team had made to his proposal.

He spent the afternoon reviewing the itinerary Alexandra had given him for the week leading up to the festivities in London. When asked, she'd listed things she wanted to do but left the timetable open.

He arranged for a rental car for the duration, making sure they had something relatively decent available. With hotel reservations and plane tickets already sorted, he tied up some loose ends at the office and went home to pack before picking Alexandra up.

He called Angel while he packed to make sure she didn't need anything before he left and to relay his father's invitation to spend Christmas with him and his wife. She was working and insisted she'd be fine on her own, as he'd expected, and deferred any decision about the holidays until after he got back. Which meant she'd pretend to think it over so she wouldn't seem rude when she inevitably said no.

Alexandra was waiting for him at the office, standing at the security desk chatting with Archie. Jealousy spiked through him, and he found himself scowling as he approached.

Archie gave him a gruff nod and Connor returned it.

Alexandra smiled, and smiled back.

"Ready to get out of here?"

"Yup." Alexandra picked up her briefcase and they waved goodbye to Archie.

For a moment, Connor wondered if they should compare notes. Sam had uncovered a lot about Whitmore through public records, including that he'd been released just under five years ago after serving three.

What a fucking joke...

Apparently, his parents still lived in Westchester, and he'd supposedly moved back in with them after his release. He bet they were just chuffed to have him back.

Sam was still working to track down his employment history and confirm his current address. It was slow going—especially using strictly legal means—but if anyone could do it, it was him.

He didn't want to withhold any information that Archie needed to do the job, but he also didn't want to share Alexandra's story with anyone unless it was strictly necessary. It wasn't his story to tell, and he wouldn't betray her trust unless absolutely necessary. Besides, it was likely that if Mr. Hughes had given him Lucas Whitmore's name, he would have given it to Archie as well.

"Sorry I'm late," Connor said, realizing how quiet he'd been. He unlocked the car and waited for her to climb in before closing the door for her and heading around to the driver's seat.

"You're not. I was early. I had nothing to do most of the day so I finally just gave up," she said with a sigh.

"No billable hours today, counselor?" Connor teased.

"Don't tell my father, but I spent at least two hours just shopping online."

Connor laughed. He couldn't see Alexandra spending two hours shopping *anywhere*. Her professional wear was tasteful and well-tailored, but mostly in basic, interchangeable colors. Her casual clothes were high quality but geared toward comfort. She wasn't flying to Milan for fashion week, but she always looked good. Or maybe she just looked beautiful no matter what she wore.

Or didn't wear . . .

"What in the world were you shopping for?" he asked, dragging his mind out of the gutter.

"Christmas presents," she said, as if it should have been obvious. As someone who typically bought everything at the last minute, the thought of Christmas shopping in October would never have occurred to him.

"Yeah?" Connor laughed. "What did you get me?"

Alexandra blushed and turned to look out the window.

Shite.

"Not that you have to get me anythin'." he said with a shrug. "I was just kiddin' ye, love."

"I did get you something... but you'll have to wait 'til Christmas," she muttered. He could see her reflection in the window and she was staring out onto the street, biting her lip.

He wanted to bite it too—but he also wanted his Hummer, and by extension *them*, to survive the trip—so he settled for kissing her knuckles. Before he could say anything—though he wasn't sure what he would have said—she continued.

"I also got Amanda this set of fancy Le Creuset ramekins she's been drooling over. And some custard cups. Also a new bag for work—she's been lugging around the same damn messenger bag since culinary school. It's a little funky, but that's her style, and it's big enough for all her stuff. I mean, really, who *travels* with knives? Oh—and I found a signed first edition of *Champagne for One* for my dad."

Connor chuckled. "Sounds like a productive day."

"It's a start. Still early, though." She shrugged. "I tend to go a little overboard, but I can't help it—watching people open their gifts is the best part of Christmas."

Connor smiled, because he knew exactly how she felt. She clearly put thought into her gifts, made sure they were personal—meaningful. That same sweetness showed in how she worried about Janie, cooked for the guys, or ordered Thai for him while he worked.

He wondered what she might've picked for him—something that met what were probably very strict criteria—considering she hadn't known him long. Whatever it was, he was sure he'd love it. She already seemed to know him pretty well.

Suddenly, he was nervous about what *he* should get *her*. He'd only been joking when he asked. He hadn't even thought about gifts this early—but even if he had, he would've told himself to wait. The fact that she'd already bought something—even if it was just a trinket—meant she had some faith in them. And two months' worth of faith was still faith.

And he wasn't going to think about *why* that made him so damn happy. Not yet.

"What time are you expecting your ma?" he asked.

"Well, I told her six thirty—which means she'll probably *already* be waiting when we get there," she said with a wry smile. "My mother is punctual to a fault. She always leaves early enough to account for any conceivable disaster—so when no catastrophe befalls her, she's inevitably half an hour early."

"And here I thought most women were always late."

"According to my mother? Early is on time. On time is late. Late is unacceptable."

"I'll make a note of that."

He was teasing again—but the idea of meeting her mother didn't bother him. In fact, he half hoped she'd ask him to stay.

Alexandra worried her mother might already be waiting when they arrived—but she wasn't. Connor escorted her in, waiting while she disarmed the alarm. He gave the place a once-over, then returned to the door looking slightly lost—like he wasn't sure if he should head out or stay.

"Beer?" she asked.

He smiled and nodded, looking a bit relieved.

"You want me to help you start dinner before I take off?" he asked.

"No, but you can keep me company for a while." She didn't want him to leave—but she also didn't want to scare him off by unleashing her mother and the inevitable interrogation.

She'd already admitted to buying him a gift for a holiday almost two months away, if she invited him to stay and meet her mother he was going to think she'd already started planning the wedding and picking out baby names.

She shouldn't be thinking about holidays or meeting each other's families—not yet. There was still a good chance that in a couple of weeks, he'd be sick of her issues and walk away. Or maybe, once the contract ended, he'd simply... drift away. It had been all of two weeks.

I must be out of my ever-loving mind...

She busied herself setting water to boil and browning sausage as the pasta sauce simmered on the stove. She preheated the oven and pulled out the other ingredients she would need to put together her lasagna.

Connor sat and watched her silently as she minced garlic, melted butter, and sliced bread. She diced tomatoes, basil and mozzarella and tossed them with balsamic vinegar, olive oil, parmesan, and a pinch of salt.

"So I talked to my da this morning," he said, finally.

"Oh?"

"Yeah. He invited me to come for Christmas."

She looked up from spreading garlic butter on the bread and studied him. He sipped his beer, looking casual, but his eyes were anxious.

"That's nice of him. How long has it been since you've seen him?"

"About six months, give or take." He'd begun peeling the label off his beer bottle.

"That's a long time."

"Yeah. He invites Angel every year, but she never wants to go—so

I usually stay here."

"That's nice of him. Why doesn't she want to go?" she asked, eyes on the sauce.

"Guess she just doesn't feel comfortable. She's only met him a few times. She's not keen on flyin' either."

"I can understand that. Still, it's a shame you can't have your whole family around for Christmas."

He took a thoughtful sip of his beer while she dropped the pasta into the boiling water.

"I was thinking of asking them to come stay here with me for a couple weeks."

"That's a great idea."

"And I was thinking that way you can come round and meet them." She paused in stirring her sauce.

"You want me to meet your dad?" She was impressed with how casual she sounded.

"Yeah, I do," he said slowly, as if he could hardly believe it himself.

"Oh." She smiled to herself. "Okay. That sounds nice."

He beamed at her as she assembled the lasagna and put it in the oven.

"That smells amazing," Connor groaned. Alexandra decided, in light of his invitation, to return the favor.

"Do you… want to stay for dinner?"

"Can I?"

"Sure." She shrugged. "If you don't mind answering a million questions from my mother."

His face lit up like a child on Christmas, and butterflies launched into aerial acrobatics in her stomach.

"Brilliant." He stood and kissed her, swift and hard. "I'll set the table."

Alexandra smiled to herself as she slid the bread into the oven. She couldn't believe how… *easy* Connor made everything. All the things that she agonized over and fretted about, Connor smoothed over with an easy smile and an affectionate gesture. It wasn't that he was dismissive or thought those things didn't matter—he just understood. He always knew exactly what to say, or do, to put her at ease.

Well, *almost* always. But it was probably better that he wasn't quite perfect. That would have been way too much pressure.

The anxiety and fear about being stalked, her panic attacks, her trauma—he acknowledged them and was sympathetic, but undeterred. He'd seen and recognized every caution sign she'd thrown up—and kept going anyway. Even the rapid pace of their relationship—and the idea of meeting each other's families—hadn't fazed him.

He was such a steady presence—honest, upfront, and open. He'd told her about some of his own issues and, while it was obvious that it hadn't been easy for him, he hadn't hesitated. He always seemed so sure of himself, so in control—not just of his own emotions, but of any situation he stepped into. Trust was a hard thing for her after everything she'd been through but she trusted him on a level she wouldn't have imagined possible after just a couple weeks.

"Alright?" Connor's low voice in her ear surprised her, sending a frisson of pleasure down her spine. He circled his arms around her waist and rested his chin on her shoulder.

"Yes," she said quietly. She reached up and curled her fingers around his nape. "Quite alright, actually."

Connor made a low hum and nuzzled into her neck. His breath skated across her skin and she let her head fall back against his shoulder.

"You smell so good," he murmured, placing warm, gentle kisses along her neck.

Alexandra felt all the tension in her body melting away. She closed her eyes and focused on the feeling of his strong arms around her and his lips moving across her skin. It was wonderfully intimate, but not strictly in a sexual sense. She felt close to him.

"I'd better change before they get here," Alexandra said, though she felt no desire to move.

"Need any help?" he drawled. She could feel his smile against her shoulder and she laughed.

"I don't think that would be wise."

"Wise? No. But it would be fun."

"Get thee behind me, Satan."

"Already there, love," he said with a wicked chuckle.

"Then take three steps back and cool off," she laughed.

Connor sighed and backed off, tucking his hands in his pockets—no doubt trying to conceal a rapidly growing (and very impressive) problem.

She bit her lip, reconsidering her position. Or rather, imagining several others. So, so many positions.

The doorbell rang, preempting any further flirtation, and a moment later Amanda followed Alexandra upstairs. Alexandra changed into jeans and a sweater and ran a brush through her hair while she got Amanda up to speed.

"You haven't said anything to mom, right?"

"No. You told me not to on penalty of torture if I recall."

"I hardly think withholding food constitutes torture."

"Excuse you—denying me paella for life absolutely qualifies," Amanda said, sulking dramatically.

"Fine," Alexandra replied. "As far as mom is concerned, Connor and I are just dating."

"Are you, though?" Amanda narrowed her eyes.

"That's not the point. The point is—that's what we're telling people. No one else needs to know about the stalker situation unless it's absolutely necessary. You *know* how Mom will react."

"Evading the question," Amanda sing-songed, flopping onto the end of the bed.

Alexandra blinked at her. "Who's the lawyer here?"

"Please answer the question, counselor."

Alexandra rolled her eyes and turned away to hide her grin. God, she was acting like a freaking schoolgirl.

"If you *must* know, it's not *exactly* a lie."

"I *knew* it." Amanda bounced up and down on the mattress, clapping her hands together. "He was practically eye-fucking you all through dinner last week."

"Amanda Renée Hughes! Language!" Alexandra scolded, face flaming.

"Oh please. As if you haven't said worse—and in court."

"Hush."

"So?"

"So, what?"

"Details, woman!" Amanda huffed. "I'm too busy at work to do anything but fall into bed and dream about tall, tattooed ex-Marines with long blond hair. You owe me something."

"Hmm… sounds strangely specific," Alexandra said, tapping her chin. "Now where have I seen someone like that before?"

Amanda rolled her eyes. "Evading again."

Alexandra tucked away that information for later and debated what she could comfortably share with her sister.

"He's… funny. Surprisingly sweet, sometimes. But also… intense. It's still really new, and a little confusing."

"What's confusing? Hot, funny, sweet guy who's clearly into you? Sounds pretty straightforward." Amanda shrugged. "Unless he's bad in bed."

"Would you shut up, you pest? What if he hears you?"

"Then say I'm wrong. Loudly."

Alexandra hesitated but decided to try it out and see how it went. Amanda wouldn't have much time to pry for details before their mother arrived, so any humiliation would be short lived and quickly forgotten, at least by Amanda.

"You are so, *so* wrong," Alexandra said giving her sister a grin.

"I knew it! God, I hate you sometimes." Amanda flopped back dramatically. "Mom and Dad's favorite. Super fancy, successful lawyer. And now you're hooking up with one of the hottest guys I've ever seen."

"Oh, shut it. You know you're the favorite. You're the baby—and a very talented chef who keeps them bribed with baked goods."

"That's fair," Amanda said, admiring her nails.

There was a knock on the door. Three precise evenly spaced raps—just loud enough to be heard, not loud enough to be rude.

"Remember—mouth shut," Alexandra hissed hurrying downstairs.

Connor was already crossing the living room toward the foyer.

She peeked through the window though she didn't need to and opened the door for her mother.

"Hi, Mom." Alexandra gave her a quick hug and a peck on the cheek, then shut the door and locked it.

"Hey, Mama," Amanda chimed in, offering her own hug and kiss.

"It's so good to see you both." Veronica stepped back to take them in. "I still can't believe how beautiful you two are. It seems like just yesterday—"

"We were in braces and pigtails," Alexandra and Amanda said in unison, already rolling their eyes.

"Yes, yes, I know. I'm becoming my mother. Terrifying, really."

Veronica gave a dramatic shudder and a wry grin.

"Mom." Alexandra cut in before the gossip floodgates opened. "This is Connor. Connor, my mother, Veronica."

Connor stepped forward, offering his hand and a warm smile. To her credit, Veronica masked her surprise well and shook his hand with a polite smile.

And so it begins…

Chapter Eighteen

Alexandra's mother was a beautiful woman who appeared to be in her late forties, though she was probably closer to late fifties. Her long hair was blonde, like Amanda's, though a shade darker and subtly streaked with silver. Her eyes were blue like Amanda's as well, but Connor could easily see the resemblance between the three women.

Veronica Hughes was shorter than both Alexandra and Amanda, and was rounder in the hips, but she was still an attractive and fit woman. He could easily imagine her on Richard Hughes' arm at a gala or dinner. They must have made a handsome couple.

She was dressed casually in jeans and a red sweater, both of which fit her well without being too tight. In short, like Alexandra, she was a woman who was beautiful without trying.

"It's a pleasure to meet you," Connor said. "I can see now where your girls get their looks."

"Hmm." Veronica raised an eyebrow in an appraising look. "You're quite the smooth talker, Mr…"

"MacLachlan. Connor."

"And to which of my beautiful girls do you belong?" she added with a knowing smile.

"That would be me," Alexandra volunteered, a grimace tugging at her mouth.

Another wave of anxiety rolled through Connor. Had he muscled his way into something she wasn't ready for? Was this too much, too soon?

"Alexandra?" Veronica whispered.

It was then that Connor understood. Her mother's eyes were a muddle of shock, sorrow, and hope—so raw it made Connor want to grimace himself. She looked as if she might cry for fuck's sake.

"Surprise," Alexandra deadpanned. "Would you like some wine?" she added casually, steering them all toward the dining room.

Her mother cleared her throat. "Yes, thank you."

Connor, remembering his manners, pulled out a chair for Alexandra's mother and received a small appreciative smile as she sat. He would have done the same for Amanda, but by then she had seated herself with small snort of laughter, the sound much like one Alexandra occasionally made.

Alexandra returned with a bottle of wine and, blessedly, a bottle of beer for him. She gave him an apologetic glance as he pulled out a chair for her. He took the place next to her—directly in front of her mother.

"So, Connor," Veronica began, sipping her wine delicately. "What is it that you do for a living?"

"I run a security firm, ma'am."

"Please, call me Roni." She patted his hand in a way that only mothers can. For a second it made his chest ache. He couldn't remember his mother ever making such a small gesture of comfort.

"Apologies. It's a bit of a habit I haven't completely broken yet." Connor gave her a small smile.

"Military, then?" Veronica asked, tilting her head. Connor nodded.

"United States Army. Twelve years."

"United States Army?" she repeated, surprised.

"Yes, m—Roni," he corrected quickly. "Don't let the burr fool ye. I'm American. Brooklyn boy, actually."

"How interesting."

"Connor's father is Scottish. He lived there for a bit when he was young and visited often growing up," Alexandra said, sipping her wine.

He appreciated the way she'd abbreviated the story while still telling the truth.

"Oh? What part of Scotland is your family from?"

"My da lives in Glasgow now, but he's from just south of Inverness. Every summer we used to spend a few weeks there."

"Beautiful country up there," Veronica said with a nod.

Alexandra and Amanda gave her a simultaneous and identical look of confusion.

"Your father and I went to Scotland on our honeymoon before heading down to England and France. You remember your great-grandfather was Scottish, don't you girls?"

"Yes, I remember." Alexandra nodded, sipping her wine.

"So I guess that means we've all got a little Scottish in us—some more than others," Amanda said, shooting Alexandra a knowing look. Alexandra's face flushed and she glared at her sister.

Connor covered his laugh with a cough and sipped his beer.

"I'll go check on dinner," Alexandra said tightly.

"I'll help you," Connor all but choked.

The evening went well. Veronica was politely curious, and Connor answered her questions with as much honesty and good humoras he could. She didn't grill him so much as ask questions that suggested genuine interest—and perhaps a little confusion.

It was obvious that Alexandra didn't introduce "boyfriends" to her family very often, and it was likely her mother was trying to figure him out. She was probably trying to decide if he deserved the honor of meeting the family.

Or maybe that was just him being a little paranoid.

All in all, he wasn't upset by it. It showed that her mother genuinely cared about her, and with what Alexandra had been through, it made sense that she'd be cautious about any man involved with her daughter.

At the end of the evening, keeping in mind the potential danger, of which Alexandra's mother was apparently unaware, Connor offered to walk her to her car. Alexandra probably thought he hadn't noticed her careful efforts to avoid leaving him alone with her mother. But he had—and he was more curious than anxious about why.

"You really didn't need to walk me out," Veronica said, though she still took the arm he offered and led the way to her pricey sedan.

"I wouldn't pass up the chance to take a wee stroll with a lovely lady, would I?" Connor said with a half bow.

"I can't tell if you're being a gentleman or a smart-ass," Veronica said with a smirk.

He could see where Alexandra got it from.

"A bit of both." He shrugged, and to his relief, Veronica chuckled.

"You remind me a bit of Alexandra's father that way," she said softly, a hint of sadness in her voice.

"Is that a good thing or a bad thing?"

"A bit of both," she said after a thoughtful pause. "He was a charmer when we first met. Still is—when he puts his mind to it."

"I can see that," Connor replied. This was delicate territory and he didn't want to overstep.

"You've met him?" she asked, a flicker of hurt in her eyes before she masked it. "I suppose you met him at the office."

Their official story was that they'd met at the firm while Connor was there in relation to a case. It was mostly true, and it was plausible enough. And they wouldn't be asked for any details—and if they were? Confidentiality. Can't discuss it.

"Yes, ma'am. He seemed decent enough."

"Decent? Yes. Driven, focused, workaholic? *Definitely*. But… he's a good father."

He was struck by her fairness. A lot of divorced people—men and women alike—wouldn't have a single kind word for their ex. His mother sure hadn't.

"This might be out of line, but my parents divorced when I was young." Connor's brow furrowed. "Mom went off about my da often enough that I could list every single thing he'd done wrong during their marriage. He was—*still is*—a good father, though. All her finger pointing and blaming him didn't make me think any less of *him*, but it did make me think less of *her*. I know divorce is hard, but it takes a good, strong woman not to turn that hurt into bitterness and put the children in the middle."

Veronica turned to him, her look one of surprise, and he experienced a moment of panic.

"I know it's not my place, but—"

"No," she said, lifting a hand to stop him. "You're right. And thank you for that."

Connor saw her eyes shining with unshed tears and was startled when she pulled him into a quick, tight hug. He gave her a sheepish smile as she unlocked her door. She turned before getting in, her expression a mix of emotions.

"Alexandra has been through a lot." She paused, clearly not sure how much to say or how to say it. "I love my daughter, and I want her to be happy. I like you, Connor. But if you hurt her—I will kill you. And I know an excellent attorney, so I'll probably get away with it."

This last bit was delivered with a smile, but Connor had no doubt she was only half joking. Veronica was a fierce Mama Bear, and— Ranger training or not—he had no desire to tangle with her.

"If I ever hurt her, I would let you," he promised.

She nodded once and slid into the car, shutting the door behind her. He watched her drive away with a small wave, then turned back toward the townhouse.

The door opened before he touched the handle—and before he even stepped inside, Alexandra kissed him. She framed his face with her hands, up on her tiptoes, kissing him positively stupid. He couldn't do much more than hold on to her waist and enjoy the ride.

The kiss was brief but searing—and when it ended, he was hard and aching. He had to remind himself that they weren't alone, *yet*, to keep from tossing her over his shoulder and sprinting up the stairs.

Alexandra pulled back and looked up at him, awed. Completely bewildered, she just stared, shaking her head.

"Not that I'm complaining—but what was that for?"

"What did you say to her?" she whispered.

He noticed Amanda standing in the living room doorway, wearing the same mix of confusion and admiration.

"We had a wee chat is all." Connor shrugged.

"Incredible," Amanda whispered. "He's like… the mom whisperer or something."

She took a step forward and Alexandra stepped between him and her sister.

"Get your own," Alexandra snapped.

Connor chuckled—he liked this possessive streak in her.

"I guess that's my cue," Amanda grumbled, grabbing her coat and bag from the hook in the hallway.

"Love you, brat," Alexandra said with a smile, pulling her sister into a hug.

"Love you, too. Call me from London."

Connor walked Amanda to her car, then returned to the brownstone, locking the door behind him.

And just like that, they were blessedly alone.

The moment the door locked behind them, her whole body buzzed with the urge to jump him on the spot. All night, Connor had been unbelievably sweet and patient with her mother—answering every question, playing host with drinks and dinner, pulling out chairs and standing whenever someone left the table. A total gentleman. While she packed with her mother and Amanda, he even cleared the table and did the dishes—like some kind of domestic unicorn.

And then, just when she thought the night couldn't possibly go better, he'd walked her mother to the car and said—or done—*something* that earned him a hug. A miracle, honestly.

Veronica wasn't cold. She'd always doted on her daughters, and back when her parents were still married, affection wasn't in short supply. But she was fiercely protective—and not easily impressed. Alexandra hadn't brought many men home over the years, and when she had, her mother had been wary at best. Polite, but never warm.

Warnings always followed. *Slow down. Be careful. Think it through.* Alexandra loved her mom, but that constant protectiveness made moving on from the past even harder. She'd never forget, but she didn't need reminders carved into every new chapter.

Somehow, Connor had slipped past every defense—her mother's and her own—with startling ease. And he had no idea what it meant to her that he'd pulled it off.

"Dinnae look at me like that." His voice was low, burr thicker than usual.

"Like what?" she murmured, stepping into his arms.

"Like I'm some white knight who's slain a dragon for ye." He smirked, pulling her in tight.

"Why not?" she whispered, brushing a kiss along his jaw.

"Because I'm not a white knight. And I'm no' fond of heights, so keep me off that pedestal, if ye please." His voice was teasing, but there was warning beneath it.

She kept kissing lower, and he groaned—deep, involuntary. He smelled like pine and clean air, crisp and sharp, but God… he tasted even better.

"If you keep lookin' at me like that, I'll haul ye upstairs and have my way with ye." His breath was hot against her ear.

"Mmm," she hummed against his throat.

Not exactly a deterrent. She nipped his neck and he grunted, gripping her tighter, hands sliding down the curve of her back. Her tongue traced the dip of his throat and he hissed through his teeth.

"Before you haul me upstairs," she murmured, "I should probably thank you for being such a gentleman tonight."

His eyebrow lifted, a slow grin tugging at his lips. "Aye? And how were you planning to do that?"

She took his hand and led him—purposefully—to the couch.

"Sit."

He dropped onto the cushions with a knowing smile, palms braced on either side of him.

"Have I mentioned how much I love this couch?"

She straddled his lap in reply, her grin matching his.

"Me too."

She kissed him slowly—sweet and coaxing—lips brushing over his with a maddening softness. Every time he tried to deepen it, she pulled back, just enough to tease.

He growled, low in his throat.

He clutched the back of her head, tangling his fingers in her hair, and took over. The kiss turned possessive, commanding—his tongue sweeping into her mouth, his teeth catching gently on her lower lip like a warning.

She melted into him, breath catching. As if he could feel the moment she gave in, he groaned—a primal sound of satisfaction. He tightened his hold, one hand gripped her thigh as he rocked up against her, slow and deliberate. Every motion was a promise of what was coming.

The ache low in her belly burned hotter.

She wanted him. *Desperately.*

But tonight, she wanted to give first.

Alexandra broke the kiss, barely managing a breath before his lips chased hers. She braced her hand against his chest, holding him back just enough.

His scowl was instant. And adorable.

She kissed his cheek, then trailed kisses to his ear, enjoying the scrape of his stubble on her skin. She nipped his earlobe and he moaned. Moving down his neck, kissing, nipping, and licking, she ran her hand down his chest, over his stomach, to the fly of his jeans.

She popped the button, eased the zipper down, and slipped her hand beneath his boxers, wrapping her fingers around him.

He groaned, deep and rough, as she stroked him slow and steady, her mouth still exploring his throat like she couldn't get enough.

"Jesus," he breathed.

He was magnificent, and she wanted to savor every inch of him.

She rose to her feet and bent to strip away his jeans and boxers. He lifted his hips, helping her—then took himself in hand, stroking lazily as he watched her.

The sight of it—the way he looked at her while he touched himself—sent fire straight between her thighs.

He looked at her like she was his entire world—all his focus, every ounce of raw hunger trained on her. It made her reckless, ravenous, desperate to please him. She wanted to brand this moment into her soul.

She sank to her knees between his thighs, her gaze never leaving his. One hand wrapped around his as he stroked himself, guiding it away. He let go with a sharp exhale, his head tipping back as she took over.

Connor's fingers found her cheek, thumb brushing across her skin like he couldn't believe she was real.

She licked a slow stripe up his length, flicking her tongue beneath the flushed tip before circling it, deliberate and slow

"Fuck," he breathed, jaw clenched tight.

Her lips curved in a smile as she took him into her mouth, slow and steady. His hips twitched, breath catching, and when she began to move—rhythmic, intentional—he groaned low in his chest, a sound of absolute surrender.

She put her hands on his thighs, fingers digging into tense muscle. He was trembling, breath ragged.

"So fucking good," he groaned, each word drenched in need and gravel.

Alexandra moaned around him, taking her time, savoring the weight of him and the raw power in her control. The sharp ache between her thighs flared hotter at the sound of his voice—at the way he was unraveling for her.

"Jesus—do that again," he growled, his hand tightening in her hair.

She obeyed, moaning low and long around him. His hips bucked up off the couch and a vicious curse tore from his throat.

"That's it. Just like that. If you don't want me to—*fuck*—say something now."

Too late.

Connor came with a hoarse shout, fingers locked in her hair, his entire body taut and shuddering as she took him through it—slow, steady, relentless.

When the tremors eased, he tugged gently on her hair, urging her to look up. She did—and his mouth was on hers in an instant, rough and claiming. By the time he pulled back, she was breathless, dazed, and somehow still on her knees.

He pulled her into his lap, crushing her against his chest like he never wanted to let go. He kissed her hair, again and again, and she held still, overwhelmed and quiet in his arms.

"Lex…" His voice cracked like something barely held together.

Her heart stuttered. This wasn't what she expected.

"You've no idea what you do to me."

Alexandra smiled to herself, remembering the night before. Connor had thoroughly enjoyed her thank-you—and repaid it in full until they were both wrecked. They'd grabbed breakfast on the way to the airport and boarded their flight.

It was a grueling seven hours, give or take—and Connor had forbidden her from sleeping. He'd declared himself the international travel expert, and therefore, his word was law. To be fair, he'd traveled more than she had—so she couldn't really argue.

They left New York around eleven and, thanks to the time difference, wouldn't land until nearly eleven that night—local time. He warned her that if she napped on the plane, she'd never be able to sleep once they arrived. It'd be hard anyway, since to them, it'd only feel like six p.m.

He kept her occupied by any means necessary—telling her stories of his misspent youth, huddling over a tablet to watch a movie, even sharing his music with her. She'd brought books for the flight, but hadn't touched a single one.

She was amazed at how easily they'd spent seven hours together in a flying tin can. They had similar taste in movies and music. They talked books, of course. She tried to sell him on Jane Austen, and he made his case for Stephen King—but neither of them got very far. As usual, talking to him was easy—and endlessly entertaining.

They grabbed a cab from Heathrow to the hotel, and Alexandra had oohed and aahed over the sights while Connor pointed things out along the way. Their suite was lovely—king-sized bed, cozy sitting area, and a big picture window overlooking the city.

Now, Alexandra stood in front of that window, staring out at London, trying to take it all in. Seven-hour flight be damned, she felt better than she had in a long time. She felt like she could breathe again.

"Nice view," Connor said casually, coming up behind her to wrap his arms around her waist, chin settling on her shoulder

"It's beautiful."

"You're beautiful." He kissed the side of her neck.

She'd noticed how physically affectionate Connor was. He touched her often—frequent kisses, constant hand-holding, casual brushes of contact.

Most of the guys she'd dated, once they knew what had happened, acted like they were afraid to touch her at all. They'd hesitate before hugging her. Even holding her hand felt like a risk. And eventually, the frustration—with her boundaries, or their uncertainty about them—always sent them packing.

Connor's casual touches and stolen kisses made her feel… *normal*. She wasn't a freak. She wasn't cold or aloof. She just needed to be loved a little differently. Connor understood and he was a quick learner.

"You're also very quiet," he murmured, straightening to rest his chin on her head.

"Just tired," she said with a sigh. Which was true.

"Come, then. Shower, food, then to bed wi' ye," he said, kissing her hair.

She let him lead her to the bathroom and start the water. When the water was warm, he pulled off her t-shirt, eased her out of her yoga pants, unhooked her bra, and nudged her gently toward the shower.

It was heavenly.

Multiple showerheads filled the ridiculously spacious stall, and she closed her eyes with a sigh as warm water soothed her back, shoulders, and scalp. London was beautiful—but in October, it was cold and wet.

Connor joined her a moment later—and as always, her pulse spiked at the sight of him in all his naked glory: dark hair, chiseled muscle, and those dancing blue eyes. She sighed, letting her gaze linger.

"Turn around," Connor ordered with a grin, pouring shampoo into his hands and massaging it into her hair.

"God, that feels good," Alexandra groaned, her voice thick with pleasure. She found herself making that sound a lot around Connor.

He was thorough, his fingers massaging gently as he rinsed and repeated with conditioner.

"Your hands are magic," Alexandra murmured, pressing a quick kiss to his shoulder as she reached around him for the shampoo. "Your turn."

He turned obediently, bending his knees just enough for her to reach the top of his head. She lathered, massaged, and smiled at the low groans he let slip.

They rinsed off, toweled dry, and pulled on the fluffy robes hanging in the bathroom before ordering room service. They sat cross-legged on the bed, eating while they talked about the sights of London and the upcoming wedding schedule.

Megan had a whole week of events planned—hair, nails, makeup, and of course, the hen night. Most were supposed to be girls-only, and Alexandra was still trying to figure out how to get around that—because there was no way Connor would be comfortable with her going solo.

"Maybe I'll say I'm too nervous to drive in London and you *have* to come with me," Alexandra mused, picking at her chips.

"Then they'll just ask why you didn't take a cab," Connor said between bites of steak.

"Hmm. I suppose that means we go with plan B," she sighed.

"What's that?"

"You'll just have to pretend you're so in love with me you can't bear to let me out of your sight. You've imprinted like a duckling."

Connor stopped chewing, looked up from his plate and raised an eyebrow. "Quack."

Alexandra laughed and he grinned.

But then—just for a moment—something shifted in his expression. It vanished so fast, she wasn't sure she'd seen it at all.

"I guess I can manage that. The hen do might be tricky," he mused, tone casual—too casual. "Depends on who's planning it."

"What do you mean?"

"Well, they all involve booze, loads of pink tat, questionable items shaped like cocks, and a substantial loss of dignity," Connor said with a chuckle. "But some of them can go on for a whole weekend. Could be just a night out—drinks, dancing, maybe a stripper. Or it might turn into a full weekend pub crawl with mortifying games and public humiliation for everyone involved."

"Ooh, now there's a thought." Alexandra beamed. "You could pose as the stripper."

She wouldn't mind watching Connor take off his clothes—or tucking bills into his G-string, for that matter. Just the thought had her pulse racing. And no, she definitely wasn't drooling over the British version of French fries. She dropped the fry back onto the plate and pushed it aside, stretching her legs out in front of her.

"Yeah? You want me to parade around the hen do and strip for your friends?" Connor gathered the plates, set them on the room service cart, and returned to the foot of the bed.

"Why not? Unless, of course, you can't dance," Alexandra teased, reclining back against the pillows.

"Is that a challenge?" he asked with a grin. His hair was still damp from the shower, and in that robe—bare-chested, relaxed—he looked downright edible.

"How about… a mattress mambo?" he asked, waggling his eyebrows.

Alexandra snorted with laughter.

"That was *so* bad."

"The Humpty dance?"

She wheezed, laughing harder until she was gasping for air.

"Stop—seriously," she begged, clutching her sides.

"Right. So, just the sex then," he said with a grin.

He undid the robe's belt, letting it slide off his shoulders and pool on the floor. Of course, he was naked underneath—blessedly, gorgeously so. He crawled toward her across the bed, slow and deliberate—and suddenly, she understood how gazelles must feel when they lock eyes with a predator.

Her breath caught. This man had made her laugh until she cried—and now he looked ready to make her *beg*.

"You're overdressed," he murmured, sliding in beside her.

He braced himself on one elbow, trailing a single fingertip over her chest, just beneath the edge of her robe. He kissed her neck, tasting her skin with teasing flicks his tongue.

Her breath hitched, nipples tightening in response. She sighed and closed her eyes, surrendering to the sensation of his touch.

The phone rang on the nightstand. Connor groaned and dropped his head against her shoulder.

His hand froze. He waited one beat—*hopeful*—then rolled away and grabbed the phone when it rang a second time.

"Connor," he snapped. A pause. Then he stood, already striding toward the dresser. He yanked on a pair of sweatpants, listening in grim silence.

So much for sexy time…

"Sorry, love. Emergency I need to handle. Get some sleep, yeah?"

Connor kissed Alexandra's cheek, steadying his breath and keeping his expression neutral as he grabbed his laptop bag and moved to the sitting area.

He laid everything out on the coffee table, powered up the hotspot, and booted up his laptop.

"Still there?" Sam asked through the line.

"Yeah. Start from the beginning."

"A friend of mine at the police department checked on his probation record. His current address is in Westchester—parents' house. Works for an uncle who does construction. Hasn't missed a check-in. No issues with probation. But get this—he's been given travel passes for Kings County four times in the last six months. Just for a day or two."

"Brooklyn? Why?"

Connor typed in his password, muttering a curse as he waited for everything to connect.

"To visit family—a cousin."

"Dates?"

"I sent the details to your email. Can't to tell exactly when the photos were taken, and he wasn't in town when they were dropped at the office. But he *was* there when the notes were left on your car. Every time."

"Okay, so either it's not him, or he's got help. What's the deal with the cousin?"

He opened his email and scanned for Sam's report.

A pause. Paper rustled on Sam's end.

"Uh—here we go. No priors. No record. Not even a parking

ticket."

"Whitmore's car—any match with the ones from the footage?"

"Doesn't look like it," Sam said.

Something in his tone was off. Hesitant. It wasn't like him.

"Doesn't *look like it*?" Connor's voice sharpened. "Is that a yes or a no, Sam?"

"No," Sam said. "It doesn't match."

"What about the cousin? He have a car?"

"Yeah. Still digging for the plate."

"Job?"

Silence

"Working on it."

"What the fuck, Sam?"

He *always* had answers—usually to questions Connor hadn't even thought to ask. But tonight, he was unprepared. And Connor wasn't in a forgiving mood.

"I'm working on it," Sam said through clenched teeth.

"Work. Faster." Connor's voice dropped to a snarl. "This is basic shit, Sam. By now, you should know what they had for breakfast, who they're fucking, and their goddamn search history."

Sam didn't respond, but Connor could *hear* the grind of his jaw through the silence.

He always went quiet before he blew.

"Find everything you can on the cousin," Connor snapped, and hung up without waiting for a reply.

Connor clenched his jaw, forcing down his anger on top of the anxiety already clawing at his chest.

That piece of shit had been in Manhattan.

Connor didn't care why—just knowing he'd been within ten miles of Alexandra made his blood boil. He wanted to pull the Barrett M82 out of storage and climb the nearest rooftop.

He allowed himself a brief fantasy: taking the bastard out from a quarter mile away.

It would be a tough shot—but he could make it. He'd made harder ones. And he'd get away with it, too.

By the time they figured out where the shot came from, he'd be gone. The rifle stripped, scattered, dumped in the Hudson. No one would ever know.

He didn't like killing. But he'd done it. And he was good at it.

Every shot had taken something from him. But Whitmore? He wouldn't lose sleep over that one.

The bastard didn't deserve to live.

But Alexandra would know. The moment she heard how it happened—she'd know exactly who pulled the trigger.

And she'd never forgive him.

No. If it came to it, he'd kill him. No hesitation. No regret. But he was a soldier, not a murderer.

And a clean shot? Quick. Painless. That was far too merciful.

He compromised. Best case scenario: get the bastard alone and turn him over to the police.

Bruised. Bloody. Broken. But alive—*barely*.

Whitmore goes back to prison, Connor stays out of it, and Alexandra's safe.

Connor spent the next hour poring over Sam's report—reading, rereading, memorizing every detail. He burned the photo of Whitmore into his mind.

Eventually, he forced himself to shut the file and go to bed. But his mind wouldn't let go of the question—how much should he tell her?

This was supposed to be her break. Her friend's wedding. A sliver of peace.

He didn't want to ruin it with something that might not even matter. Still, relevant or not, Alexandra would want to know. And she deserved the truth. He'd tell her as soon as they got back from London.

He turned out the light and climbed into bed. He pulled Alexandra close, tucking her snug against his chest. He buried his face in her hair and inhaled. The hotel shampoo was flowery—but underneath: honey and almonds.

Alexandra.

She sighed—a small soft, sound. Content.

His chest warmed. He was already gone for this woman—completely.

Then fear gripped him, sudden and sharp. He had to keep her safe. No matter what.

What he would do—
how would live with himself—
if anything happened to her?
He didn't think he could.

Chapter Nineteen

Alexandra woke to a gray, drizzly day beyond the picture window—but with Connor snuggled behind her, his arm draped over her waist, she was warm and cozy. She had no desire to move—maybe not for the rest of the day.

Unfortunately, nature had other plans.

She slipped away as gently as possible, not wanting to wake him, and pulled on her bathrobe against the morning chill. She went to the bathroom, brushed her teeth and hair, and tiptoed back to bed.

She sat for a while, legs tucked beneath her, just watching Connor sleep. He was always handsome—but asleep, he was breathtaking. With the burden he always carried briefly set aside, he looked so peaceful.

Her heart squeezed.

She wished he could hold onto that peace even when he was awake—but he wouldn't be Connor if he didn't pick that yoke back up every single morning.

Despite what she'd once thought, Connor was loyal, responsible, and cared deeply for the people in his life. He would do anything to keep them safe, healthy, and happy—and his own happiness came from making sure they were.

He was, without a doubt, the best man she'd ever met—

not perfect, but maybe perfect for her.

The only question left was whether she deserved him.

As Alexandra watched, he frowned in his sleep—his face contorting with anguish, his body twitching restlessly. He started to thrash, mumbling incoherently.

But she didn't need to understand the words to know—he was afraid.

He was in pain.

She froze, unsure what to do.

It was clearly a nightmare—but she didn't know how to wake him. She'd heard stories about how dangerous it can be to wake someone from a nightmare.

Especially someone like Connor.

Her own nightmares left her shaken and reactive, even after waking. She knew it would be the same for him.

Connor had told her himself—he was scared of what he might do during a flashback.

She wasn't afraid of him.

Despite his fears, she was confident he wouldn't hurt her. That was something she'd need to think more about later. But if she came away with even a scratch, the guilt would destroy him.

"Connor?" she said softly, resting a gentle hand on his leg.

He mumbled something indecipherable, twisting in the sheets, reaching out for something—or someone.

"Connor, wake up," she said louder. "You're safe. We're in London. I'm here with you. You're okay."

She didn't know what to do other except keep talking. Until he came to… or slipped back into a peaceful sleep.

She squeezed his leg gently and continued to talk in calm, soothing tones—even as her heart pounded and a cold sweat clung to her skin. She could *not* afford to fall apart.

Connor needed her.

"Connor, wake up. It's me—Alexandra. I need you to wake up for me now, okay? Can you do that? Please?"

Connor stilled—then his eyes snapped open.

His chest heaved like he'd been running for his life.

"You're okay. You're safe," Alexandra said, praying that her voice didn't sound as shaky as it felt.

"London. We're in London," he muttered, like had had to remind himself. He took a few deep breaths and closed his eyes, trying to wrestle his body back under control. Alexandra had been there before. She knew the drill.

Knowing he was awake and aware, she scooted closer and laid her hand on his chest.

His heart thundered beneath her palm.

"Are you okay?"

He drew one last deep breath, letting it out slow.

Then he blinked up at her and offered a strained smile.

"I'm fine," he said, voice tight. He sat up, gave her a quick kiss on the cheek, and disappeared into the bathroom.

He definitely *wasn't* fine—and he definitely didn't want to talk about it. It felt like he was pulling away and her heart sank at the thought. She wanted him to talk to her.

To let her in.

To let her be there for him the way he'd been there for her.

She'd broken down in front of him more than once. He'd seen her in the grip of a panic attack, after a nightmare. Heard her tell the story of the worst night of her life.

She'd opened up to him like she never had with anyone else.

And It hurt that he couldn't do the same.

She knew he had to go at his own pace. He hadn't pushed her—just offered to listen, and waited. But still—she wanted him to trust her with this. She wanted to soothe the fear and loss she'd seen etched on his face.

To give him back a sliver of peace.

No matter how often her therapist's voice whispered that he was the only one who could do that—it didn't make the feeling go away.

"What time is it anyway?" he asked, emerging from the bathroom and rummaging through drawers.

"A little after seven," she replied.

She hesitated—then crossed the space between them, wrapping her arms around his waist and resting her cheek against the broad expanse of his back.

"Are you sure you're okay?"

He froze—just for a breath. But it was enough to gut her.

Then he recovered, covering her hand with his where it rested against his stomach.

"Yeah. I'm fine, love."

His voice was gruff—but steady.

"Do you want to talk about it?" she asked, pressing a soft kiss between his shoulder blades.

"I—"

He cleared his throat and shook his head.

"I don't think so. Not right now."

Alexandra tried not to let it sting. It was hard, opening the door to your own private hell—she knew that.

He'll tell me when he's ready…

As if reading her thoughts—or maybe just sensing the shift in her—he turned in her arms and hugged her tightly, kissing the top of her head.

"Soon. I promise. I just… it's still too fresh," he said quietly. Alexandra tried to keep the disappointment out of her voice.

"It's okay. Whenever you're ready… you know where to find me."

She'd just have to be patient and wait until he was ready.

And she wasn't going to think about what happened if that day never came.

Connor wasn't sure he'd ever be ready. He only knew there'd come a day when he couldn't hold onto it in anymore—when it would rip its way out. And it would be hell.

But not today.

Only four people knew the whole story—the three who'd survived that godforsaken desert with him, and the counselor he'd seen when he came home. He hadn't even told Angel a fraction of it—and he honestly didn't think he ever would.

It wouldn't help.

She didn't need to carry that kind of weight around every day.

Hell, that was the whole point—to keep it all far, far away from the people they cared about. To spare them the sleepless nights, the blood, sweat and tears. The fucking sacrifices. To make sure everyone on this side of the world lived their lives without seeing what they'd seen—things that still showed up in his nightmares.

They were always the same.

That shithole outside of Mosul.

Watching through his scope as everything went to hell—

and not being able to do a goddamn thing to stop it.

Except now, Alexandra was there too—

on the wrong side of his scope.

He shoved the surge of emotion back down where it belonged

and forced himself to focus on the here and now. He dressed quickly and checked his email while Alexandra got ready. It was oddly soothing to sit there while she picked out clothes, styled her hair, and did her makeup.

So mundane. So normal.

It grounded him.

Maybe, for a few minutes, he could believe he was just a regular guy—a man without scars or nightmares, without blood on his hands. He could pretend he wasn't so broken.

Pretend he was the kind of man Alexandra deserved.

He forced himself out of the spiral—for her. She needed someone who could focus on *her*, on what *she* needed, not sit in a dark corner brooding like a cliché. Sooner or later, she'd realize she could do better. Until then… he'd make the most of every second.

He would try to make her happy.

He'd keep her safe.

Or die trying.

There was a knock on the hotel room door—and Alexandra bolted past him to look through the peephole.

She squealed. And someone squealed back from the other side of the door.

Alexandra flipped the latch and opened the door, and before Connor could blink, a petite brunette launched herself into Alexandra's arms, wrapping her legs around her waist.

Connor watched in amused awe as Alexandra spun in circles, giggling.

His heart cracked wide open. The sound was so sweet—so free, so full of joy. He'd give anything to let her feel like that every single day.

"Oh. My. *God*." The brunette—presumably Megan—shouted.

She punctuated each word with a smacking kiss to Alexandra's cheek. "You are still such a sexy Amazon."

"And you are still the most beautiful little Hobbittses," Alexandra laughed, setting Megan down.

Connor chuckled—because the comparison was *painfully* accurate. Alexandra really did look like an Amazon towering over the smaller woman.

"And who is *this*?" Megan asked, shoving Alexandra aside and strutting up to Connor, hands on her hips. She narrowed her eyes and gave him a frank once-over.

"This is Connor," Alexandra said with a smile, moving to his side.

He slung an arm over her shoulder and tugged her tight against him. He kissed her temple and then extended a hand to the little brunette.

"Megan?" he asked. She nodded, shaking his hand—still clearly assessing him.

"Dear God, you're handsome," Megan muttered, shaking her head. She looked displeased.

Connor was very confused.

"Yes, but he's also *nice*," Alexandra said. Connor just looked from one woman to the other. He wasn't sure what was happening, but at least Alexandra was defending him.

…I think.

"Megan insists that men who are too handsome must be jerks," Alexandra said with an apologetic look up at him.

"Not jerks—*douchebags*," Megan corrected. "And it's not just an opinion. It's a well-tested theory at this point."

"Anecdotal evidence, at best," Alexandra muttered.

"Well, I hope I'm neither," Connor offered. They ignored him completely, still locked in their unspoken chaos duel.

"Besides, your groom is pretty damn handsome," Alexandra said with a pointed look.

"Yes, but he's not *too* handsome," Megan argued. "He has a scar through his left eyebrow—mars the perfection."

"One might argue that makes him *more* handsome, not less."

"And *one* might mind their own business," Megan said with a grin.

"True," Alexandra laughed.

"In that case, it's a win/win for me," Connor said smugly.

"Oh?" Megan quirked an eyebrow.

"Yup."

Connor stepped forward and tilted his head to the left, letting the light catch the inch-long scar along his jawline. It was old and faded—easy to miss.

"See this?" he said, pointing without hesitation.

"Hmm. I do."

"So according to you, I'm not *too* handsome to be a decent—and according to Lex, I'm even *more* handsome than I was before. Which, honestly, I didn't think was possible."

Alexandra snorted and rolled her eyes, pretending to be unimpressed.

It was fucking adorable.

Megan burst out laughing, and Alexandra couldn't hold her straight face for long.

"So, what happened here?" Megan asked, stepping closer to get a better look.

"You don't—" Alexandra began quietly.

"Riding accident," he said, giving her shoulder a squeeze—grateful that she'd been ready to jump in if he didn't want to answer.

He told them the story of how he'd fallen off a horse one summer in Scotland, and how his father had panicked—rushing him to the hospital, shouting for every test possible at the top of his lungs.

By the end, he'd gotten six stitches. And both women were nearly doubled over with laughter.

"Alright," Megan announced after her laughter had subsided, clearly having come to a decision.

Connor was more anxious about the verdict than he wanted to admit. He wanted Alexandra's friend to like him.

"I suppose you pass the first test."

Megan flashed a mischievous grin that lit up her heart-shaped face and made her dark eyes dance. He could see how she'd snagged herself a handsome—but not *too* handsome—fiancé.

And since that fiancé was the man who'd quite possibly saved Alexandra's life, Connor was glad that Megan was a lovely girl. And charming.

Alexandra's hero deserved that much.

He added it to the list of things he didn't want to examine too closely—the sharp little pang of jealousy that came when he thought of someone else as Alexandra's hero.

He was glad someone had been there for her. Truly.

But still...

Megan's opening salvo turned out to be only the beginning—of both the wedding week festivities *and* the inquisition. Connor tagged along to nearly every event that week, under one pretense or another, unless it was at a reasonably secure location, like Megan's home.

Even then, he was never far.

And at every turn, Megan had a new list of questions to fire at him until she was satisfied. *For the moment.*

It became a ritual of sorts. They'd arrive. Megan would give Alexandra enough time to get distracted—then she'd pounce.

Connor would spend twenty minutes cornered and questioned—and then he'd be released for the rest of the day, like a very polite hostage. Or a large mouth bass.

By the weekend, he was *pretty* sure Megan worked for the FBI—and he was now on some kind of watchlist. He just hoped they let him on the plane when it was time to go home.

Connor was handling everything better than she'd expected. He was amazing—capable, charming, handsome—but the week had been a blur.

Megan would've eaten most people alive by now.

It was a good thing she'd been going easy on him, since Alexandra had been too busy to run interference like she'd planned.

She'd barely had time to breathe, let alone go sight-seeing. But thankfully most of it was fun. No Bridezilla importing Russian swans or trying to convince Elton John to perform at the rehearsal dinner.

They went shopping, ate at all the best restaurants, drank wine by the bottle, and weighed the pros and cons of eloping whenever the stress got too high.

She and Megan caught up on everything they'd missed since the last time they'd seen each other. It was like summer camp—except at the end of the day, she got a slumber party with Connor.

Which involved very little actual sleep.

They ordered room service. Watched movies. Snacked on junk food.

They talked. Laughed.

Had sex.

Incredible sex.

A lot of incredible sex.

It was perfect. Like living in a romance novel.

Which worried her.

In the books, as soon as everything seemed perfect—that was usually when everything went to shit.

And that's how her life had been, too. The moment things started to look up, the floor fell out from under her. She scolded herself for being so stupid. Told herself to just enjoy it—enjoy the trip, enjoy Connor—one day at a time. Deal with whatever comes *when* it comes. It was the only way she'd survived the last nine years.

Friday night was the "hen do," and Connor had gone to run some errands—but not before making Alexandra promise to stay in the hotel suite with the door locked until he got back. She'd used the time to get ready for the party, wondering what to expect.

Megan had come by earlier to help pick out clothes and weigh in on shoes. But she'd refused to answer any questions about the night's festivities.

Whether she genuinely didn't know, or just thought it would be more fun to keep Alexandra in the dark, she wasn't sure. Honestly, it felt exactly like the kind of thing Megan would do.

She was just finishing her makeup when she heard Connor's deep voice through the door.

"It's me."

Still, she checked—just to be sure—before opening it. He was reading something on his phone as he wandered in, not looking up until she shut and locked the door behind him. When she turned around, he was standing stock still.

His eyes swept over her from head to toe.

Slow. Stunned.

"Well?" she asked with a smile, doing a little twirl. "How'd I do?"

Connor blinked.

Once.

Twice.

"Fuck me," he breathed.

She tilted her head, raising an eyebrow, waiting for an answer.

That can't be a serious question.

Alexandra was sexy in anything—suits, jeans, gym clothes—you name it.

But this…

There were no words for *this.*

His mind had gone completely blank.

Her hair was wavy and artfully tussled like she'd just rolled out of bed after a night of incredible sex—a look he was pleased to be familiar with. Her didn't know what she'd done, but her eyes glowed gold under smokey shadow and long, dark lashes.

And her mouth—soft, glossy, pink—gave him all sorts of ideas,

That dress had looked plain on the hanger. But on her?

Spectacular.

It skimmed her waist and hips like it was made for her. Knee-length with long sleeves, it was modest in design, but lethal in effect.

High heeled boots in cream-colored suede? Inspired.

He was inspired to do a lot of things.

Most of which involved those boots up on his shoulders and that dress on the floor.

Or maybe the boots on the floor and the dress up around Alexandra's waist.

Or maybe—

Not the time. Use your words.

"You look stunning," he said, voice rough as sandpaper.

He took her hand and brushed a kiss across her knuckles. She looked away, blushing and he stepped forward, wrapping his arms around her and kissed the top of her head.

Then her shoulder. "You look breathtaking."

Her collarbone. "Exquisite."

The side of her neck. "Perfect."

The hollow of her throat. "Enchanting."

"You, lass," he whispered. "Look positively edible."

He took her earlobe in his mouth and nibbled—just enough to hear her gasp. It was all he could do not to pick her up and toss her on the bed.

But women generally got peevish about spoiled hair and makeup. So he came up with a better idea. His hands skimmed down her hips to the hem of her dress, inching it up over her smooth, bare thighs.

"What are you doing?" she whispered, breath catching.

"Hush, love," he murmured, kissing just below her ear.

He nuzzled her neck, inhaling the warm sweet scent of her skin as he bunched the dress around her hips. He took a step back and smiled.

Silky, blue underwear, trimmed with lace.

He crouched, hooked his fingers beneath the waistband, and slid them down.

She steadied herself with a hand on his shoulder, stepping out of them with a grace that made him ache. He pressed a soft kiss to her thigh, then stood, pocketing his trophy.

"You stole my undies," she said, voice breathless and stunned.

He smoothed the material of her dress back down over her hips.

"Yes. I did," he said with a grin.

She blushed and the growing bulge in his pants pressed against the seam of his trousers.

"You want me to go out dancing without underwear?" she asked, trying to sound stern.

But he could see the spark of excitement in her eyes.

"Yes," he said, voice low. "Your skirt's long enough. No one will know but me."

His hands slid up from her waist; thumbs grazing the undersides of her breasts.

He leaned in, his mouth brushing her ear. "It'll be our little secret. And Maybe we'll find a quiet corner of the pub later on."

She shuddered. She liked the idea as much as he did. Connor had never considered himself adventurous in bed. Sex was just sex. Simple.

He'd never been possessive. Or jealous. No kinks to speak of. But Alexandra brought things out of him he hadn't even known were there.

He wanted her everywhere.

All the time.

Yes, because she was fucking irresistible—but also because he wanted the world to know she was *his*.

He was protective by nature—of his sister, his team, even his father. It was who he was and what he did. But this? This was something else.

Something he wasn't ready to name.

He gave her a quick kiss—careful not to smudge her makeup—and stepped back.

"Get your coat, gorgeous. It's a wee bit nippy." He winked at her.

And when she giggled, he thought his heart might burst.

Chapter Twenty

Connor delivered Alexandra into Megan's waiting hands, and was immediately shooed toward the bar to wait out the evening. He ordered a pint. A good stout—*thank God and all the saints*—and tried to keep his nerves in check.

The pub was loud, dark, and crowded. Which made Connor's skin crawl. A thumping bass line tried to rattle his bones loose, and somewhere, a strobe light was flashing like it got paid by number of seizures induced.

He closed his eyes, reminding himself he was in England, not Iraq. Pub. Not desert.

His heart was still pounding, and his ears were ringing. But he focused on Alexandra and the panic lessened.

She was dancing with a gaggle of other women, wearing a hot pink sash that read "*Bitch of Honor*," a perfect match for Megan's "*Bridezilla*." The drinks were flowing and the chaos was well underway. They seemed to be having a grand time.

Alexandra was a sight—laughing, dancing. *Free.*

More radiant than he'd ever seen her.

She tossed her head back and laughed at something Megan said—and Connor couldn't take his look away.

She lit up the room.

"Now there's a man in love if I've ever seen one." The man who sat down beside him was tall, ruddy, blond—with a posh British accent that said his family kept hounds and owned a polo club.

He didn't wait for a reply—which was good, because Connor had no idea what to say to that.

"Which one's yours?" the man asked, flagging down the barman.

Yours…

Connor liked the way that sounded. He *wanted* everyone to know that Alexandra was his—but he was also a little unsettled by how obvious it apparently was. He'd always thought his poker face was better than that.

"The one in the blue dress—dark hair, boots. She's mine." Connor smiled. He'd have said it anyway—he had a part to play, after all—but it helped that it was mostly true.

"Alexandra?"

Ah. This must be the fiancé.

Ryan's expression shifted—surprise, then wariness—as he gave Connor a thorough once-over. He was sizing Connor up—and while that usually didn't end well, Connor reminded himself Megan's fiancé had every reason to be on guard.

"None other," Connor said with a nod.

"You must be Connor then," Ryan said, extending a hand. Connor shook it without hesitation.

"Which must make you the fiancé."

"Ryan," he confirmed with a nod. "Good to finally meet you. Megan's mentioned you a time or ten."

Connor wasn't sure if that was good or bad—so he went straight for the compliment.

"You've got a good one there. Bit of a handful, but she's class. And she's been good to Lex—so hell, she could be an axe murderer and I'd still post her bail."

That made Ryan laugh and he seemed to relax a bit.

"Thick as thieves, those too," he said with a grin.

"So I've heard. This week's been... an experience." Connor chuckled, thinking of the way they bickered until they both broke down laughing—and all the impromptu carpool karaoke he'd had to sit through.

"Oh, I bet. I would've loved to be there myself, but work's been hell. Trying to catch up so I can actually *take time off* for the wedding and honeymoon has kept me chained to my desk."

Ryan looked genuinely disappointed to have missed it—and Connor didn't blame him. If Connor had been anywhere but right next to Alexandra this past week, he'd be a miserable bastard too. And not just because of safety concerns.

"I've heard quite a bit about you from Alexandra, actually," Connor said, sipping his pint. Ryan frowned slightly, suspicion flickering across his face.

"What have you heard, precisely?" Ryan sipped his own pint.

"That you and Megan have been her friends since college. And that you… helped her out." Connor glanced into his pint, recalling the story Alexandra had told him. "That you probably saved her life."

"She told you that?"

"Aye."

"That's… surprising. She never talks about it—she doesn't open up easily, even to us." Ryan pursed his lips, spinning his glass on the bar, lost in thought. "She must trust you a great deal."

Connor noticed his sidelong glance and turned to face him.

"I hope so," he said truthfully. He shrugged, suddenly feeling a little uncertain. "I told her I wanted to shake your hand—now I have. And I wanted to thank you for being there when she needed someone."

"I can't say it was a pleasure, but I'd do it again in a heartbeat, mate," Ryan clapped him hard on the back. "I only wish I'd found a more permanent solution while I had the chance."

Connor recognized the murderous glint in the man's eyes. He'd seen it before—on other faces, and in the mirror more times than he cared to admit. Ryan might think he wasn't being serious—but Connor wasn't so sure. Given the chance, he suspected Ryan would make good on his words.

Most people lived their whole lives never knowing what they were truly capable of—and that was how it should be. But beneath the swank exterior, Ryan had mettle.

"I ken what ye mean," Connor muttered, his fist tightening on the bar.

"Good. Then you also *ken* that I have to warn you. If you hurt our Alexandra—"

"You'll have me bollocks," Connor finished for him. "Understood."

"Oh, *I* won't—but my blushing bride over there most certainly will," Ryan said with a chuckle. "As you may have noticed, '*though she be but little, she is fierce.*' I *will*, however, be obliged as a dutiful husband to help my lovely wife hide your body."

"Of course," Connor said with a nod. "I'd do the same in your shoes."

"Good to know." Ryan smirked and turned back to his beer, and Connor had the feeling they were going to get along just fine.

"What are ye doin' here anyway? I thought this was just for the lasses. Aren't you supposed to be at your stag party?"

"Oh, this is revenge, you see. My stag do was last night. My mates took me out for a pub crawl and got me properly pissed. We get to the last pub and before I know it I'm being dragged into some rank back room and in comes my best man wheeling in this enormous cake. On goes the music, and then out pops—not a stripper—but my stunning fiancé."

If Ryan's expression was anything to go by, he really hadn't been keen on that surprise. Connor couldn't say that he blamed him. If Alexandra popped out of a cake in front of his friends—his *men*—Connor would lose his damn mind.

"So you're crashin' her hen night?" Connor asked. He was tempted to offer to help—but he wasn't sure how Alexandra would take it. Not to mention he needed to keep his attention elsewhere. Still, that didn't mean he couldn't enjoy the show.

"Oh no, not *just* crashing. She was wearing little more than cake frosting—in front of a room full of men. Men I now have to see. And be polite to. And certainly not punch in the face. It's bloody hard *not to* when you know they've seen your soon-to-be-wife half-naked."

"Dinnae tell me you're gonna return the favor." Connor grimaced.

"Oh, yes, my friend. *Our* lovely Alexandra even went to the trouble of cancelling tonight's hired entertainment."

Our Alexandra…

Connor liked the sound of that too—and that answered his question about how she'd feel if he'd offered to help. He should have known.

"You dragged Alexandra into the line of fire? Not very nice of you."

"She volunteered," Ryan said with a grin.

Of course she did.

A rowdy cheer rose from the dancefloor as the women began herding Megan toward the back of the club.

"That's my cue." Ryan winked and sauntered away.

He was a tall, good-looking fella and Connor was sure no one would complain about him standing in. Even knowing the man was getting married in the morning, Connor didn't like the idea of Alexandra watching him strip.

For safety's sake, he should probably move closer to the private rooms. There was a back entrance he really should keep an eye on. He was just rising when he saw Alexandra walking toward him.

Time slowed. The crowded dance floor seemed to part for her. She was smiling, cheeks flushed from dancing. Her dress had ridden up, revealing long, bare inches of thigh above the knee.

He stood, one hand in his pocket, rubbing the silk of her panties between his fingers—remembering how she'd looked when he slid them off her.

As soon as she was within reach, he slipped an arm around her waist and pulled her close. His fingers threaded through her hair, sifting the soft strands—marveling that they felt even better than the silk in his pocket.

With a firm grip on the back of her neck, he leaned down and kissed her. Hard. He hadn't thought about it. Hadn't planned it. His body had moved on instinct, wanting—*needing*—her mouth under his.

He slanted his mouth over hers, teasing one lip, then the other, with slow sweeps of his tongue. He nipped her lower lip between his teeth and tugged on it until she sighed softly and opened for him.

"Good girl," he growled.

He angled her head back, delving deeper—and she met him with matching heat, every slide of her tongue fanning the fire between them.

It was maddening how much he wanted her—until there was nothing else. It was dangerous, and he knew it.

He pulled away and leaned his forehead against hers as they both regained the ability to breathe and speak.

"Let's get out of here," Alexandra whispered. There was mischief in her eyes and her smile screamed the best kind of trouble.

"Surely the party's no' over?"

"Close enough. Once Megan gets her *surprise* I doubt she'll stick around long. And I don't really want to be in her path if she does."

"Aye, I met her *surprise*," Connor replied. "I think it's safe to say she'll be in good hands."

"Oh, most definitely," Alexandra agreed with a smirk. "But it's a little hard to focus on that at the moment."

She bit her lip and looked up at him through her lashes, cheeks flushed. She shifted awkwardly, pressing her legs together and tugging the hem of her dress down to where it should be.

"Distracted, are ye?" Connor laughed, running his thumb along his lip—thinking about finding that quiet corner and taking care of her once before dragging her back to their room.

It was all too tempting knowing she was standing there, wet for him, with nothing in the way of his hands or his mouth.

He shook his head, choosing the wiser path—hoping he wouldn't regret it.

"Come." He took her hand, led her to the car, and helped her climb in.

On the drive back to the hotel, he forced himself to focus—drive with caution. Right up until she put her hand on his thigh. He glanced over—she was turned toward him, one hand on his leg, the other skimming the neckline of her dress.

Oh, you wicked little minx…

"Eyes on the road." She quirked an eyebrow at him and he obeyed, silently promising he'd get his revenge as soon as they walked through the door.

She kneaded his thigh, fingers digging into the muscle already tense beneath her touch. Her hand slid upward—fingers brushing dangerously close to his aching cock beneath the fly of his trousers.

"Lex," he warned, voice tight, shooting her a quick, hard look.

"Hush." She shifted to face him more fully, skirt hiked well past mid-thigh. She was close enough he could simply reach over…

No. Very bad idea.

He shook himself mentally.

"It's not safe to distract—*fuck*—the driver."

Her hand closed the gap—squeezing him gently, rhythmically. His hips bucked involuntarily—and only years of combat driving kept him from swerving into a line of parked cars.

"Oh, I fully intend to fuck the driver," she purred.

"*Alexandra,*" he said tightly, and this time it was a warning *and* a promise.

She gave him a cherubic smile—pure innocence—then moved her hand from him… to herself. Her fingers traced her neckline, then lazily drifted to her thigh. Just a fingertip at first… then two. She ran her fingers along the hem of her dress—which, by now, barely covered anything at all.

"You're playing with fire, lass," he growled. "Hope you're prepared to burn."

She smiled at him, and spread her legs slightly, inching that naughty hand of hers up under her skirt.

He tried—and failed—not to notice the sweet, musky scent of her arousal filling the car, thicker by the minute.

By the time he parked, he was ready to explode. She'd straightened her skirt and now sat prim—and *very* smug—in the passenger seat, waiting to see if he'd pounce on her here or if he could wait until they had more privacy. He did neither.

He opened her door and waited patiently while she got out. He took her hand and, just as casual as you please, led her into the hotel and toward the elevators. She looked wary—maybe a little confused—as the elevator doors closed and she realized they were alone.

He tugged her back against him—close enough to feel exactly what her clever little game had done to him. She gasped—then pressed back into him with a soft, deliberate arch of her back.

Fuck me sideways.

He caressed the back of her thigh with his free hand and felt her shudder. He slid it higher—until he was palming one firm, perfect cheek. The elevator chimed and the doors began to open. She froze, but he continued to knead and shape the taut flesh in his hands ignoring her subtle, futile attempts to tug her dress down.

An older couple boarded the lift with polite nods, then ignored them in the way that is not only acceptable—but *required*—on an elevator.

Alexandra tried to pull away from him, but he simply tugged her more firmly against him, bending his head to kiss the back of her neck, the pulse point just below her ear, her shoulder…

Alexandra began to melt back into him, little by little. He grinned against her neck and bit her nape—just a scrape of teeth—as he slid his hand between her thighs. He shifted slightly. He pushed a knee between her legs, forcing her feet farther apart.

He started slowly, observing her reactions closely for any sign he was pushing her too far, too fast. Her breathing was even, but a little fast. Her heart was pounding, but her skin was flushed, not pale. He began dragging one thick finger back and forth, teasing. She stifled a moan and it came out as a squeak.

She was gloriously, deliciously wet and he had to stifle a groan of triumph as he slid his middle finger in deep. She sagged against him, legs trembling as he began to thrust slowly.

He relished the perfect weight of her in his arms as her head came back against his shoulder. He kissed her temple and whispered in her ear.

"Just remember that you've earned every last bit of this," he said softly, adding a second finger and increasing his pace.

She turned to him, eyes glazed and heavy lidded—her whole body was shaking with need.

"Do you want to come?" he whispered.

She made no sound, but she shifted, widening her legs a little more, opening up for him. He let out a satisfied hum and added a third finger, keeping the rhythm slow and steady.

He slid his other hand down her stomach until the palm of his hand rested where her thighs met. He pressed in with the heel of his hand, circling slow and steady—until she was whimpering.

Her body began moving in counterpoint, fingers digging into his arm as she held on tight. She was so close that just about anything would send her over the edge.

"I've got you," he murmured, kissing her neck. "Now be a good girl and come for me, love."

Her whole body tensed—then sagged back into him with a soft, broken sound. She inhaled sharply and then the breath froze in her lungs for a long minute as her body spasmed around his fingers. He kept moving—slow, deliberate—carrying her through it. When she began to breathe again it was deep and ragged.

Her body was warm, soft, and pliant against his.

She leaned her head back against his shoulder, eyes closed, a small smile curling her lips, it was the most beautiful thing he'd ever seen.

God, I love this woman.

Connor unlocked the door and locked it again behind them. She pushed him against the door, fingers buried in his dark hair, her mouth claiming his like a brand.

"I can't believe you did that," she rasped. "I can't believe I *let* you do that," she added with a surprised laugh.

She really couldn't. She couldn't believe she'd teased him in the car—or that he'd made her come in the elevator with people standing inches away. That had almost certainly been illegal.

And she couldn't believe how much she'd loved every second of it.

For years, ever since that horrible night, sex had been an ordeal. The few times she'd tried to explain her issues, it was just humiliating and painful.

Telling Connor had been humiliating and painful too, but Connor made it worth it. He didn't treat sex with her like a minefield. He wasn't overly cautious, he wasn't hesitant.

He trusted her to tell him when it wasn't right—when she was scared, or uncomfortable. And she trusted him to listen. That—*that* was what had always been missing. She'd never been able to fully trust any other man since that night.

With Connor, everything just… *worked*. It was amazing and spontaneous and hot, but she also knew she was safe with him. She kissed him, deeply, sweetly, trying to tell him what she didn't trust her voice to say—thanking him for giving her hope and making her feel joy again.

He picked her up and carried her to the bed, setting her down with a lingering kiss before kneeling to remove her boots. Once she was bare, he just stood there—*staring*. Her cheeks flamed and she wanted to cover herself.

He'd seen her naked, but he'd never spent so much time just looking. It was… intimate. Unnerving. Overwhelming.

"You are so beautiful, Alexandra," he said quietly.

His gaze was focused and intense, his eyes so dark not a hint of blue remained. He continued to look at her as he pulled his shirt over his head and tossed it aside. He didn't take his eyes off of her as he toed off his shoes and undid his belt.

By the time he finally stepped free of his pants, she'd felt his gaze on every inch of her skin—like a touch. At last, he wrapped his arms around her—and just held her. His hands worked up and down her back and her arms, over the back of her neck, leaving trails of warmth in their wake. It was as if he was trying to touch her everywhere—*be* everywhere at once.

When he kissed her, it was slow and sweet and so tender that she nearly cried. Every time he looked at her, touched her, held her like she was precious, the broken places in her heart—the pieces of her soul—mended just a little more.

She felt… *loved.*

He urged her to lie back on the bed and she didn't feel a single second's hesitation. She never thought she'd want the weight of a man on top of her again. She thought she would always feel suffocated and terrified to be in that position. Now she wanted it with every fiber of her being.

She closed her eyes, stunned by the revelation.

She wanted him to make slow, sweet love to her while he surrounded her with his strength. From him, it would be protective, not threatening. She would be safe—not exposed.

But Connor didn't push.

He never did.

He gently rolled her to her side and pressed himself against her from behind.

She opened her eyes and was surprised to find that she had a full view of herself in the mirror above the dresser. She took in her wild hair, her kiss-smeared makeup and flushed skin—then quickly shut her eyes again.

"Oh, no, love. Don't hide." He kissed her temple. "Eyes on me."

Alexandra hesitantly obeyed, meeting his stare in the mirror as his hands moved over her skin. He stroked her arms, her slightly-too-wide hips, her not-toned-enough stomach.

"Look how gorgeous you are."

Connor wedged a knee between her thighs, then bent it, bracing his foot on the bed behind her. Her leg draped over his, leaving her wide open—every part of her reflected in the mirror.

"Have I told you how much I love this?" he murmured, sliding his hand between her legs. "So warm … so sweet."

She shuddered and arched into his touch. His fingers found that perfect spot as if he knew every inch of her body by heart—and precisely how she needed to be touched.

He withdrew his hand. Before she could protest, he was sliding into her with excruciating slowness. She moaned and shifted but had no choice but to take what he gave her at whatever pace he set. Still sensitive and still craving him, she was close to unraveling.

"And here," he said, his hand skimming up her thigh and resting on her hip. "You're so soft. You fit my hands perfectly." He squeezed, fingers sinking in as he began to move with agonizing care, going a little deeper on each thrust.

Alexandra could do nothing but watch—his face, his hands, the place where their bodies joined—as he set a slow, torturous rhythm that made her burn.

"God, I love your breasts," he moaned, cupping the weight of one in his hand, gently teasing the peak until it was stiff and flushed between his fingers.

"Connor," Alexandra pleaded. "Please."

She tried to move her hips or arch her back; anything to get him deeper, faster. He was stoking the fire hotter and hotter and she felt as if her bones were going to melt before she found release. She needed him to *move*.

"Hush now," he whispered, throwing her words from the car back at her as he nipped the skin just below her ear, drawing a whimpering sigh from her throat.

Her overloaded mind finally caught up—remembering what he'd whispered in the elevator about earning this.

She moaned, loud and helpless.

"I'm sorry," she whined, breathless.

She was so close. If she could just—

Connor caught her hand before it reached its destination, gripping it lightly but firmly.

"No touching," he instructed, before releasing her.

She knew she didn't *have* to listen to him. He wouldn't physically stop her because he knew she would hate it. But somehow… she couldn't bring herself to disobey. As frustrating as it was, she didn't want to disappoint him.

And she *had* earned this.

He wouldn't leave her hanging forever.

"That's my girl."

Alexandra closed her eyes and let his muttered praise wash over her, taking the edge off her frustration and making her heart pound even harder.

"Oh, God," she moaned, savoring the feel of his hips finally pressing fully against hers and being completely full of him.

"And I love this," he murmured, placing his hand over her chest, right between her breasts. "This fierce heart." He continued placing kisses down her neck, some soft and sweet, others gentle nips or teasing swipes of his tongue until she was dizzy with need.

"And this smart mouth," he said, his voice thick and strained as he stroked her bottom lip with his thumb. "It gets me hard every fucking time." Alexandra nipped the pad gently—then sucked his thumb into her mouth, slow and deliberate.

He nipped the back of her neck and sent shivers all the way down her spine. He followed it with open mouthed kisses and his hand rested on her neck, stroking her jaw with his thumb.

"And I love how smart you are. How passionate. Funny. Sweet," Connor's voice was rough and he was breathing heavily. He was torturing her, yes, but he was also torturing himself. "You're a goddess, Alexandra. Look at you."

She did.

This time she saw her flushed skin, too-bright eyes, parted lips… the slow sinuous movements of her body. The soft sway of her breasts, rosy tipped and perfect.

She met Connor's stare and saw tenderness, affection, frank male appreciation, and fierce pride. Her breath hitched as she realized that she was seeing herself the way he saw her.

"Do ye see now?" he gritted out, thrusting deeper—unhurried. Patient.

She looked again—and saw something that transformed every part of her into a thing of beauty.

Love.

Love for herself—for the broken parts and the brave parts. For the woman who had clawed and crawled her way back from the darkness.

And for him—for the patient, funny, kind, generous, brave man that he was.

She felt her eyes sting with welling tears and she bit her lip to keep from sobbing.

Connor pressed one reverent kiss to her neck—then snapped his hips forward, finally giving them both what they needed.

It was only a matter of seconds before her orgasm rushed over her like a forest fire—steady, all consuming. Clearing space—room for her to breathe.

Her body tensed, wracked by wave after wave of aftershocks—every one making Connor feel impossibly deep, impossibly perfect inside her. He swore and tensed, holding himself still deep inside her as he came. Alexandra watched the soul-shattering pleasure sweep over him, holding his eyes as their orgasms faded.

She drifted off—warm, safe, aching with joy—thinking just one simple, wonderful thing.

I love him.

Chapter Twenty-One

Megan's wedding was nothing short of magical.

The ceremony took place at St. Pancras Old Church in Camden—the aisle flooded with so many white flowers it looked like they'd grown up through the floorboards. Fairy lights lined the chapel, and dozens of candles burned on the dais making the small space feel like something out of storybook.

The effect was breathtaking. Ethereal.

Alexandra considered it a miracle that she'd only cried three times.

She'd made it through the ceremony without tripping over her blush-colored gown, and even posed for wedding photos without dragging her hem through the dirt or bursting into tears.

She considered that a victory. Especially with Connor there watching her the entire time.

He looked so good in his tux that it was criminal. The moment she stepped out and saw him tying his tie—actually *tying it*, not clipping it on—it was game over. She'd thought of little else but getting him back out of it.

Turns out, neither of them needed to strip for her to get a fantastic orgasm before leaving the hotel room. They'd arrived a few minutes late—which really just meant not as early as planned—but she was satisfied. At least momentarily, anyway.

And, according to Megan, "glowing."

Honestly, it was incredible she could string two words together.

She gave her speech with minimal waterworks and maximum poise—under the circumstances.

Everyone laughed at the right parts, a few cried at the sappy bits—so all in all, she'd nailed the Maid of Honor gig. And now that the reception was well and truly underway, and her job was done, it was time to reward herself.

She found Connor leaning against the bar holding a rocks glass filled with brown liquid. He sipped his drink, watching her from the bar—and her legs went wobbly. He looked at her like she was dessert.

That smile—so warm and genuine—turned her insides to goo and made her heart skip a beat.

When she finally reached him, he wrapped an arm around her waist—hand warm on the small of her back—and kissed her. It was soft and sweet and oh so perfect.

"Are you off the clock?" he asked, humor dancing in those bright blue eyes.

"Yes, sir. Maid of Honor duties officially complete."

She wiped her brow with the back of her hand. He chuckled and she could feel the sound resonate deep in his chest.

"Sir, huh? I kind of like the sound of that," Connor murmured, his hand sliding lower than was strictly appropriate. Luckily, their backs were to the bar.

She laid a hand over his chest—*this fierce heart*—and rose on tiptoe to whisper in his ear.

"Do you now? I'll keep that in mind. Right now, I'm thinking about thanking you for earlier... *several times over*."

He grinned at her and the gleam in his eye was diabolical. "I will accept your thanks whenever, and wherever, you decide. Just say the word, love."

She was about to suggest "here and now" when his phone buzzed in his breast pocket. He frowned, looking at the screen. As he answered it, he tugged her toward the ballroom exit.

"Go ahead."

His tone was brisk and his smile had completely vanished. His jaw was clenched as he listened, his posture rigid.

What? What is it??

Had someone been hurt? She told herself not to catastrophize—there was no point in spiraling until Connor hung up and told her what was happening.

Of course, she completely ignored herself and continued to run through the list of all the bad things that could possibly happen.

"Have Jackson and Parker secure it once the police are finished," he said in a low voice. "Call me with any updates."

Alexandra looked around, suddenly remembering there were people everywhere. Connor ended the call, pocketed his phone, and gently steered her farther down the hall.

"What is it? What's going on?" she asked, voice low.

"Relax, love. Everyone's alright." He stopped and put his hands on her arms, rubbing up and down in slow soothing strokes.

"Okay, that's good. But what happened?" she demanded.

Facts. Facts were helpful. If I have facts, I can make a plan—deal with whatever this is.

"The security company called because the alarm at your house was tripped. Jackson and Parker went over to check it out."

He paused, his mouth set in a grim line. Pausing couldn't be good. Grim *certainly* couldn't be good.

"Someone broke into my house?" she asked, trying to clarify.

"It looks like it."

"Looks like it?" she replied, trying, and failing, to keep her voice from pitching up in her near panic. "Or they actually *did* break in?"

"Yes. Someone broke in," Connor said evenly.

How the hell could he be so calm with this many unanswered questions?

How'd they get in?

Was anything taken? Did they just trash the place?

Did the cameras catch anything?

Who was it? Was it the same person who was stalking her?

It had to be. No way she was unlucky enough to have a stalker *and* a completely unrelated break-in.

The only question that actually came out of her mouth was—

"When?"

"It's all right. You're safe," he said softly.

She knew he was trying to be comforting and reassure her, afraid that she might have an anxiety attack, but honestly, as afraid as she was, she was more furious than anything else. And his not answering her questions was only adding fuel to the fire.

"I'm safe because I'm *here*. *When*, Connor?"

"It was about two this morning, local time."

If I'd been in New York last night… I would have been home. Alone. Oh, God…

Suddenly, she couldn't get enough air into her lungs.

"Breathe, love."

He guided her into a chair and crouched in front of her, steady and close.

"You wouldn't have been alone," he said, like he already knew what she was thinking. "I would've been there too. And even if you were there alone, Jackson and Parker said the police were there within ten minutes, I'd reckon. You would have been okay. You would've done just what I showed you, right?"

She nodded dumbly. That's right. She'd have followed instructions—panicked later. She would have kept quiet. She would have locked her bedroom door with the new deadbolt he'd installed, then she would have taken her phone into the bathroom and locked that door too.

She would have left the lights off, stayed quiet, and called 911 and waited for help to arrive. And if she'd been found—

Her mind balked at that and she had to refocus.

Think. You'd do what Trey taught you. Stay calm. Use what's around you. Make an opportunity to run.

She thought it over and over again like a mantra. She concentrated on keeping her breathing even, counting each inhale and exhale. She was doing fine, until she had one brief thought that made her blood run cold. It could happen again.

Her panic hit critical mass. She couldn't contain it. She clutched both sleeves of Connor's jacket, holding on so tightly her fingers ached.

No air.

Her dress squeezed like a vice. Her vision narrowed to a tunnel, until dots filled her vision. She tried to focus; she tried so hard.

Connor was talking, but it was drowned out by the roaring in her ears. Her head felt like a balloon that was about to float away, if it could ever untether itself from her body which was suddenly made of lead.

"Alexandra, breathe!" He put a hand on either side of her neck, cradling her jaw and tipping her head up to catch her eyes. "Breathe for me, baby."

She gasped, filling her lungs—only for the air to vanish again, yanked out of her. She inhaled again, playing tug of war with the atmosphere and fearing she would lose.

"That's it. You're doing great, Lex. Just keep breathing, love." He scooped her up and she concentrated on pulling air into her lungs each time it escaped, closing her eyes and trying to fight the growing nausea.

She pressed her face into Connor's neck and the scent of him encouraged her to keep breathing. He smelled like fresh air and warm memories and safety. He smelled like joy and peace.

His arms around her were solid, his steps were sure and she could feel some of the panic beginning to ebb away. Connor shoved through the doors of a small, dark meeting room.

He didn't put her down. Instead, he used his foot to pull out a chair from the large conference table and then sank into it, positioning her on his lap.

For a few minutes he just sat there, silently rubbing her back in soothing circles and occasionally kissing the top of her head. He was waiting. He'd found a quiet place to hold her—for as long as she needed.

I love this man.

Once she got her breathing under control she kissed his jaw. "Thank you."

"Are you alright?" The genuine worry in his voice made her heart squeeze.

"I will be," she whispered.

"It kills me to see you like that." He hugged her tighter, burying his face in her neck.

"I know. I'm sorry." The response was automatic at this point. His head whipped up and his gaze was hard.

"Never apologize. Not for this. None of this is your fault."

She nodded, choking back more tears, even as some knot deep within her chest unraveled. She took a deep, easy breath for the first time in what seemed like years and kissed him gently.

Alexandra took her time getting herself together and repairing her makeup before finding the bride and groom to say her goodbyes. She needed to leave, but she didn't want to ruin their day.

She hugged them both and wished them all the happiness they deserved and even some they didn't. Then she let Connor lead her out to the waiting car.

Back in the suite, Connor undressed her gently and helped her into a tub of warm water and lavender-scented bubbles.

Climbing in behind her, he washed her back, kneading away the tension with long, firm strokes of his strong hands. Once he deemed her sufficiently relaxed—meaning half asleep—he lifted her out of the tub, gently dried them both with a towel and wrapped her in a clean, fluffy robe.

"I'm stealing this robe," she mumbled.

She could feel the rumble of his laugh as she leaned her head against his chest while he carried her to the bedroom and laid her gently on the turned-down king-sized bed.

"Stay there," he ordered, disappearing into the bathroom.

She watched him prowl, still gloriously naked—broad shoulders, narrow hips, tight round glutes on full display. Even so, now that the panic had faded, she was so exhausted she could barely keep her head up. She sighed, knowing only sleep awaited her.

He returned with a spray bottle and a comb, smirking as he set them on the bedside table and positioned himself behind her. She hugged her knees, resting her chin on them as Connor started combing out the knots.

A comfortable silence stretched between them as Connor massaged her scalp and ran his fingers through her hair, making sure all the tangles were gone. She could've slept sitting up, but Connor clearly had other ideas.

He untied her robe and slid it from her shoulders, tossing it toward the foot of the bed. He tugged her back against his chest, cradling her between his legs, and pulled the down comforter over them. She nestled against his chest, savoring the warmth of his skin.

"Sleep, love."

She pressed a kiss his chest, right over his heart, and let her eyelids slide closed. She was surrounded by his heat, his scent, and that rare feeling of safety that was all Connor.

What if it hadn't been him that day?

Would she have ever known what it felt like to have someone really see her... and stay?

No... I would never have known.

She tried not to think about it. Thankfully, it wasn't long before sleep claimed her.

Connor didn't sleep. He couldn't.

She'd needed him solid so she could safely fall apart—so he'd held the line. But inside, he was fire and fury. Under any other circumstances, it would have been impossible to contain. The overwhelming need to choke the life out of the bastard with his own two hands would have terrified him if he'd had any space left for rational thought.

He wanted to scream and break things. He wanted to kidnap Alexandra and take her to Scotland where he could find them a little cottage and spend the rest of his life holding onto her to make sure she was safe.

Instead, he held her as she slept—working the problem over and over in his head.

She couldn't go back to her place any time soon. She would probably refuse to stay in London, and he doubted he'd convince her to stay away from the city until this was over.

No. As stubborn as she was, she'd insist on going back to work—living like nothing had happened. Which meant he was going to have to tell her everything.

She needed to know. But that conversation was going to go sideways—and the longer he waited, the worse it'd be when it finally blew up. He just hoped she'd forgive him. *Eventually.*

By the time their plane descended into JFK the next afternoon, Connor had a solid plan—one that didn't improve his odds of coming out clean. This could very well end everything, and he didn't want to consider it. Just thinking about it made his chest tighten to the point of pain.

Parker was waiting at baggage claim, and Connor was itching to get the hell out. Too many people. Too many entry points. And he didn't have any of the gear he normally carried.

Unfortunately, Alexandra's suitcase took a goddamn eternity. His had been one of the first bags off the carousel. Hers? Nowhere. Odd, but baggage logistics were black magic on a good day.

Still he was relieved when her bag finally appeared and Parker led them to where he'd parked the Hummer.

"Where to?" Parker asked as they pulled out of the garage.

"My place," Alexandra and Connor said in unison.

Alexandra narrowed her eyes. Connor took a breath—and prayed for luck.

"You can't go back to your place right now," he said quietly.

He hadn't told her how bad it was. Last night, she'd needed

rest—not another spiral.

"They broke a window on the ground floor. Until it gets fixed, the house isn't secure."

Alexandra looked like she was going to argue, but he pressed on before she could speak.

"Besides, I don't like the idea of you there alone." He kept his voice low, tried to keep the fire out of it.

He didn't want to spook her, he wanted her to see the logic of it. "They're getting bolder. Their behavior is escalating and we don't know what they might do next. We need to find a secure location for you temporarily. It makes the most sense for you to stay with me for the time being. Unless you'd rather stay with your father."

He knew damn well that was the last thing she wanted.

Was it manipulative? Absolutely.

Would she see it? Of course.

Did it matter? Not in the slightest.

He wanted to tell her he was taking her home whether she liked it or not, but that would almost guarantee that she would tell him to fuck off. So he gave her a choice, and hoped like hell that she would choose the option that put her in his bed for the foreseeable future.

She tensed, arms crossed like a barricade. Now she was leaning just far enough away to make her point—silently glaring.

Yup, she's pissed...

"Do I actually have a choice?"

"Of course you do." His voice was calm. "But we both know I'm right."

She sighed, pinching the bridge of her nose.

"Fine."

And fuck, did he love the way she said it.

Connor exhaled, a silent breath of relief. First hurdle cleared.

"At least now I get to see your man-cave," she joked, bumping his shoulder with hers. He chuckled, wrapping an arm around her waist and tucking her against his side.

Some time later, Parker pulled up outside his building and helped Connor gather their luggage from the trunk. They rode the elevator to the top floor and he unlocked the door to his apartment.

It wasn't quite a penthouse, but the three-bedroom apartment took up the whole floor—and he had the only key to the roof.

"Wow." Alexandra stood looking around his living room. His taste ran towards simple and comfortable so there was nothing spectacular. He had a large sturdy black leather sectional with a few throw pillows in greys and blues. The coffee table was reclaimed wood that was grey and weathered. And of course, he had a large screen television mounted on the opposite wall.

Bookshelves lined the far wall except for where a desk sat in front of the window in the center of the wall.

"I like it," she said, clearly surprised.

"Thanks?"

"It's very… *you*. Simple and practical, but classic. It's honest." She shrugged.

"Interesting way of saying 'boring,'" he said with a smirk. "Most people just ask if I'm colorblind."

Alexandra laughed. "No. It means… what you see is what you get. With the occasional fun surprise."

He grinned at her. He liked the way she looked in his living room.

"Make yourself at home. You hungry?"

"*Starving.*"

She probably was. They'd left the reception early yesterday and spent the rest of the night in the hotel. They'd been on a plane for seven hours today without much to eat aside from pretzels.

Add in the jet lag and it felt like ages since breakfast that morning, even though the local time was only mid-afternoon.

He ordered a large pizza, loaded with toppings and extra cheese, and then moved their suitcases to the bedroom. When he returned, he found Alexandra sitting on the hardwood floor in front of his bookshelf.

"Of course you went straight for the books."

"You can tell a lot about a person by the books they keep."

"I haven't read them all," Connor admitted, feeling oddly guilty.

"Everyone has books on their shelf they've never read," she said waving away his confession. "And nobody owns *every* book they've ever read. It's the ones you *keep*, whether or not you've read them, that tells a story."

"You're making this up."

She looked affronted and then grinned at him a little sheepishly.

"Okay, I kind of am. But now that I say it, it makes sense."

Connor laughed but nodded. "I get it. The ones you keep are the ones you've read and liked, or want to read again. Or, they're the ones you aspire to reading. It's who you are and who you want to be—but alphabetized."

"Exactly," she said, excitedly. "And thank God you alphabetize," she added, narrowing her eyes. "I don't associate with heathens."

He offered her a hand and pulled her to her feet. She stretched, flinging her arms over her head and arching her back. He tried—and failed—not to stare as her shirt stretched tight across her breasts, riding up just enough to reveal a sliver of bare skin beneath her bellybutton.

"Pizza will be here in a few minutes. You want something to drink? I have beer, water, coffee, tea…"

"Water is good," she answered following him into the kitchen.

She perched on a barstool at the island, taking in her surroundings. His kitchen was smaller than hers, but sleek and newly remodeled—stainless appliances, white cabinets, black granite countertops, even on the island.

He opened two bottles and handed one to her while he took a swig from the other.

"Oh, and before I forget, you'll need this." He dug in his pocket and handed her his spare key. "If you're going to stay here for a while, you'll need it. Jackson is picking you up in the morning and I'm not sure what time I'll be home."

"Thanks." She tucked it into her pocket.

"Would you like a quick tour?"

"Please."

"You've seen the living room and the kitchen." He said, gesturing broadly at the open space. He led her to a short hallway to the right. "Guest bedroom." He opened the first door on the left and she poked her head in briefly. "Guest bathroom." He opened the door on the opposite side of the hall and she repeated the cursory inspection.

At the end of the hall, he opened two more doors. "Gym and laundry room."

"Very nice."

He closed the doors and led her across the living room to a another door. He opened it and led her into the master suite.

"And this is the *man-cave*." He smiled.

This time she wandered in and took her time, eyeing the space with open curiosity. A king sized bed took up the center of the far wall with a nightstand on either side. He had an overstuffed leather chair and a small table tucked beneath the window to the right and a wardrobe stood in the corner by the door.

She opened a door and peeked into a sleek grey bathroom—double sinks, slate tile, a massive shower.

"This room is huge," she said, crossing to the bed.

She ran her hand along the bedspread, one of the few colorful items in the room. He'd picked it because he'd read somewhere that blue was supposed to be soothing and the pattern was a simple trellis design that wasn't too boring.

"But it's a little sparse," she added, pushing on the mattress as if testing the firmness.

"Yeah, another leftover habit from the Army. Not used to… *decorating.*"

He cringed at the thought of picking out throw pillows or rugs and trying to coordinate things so that they looked like they belonged in the same room. The best he could do was make sure the colors didn't clash.

She laughed and he tried not to dwell on how *right* it felt seeing her in his room—or how badly he wanted her naked in his bed, screaming his name.

A knock on the front door saved him from himself. He left her there to answer the door, silently berating himself for having the self-control of a horny teenager.

He needed to talk to her and it wasn't going to be easy or comfortable. But after what happened, she needed to know. He just hoped she'd let him explain before she castrated him—though he was fully prepared to beg if it came to that.

Chapter Twenty-Two

Connor seemed tense while they ate, and she couldn't blame him.

Alexandra was practically a ball of nerves after the events of the last two days. She wanted to go home. She wanted the comfort of her routine and the familiarity of her own things and her own space, but she knew why that wasn't an option right now.

Surprisingly, if she couldn't be home, she didn't mind being here. She liked being with Connor, in his natural habitat, and she found that she was actually looking forward to seeing him everyday. She just hoped that he was okay with it.

She hated the idea that he'd offered out of obligation—or worse, pity. He'd never invited her over before, and it made her anxious to think that maybe circumstances had pushed him into it before he was ready.

She wondered if maybe he'd mentioned staying with her father because he didn't really want her here, but he just didn't want to hurt her feelings. What if he'd only offered to be polite, thinking she'd turn him down.

That's insane. You were already in the car before he even asked. If he didn't want you here—or didn't think you'd say yes—he would've waited to hear your answer before telling Parker where to go.

She wiped her hands on her napkin and drained her water, trying to stay calm—trying to stop the spiral before it started.

"You okay?"

Dammit, how does he always know?

"Yeah. I was just thinking. Are you sure you don't mind me staying here? I don't want to be in your way."

"Of course," he said, taking her hand from across the table. "There's no place I'd rather you be than here."

There wasn't a hint of hesitation, and he looked so earnest she believed him—until some unreadable emotion flickered across his face and made her doubt.

"As long as you're sure…"

"Absolutely." He stood up, clearing away their plates. "Why don't you get comfortable in the living room while I clean up?"

She curled into the corner of the sofa, tucking her feet beneath her. It was late afternoon, but she was jet-lagged and exhausted. She suddenly wished she had a cozy blanket so she could curl up right there and go to sleep.

She must have dozed off, because the next time she opened her eyes, the room was dark.

She was stretched out on the couch, draped in a soft fleece blanket and Connor sat beside her with her feet resting in his lap. He was staring off into space, a beer in his hand.

"Sorry. I must have fallen asleep."

"You needed it," he said, leaning forward to set his drink on the coffee table. He looked tense—brooding.

"Something wrong?" she asked, sitting up.

He put his arm around her and gathered her to his side. She placed a hand on his chest and leaned her head against his shoulder.

"There are some things you need to know." His tone sent a frisson of fear down her spine.

"About what?"

"About your stalker."

She swallowed hard, but encouraged him to continue. "Okay, so tell me."

He reached over to the coffee table and picked up a few pieces of paper, handing it to her. "These were left on my car at different times over the last two weeks."

She took the notes but her hand was shaking so badly she barely managed to read them. When she'd finished, she looked up at Connor and he handed her a fourth note. From the set of his jaw and the furrow in his brow, she knew this one was different—much worse.

"This was found in the townhouse after the break-in." His voice was tight and laced with some barely suppressed emotion. Fear? Anger? She couldn't tell.

She unfolded the note and held it carefully in both hands. She had to read it three times to be sure her eyes weren't playing tricks on her. They had to be. This couldn't be happening.

YOU CAN'T SAVE HER.
NO ONE CAN.

Memories of that night rushed back to her and she could hear him, clear as day.

"No one can save you."

She'd forgotten. She'd *forgotten* how Lucas had hissed those words, sneering at her while she'd screamed. How could she have *forgotten?* Some details were so permanently seared into her memory that she would never—*could* never—forget them.

"Alexandra, what is it?" Connor framed her face in his hands and looked at her, searching.

"It's him." It was barely more than a breath.

"Fuck," he muttered.

His voice had a violent edge, and his eyes—so dark now you'd never know they were usually a vivid, brilliant blue. They were cold and hard and glittering with barely contained fury. He looked very capable of killing someone.

For her.

It was terrifying and comforting.

"Tell me," he said softly.

"He said something… that night. Something very similar. He told me no one would save me. It's *him*, Connor. I *know* it's him." She was shaking, her voice unsteady—and she hated it.

Hated the fear. Hated the weakness.

"Proof enough for me." Connor gave her a quick kiss before he picked up his cell phone and dialed. Someone answered quickly. "Put a tail on Whitmore and the cousin. I want to know where they are every *fucking* second of every *fucking* day."

Alexandra was still reeling from the notes and the memory she'd recovered that it took her a few seconds for her sluggish brain to point out that something significant had just happened. Something she should focus on.

When she realized what it was, it was like she was jolted awake.

"Who was that?" she asked, her breath was coming quickly now. She was going to panic, but not before she got the answers she needed.

"Sam," Connor answered, examining her closely.

"You told him?"

"Lex—"

"Who else, Connor?" Her voice sounded hysterical, desperate, even to herself. She didn't care. It felt like the walls were closing in and the sky was falling.

"Lex, you had to know he'd be a suspect," he said calmly.

He was hesitant, looking wary as if he was dealing with a wild animal. And she felt like one. She wanted to lash out at anyone and everyone.

"I didn't tell Sam the whole story—just that he was a piece of shit and he'd hurt you. I needed Sam to track him down."

"Does Archie know, too?" she asked, her voice shaking.

He put a hand on her arm and she jerked away instinctively. She was feeling too raw, too vulnerable to be touched.

"I didn't tell him anything," he replied. But that didn't answer her question and she understood what he didn't say.

"But he knows."

She couldn't look at him. She focused on the pattern of the blanket that still covered her legs.

"Lass, look at me."

She shook her head firmly refusing to meet his eyes. She heard him sigh and felt the couch dip as he sat down next to her.

"Archie already knew," he confirmed.

"How?"

"The same way I did, I reckon. Your father gave me his name the day we met."

"You knew?" she hissed. "All this time?"

"I only knew his name," Connor insisted. "He didn't give me details."

Still… he'd known all along and didn't say a word when she'd told him her whole humiliating story.

"Who else knows?" she whispered, barely holding back tears.

"Lex—"

"*Who. Else?*" she gritted out between clenched teeth.

"I gave his name and photo to Jackson, Parker, Ian, and Cam. They needed to know what he looked like and that he was a threat in case he ever came near you. I know you—"

"You had no right," she hissed coldly. "That was private. *I get to decide who I tell.* You had no fucking right."

She stood up and headed for the door, jamming her feet into her sneakers. Connor cut her off, but wisely didn't touch her.

"You can't leave, Lex," Connor said thickly. "I know you're angry—you've got every right. But you can't go out there alone. Not now. If you want to go to your dad's I'll—"

He stopped and cleared his throat but it was still rough as he continued.

"I'll take you there, if you want to go, but you can't go out alone."

Her father… She'd deal with him later. She didn't even want to think about him, let alone see him right now.

"Please, just *talk* to me, love," Connor begged.

"I can't. I can't talk to you. I can't look at you," Alexandra whispered. She swiped at the tears she could no longer hold back and turned away.

She marched down the hallway and went into the guest bedroom, slamming and locking the door behind her. She stood with her back to the door, sobbing. Then slid to the floor, crumpling into a heap, head in her hands as her heart splintered all over again.

She should have known. No, she *had* known. She had *always* known this would end badly. Things always did. Why had she ever thought that things would go differently this time?

She felt so incredibly stupid for having trusted someone again. The fact that it was Connor gutted her to the core.

A moment later she heard a soft knock on the door.

"Alexandra?" Connors voice sounded muffled coming through the closed door, but even so, just the sound of his voice made her heart ache. "Baby, please listen to me. I understand why you're upset. But they needed to know. I trust them with this, Lex. They're not going to tell anyone."

He trusted them? That was his excuse? He couldn't have just asked her? Or even given her a heads up? How long had they known?

And her father—how could he do something like this without any warning?

"Lex?" He sounded so worried that it just made her feel worse.

This was why she was so careful. When you let people in, you give them the power to hurt you.

Her family had been through hell after her attack and every ounce of pain she'd felt was reflected back at her in three pairs of eyes. Three worried, haunted faces staring back at her every day, and then another one in the mirror.

That concern—that *pity*—ripped open the wound over and over and over again, never letting it heal. At this point, she wasn't sure there was enough left of her heart to stitch back together.

It was the feedback loop from hell. Her pain hurt them and that just made her pain worse. She'd told Connor because she needed him to understand her boundaries. She'd thought she could trust him.

He'd seen her panic attacks and heard her story but he'd never made her feel pathetic or weak. She knew he had his own demons and she thought he would understand.

But now she didn't know how she'd look any of them in the eye.

She'd be too afraid to see that damn look in their eyes. And Archie—*oh, God*. She had to *work* with him.

"Alexandra." The concern was still there—but now it was tinged with something else. Frustration? Anger?

Well, back at ya, buddy.

"Go away," she snapped.

"Let me in. Please?"

"No," she said flatly. She couldn't right now. Couldn't think. Could barely breathe.

"I'm not going anywhere," Connor promised softly. "No matter what. I go where you go. It's that simple."

"Fine," she ground out. "It's your house. You can stand there all night if you want. But I'm going to sleep."

She took off her bra, stripped out of her jeans, and climbed into the guest bed. The sheets were cold but soft, and she snuggled under the comforter, crying until there were no tears left. She had a splitting headache and the bed was littered with tissues by the time she was done, but she felt oddly calm.

Completely exhausted, she sent a couple of texts, set her alarm, and lay there focusing on her breathing. She could still hear Connor moving around in the hallway, and she tried to ignore him.

She tried to think rationally, but the hurt and humiliation blocked out everything else. Eventually, sleep took her—and mercifully, she didn't dream.

Connor hadn't slept. Not until he knew she was asleep. She hadn't bolted. *Yet.* That didn't mean she wouldn't. If she did… he didn't know if he could stop her. He was prepared to grovel, and gladly would have already if she'd opened the damn door.

Instead, he turned on the TV, with the volume down low, and stretched out on the couch. He was used to sleeping anywhere and everywhere, and he'd certainly gotten plenty of shut-eye sleeping on dirt floors and Army cots that one night on the couch wasn't a hassle. He wasn't a deep sleeper, so from there, he'd know if she left the guest room.

Anxiety was a trigger for him, so he didn't really relish the idea of sleep anyway. He was sure the nightmares would come. He must've dozed off sometime around dawn because the next thing he knew, the sun was rising. He scrubbed his hands over his face, reminding himself where he was.

He heard one door open and close and then another. Alexandra was up and apparently in the guest bathroom. He rolled off the couch and headed into the kitchen to make coffee. Once that was brewing, he went into his bedroom long enough to clean up and use the bathroom.

When the coffee was done, he fixed a cup for Alexandra, poured one for himself and settled in to wait. And wait. And *wait.*

He was about to check on her to make sure everything was okay when there was a knock on his door. He checked to see who the hell it could be at this hour and immediately swore under his breath.

"What are you doing here this early?" he demanded, opening the door. Jackson frowned and gave him a confused look.

"I got a text *asking* me to come this early. Seven on the dot." He checked his watch to make sure it was correct.

"I—"

"Oh good, you're here," Alexandra said, breezing past them. "Just let me grab my things." She kept walking, disappearing into Connor's bedroom.

"Just a sec," Connor said, dashing after her. She already had her suitcase and was wheeling it out the door when he stopped her. Her hair was wet from the shower and she wore the same t-shirt and jeans that she'd worn all day yesterday. "Where are you going?"

"To Janie's to drop off my bag and get ready, then I'm going to work." Her response was carefully neutral and he realized she'd donned her mask. Emotionless, impassive.

"We need to talk about this."

"Do we?" she said, cocking her head to the side and affecting an innocent expression. "I can't go home so I've made other arrangements. Janie's apartment is closer to the office so I assume it won't make much of a difference in terms of travel time." She shrugged and moved to brush past him.

"Don't go cold on me now," Connor said softly, an ache blooming in his chest at the memory of how soft and warm she'd been waking up next to him—just yesterday.

"What?" Her eyes flashed, but it was quickly gone, replaced by bland indifference.

"Don't shut yourself off. Not from me. Yell at me, fight with me—hell, *punch* me if you want. Just… don't go cold."

"I don't know what you're talking about." Her chin went up stubbornly and she shoved past him.

Connor had a choice. He could try to keep her here, chipping at the walls with sheer persistence—or let her go, give her some time to cool off and hope that they would soften a little bit before he had a crack at them.

He took a deep breath and followed her to the door, swallowing all the things he nearly said. Words she deserved to hear, but not like this.

She practically walked through Jackson on her way out the door, but luckily he'd been smart enough to step aside to avoid being trampled.

She stood in the hallway waiting for the elevator, all calm professionalism—like it was just another Tuesday. Arms crossed, one hip cocked and checking her watch like she was late for a meeting.

But her eyes were just slightly unfocused, and her shoulders curved inward more than usual. Connor saw it—even if no one else would.

He could see the hurt and it nearly killed him.

"What the fuck did you do, man?" Jackson asked quietly, bewildered.

"Just keep her safe," Connor growled. A command. A warning.

Jackson looked at Alexandra and then back at him before giving him a quick nod.

Connor waited until the elevator doors had closed behind them before he slammed the door and swore. This was going to be a long day.

Chapter Twenty-Three

Thank God for Janie. Alexandra wanted to hug her when she walked in and Janie immediately handed her a mug of coffee with tons of cream and sugar.

"So what's going on?" Janie asked, casually sipping her own coffee. No judgment, no worry. She wore a plain pink tank top and a pair of fuzzy pajama pants. Alexandra could just barely see her red painted toenails poking out beneath the hems. Her hair was in honest-to-God hot rollers.

Alexandra dropped onto Janie's couch and took a sip of her coffee for fortitude before answering.

"Connor and I had a fight. I slept in the guest room at his place, but I couldn't stand to stay another second this morning."

"What happened?" Janie looked curious, but again, not a "*poor thing*" or "*oh, no*" in sight.

"It's complicated," Alexandra said simply. She didn't know how to explain without going into things she'd rather not. "Mind if I stay here for a few days?"

"I don't mind. Make yourself at home," Janie said with a shrug. "But why can't you go home?"

Shit…

Alexandra hadn't thought to come up with an excuse—and she didn't have the energy to invent one on the fly. She might as well keep it simple and stick as close to the truth as she could.

"Someone broke into my house while I was in London, and they broke a window so I don't really feel safe being there until it gets fixed."

"Holy shit!" Janie nearly spilled her coffee. She set the mug down and plopped onto the couch beside Alexandra. "Was it a burglary? Robbery? What's the difference anyway? *Wait*—that doesn't matter. Did they take anything?"

"Not that I know of. My security company checked it out and there was nothing obviously missing, but I won't know for sure until I check it out myself." Which was technically true.

"Damn. That sucks. Will insurance cover it?"

"Yeah, probably. I'll call them today."

Just one more thing to add to the to-do list. And that was fine. The busier she stayed, the less time she'd have to think about Connor. Or hurt.

"Can I use your hair dryer?" Alexandra asked, wanting to end the conversation before her mind wandered too much farther down that road.

It had been hard enough to keep her tears in check on the ride over. Poor Jackson had looked like he wanted to launch himself out the driver's side door the entire ride.

"Yeah, bathroom's through there. I've got to let these bad boys set for another ten minutes for maximum body and bounce, otherwise it's less Sophia Lauren and more Texas drag queen."

She gestured to her hair and Alexandra assumed she was talking about the rollers. Alexandra just shook her head as Janie sauntered off toward her bedroom.

"Holler if you need me," she called over her shoulder.

Alexandra grabbed her toiletries and headed for the bathroom. After drying her hair and putting on some makeup, she rifled through her suitcase for anything even remotely work-appropriate. She hadn't packed much for London except for a few party dresses, her bridesmaid's dress, and some casual clothes.

She did have a knee length suede skirt and some knee high boots, but she didn't have a clean blouse or a jacket. She mentally added getting clothes from her apartment—*somehow*— to the to-do list.

"Hey, Janie?" She knocked on the bedroom door, which was still ajar, before poking her head in.

"What's up?" Janie asked, not taking her eyes off the vanity mirror where she was applying mascara.

"Do you have a blouse I could borrow? I only have the clothes I took with me to London and I can't go in looking like this."

"Sure. Take whatever you want." She gestured toward the closet as she began taking rollers out of her hair.

She picked a plain white button-up. A little large in the bust, a little short at the hem—but once it was tucked into the suede skirt, it didn't look half bad. It actually worked with the boots. It was a far cry from the usual suit and pumps she normally wore, but it would have to do.

"I like this look," Janie said, surveying her outfit in the mirror.

"Really?"

"Yeah, it's a nice change. Makes you look… *human*. Almost."

"Is that a compliment or an insult?" Alexandra snorted.

"Neither. You look fierce any day of the week, and you know it. But this is a little softer—a little more approachable than the usual boss bitch vibe you've got going on."

"Boss bitch?" Alexandra laughed.

"Yeah. All badass business." Janie grinned.

She knew Janie was just teasing her. She'd be the last to judge anyone's style choices, or choices in general. But something about that descriptor felt… off. She didn't like it.

"Do I come off as… cold?"

Janie frowned, tilting her head like she was debating how honest to be.

"I suppose you could call it that," she said slowly. "I've always considered it a sort of professional detachment. At least at work. You don't give anything away. But isn't being unreadable a good thing in your line of work?"

"I guess." Alexandra shrugged.

So why does it feel so…

"Come on, boss lady. We're gonna be late." Janie grabbed her purse. "Driving separate, or do you want to carpool?"

Double shit…

"Yeah, about that… just promise me you'll have me buried in my Chanel suit."

Connor wanted to tear his damn hair out. It had only been two hours since Alexandra had stormed out of his apartment and he'd already picked up the phone to call her a dozen times. After checking in with Jackson twice, he finally got so frustrated he chucked his phone in a desk drawer and slammed it shut.

He didn't know what to say or how to make her understand that he would do anything—*anything*—to protect her. That he'd never be able to live with himself if anything happened to her. That she was the most important thing in the world to him. He *loved* her.

You could tell her that, you fucking tool.

If she walked away from him now, he didn't know what he would do.

He had to focus on keeping her safe so that he'd have a chance of making things right. He wanted a future with her, one that he'd never even bothered to consider until now.

"What the fuck is your problem?" Jackson snarled, marching into his office. He stood in front of Connor's desk, feet planted, arms crossed and eyes narrowed.

"Hell if I know." Connor scrubbed a hand through his hair, jaw tight.

"What did you do to her?"

Connor explained the situation and Jackson sank into one of the leather chairs.

"Shit," he muttered. "You screwed the pooch, brother."

"I know," Connor snapped. "What do I do now?"

Jackson frowned. "Look. She's a smart woman and she's given us no trouble so far—"

Connor gave him a pointed look and Jackson smirked.

"She's given *us* no trouble. All the shit she's given you? You've earned it, fair and square, and we both know it."

Connor glared, but couldn't argue. He had earned every bit of it. Apparently, he'd been fucking things up from the very beginning.

"Even this morning when she looked like she wanted to *geld* you, she still followed all the rules. She *knows* how serious this is. Eventually she'll get why we needed to know. But you're gonna have to get down on your knees and beg her to forgive your sorry ass for blindsiding her."

"I will as soon as she gives me a chance."

"Good." Jackson nodded grimly. Then a grin spread slowly across his face. "Can I watch?"

"Fuck you, Hunter."

"Hard pass. If you're into that, hit up Sam," Jackson replied with a grin. "Does that mean you're picking her up after work?" he asked.

"I can't. I have a goddamn dinner meeting that I've already rescheduled *twice*. But do me a favor and see if you can't put in a good word for me? For some reason, she claims to like you."

"Southern charm works every time." Jackson winked and Connor resisted the urge to throw something at his smug face.

"Get out of my office before I fire you again," Connor said instead.

"Sure thing boss. Final word of advice?"

"What?"

"Don't fuck it up this time."

Jackson hightailed it, closing the door just as Connor's stapler sailed into it.

As if I didn't already know that, jackass. I just don't know how *to* not *fuck it up.*

Janie knocked on Alexandra's door around lunch time and came in toting a large take out bag. Without a word, she began unpacking cardboard boxes of what smelled like greasy Chinese food. Which could only mean one thing.

"Uh oh. What happened now?" Alexandra asked, setting aside a brief one of the Paralegals had put together while she was gone. Janie only broke out the greasy takeout and lunchtime vent sessions when she had man trouble.

"I don't know. You tell me," Janie said, still unpacking boxes.

"What do you mean?"

"Alexandra, sweetheart, this is your first fight with the first boyfriend you've had in years. *Years.* I think that warrants convening the war council, don't you?"

"It's not *that* bad."

Is it?

"So then tell me." Janie shrugged, sitting down with a carton of orange chicken and a pair of wooden chopsticks.

"It's…"

"Complicated, yeah, yeah—you mentioned that. Now speak slowly and use small words so I can keep up," she added with a self-deprecating smile.

"It's not that, it's just… really personal."

"Does it have anything to do with him being your bodyguard?"

Alexandra froze reaching for a container and tried to cover it by feigning indecision.

"What do you mean?"

"Come on. I'm not stupid," Janie snorted. "How long have I worked here?"

"Three years, give or take."

"And how many guys have you brought to the office, or out to drinks, or to the gym in that time?"

"I don't know," Alexandra hedged.

"None. Not one." Janie shook her head. "Now, suddenly, you have a boyfriend who is spending every second with you, meeting your friends, going to *London* with you?"

"What? It's so hard to believe I finally found someone I actually like?"

Who I love?

"I'm not saying that," Janie huffed, setting down her container and handing Alexandra the dumplings. They were Alexandra's favorite, and Janie knew it.

"Lex, you're gorgeous, smart, funny, and stubborn as hell. You're a catch. But you haven't *let* anyone catch you. I don't know why, and that's your business, but it makes the whole thing suspicious as *fuck*. And it's no secret that Connor is the head of MacLachlan Security Group. I mean he gave me his business card, for crying out loud."

Alexandra was a little embarrassed at how poorly she'd covered their tracks. Maybe she and Janie should switch jobs.

"And all those fine-ass men—*friends* of Connor's—you had for dinner? Please."

"Hey, you asked me where he'd met them. And would he take you!"

"Yeah, dumbass. That was me giving you a chance to fess up."

"Oh," Alexandra said quietly.

"Yeah. And if all that wasn't enough? Jackson, who *works* for Connor just *happened* to offer to give you a ride because your car—which you haven't driven because you've been out of the country for the last week—is in the shop?"

Alexandra sat, stunned, holding a dumpling and wondering where the hell to even start.

"So you wanna tell me what's going on?" Janie asked, real concern in her eyes. That should have shut down any inclination to explain, but there was also hurt and anger, which made her reevaluate.

So, Alexandra took a deep breath and started at the beginning. She meant to gloss over the worst of it—just the relevant parts. But once she started talking, she couldn't stop. She couldn't seem to stop the tears, either, which should have mortified her, but oddly… didn't.

Janie stayed quiet. No platitudes, no pity. Just held Alexandra's hand across the desk, squeezing gently now and then, saying nothing. It was still hard to talk about. Still painful. But it was a little easier the second time around.

When she finished she dared a glance at Janie's face. Janie had been quiet the whole time. Almost *too* quiet. When Alexandra looked up, Janie's face was filled, not with pity, but with rage.

"That goddamned, fucking, low-life, son of a whore," Janie said through gritted teeth.

"Pretty much." Alexandra gave her a watery smile.

"Why didn't you tell me any of this before?" Janie asked, looking hurt again.

"Because I didn't want to burden you." Alexandra shrugged. "Same reason I didn't want Connor telling everyone under the damn sun, either."

"That's bullshit, and you know it." Janie's voice was low and fierce. Alexandra flinched.

"It's not *bullshit* to want to be treated like a normal human being, and not like a perpetual victim," Alexandra said defensively. "It's not *bullshit* to try and prevent your family and your friends from worrying about you."

"It *is* bullshit," Janie shot back. "You think I'd see you any differently because some worthless fuck hurt you? You think I'm gonna think less of you? Get yer head outta yer ass and look around. A lot of people have been through a hell of their own. Everyone gets hurt. The only way we get through it is knowing we're not alone."

Alexandra had never seen her this angry before. It was more than a little scary. Her Mississippi accent never showed up unless she was tipsy—or furious. Janie paused to breathe and Alexandra sat very still.

"As my grandmother used to say, 'a burden shared is a burden lessened.' And keeping quiet about it gives him *more* power, not less. And you? You're not quiet, Lex. You're a goddamn force of nature."

Alexandra thought about that for a minute. She thought about Janie's reaction, which was not what she'd been expecting. She thought about Connor's reaction. There had been no pity, no treating her like she was made of glass. They'd been angry. They'd been *furious* for her. And *at* her, in Janie's case.

And maybe the hurt in her sister's eyes, and in her parents' eyes, wasn't pity. Maybe they were hurt because she'd shut them out.

Alexandra had a quiet epiphany. She'd been playing the martyr—not because of how she'd been hurt, but because she'd clung to suffering in silence, like it made her stronger. She'd underestimated her family, and her friends.

All this time, she'd been so obsessed with not being treated like something fragile—and yet here she was, bending over backward to convince everyone she was fine when she wasn't. She hadn't trusted them enough to lean on them. Instead, she'd taken it on herself to protect them.

She'd been so upset thinking that they couldn't get past it and that every time they looked at her they were only seeing who she'd been at the worse moment of her life and not who she was now.

But the truth was, *she* was the one who hadn't moved on.

She hadn't been able to let it go enough to have a normal relationship or to be able to talk about it without having a panic attack. She hadn't dealt with it, really, she'd just pushed it down and tried to ignore it.

Her rules and boundaries had kept her safe. Given her peace of mind. But they also kept everyone at arm's length. Because if she just ignored it, if she just didn't think about it, she could pretend it never happened and she wouldn't have to really deal with it.

That's what she'd been doing for years—pretending. Telling herself she'd healed, moved on. But really, she'd just put on a mask. One that only worked if no one ever got close enough to see it slip.

"I'm sorry, Janie," Alexandra said quietly. And she was. Sorry she'd shut her, and everyone else, out of so much of her life for so long.

"Good." Janie nodded, smoothing her skirt on her lap. "Now, how are we going to fix things with you and Connor?"

"I'm not sure."

"I'm not about to let you throw away a man with *that* face, *that* body, *that* sense of humor—and, I'm assuming, *a spectacular dick*—over this."

"And what exactly do you know about his dick?" Alexandra said with a frown.

"Oh, honey. I've seen the way you look at him—like he's your favorite midnight snack. That's all the evidence I need."

After three unanswered calls to Alexandra, Connor gave up, at least for the moment, and threw himself into catching up on a week's worth of work. He soldiered on until lunch time, but by then he needed a break. And possibly a stiff drink.

Two taps on the door were the only warning he got before Sam walked into his office carrying two take-out containers. He plunked one down on Connor's desk, right on top of the report he'd been reading, and sat down in the chair opposite the desk.

"Thanks," Connor mumbled, opening the container. A medium rare burger and hot fries with plenty of salt.

Sam might be a pain in the ass, but he wasn't all bad. He always knew exactly what Connor needed when he was in a black mood—usually meat, booze, or both.

They sat in silence for a minute. Both focused on their food.

Finally, Connor set his burger down and sighed.

"I fucked up, Sam."

"I heard," Sam said quietly. "But you'll fix it."

"I'm not sure I can," Connor said. He hated to even think about it, but he knew it was true.

"Listen," Sam said, leaning back in the chair. "I know you, man. You're dense—"

"Asshole."

"—but you're a good guy. I don't know what you did, but I know it was probably just… dumb. You'd never hurt her on purpose."

"Of course I wouldn't."

"So just talk to her. Explain. Let her knock you around a little bit."

Connor snorted and Sam offered him a small crooked smile.

"Like I said, you're dense—but doing the right thing is your basically your whole fucking personality. You'll fix it."

"Thanks," Connor muttered.

He took a deep breath, some of the weight lifting off his chest. But there was something else they needed to talk about.

Connor and Sam had served together in the Army. They'd been through a lot—good and bad. And once they'd walked straight through hell and somehow made it out the other side. They weren't just friends.

They were brothers.

"I know I was a dick," Connor admitted. He wouldn't apologize because he hadn't really been wrong. But he could acknowledge that much.

"Yeah," Sam scoffed, looking down at his half eaten lunch. "But you weren't wrong."

"Something goin' on?" Connor asked.

Sam hesitated, then flashed a grin. A little off-kilter. A little dim.

"Nah, man. I think I just need a fucking vacation."

"Help me get rid of Whitmore and you can take as much time off as you want."

Sam crammed a handful of fries in his mouth.

"I'm gonna hold you to that."

"Don't talk with your mouth full," Connor grumbled.

In response, Sam shoved at least a dozen fries in his mouth and chewed loudly with his mouth open.

"I thought you lot were supposed to be all about manners and shite."

"*You lot?*"

"Yeah. You nancy-boys," Connor joked.

Sam snorted and shook his head, continuing to devour his lunch.

Sam had been kicked out by his conservative Midwestern parents at eighteen when they found out he was gay. With few options and a desperate need to get far away from what he called "*that backwater shithole,*" he'd enlisted. They'd ended up in the same unit. The rest was history.

Sam had never hidden who he was. And not one of them had given a damn. They *had* treated him like the smartass he was—complete with name calling, teasing and the occasional smack upside the head when he needed it.

Nothing more and nothing less.

"My manners are still better than yours, dumbass," Sam said. "Even I know to send flowers when you've fucked up."

Eager to change the subject, Connor decided now was the perfect time to talk to Sam about something that had been bothering him.

"Why do you think he's escalating now? From photos taken weeks or months ago, to a note on my car, to B&E—all in two weeks. It seems off."

Sam shrugged. "Could be he panicked."

"How so?"

"Think of it this way. Whatever game he's playing, he's been setting up the board for weeks, maybe months, like you said. Then all of a sudden, she disappears. He loses her, not just for a day or two, but a whole week. Maybe he wigged thinking she'd gone into hiding—or left town."

"Why break into her apartment if he knew she wasn't there?"

"Maybe he wanted to see if her stuff was still there. Maybe he figured someone would call her and she'd come to look over the damage. Who the hell knows how this asshole's mind works."

"Good point. I know I'd lose my damn mind if she disappeared on me for even a day."

Sam grinned, chewing. "You are so screwed."

"Fuck off," Connor muttered.

"Yes, sir." Sam stood, grinning from ear to ear, turned on his heel and marched out of the office with the precision of a soldier on inspection day. Connor finished his lunch in silence, then went back to work—keeping one eye on the clock the whole time.

He tried Alexandra's cell phone one more time and got no response. In desperation he called the office. Janie answered on the second ring with her usual cheerful professionalism.

"Janie, hi. It's Connor."

"Hi." She sounded… relieved, as if she was glad he'd called. Was something wrong?

"How are you?"

"I'm fine. Your *girlfriend* on the other hand—"

"Is she okay?"

"She will be. We had a bit of a chat…" Janie trailed off.

Ah. That *kind of chat.*

"What's the verdict?" Connor asked, anxiously. "Firing squad? Electric chair?"

"Slap on the wrist. Maybe some community service. Play your cards right and you might even earn a full pardon."

"Pardons come from the governor or the President, not a judge, Janie." Connor smiled, relieved beyond words.

If Alexandra had been absolutely done with him, he doubted very much that Janie, as her Assistant/Best Friend would even be talking to him right now. He probably would have gotten a polite *"may I take a message"* at best and at worst, she probably would have just told him to fuck off.

"I work at a law firm, *of course* I know that. But Judges dismiss cases so I thought pardon sounded better than dismissal. *Nobody* wants a *dismissal* from their girlfriend."

"You're a brilliant and lovely woman, Janie." Connor didn't care how shameless he sounded. He meant every single word at that moment. "Is Alexandra there?"

"She is, but she's in a conference and told me not to disturb her."

"Can you tell her I called?"

"I can do you one better. I'll text you my address and you can surprise her after work."

"How are you still single, beautiful genius that you are?"

"By choice," she snorted.

Almost as soon as he ended the call, his phone dinged and he started making plans to get himself that pardon. Though he'd gladly take a slap on the wrist—or anywhere else for that matter—if that fixed things.

Now all he had to do was get through this horrible dinner meeting and he could see her. He could hold her, touch her, and make sure that she was alright and hopefully he could take her home.

Home.

He wanted it to be her home, too. Wanted her in his apartment, in his bed, in his life—tonight, tomorrow, and every day after that.

One step at a time.

He'd fix this. And then he'd make her his.

Chapter Twenty-Four

Something was up.

Janie had been cheerful all afternoon—nothing unusual there—but she also seemed a little too pleased with herself about something. Alexandra suspected she was planning to kidnap her for a girls' night or something, but the last thing she wanted to do was go out after work. She was tired—seven hours on a plane yesterday and barely a wink of sleep last night.

She wanted nothing more than a long hot shower, some PJs and maybe a pint of ice cream. She needed to talk to Connor, but she hadn't decided what to say to him yet. Her phone had died that morning—her charger still tucked in her suitcase all night, in Connor's room, where she hadn't set foot.

She'd left it charging in her office for a while with the ringer off. And then she'd left it there simply because she didn't need the constant distraction. She knew she'd have checked it every five seconds if it had been with her.

And if he'd called, she wouldn't have gotten a single damn thing done. When she finally checked it late in the afternoon, she knew that had been a good call. She'd missed four calls from Connor. Her heart leapt—traitorous little organ—but it sank just as fast when she saw he hadn't left a single message.

Maybe after some food and a little time to screw up her courage, she'd call him tonight and talk things out. She could admit she'd overreacted—just a tad.

Yes, he should've told her sooner. But she could see now—he'd used every tool he had to do his job the best way he knew how. Objectively, he'd made the right call.

She also realized, with Janie's unexpected but apparently much needed help, that she didn't have to do this alone. Connor could be supportive—hell, he *wanted* to be. She just had to let him. Maybe then he'd see she wanted to be there for him too.

That was the other thing she'd realized. She'd been frustrated that he hadn't confided in her the way she'd confided in him. He'd stood by her during not one, but two panic attacks—and a dozen other less-than-stellar moments.

He'd been nothing but patient and sweet and understanding. He'd gone out of his way to make her feel safe and cared for. Connor had given her the space to fall apart—and made himself the soft place she landed. She wanted to be that for him too.

He'd earned her trust a hundred times over—and she wasn't sure she'd done a damn thing to earn his.

All of it spun through her head as she packed up for the night. The jig was up about her protective detail, so she grabbed Janie and the two of them waited together in the lobby for Jackson.

Jackson looked adorably bewildered to see both of them, but he recovered fast—offering a charming smile and a quick, "You ladies ready to roll?"

"Cat's out of the bag, Jacks," Alexandra said, offering him a tired smile.

"Yeah?" He actually looked relieved as he hustled them into the backseat of the Range Rover. "Where to, ladies?"

"My place," Janie replied with a mischievous grin. Alexandra practically heard Jackson swallow comically as he turned back and pulled away from the curb.

Poor man.

"Be. Nice," Alexandra mouthed when Janie finally looked her way.

Janie rolled her eyes and asked Jackson some polite getting-to-know-you questions. Which was good because Alexandra wasn't feeling particularly chatty. She tuned them out and stared out the window at the dreary gray evening. It suited her mood perfectly.

Jackson parked and walked them into Janie's cozy little apartment. He and Janie were still chatting in the living room when Alexandra shut the bathroom door behind her. She turned on the water, stripped out of her clothes and was under the hot spray in record time.

A knock sounded on the door and Janie popped her head in.

"Just me," she called out.

Alexandra peeked around the shower curtain, blinking water from her lashes.

"Need something?"

"Just wanted to tell you that I'm going for coffee with Jackson." Janie grinned and wiggled her eyebrows. "I'll be back before it gets too late and I'll lock up on the way out."

"Okay. Have fun. Just don't do anything I wouldn't do," she warned.

"I thought you said have fun," Janie teased, sticking out her tongue before shutting the door.

Alexandra washed her hair, then stood motionless beneath the spray, letting the heat and white noise work their magic while she tried to figure out what the hell to say to Connor.

She felt ridiculous for how she'd reacted—storming off like some drama queen, locking herself in the spare bedroom, and running at the first chance she got.

She hadn't given him a real chance to explain. And to his credit, he had told her the truth. He could've kept all of it to himself—especially his suspicions about Lucas. That would've been so much worse.

Alexandra dried off and carefully combed and dried her hair. She dug pajamas from her suitcase and wondered what she was going to do in terms of clothes. She had nothing suitable for work, and she would run out of basic necessities in a day or two.

Tomorrow, she'd have to ask someone to swing by her place—just long enough to grab some clothes. She hadn't had the time or energy to deal with it today.

Seriously, how long could it take to fix one damn window?

She changed, made a cup of tea, and curled up on Janie's overstuffed couch. When she checked the time and saw it was still relatively early, she gave herself another hour.

Connor often worked late, and he'd probably be buried catching up after a week away—she certainly had been. Honestly, she should still be at the office—but she hadn't been able to focus another damn second.

Okay, yes—she was stalling. And she felt like a coward. But under the circumstances? She decided to give herself a pass.

She turned on Janie's TV and flipped channels until she landed on an episode of *Doctor Who*—judging by the hairstyles and questionable wardrobe choices, it was definitely from the mid-'80s.

She hadn't seen much of the show and was quickly, hopelessly lost. If Connor were here, he'd probably be able to explain it frame by frame.

That was her last conscious thought before sleep snuck up on her.

She jolted awake in a blind panic, heart pounding, disoriented by the unfamiliar couch and the choking silence. The hair on the back of her neck stood on end, adrenaline spiking sharp and fast in her veins.

It happened sometimes—after a nightmare, after too little sleep—but she didn't remember dreaming at all.

Her surroundings clicked into place soon enough, but something still felt... *off.*

The glowing numbers on the cable box told her she'd only been out for ten minutes, maybe less. So what the hell had woken her?

She stayed perfectly still, straining to hear anything that didn't belong. Just when she was ready to chalk it up to anxiety playing tricks again—she heard it.

A faint crunching noise.

Like someone walking across gravel—but muffled, distant. *Wrong.*

She couldn't place it, but whatever it was—it wasn't good. And it was coming from Janie's room.

She reached for her phone on the coffee table, slow and silent. Once it was in her grip, she rolled off the couch and onto the floor. She needed to get out. Once she did, she'd bang on doors until someone answered—or called the police.

If they opened the door, she'd call the police. And Connor. And Jackson. Not necessarily in that order. If *they* called, even better—cops would already be on the way. In fact, it might be best if several of them called.

It was a solid plan. At least, that's what she told herself as she slowly rose, staying low. Her heart was pounding in her ears so loud it had to be echoing through the whole building.

She glanced around the edge of the couch, then crept toward the front door—silent as she could.

She stood and eased the deadbolt back. It opened with a metallic click.

Too loud.

She cringed.

Between one heartbeat and the next, she could feel someone behind her.

Maybe it was a hinge squeak. Maybe a footstep. She didn't know how—only that she *knew.* She fumbled for the second lock. Her fingers wouldn't cooperate. Her phone slipped from her hand, clattering to the floor.

A hand tangled in her hair and *yanked.* Pain seared her scalp and she shrieked. She screamed louder, praying someone—*anyone*—would hear her.

A gloved hand clamped around her throat and *squeezed.* Her voice died in her mouth.

"Quiet," a voice hissed in her ear—familiar.

Too familiar.

As soon as she heard his voice, something inside her *snapped.* She *heard* it—a pop, sharp and electric—then everything else vanished beneath the roar in her ears. Fury like nothing she'd ever known flooded her veins, her vision going red with rage.

Trey's training surged to the surface. She fought, throwing an elbow into his ribs—but trapped between him and the door, she couldn't get the leverage she needed. She stomped on his foot—nothing. Thick boots. Bare feet. It only hurt her.

She clawed at his face—nails deep. He flinched, releasing her hair to grab her wrist. She yanked her head forward—then slammed it back, aiming for his nose. He turned—just enough. Her skull caught his jaw instead of his nose. Not perfect, but it rattled him.

He staggered sideways, grip loosening as he fought for balance.

She twisted, snaking her free arm up through the one still choking her. She pushed through, pinned it against her chest, and spun—*hard.* He lost his footing. Went down. His head cracked against the wall as she reversed their positions.

He nearly took her down with him, but she wrenched her hand free—just in time.

She bolted for Janie's room, praying to *anyone* listening that the taser was still there. She was a single woman living alone in the city. Even if the taser wasn't there, there had to be a baseball bat or something.

Suddenly she went down hard. Smashing her face into the floor. White-hot pain exploded behind her eyes. Her vision flared.

She tasted blood.

Lucas had her by the ankle, cursing a blue streak as he sprawled on the floor. She flipped onto her back—blood pouring from her nose, vision swimming—and kicked with her free leg. She kicked again. And again. Aiming for his head. He blocked with one hand, still swearing.

He caught her other ankle mid-kick and yanked—hard. Her skull cracked against the floor, stars bursting behind her eyes. Everything went black.

She couldn't black out. If she slept, she'd die.

She had to keep him here. If he got her out that door—she was dead.

Stay awake. Stay alive.

She chanted it silently. Over and over. Like a lifeline.

He had a hold of both ankles now. She looked around, desperate for something, anything, she could use as a weapon.

He continued to drag her away from the door into the center of the living room. She tried to scream, but she could hardly breathe for all the blood in her mouth and nose, and her throat felt tight and painful.

She kicked, thrashed, clawed at the furniture—anything to slow him down—as he dragged her across the floor. She tuned out the hissed insults. They didn't matter. *Survival did.*

He stopped. Dropped to a crouch. She forced herself upright through the pounding in her skull and swung—nailing him in the jaw. It wasn't clean—too rushed, bad angle—but it startled him. He ducked sideways.

She shoved, pulled her knees up, tried to twist free. He dropped his weight, kneeling on her thighs—pinning her fast.

A quick, hard punch to her stomach—the air left her lungs is rush. She couldn't breathe. Couldn't move. Pain locked her in place. He took advantage—straddling her thighs, his weight like concrete across her legs.

By the time she dragged in a ragged breath, he had her arms pinned—and wore that smug, sick smile.

"That was unexpected," he sneered. "You didn't fight like this the first time."

"Fuck you," she wheezed. It hurt like hell, but she forced it out loud and clear. If she could've screamed it, she would have shattered windows.

"No, Fuck *you*," he snapped. "You and your self-righteous prick of a father."

"What?" she rasped. Her father? What the hell did he have to do with any of this?

"He offered me an internship—your dad. Before you dumped me. Said it'd be a chance to see if law school was right for me."

He pulled her hands together in front of her and held them both with one hand. She twisted her hands, trying to break his grip, but he was stronger than he had been nine years ago.

He pulled a roll of duct tape from his cargo pants and started winding it around her wrists.

"You didn't really want to go to law school. You were some wishy-washy Lit major. I figured you'd vanish after college—become a teacher, maybe some broke-ass writer."

Alexandra was trying hard to pay attention, trying figure out what the hell he was talking about. She was also trying to figure out some way to make use of his distraction as he chattered away while binding her hands.

There had to be something—*anything*—she could use, do, reach.

"Hell, I thought maybe you would've gotten married and had a few babies and that would be that. But no. *I'm* stuck in some dead-end job, being watched like a goddamn zoo animal—and there you are in the paper, Alexandra Hughes, hotshot lawyer. Working for dear old dad at one of the city's best firms. You—*you*—with no ambition, no drive. It should've been *me*. It would've been me, if you'd just listened. Given me another chance. None of this had to happen."

Oh God. He wasn't just angry—he was completely unhinged.

He was so delusional that it was beyond her punch drunk brain's ability to comprehend. He was upset… because she'd become a *lawyer*? He was upset because he was being treated like the criminal he was and Alexandra had actually made something of herself? And what had happened ten years ago was… because of an *internship*?

"So, I *deserved* what happened—because I dumped you? Because you lost a fucking *internship*?" Alexandra hissed.

Her nose throbbed, voice warping into a nasally rasp. She hated how much it sounded like a whine.

"Are you *fucking serious* right now? You're a goddamn lunatic! Nobody owed you shit then, and you don't deserve a goddamn thing now—except maybe a needle in your arm!"

Lucas sighed—long, theatrical—like he was explaining calculus to a toddler. She hated that *so much.*

"If you'd just reconsidered," he seethed, "I could've done my internship, gone to a top law school, landed a job at your dad's firm. I tried to reason with you. Remind you how good we were. But you just—made me so *angry.*"

That last part came through clenched teeth, rage simmering just from the memory.

"I was willing to let sleeping dogs lie," he snarled. "You cost me everything—my internship, the four years I spent in prison, my future. *You* ruined my life, and I let it slide. But now you're living *my* life. That degree, that license, your job—*mine.* They should be *mine!*"

She couldn't help it. A bitter laugh broke from her throat. Disbelief, rage, and horror all collided.

"I always knew you weren't the brightest, but I didn't think you were *this* stupid," Alexandra spat.

He clenched his jaw, red-faced.

"My father wouldn't have pulled your internship, even if we broke up. You *idiot.*"

"What?" he asked, confusion flickering.

"Unlike you, he's not a selfish *prick* who fucks with people's lives for fun. If he offered you an internship he would have kept his word, *dipshit.* It's called *integrity,* asshole. Not that you'd recognize it."

He stared, shaking his head like she was speaking a foreign language.

"You're lying," he growled. But his voice wavered.

"All of this? The prison time? Your pathetic life? You did that to yourself. For *nothing.*"

"YOU'RE LYING!" he screamed, and the backhand came fast and brutal—pain exploding behind her eyes.

Stay awake. Stay alive. Stay… awake…"

"The person who ruined your life… was *you,*" she slurred.

Uh-oh. Not a good sign.

"Shut up," he hissed. "It doesn't matter now."

He scooted back, keeping her legs pinned with his weight, kneeling painfully on her shins as he turned around to tape her legs. She gasped and bit the inside of her cheek to keep from crying out.

He yanked hard on the tape, wrapping it too tight around her ankles.

Her hands were already numb. The fury that had kept her upright bled out, leaving only cold panic in its place. She tried to swallow past all the blood. She was having trouble breathing and her head was pounding with each beat of her heart.

She couldn't move. Couldn't scream. Couldn't fight. Every inch of her body ached—and God, she missed Connor. Missed his voice. His touch. She hated how they'd left things. Hated herself for not picking up the phone.

If she'd called, he might be here. And Lucas? He never would've made it past the front door. Connor would've *ended* him.

And now Connor would blame himself—because of course he would—even though it was her fault. All of it. She should have listened to him. The tears came, hot and silent. It didn't matter anymore. Nothing did.

I'm sorry, Connor.
I love you.
Always.

Connor could've sworn time was moving backward. Hell, at this point, he was willing to put money on it.

He'd pitched his system update proposal, laid out a full cost analysis showing how they'd save money long-term with fewer boots on the ground—*and still*, these assholes kept asking the same questions over and over, forcing him to invent new ways to say the exact same thing.

Every. Damn. *Time.*

They'd eaten their overpriced steak—on his dime—and now they were wasting his goddamn time. Alexandra would be home by now. He needed to see her.

Touch her.

Hear her voice.

He needed to make sure she was okay—make sure *they* were okay.

When his phone rang, his first thought was: "Thank God—*and Sam*—for the escape plan."

His second thought chilled him—Sam knew where he was. Sam wouldn't call unless it was serious.

"Excuse me, gentlemen. I need to take this."

He was already up, striding for the exit. His heart was hammering, but he kept his face neutral until he was out of range.

"Sam?"

"Something's up," Sam said flatly. "Archie's men were watching Whitmore—soon as we had eyes, I had them tail him. But… they lost him."

"What? When?"

Sam's voice was taut, strained—like he was chewing broken glass. "Didn't show at work. They doubled back to his apartment. Nothing."

Connor swore viciously and sprinted for the lot.

Connor swore under his breath and took off for the parking lot.

"What about the cousin?"

"Gone."

"Goddamn it."

"There's more," Sam said, and Connor's pulse jumped. He forced himself to breathe.

"Paul from Probation called. Whitmore missed his check-in this afternoon—got flagged by Westchester PD."

Connor cursed some more as he sprinted for his vehicle.

"Call Jackson," he barked. "Send him back to Janie's. Tell him not to move until I get there."

"Got it." Sam hung up without another word.

Connor had the SUV flying down the road before he hit dial on Alexandra's number.

Still no answer. His stomach turned to stone.

He never should've let her leave. Never should've given her the option. If she'd stayed—locked herself in the guest room, refused to look at him, screamed at him every time he walked past—at least she'd have been safe. He'd fucked up. Again.

Now someone he *loved* might pay for it.

He called Janie. Still no answer.

He was already breaking half a dozen traffic laws tearing toward her apartment, and that knot in his chest pulled tighter with every passing second.

He told himself he was overreacting. That he'd bust through that door and find her sipping tea in her pajamas.

But his gut said otherwise—and it had never been wrong before.

Whitmore had played the part of a model ex-con. Showed up to every appointment, followed every rule, not even a damn parking ticket. And now? Now he vanishes—*today*. The day Alexandra comes back. The *first* night she's not under Connor's roof. Not at her well-secured brownstone.

No fucking way that was coincidence.

He skidded to a stop out front, yanked his P99 from the lockbox under the seat, and sprinted for the apartment entrance.

Locked. Of course.

His finger hovered over Janie's buzzer—then froze.

If everything was fine, he could wait.

If it wasn't—if she was in danger—ringing that damn bell might tip the bastard off. He needed another way in. Quiet. Fast.

He called Alexandra again. Six rings. Voicemail. Not dead—just unanswered. Not good.

He stabbed Jackson's number and it connected on the first ring.

"We're on our way, we'll be there in five."

"Got it. Where is Janie's apartment located in the building?"

"Third floor, second unit north of the southeast corner."

"Got it. Call me when you get here."

He hung up the phone and jogged around until he found an alley he could slip through to get to the back of the building. He looked up to the third floor and swore. All the unlit windows reflected the ambient light from the city, except for one. The third window from the left was either broken or open. Being late October, he doubted very much that Janie had intentionally left a window wide open.

He tucked the gun into the waistband of his slacks—no time to grab a holster—and ditched his jacket and tie. Rolling up his sleeves, he started up the fire escape, every muscle strung tight with urgency.

He wanted to race up the rungs. Everything inside him was screaming at him to hurry. The thought of Alexandra in the same *room* as Whitmore made his blood boil and his stomach churn. In the same city was bad enough. This? This was unthinkable.

Please be okay. Please be okay.

He climbed through the window, being very careful not to make too much noise. The only sounds coming from the other room was the television. Quiet was good, right? Alexandra had been training with Trey for a while now. She would put up a fight this time. Unless she already had… and lost.

He crept to the door, sidestepping broken glass. It hung slightly ajar. He paused, listening. Still nothing. He craned his head, trying to see as much as possible through the small crack in the door.

He couldn't get a visual on anyone so he pulled out his weapon, taking the safety off and moved carefully to the other side of the door. He still couldn't see anything or anyone.

He nudged the door open, holding his sidearm down at the floor in front of him. When the door was fully open and he'd visually swept the room, he straightened, staring at the floor.

Her phone lay on the rug beside the door.

In front of the couch—a pool of blood.

A roar filled his ears, drowning everything else. His vision narrowed until there was only red—smeared across the floor.

"*Fuck!*" *h*e roared and kicked the coffee table, sending it crashing across the floor.

He dropped into a crouch, head in his hands, every instinct screaming for action even as his brain fought to think. Fast.

Where would he take her? How would they get there? She had to still be alive or he wouldn't have taken her. How long would she stay that way? What was his plan?

It had to involve Mr. Hughes somehow. He must want something from him. This wasn't about money, it was personal. He wanted revenge. On Alexandra and on Mr. Hughes…

"Connor?"

He looked up and saw Jackson standing in the doorway, holding Janie behind him with one outstretched arm. He looked concerned.

"You wanna put that down, boss?"

Connor was confused for a second until he realized he was still holding his weapon and it was more or less pointed at the door. He immediately lowered it and put the safety on as he stood up.

"Where's Lex?" Janie whispered, voice barely steady.

Connor's throat closed. He had to force the words out past the ache in his chest.

"Gone."

Just saying it nearly broke him.

Chapter Twenty-Five

Fuck… FUCK! Think. Don't panic, just… think. Sam. Call Sam.

Connor pulled out his phone and hit two on his speed dial. He heard the call connect and spoke before Sam could even answer.

"What have you got?"

"CCTV across the street from Janie's apartment shows a black sedan circling the block three times before finding parking close to the building," Sam said, tone calm but brisk.

"Shit."

Black sedan. Just like the car they'd caught on camera when the photos were delivered. It wasn't Whitmore's. Had to be the cousins.

"Yeah. I confirmed it belongs to the cousin. Plate matches the partial from the video. He's our accomplice."

Sam paused a beat, letting Connor process before he moved on.

"Two males. Caucasian. Height and build are consistent. Car slows, one gets out—disappears behind the building. Car circles a few more times. Twenty minutes later—the cameras lose 'em. Don't pick 'em again until they're on the way out. *Both* of them."

"Cameras in the building? They got in via the fire escape, but they couldn't have left that way. Not with—"

Alexandra.

She'd fought. They'd have to carry her out.

He felt like his chest was caving in. It was hard to breathe.

"No CCTV in the building, but it's not a total loss. Neighbor has one of those doorbell cameras—went off when someone went by…" There was a pause that made Connor's heart sink into his stomach. "She called the police as soon as she saw it."

"When was that?" Connor's voice was a hoarse whisper.

"Seventeen minutes ago." Connor could hear the steady clicking of the keyboard in the background and for a moment Sam had that distracted quality to his voice that meant he was doing about eight things at once, seven of which Connor would never be able to understand.

"So we *just* missed them."

Connor ran his hand through his hair, trying desperately to keep his brain from short-circuiting and sending him on a downward spiral like none other.

"The video…" he asked.

"I don't know," Sam replied, the frustration evident in his voice but the keystrokes still steady in the background. "Lopez is *off* today, so I've got nothing. Archie's working on it."

"Fucking, *Archie*."

"For what it's worth," Sam said. "He ripped his guys a new one. I'm pretty sure he canned both of them on the spot. Not sure, but I *think* he threatened kill them—but the way he worded it? It would never hold up in court. He's… *terrifying*."

Connor didn't give fuck. If anything happened to her—CIA, FBI, fucking *KGB,* it didn't matter.

He'd be *dead.*

"Whatever it takes, Sam," Connor said, voice low and razor-sharp. "And I mean *whatever.*"

"I know," Sam cut in. "We'll get her back in one piece. I *promise.*"

Connor exhaled slowly. Alexandra needed him sharp. He could break later—once she was safe.

He dropped the phone for a second. "Jackson?"

Jackson was standing by—one arm around a pale, shaken Janie.

His jaw worked and his face was drawn tight—quiet fury simmering beneath the surface.

"What's next?"

"Neighbor's doorbell camera. Find it. Talk to them."

Connor flicked a glance at Janie, tilting his head toward the door. Jackson gave a silent nod.

Jackson led Janie into the hall, their voices dropping as they moved out of sight.

Connor put the phone back to his ear. "Call everyone. They're on standby."

"Handled," Sam confirmed

Something still bothered him.

How the *fuck* had they found her? She'd been out of his sight for *one goddamn day*—not even. And she wasn't *supposed* to be there. The only people who knew where she was were his team and Janie.

Could it be Janie?

He trusted his team with his life and their comms were secure. But Janie?

She knew where Alexandra was.

She'd left with Jackson—left Alexandra alone.

He considered it—then dismissed it. Her shock was too real. No way her acting was that good. He'd seen them together—his gut said it wasn't her.

"How the hell did they even *find* her?" Connor muttered.

"Good question," Sam muttered, keystrokes still steady in the background.

"Could be a bug in her office?"

"No chance. You've seen their security. And Archie's been sweeping regularly."

Archie. *Again.*

"Maybe—"

"Nope," Sam cut him off. "I thought of that, too. Already checked—there's no way."

"Phone tracking?"

"Not impossible, but not likely. No indication either of them is tech savvy enough for that."

"Was she followed?" That was a low tech as it got. They knew where she worked. It would be simple to wait for her near her office and follow her to Janie's apartment. And when the opportunity presented itself…

"Jackson's sure they weren't followed."

"Then how the fuck—"

"*Wait,*" Sam said, urgently. "You flew in to JFK, right?"

"Yeah," Connor replied, a pit forming in his stomach. "Why?"

"*Sonofa—*" Sam shouted before cutting himself off. "The cousin—Daniel Whitmore? Works at JFK. Baggage handler."

It took Connor a second to catch up.

When it dawned on him, his blood ran cold.

Tracker?

Connor backtracked into the bedroom. Alexandra's bag sat on the floor by the door. He hoisted it up onto the bed.

He unzipped it, dumping the contents onto the bed. He clenched his teeth, trying to ignore the almond and honey scent that clung to her clothes—even as it haunted him while he searched her bag.

He was good at compartmentalizing—turning off his emotions. Usually.

Now? It was impossible.

He felt like all his nerves were raw—*exposed.*

But he kept his hands moving—unzipping every compartment, feeling the lining of every pocket. Feeling for anything that shouldn't be there. He turned it over, looking for cracks, scuffs, broken pieces. Any place you could hide something or any sign it had been tampered with.

And then he heard it.

It was faint, but he shook the suitcase and heard it again. A rattling noise, like plastic on plastic.

At first he thought it was just the wheels but the sound was different.

He isolated the noise to one wheel in particular. With a silent apology to Alexandra and a promise to buy her twenty new ones, he picked up the suitcase—slamming it into the floor. He made sure the point of impact was the wheel.

They were plastic, so after two sharp cracks, they shattered and the wheel assembly snapped off. He tossed the bag aside and picked through the pieces.

There, amid the plastic shards, was a small, round tracking device. commercially available—no tech savvy required.

Son of a bitch…

They'd stood there and patiently waited while he'd planted a fucking tracking device in her suitcase.

His phone rang and he picked it up with equal parts dread and hope.

"What've you got?"

"The apartment," Sam said instantly.

"Which one?" Connor was already on his way out the door.

"The one that was already rented out—a month in advance? Without the landlord actually *seeing* anyone?"

"I thought you ran the name," Connor barked, racing down the stairs.

"I *did*. Some guy in Florida—but it wasn't easy tracking him down. Now I know why," Sam said. "He's been dead for a month."

"*What?*"

"They used his information to fill out the rental application. Paid the rental fees and deposit by money order."

"How *the hell* did they do that?" Connor rounded the corner of the building and jogged to the Hummer.

"Get this. He lived in Florida, but he was transported to New York for burial via American Airlines. Guess which airport."

"JFK," Connor muttered, climbing behind the wheel. "Call *everyone*—get them over there *now*."

"I already promised to cover speeding tickets—and bail money, if necessary. They'll be there in ten, max."

Connor threw the car in gear, peeling out of the parking lot.

"Fuck it. Tell them whoever gets there first gets a bonus, a raise, and my first born child."

"I'm not sure Alexandra would like you promising that."

Connor's chest squeezed at the thought—Alexandra, a ring on her finger, a baby in her arms. Of course his firstborn would be hers, too.

And then Connor did something he hadn't done in years.

He prayed.

Connor parked around the corner, eyes scanning for the black sedan—or any sign of Whitmore and his cousin. Nothing. No sign of his team either. Jackson was on the way—he'd called from the car—but right now, Connor was alone.

He should wait for backup. Make sure they had the tactical advantage, superior fire power.

But Alexandra was in there. Scared. Injured. Alone.

He couldn't wait.

The basement apartment windows were too small to climb through, and there wasn't time to scope out a second entrance. But he couldn't go in blind. He crept to one of the windows and peered inside.

There was a common area—living room and kitchen combined. But no furniture. And no people. There was a door to the side that probably led to a bedroom.

His stomach twisted. Bile rose in his throat.

He checked the doorknob—surprised to find it unlocked.

Were they that confident… or just that stupid?

He eased the door open carefully, making sure it wouldn't creak or groan. Luckily the door was new and the hinges were well oiled. Sliding inside, he shut it silently behind him.

Hugging the wall, he moved toward the interior door. Steps slow—silent.

He heard faint scuffing, as if someone was shifting around. Then a voice. The door was cracked an inch or two—just enough. There was one piece of furniture in the room: a bed.

A twin size mattress covered in a sheet and a threadbare blanket.

It stuck out from the wall beside the door, essentially in the center of the wall.

Someone was standing on the other side.

One subject—male. Back to the door. No visible weapon.

He couldn't see Alexandra, but the view of the floor on the other side was obstructed. One subject meant the other could be coming back any minute. That would explain why the door was unlocked.

The subject bent down, and Connor strained to see if he could hear anything over the pounding of his pulse in his ears.

"Don't worry. I'll make sure you're nice and comfortable," he said, his voice oozing smug hostility. "It'll be like old times."

Connor's vision went red and he raised his weapon in the blink of an eye, finger already squeezing the trigger.

Until there was a scream—*two* screams.

One man—

and a woman.

Connor burst through the door, sidearm raised, circling the bed. And noticed the blood.

Lots of blood.

God, no…

Alexandra was on the floor, the subject's body blocking his view. All he could see was her legs, taped at the ankles, sticking out from under his body.

They began to flail and Whitmore slumped off to one side—accompanied by a groan and a wet gurgling sound Connor was familiar with.

He lowered his weapon, pushing Whitmore's still body aside with his boot as Alexandra—sobbing, frantic and covered in blood—scramble backwards. A bloody hunting knife dropped from her bound hands.

Connor holstered the gun and scooped her up as soon as she was free of the dead weight.

He carried her—thrashing and crying, into the kitchen. His gut twisted and his heart broke as she struggled, terrified. Incoherent. He tried to calm her down and assess her injuries.

There was *so much blood.*

Guilt punched through him.

He had *one* job.

One. *Goddamn.* Job.

And he'd failed.

Again.

"It's me, love—it's Connor," he murmured. "It's okay. You're okay. You're safe now."

He held her carefully—firmly enough that she didn't hurt herself flailing, but not so tight that *he* hurt her. He stroked her hair, rocking gently as she sobbed. He kept up a soothing stream of words.

After a lifetime, her breathing slowed, she grew quieter, and her body relaxed—just a little—into him.

"Shh. Hush, lass. You're safe," he whispered softly.

"Connor?" she whispered.

"I'm here, love. I'm here." His voice was thick and his eyes stung.

He loosened his hold enough to pull back and look her over. Her face was a mess, but it looked like the rest of the blood wasn't hers. The blood at the apartment must have been from her nose, which looked like it was probably broken.

He sent up a silent prayer of thanks that she was okay. And that Whitmore was already lying motionless in the other room. Otherwise Connor wasn't sure what might have done.

"D-dead?" she whispered.

The way her voice broke was a stab to his heart.

"I don't know, love. But he won't hurt you again—*ever.*"

"I s-stabbed him," she choked out. "He had a-a knife in his boot. I s-stabbed him."

"Yes, you did, and I'm *so proud of you.*" Connor squeezed her a little and kissed the crown of her head. "Are you alright? Where are you hurt?"

"My nose. I think it's broken. My head hurts. And my neck."

Connor swore silently to himself. He shouldn't have moved her. But she'd been desperate to get away and she could have done more damage to herself thrashing around than he was likely to do by moving her.

"I need to make a call, okay?"

She nodded gingerly and he dug the phone out of his pocket. He dialed Jackson, telling him the situation and to watch out for the cousin who was still floating around out there somewhere. He asked him to call the police and get at least one ambulance there ASAP.

In the meantime, he needed to get Alexandra out of there. He used his pocket knife to cut the tape on her ankles and wrists and helped rub some feeling back into them.

"Okay, we're getting out of here, and we're going to get you cleaned up and looked at. You'll feel better soon, love. Lean on me and go as slow as you need to."

He tucked her under his left arm so that he was between her and the bedroom where Whitmore's body was. The less she had to see the better.

They were almost to the door when something caught Connor's attention.

A noise, a slight shift in the light—he couldn't say which, but he turned, raising his sidearm before he even had time to think.

Whitmore stood there, clutching his stomach, a gun in his hand.

He pulled the trigger.

Connor returned fire—

and put a 9mm bullet square between his eyes.

He immediately turned to Alexandra, praying Whitmore's aim was a shitty as he was.

"Are you hit?" He scanned her frantically, looking for fresh blood.

He didn't see anything, but her face had lost what little color it had a minute ago.

"You're bleeding," she gasped.

Her voice shook and her eyes were wide. He looked himself over and was surprised to see a rapidly growing red stain spreading across his chest. He pressed a hand over it.

That was when the pain hit him—sharp, searing. He grimaced.

"Don't worry, love," he said. "You're not getting rid of me that easily."

And he meant every word.

He wasn't dying here. Not like this. Not in front of her—when she was hurt and scared. Vulnerable. Gritting his teeth through the pain, he kept pressure on the wound with one hand. Gun still in the other, just in case.

"Let's get out of here, yeah?" he said. He tried to give her a reassuring smile. The devastation on her face hurt more than the bullet wound.

She nodded quickly, sticking close as she followed him out the door. He kept an eye out for the cousin, but the street was clear.

Until he saw them—Cam and Parker, racing down the street toward them, their car parked down the block, doors still open.

On the ground beside the car was the other subject—the cousin. Face down, hands cuffed behind his back, casually pinned to the pavement by one of Ian's boots on his neck.

Ian leaned against the car, arms crossed over his chest, unphased. Like he was just killing time. But Connor knew better. Knew the shoulder holster under his jacket was loaded with a Sig P320. Possibly two.

Those casually crossed arms meant he could draw and shoot before a normal man could even blink.

Parker and Cam reached them in seconds. Then Connor was lying on the ground—grass underneath him. He didn't know if he fell or if they'd helped him down. Either way, Parker was leaning over him applying pressure to the wound with... what looked like someone's shirt.

He looked over at Cam and laughed—or tried to.

Of course it was Cam.

Shirtless. In *October*. Obviously.

He was feeling a little lightheaded. It didn't hurt anymore—that was probably a bad sign.

Alexandra was there, holding his hand. She was banged up, shaken—but alive. She'd made it. She'd survive this too.

And Lucas Whitmore would *never* touch her again.

Beautiful, brave Alexandra. So strong. Still fighting, even when she was terrified.

He was so fucking proud of her.

And he loved her. So much it hurt.

"Stay with me, baby," Alexandra said. Her voice sounded far away. Muffled. Like she was underwater.

She's never called me that before. I like it…

She squeezed his hand. *Hard.* "Don't you *dare* leave me, you understand?"

"I… would never," he murmured. Too quiet.

"If you do, I'll kill you," she choked out, sobbing.

Tears streaked down her face. He tried to wipe them away, but he didn't have the strength.

"Shh, it's okay," he breathed.

"It's *not* okay. And it *won't be* until *you're* okay. So don't you fucking *dare* die on me, or I swear it will *never* be okay."

He tried to respond—to promise—but he was fading. His vision narrowed, dimming around the edges.

Someone was talking. Couldn't tell who. Didn't understand.

The last thing he heard was, "Ah, shi—"

Then the world was silent.

Everything went black.

"They won't tell me anything," Alexandra snapped, frustration boiling over.

Her nose had been treated—luckily it wasn't broken. But she had a mild concussion and had been poked, prodded, and x-rayed from head to toe. And *still,* no word on Connor.

They tried to convince her to stay overnight for observation, but unless she could be with Connor, she'd rather be in the waiting room with Jackson and Janie.

The police had taken her statement while EMTs, then doctors and nurses, examined her. She still had to go down to the station to sign a formal statement, but right now all she cared about was Connor. Lucas was dead. He didn't deserve a single second of her attention.

"You sure you're okay?" Janie asked gently, giving her hand a squeeze.

"I'm fine. I just need to know he's okay," Alexandra murmured, rubbing her aching temples.

A petite woman in scrubs burst through the ER doors, breathless, and hurried to the check-in desk. Curvy, with long dark hair and brown eyes, she was lovely. And looked vaguely familiar.

"Connor MacLachlan? I'm Angel Alvarez—his sister, emergency contact, and healthcare proxy."

She handed a paper through the glass. The nurse skimmed it, then set it aside

"He's in surgery now. I'll let the doctor know you're here and I'm sure someone will be out to talk to you shortly."

"Thank you." She turned and took a seat in the waiting area.

She looked calm, but it was obvious she was upset. The way she shifted, crossing and uncrossing her legs, gave away how anxious she was. But her face was blank.

It reminded Alexandra so much of herself—and that last moment with Connor—she fought back tears. He'd begged her not to put the wall back up, not to shut him out, and she'd simply walked away.

And now she might not get the chance to apologize, or tell him…

She couldn't let herself think like that or she'd fall apart.

Connor would hate that. And he'd hate his sister sitting here worrying about him.

That was one thing she could do for him. She got up and walked across the waiting room, sitting down next to her.

"Angel?" she said nervously. Her throat still felt raw and her voice was little more than a croak. Angel looked up, startled.

"Yes?"

"I'm Alexandra Hughes. Connor's…" *Friend? Girlfriend? Client?*

"You're Connor's Alexandra," Angel said as if that was explanation enough. She held out her hand and Alexandra shook it. "He's told me a lot about you."

Angel studied her face—no doubt a mess.

Wide eyed, she asked: "What happened?"

"It's a long story," Alexandra admitted—and then she started at the beginning.

It felt good to get it all out, even though by the end she was barely holding it together. She told Angel everything—about Lucas, her feelings for Connor, the fight, and how he'd saved her. Angel listened without interruption, then pulled Alexandra into a gentle hug while she wiped at the tears streaming down her face.

"He loves you, you know," Angel whispered softly.

Alexandra couldn't speak. Her throat locked, and the tears came harder. She let them. Please, God—don't let it be too late to tell him how she felt.

Two unbearable hours later, a doctor finally appeared. He told them Connor had been lucky—if any one who'd been shot could be called lucky. The bullet had missed everything vital and was relatively easy to remove.

He'd needed a lot of blood, but there would be no lasting damage. They suspected the bullet had glanced off his collarbone—leaving a hairline fracture that would heal with rest and time.

With Connor out of surgery and resting while the anesthesia wore off, both Janie and Jackson tried to convince Alexandra to go home—but she refused. Connor had nearly died saving her. She needed to be there when he woke up. She wouldn't waste another second before telling him she loved him.

The past twenty-four hours had been a nightmare—one she might've avoided if she hadn't been so afraid. For nearly a decade, she'd let Lucas Whitmore keep hurting her. It was over now—but it should have ended years ago.

Still, if she hadn't fought with Connor and taken off… who knows how long it would've taken for Lucas to strike—or for them to gather the evidence they needed to stop him. It wasn't the ending she wanted—but it was an ending. One where she and Connor were alive… and Lucas Whitmore was dead.

"You sure you don't want to get some rest?" Janie asked softly. Jackson had offered to give her a ride wherever she needed to go, and considering it was getting late, Alexandra convinced her to go.

"No. I want to see him. Besides, where would I even go?" She tried to smile, but Janie's reaction told her it hadn't quite landed. "What about you? Where are you staying tonight?"

"Hotel for now. I'll figure out something longer-term tomorrow. No way I'm going back to my place—who knows how long the police will keep it locked down."

"I'm sorry, Janie."

"Yeah, because clearly this is all your fault." Janie rolled her eyes, then winced. Her cheeks flushed and she gave Alexandra a sheepish smile. "Sorry. Sarcasm's a reflex."

"It's okay." Alexandra gave her friend a hug. "Tell you what—once the window's fixed, you can stay with me as long as you want. I've got plenty of space, and hey… could be fun to have a roommate."

"Seriously?" Janie grinned.

"Yeah, and we can carpool—since I'm pretty sure I'm about to lose my personal driver." Alexandra gave Jackson a smile and he wrapped her in a Texas sized (if not Texas strength) bear hug.

"Hey, I'm still around. And you've got my number," he said with a wink. He gave Angel a hug too, whispered something in her ear, then kissed her temple. Janie watched a little too closely—then quickly looked away, pretending to rummage through her purse as Jackson turned to escort her out.

Fifteen minutes later, Parker and Cam arrived. Angel spoke quietly to Parker when he hugged her, but she ignored Cam completely and went back to scrolling through her phone.

Alexandra was surprised when Parker gave her a careful hug. He even sat beside her, while Cam took the seat next to Angel. And then he surprised her again.

"I called your sister," he said quietly. "She'll be here soon—with some clothes."

Alexandra blinked. He had Amanda's number? He *called* her?

"Thank you, Parker." Alexandra gave him a quick kiss on the cheek. He looked away, rubbing the back of his neck.

"Don't mention it," he muttered, standing abruptly. "You want coffee?"

"No, thanks."

She smiled as he walked away. Bashful Parker. That was unexpected.

Half an hour later, dressed in clean clothes thanks to Amanda, Alexandra was finally allowed to see Connor—with Angel at her side. He'd been moved to a regular room and opened his eyes the moment they walked in.

Angel, who'd been calm and stoic in the waiting room, broke into sobs the instant she saw him. She rushed to his bedside and grabbed his hand.

"Shh. It's okay. I'm fine," Connor rasped. Angel slumped into the chair beside the bed, resting her head on his arm as the tears kept coming. He looked at Alexandra over Angel's head and swallowed hard.

Alexandra moved to the other side—his injured side—and gently took his other hand. It was warm and dry, and she wanted to weep with relief. He was really okay. She sat quietly holding his hand while he comforted his sister. Watching the way they cared for each other—if she hadn't already fallen in love with him, she would have right then.

"Are you okay?" he asked, once Angel had regained her composure and was busy examining his chart.

"I'm fine," she said softly.

"Your nose?"

"Not broken."

"She has a concussion," Angel added, frowning at the clipboard in her hands. Alexandra glared at her.

"*Mild* concussion," Alexandra clarified. "Just some bruises."

Connor surveyed her thoroughly, taking in her swollen nose, black eyes, and bruised throat. She hadn't been able to wash away all the blood without a proper shower. She'd made do with a pack of wet wipes and a change of clothes.

"God, Lex. I'm…" His voice was thick and his eyes shone. If he cried, she was going to lose it too—no question.

"I'm going to get some coffee," Angel interrupted. "You want some?"

"Sure. Thanks." Once Angel was gone, Alexandra turned back to Connor. "Does it hurt much?" she asked.

"No. They gave me something for the pain… I think." He didn't look at her—just at their joined hands. "Lex, I'm…"

He cleared his throat and started again.

"I'm so sorry," he said hoarsely. "So fucking sorry."

"Shh." She brushed the hair off his forehead. "Only one person's to blame for all this, and it isn't either of us."

"I shouldn't have let you go. I should've made you stay. I'd rather have you angry and cursing my name than see you like this. I was supposed to keep you safe… and I failed." His jaw clenched.

"I doubt there's anything you could've said to make me stay. I've been told I'm a bit stubborn." She tried to lighten the mood, but Connor wasn't having it.

"I fuck everything up," he muttered, scrubbing a hand over his face.

"Hey." She squeezed his hand. "You saved my life."

"After putting it in danger in the first place."

"I put *myself* in danger because I was too pigheaded to realize that you did the right thing. I overreacted and that's on me, Connor."

"I should've told you what I was doing. I should've..." He shut his eyes, wincing. "I fucked up."

"Maybe." She shrugged, the part of her that hated being vulnerable refusing to let him completely off the hook. "But I understand, Connor. I know you'd never do anything to hurt me on purpose. I trust you."

She took a deep breath as her stomach flipped.

"That's one of the reasons I love you."

I love you.

On top of the guilt and regret already crushing his soul, those words cut like a rusty blade—jagged, brutal, and deep. She trusted him. She loved him. And he'd let her down—utterly, completely, spectacularly.

His actions had hurt her. His poor judgment had put her in danger. And instead of cancelling one goddamn dinner meeting to make it right, he'd waited—almost until it was too late.

If she had died...

He couldn't even imagine a world without her in it. And it would have been his fault.

She deserved someone better. Someone whose protection wasn't a gamble. Someone whose track record wasn't littered with failure. Someone who hadn't lost lives that were placed in his care.

He loved her. More than he'd ever loved anyone. But she'd be better off without him. Sooner or later, she'd see that.

"Alexandra—"

"Connor?" Sam's voice came from the doorway.

"Hey, Sam." Connor sighed. He was surprised when Alexandra let go of his hand and stood to give Sam a hug. From his expression, Sam was surprised, too.

"Thank you, Sam," she murmured, her voice still thick. Sam looked pained, but hugged her back.

"I mean it. Jackson told me what happened. If you hadn't figured it out in time…"

Sam flinched, and Connor caught the guilt buried behind his crooked smile.

"I'm just glad you're both okay."

"Me too." Alexandra grinned at both of them, and Connor's heart broke a little more.

Sam filled him in on what happened after he'd been shot. The cousin had just been coming back when Cam, Ian and Parker showed up, which explained the crazy parking job.

It hadn't taken much persuasion to crack the little bugger. He admitted to everything but of course insisted it was all Whitmore's idea. They already knew that much and it didn't make one good goddamn bit of difference in his charges.

They were waiting for the District Attorney to decide what to do with him. Connor was relieved to have all the pieces of the puzzle accounted for, but it didn't remove the guilt of having let Alexandra down when she needed him.

Connor didn't get another chance to talk to Alexandra alone that night, or for the next three days, even though she hardly left his bedside.

Angel hovered around like a mother hen, and the guys had apparently set up some kind of rotation for visiting hours because one of them was *always* there.

They brought him food so he didn't have to suffer through hospital trays. Magazines, books, and enough banter to make the hours pass. They even played cards with him once or twice—while roasting him mercilessly, which, strangely, helped.

On Friday morning, he was told that the incision site was healing as expected, there were no signs of infection and that he'd be free to go home that afternoon. Alexandra and Angel arrived together to pick him up once his discharge paperwork was signed, and he was fucking ecstatic to put on his own clothes and go home. He didn't even mind the sling. *Much.*

Once he was settled in at home, Angel insisted on staying the weekend in case he needed anything, Alexandra had to leave to help Janie move her things into the brownstone.

"This shouldn't take long. I'll be back in a couple hours."

"That's okay. You should stay and help her unpack. I'm just going to crash anyway."

"You sure?" she asked, anxiety clear in her expression. The lie twisted his guts, but he didn't have the energy to do what he knew needed to be done. A few days to get his head straight would help.

"Yeah. And Angel's here if I need anything."

"Okay. I'll call you later." She gave him a soft, sweet kiss that left him feeling more broken than the gunshot wound.

He slept. For the next three days, he did little else. The pain meds made him drowsy and being awake wasn't very appealing anyway. His shoulder hurt, he couldn't use his hand much without making his shoulder hurt *more*, and every time he thought about Alexandra an ache in his chest that had nothing to do with his injury made it hard to breathe.

Angel stayed, checking on him, making sure he ate, reminding him when it was time to take his meds, and generally doing what came naturally to her—*caring*.

"You know your phone's got, like, five voicemails," she said, setting his dinner on the nightstand.

"Yeah?"

"Yeah. And Alexandra hasn't been around the past couple days."

"Yeah."

"You're being an ass about something, aren't you?"

"No," Connor sighed.

Angel rolled her eyes in that uniquely younger-sister way that said everything at once:

You're such an idiot.

Why do I even bother?

Please tell me I was adopted.

"Okay, whatever."

Yet another code used by younger sisters meaning they knew damn well you were being stupid and the only reason they weren't going to call you on it was because you wouldn't listen anyway.

"What would she even do? Watch me sleep? She's got better things to worry about."

"Oh, I don't know—comfort you, maybe? Help you? Actually give a damn?" Angel scowled. "You know, the kind of thing people do for someone they love—unless that someone's too damn stubborn to let them."

"What are you talking about?"

"You don't have to carry everything by yourself, you know."

Angel sighed, dropped the plate on the nightstand, and left—quietly shutting the door behind her.

Connor stared at the wood grain.

Ah, hell…

Chapter Twenty-Six

"I'm starting to really worry." Alexandra stared into her tea, frowning like it held answers she couldn't find.

She had taken two weeks worth of sick time, a week of which had already passed, and she was sitting around her house when she *should* have been at Connor's taking care of him.

"So go over there and find out what the hell is going on," Janie said, sipping her cocoa. She didn't do tea, but hot chocolate was her gospel.

"I talk to Angel every day, and she says he's sleeping a lot. I don't want to disturb him if he's resting, but—'a lot' isn't all the time. I call, he never answers. He doesn't call back."

"Again, go over and hang out until he wakes up and find out what's up."

"What if I scared him off when I told him I loved him?"

"Maybe, but I doubt it. That boy is crazy about you." Janie snorted. "He took *a literal bullet* for you, sugar. If that ain't love, I don't know what is."

"Taking a bullet for people is *literally* his job," she said, trying to joke but only managing a tremble.

If they managed to work things out she didn't know how she would deal with knowing her boyfriend was going to be in danger on a regular basis. When she'd seen that blood…

She couldn't even think about it without wanting to cry. Not even thinking *she* was going to die had terrified her as much as the thought of losing Connor.

"I don't know. I feel like he's… pulling away for some reason. I don't know if it's something I did or if he's freaking out about something else or if this is just some stupid macho '*I can't look weak in front of my woman*' thing." Though she knew he wasn't the type, really.

"Well, if you're not gonna storm over there, call in the cavalry. Start with Jackson."

"Jackson?"

"Call him and pump him for information. He likes you. If he can help, I think he will." Janie shrugged.

"Maybe…"

"Think about it. I'm going to bed. You gonna sit here and spiral some more or are you going to bed?"

"Just a few more minutes."

"Night, Lex. Don't let this keep you up. You need your sleep."

"I won't. Night."

She *did* need sleep. The bruises had mostly faded, her nose was back to normal—tender but intact—and the faint marks on her neck were the only lingering shadows.

But she was so tired. The whole experience had made her weary to her very soul. She'd met with her therapist who was, as always, supportive and helpful. But she knew it would take time to put everything finally, completely behind her.

She finished her tea and rinsed out her cup before heading to the laundry room. She'd been putting off the chores all week. Between her parents and her sister constantly popping in to check on her, feeling as though she'd been hit by a truck and everything that was—or *wasn't*—happening with Connor, she hadn't had the energy to put her house to rights.

Today she had finally checked some things off her list, including her laundry. The last load was ready to come out of the dryer and if she did it now, she wouldn't have to worry about it in the morning.

She carted the basket upstairs and got started on folding. She was down to the last pair of jeans when something dropped into the basket with a soft thud.

She picked it up, confused for a second. But then recognition dawned—followed quickly by inspiration. She hurriedly folded her jeans and put the rest of her clothes away. Then, she started to make a plan.

For the past week, Connor had been haunted by strange dreams. He blamed the pain meds—and the PTSD. Monday night alone had been enough to trigger a full-blown episode.

He dreamt of Ramirez and Thomas dying in the desert while he stood by, helpless. He dreamt of Alexandra—bruised, bleeding—lying beside him while he couldn't move, couldn't save her.

Maybe God had taken pity on him. Or maybe his subconscious had just decided he'd suffered enough. Because last night, he dreamt of Alexandra lying beside him in bed.

He could smell her—honey and almond—and hear her soft voice whispering him back to sleep. It was so vivid, so tender, it nearly broke him.

He woke to an empty bed. And that, somehow, felt crueler than the nightmares. To dream of her… only to wake up alone. He could practically smell her on his pillow.

The sun was up, but the way it angled through his east-facing windows said it was still early. Footsteps and cabinet doors clattered in the kitchen—Angel was already up, probably making breakfast.

He shuffled to the bathroom, testing his shoulder as he moved. Still tender—but manageable. The incision had surprised him the first time he saw it—smaller than expected. Now it was healing fast. Just another scar in the collection.

He took a shower, grateful he could wash his hair with both hands. Small victories. He still had to take it easy—doctor's orders: no boxing, no lifting—but he'd be cleared for work next week. Another week stuck in this apartment—either alone or with Angel hovering—and he was going to lose his damn mind.

He slept as much as he could to avoid thinking about Alexandra. Getting back to work couldn't come fast enough—he needed something to fill the space. He knew he owed her a conversation. Disappearing wasn't fair. She deserved better than that. Better than him.

He scrubbed the towel over his hair, wrapped it around his waist, and headed toward the bedroom—only to stop short the second he stepped through the door.

"Good morning." Alexandra smiled at him from his bed, relaxed and impossibly sexy in one of his t-shirts. A tray of food sat beside her, complete with a single daisy in a glass of water.

"Lex? What—when did you get here?"

"Last night," she said with a shrug. "You were sleeping. I didn't want to wake you."

"How did you even get in?"

"You gave me this, remember?" She held up the key he'd forgotten she had.

"How are you?" he asked, his throat tight. His chest ached, knowing this might be the last time she looked at him like that—and maybe it should be.

"Physically? I'm fine. But my boyfriend—who recently got *shot*—hasn't been returning my calls, so yeah, I've been a little worried."

"Lex, I—"

"How are *you*, Connor?" Her voice was soft, but the concern etched on her face hit him like a gut punch.

"I'm…" He ran a hand down his face and sat on the edge of the bed, facing away. "I don't know."

The bed dipped behind him, and a moment later she was there—legs bracketing his hips, arms wrapped tight around his waist. Her cheek pressed between his shoulder blades. He closed his eyes, breathing her in.

"You can tell me anything," she whispered. "Whenever you're ready. I'll listen." She sealed the promise with a kiss to his shoulder.

"I don't deserve you," he whispered before he could stop himself.

Alexandra, bless her, didn't argue. She just hugged him tighter, her thumbs sweeping slow, soothing strokes across his skin. He went quiet, searching for the right words, for a way to explain the weight on his chest.

"No matter what I do… I let people down."

"That's not true," she murmured.

"It is. I left Angel alone every summer with my grandmother when I should've been there to protect her."

"You were just a kid, Connor. That wasn't your job."

"I knew nobody else would. My gran was…" He hesitated. "I didn't even know half of what Angel went through until I got back from the Army."

He paused, taking a long breath. "I let my father down too. D'you know why I joined the Army? My da wanted me to move to Glasgow with him. Said he'd help me with university if I could get in. Said if I didn't want to go to school, he'd help me get a job. I wanted to go. Desperately. Mom wouldn't have cared—except to spite him. But I felt like leaving meant giving up on Angel, and I couldn't do that. So instead of choosing one, I ran from both. I joined the Army and lied to myself about why."

She squeezed him, pressing another kiss to his shoulder. The quiet comfort of it made his throat go tight. They were sitting just like they had when she told him her story—and somehow, that felt right.

"And in the Army… I did things. Things I can't take back." His voice broke. She held him tighter.

He was silent, then—just long enough to gather the courage. "I made a mistake. Three of my team died in a shack outside Mosul. I missed something… and they paid for it."

"Shh. It's okay," she whispered. "You don't have to say more if you're not ready."

Alexandra climbed into his lap and cupped his face in her hands. His eyes were distant—somewhere else entirely. She had to bring him back.

"Connor," she said, her voice firm and steady.

His eyes snapped to hers, and the raw despair in them made her throat close around a sob.

"It wasn't your fault. You did your best. Sometimes our best isn't enough, but that doesn't mean it's your fault. You *saved lives*, Connor. You did what you did to *save lives*, and so did every one of them. I won't tell you they knew the risks, even though they did. I won't tell you that it's the cost of freedom or any bullshit like that. It's awful and it sucks and it's *so* unfair. But it's *not your fault.*"

He nodded and a single tear trailed down his cheek. She swiped at it with her thumb and he dropped his eyes.

"You sound like Sam," he murmured.

"Sam's a smart guy," she said, brushing another tear away.

"He was with me… that day," he said quietly.

"Then he knows," she said softly. "And *I* was there this time. You didn't let me down, Connor. You saved me."

"You did pretty well on your own."

"True, but I was in shock. I didn't know he had a gun. I wouldn't have been able to get myself free and away from him in time if you hadn't been there."

"It kills me that he hurt you." His arms finally wrapped around her, and she exhaled a little of the tension she'd been carrying.

"He did hurt me. But seeing him hurt you? That was worse. I love you, Connor. I couldn't stand it—I almost lost you."

For a long moment they simply held each other in silence. Arms wrapped around each other. She put her head on his shoulder and kissed his jaw. He was fresh from the shower, and she could smell the woodsy scent of his soap and the scent that was something uniquely Connor underneath.

"I'm sorry," he whispered, voice rough with emotion.

"For being stubborn and shutting out the one person who cares about you most because you think you have to carry the world alone?"

"Something like that." His lips brushed her neck in a faint smile, and she smiled too.

"I get it. Been there. You're forgiven," she said, kissing his jaw. "And I know exactly how you can make it up to me."

She kissed him quickly and scooted off his lap. She stripped out of his shirt and tugged him to his feet. His towel fell to the floor and for a moment she simply stood there, devouring him in all his naked glory.

She kissed him again—slow, teasing—until it deepened into something soul-shattering. With one arm wrapped around his waist and her hand furrowed into his hair, she maneuvered between him and the bed.

She held him tight and let gravity do the rest, pulling him with her as they sank onto the bed. He froze for a moment when he realized he was now lying on top of her, but she held him to her and kissed from one corner of his mouth to the other.

She kissed his cheek, along his jaw, and pulled his earlobe between her teeth. He relaxed a fraction and groaned as she nipped at the skin of his neck, just below his ear.

"I trust you," she whispered between soft, open-mouthed kisses to his shoulder.

His arms tightened around her and his body relaxed over her, a comforting, calming weight. He nuzzled her neck, kissing a trail up the side of her neck.

"I love you, Lex," he murmured against her ear. "So damn much."

"Then love me," she said, kissing his shoulder and wrapping herself around him. And he did—slowly, reverently, like she was everything.

Twice.

Epilogue

CHRISTMAS EVE

Alexandra finally—*finally*—crawled into Connor's—*their*—massive bed and snuggled under the covers, shamelessly watching as Connor stripped out of his dress clothes and prowled toward the bed, all hard lines and masculine grace. He caught her staring and gave her a wide, lazy grin before flopping down beside her.

"You're tired, remember? Don't be lookin' at me like that," he growled, nuzzling her neck.

"I *am* exhausted, and you know it." She yawned then, proving her point.

"Then get some sleep, love." He pulled her close, wrapping her in his arms and rubbing slow, soothing circles on her back with those big, warm hands. Heaven.

"I like your dad," she murmured, eyes drifting shut as she melted into him. "And my parents like him."

"They all got on well. The three of you talked law, he talked Scottish scenery with your parents, Angel and Mary Fran swapped gardening tips, and everyone stuffed themselves with your sister's pastries."

"I'm so glad you convinced them to come here for Christmas."

"Mmhmm."

"How did they meet anyway?"

"Mary Fran was a client. Nasty divorce, from what he says. Her ex was a right bastard. Da took her case, pro bono, and got her half of everything and a protection order. Then he gave her a job. The rest is twenty years of history."

"Ah, so the heroism runs in the family."

"I suppose so," he said with a chuckle.

Alexandra sat up suddenly. "That reminds me. I wanted to give you one of your gifts tonight."

She scrambled out of bed and pulled a wrapped box from the closet where she'd hidden it earlier. When she'd ordered it months ago, it had been a joke—now it felt like something real. A symbol. And she wasn't sure how he'd take it.

Connor unwrapped it carefully and lifted the lid. He stilled, then reached inside to withdraw the small statue. It was carved from pale stone—a beautifully detailed knight on horseback, sword drawn, charging into battle.

Alexandra bit her lip, watching him turn it in his hands, taking in every detail.

"It's silly, I know," she said quietly. "But you really are my knight in shining armor."

Connor looked up, and the slow, wide grin that spread across his face made her breath hitch.

"I love it," he said, and kissed her softly before setting the statue on the nightstand.

"I suppose you'll want yours now, too."

"I can wait."

"Well, I can't."

He opened the drawer and handed her a flat box wrapped in gold paper. She tore into it, peeled back the tissue, and gasped.

"It's beautiful." She lifted a scarf from the box—rich blue and red plaid, with thin stripes of green and gold. "It's so soft."

"Proper Scottish lambswool," he said, preening.

She laughed, wrapping it around her neck.

"That's the MacLachlan tartan," he explained. "My family's been wearing it for generations. Go have a look."

He guided her to the mirror with a gentle hand on her elbow. She admired the scarf, smiling.

"It really is lovely," she said. "But am I even allowed to wear it? Isn't there some rule against wearing someone else's tartan?"

"Not if you're married to a MacLachlan."

She turned, startled—only to find him down on one knee, ring in hand, smiling nervously.

The tears came fast. She could barely breathe around them.

"Yes!" she cried, dropping to her knees and flinging her arms around his neck, kissing his face, his shoulder, anywhere she could reach.

"You didn't even let me ask the question!" Connor scolded, though his grin betrayed him.

"I'm sorry," she sniffled. "Ask."

"Alexandra Hughes," he said solemnly, "will you do me the very great honor of being my wife? Of letting me love you? Of forgiving me when I'm a stubborn ass?"

"Yes," she whispered through her tears. "As long as you'll let me love you, and forgive *me* when I'm being a stubborn ass."

"I will." He kissed her then—slow and sweet, deep and certain—and when it ended, he swept her up into his arms and carried her back to bed.

"Happy Christmas, Lex."

"Merry Christmas, Connor."

About the Author

RIANNA CAMPBELL is a wife, mother, and self-proclaimed Jack of all trades—thanks in large part to a late ADHD diagnosis that explained *a lot*. Her hobbies include painting, drawing, board games, video games, tabletop RPGs, woodworking, crocheting, home and auto repair, archery, graphic design, photography, cooking, and—most importantly—reading.

She's a Pisces from Upstate New York—either of which may account for her emotional instability, desire to escape from reality, and preference for never leaving her house.

As a self-published author, Rianna wears all the hats. She designs her own book covers, handles her own PR and marketing (usually via badly written, questionably lit, dramatically under-rehearsed and poorly performed TikToks), and yes, she even wrote this "About the Author" blurb in third person. Which, honestly, felt weird as hell.

She just asks that you be kind—and maybe pretend you didn't notice how many hobbies she has.

She's currently working on five more books in this series and has more ideas than she has the time, caffeine, or sanity to handle. Stay tuned.